PhBu
JoWi

The Big
Over Easy

*Also by Jasper Fforde
in Large Print:*

The Eyre Affair

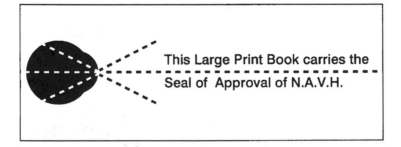

This Large Print Book carries the
Seal of Approval of N.A.V.H.

THE BIG OVER EASY

A Nursery Crime

Jasper Fforde

Thorndike Press • Waterville, Maine

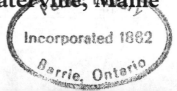

Published in 2006 by arrangement with Viking Penguin, a member of Penguin Group (USA) Inc.

Thorndike Press® Large Print Basic.

The tree indicium is a trademark of Thorndike Press.

The text of this Large Print edition is unabridged.
Other aspects of the book may vary from the original edition.

Set in 16 pt. Plantin by Ramona Watson.

Printed in the United States on permanent paper.

Library of Congress Cataloging-in-Publication Data

Fforde, Jasper.
  The big over easy : a nursery crime / by Jasper Fforde.
    p. cm.
  "Thorndike Press large print basic" — T.p. verso.
  ISBN 0-7862-8233-9 (lg. print : hc : alk. paper)
  1. Nursery rhymes — Adaptations.   2. Large type books.
  I. Title.
  PR6106.F67B54 2005b
    823'.914—dc22   2005026730

For my brother Mathew,
whose love of the absurd —
and the profound —
enlightened my childhood

National Association for Visually Handicapped
------------------------- serving the partially seeing

As the Founder/CEO of NAVH, the only national health agency solely devoted to those who, although not totally blind, have an eye disease which could lead to serious visual impairment, I am pleased to recognize Thorndike Press★ as one of the leading publishers in the large print field.

Founded in 1954 in San Francisco to prepare large print textbooks for partially seeing children, NAVH became the pioneer and standard setting agency in the preparation of large type.

Today, those publishers who meet our standards carry the prestigious "Seal of Approval" indicating high quality large print. We are delighted that Thorndike Press is one of the publishers whose titles meet these standards. We are also pleased to recognize the significant contribution Thorndike Press is making in this important and growing field.

Lorraine H. Marchi, L.H.D.
Founder/CEO
NAVH

★ Thorndike Press encompasses the following imprints: Thorndike, Wheeler, Walker and Large Print Press.

Humpty Dumpty sat on a wall,
Humpty Dumpty had a great fall;
All the king's horses
And all the king's men
Couldn't put Humpty together again.

— Traditional

Briggs waved a hand in the direction of the corpse. "It looks like he died from injuries sustained falling from a wall."

Contents

Author's Note

The Nursery Crime Division, the Reading Police Department and the Oxford & Berkshire Constabulary in this book are entirely fictitious, and any similarities to authentic police procedures, protocol or forensic techniques are entirely coincidental.

All Nursery Crime books have been designated as Character Exchange Program Safe Havens, and all characters are protected by the Council of Genres Directive GBSD/211950.

The Big Over Easy has been bundled with Special Features including: the "Making of" documentary, deleted scenes from all Fforde's novels, outtakes and much more. To access all these free bonus features, log on to www.nurserycrime.co.uk/special/js1.html and enter the code word as directed.

1. Mary Mary

If Queen Anne hadn't suffered so badly from gout and dropsy, Reading might never have developed at all. In 1702 the unhealthy Queen Anne, looking for a place to ease her royal infirmities, chanced upon Bath; and where royalty goes, so too does society. In consequence, Reading, up until that time a small town on a smaller tributary of the Thames, became a busy staging post on the Bath road, later to become the A4, and ultimately the M4. The town was enriched by the wool trade and later played host to several large firms that were to become household names. By the time Huntley & Palmers biscuits began here in 1822, Simonds brewery was already well established; and when Suttons Seeds began in 1835 and Spongg's footcare in 1853, the town's prosperity was assured.

Excerpt from *A History of Reading*

It was the week following Easter in Reading, and no one could remember the last sunny day. Gray clouds swept across the sky, borne on a chill wind that cut like a knife. It seemed that spring had forsaken the town. The drab winter weather had clung to the town like a heavy smog, refusing to relinquish the season. Even the early bloomers were in denial. Only the bravest crocuses had graced the municipal park, and the daffodils, usually a welcome splash of color after a winter of grayness, had taken one sniff at the cold, damp air and postponed blooming for another year.

A police officer was gazing with mixed emotions at the dreary cityscape from the seventh floor of Reading Central Police Station. She was thirty and attractive, dressed up and dated down, worked hard and felt awkward near anyone she didn't know. Her name was Mary. *Mary* Mary. And she was from Basingstoke, which is nothing to be ashamed of.

"Mary?" said an officer who was carrying a large potted plant in the manner of someone who thinks it is well outside his job description. "Superintendent Briggs will see you now. How often do you water these things?"

"That one?" replied Mary without emotion. "Never. It's plastic."

"I'm a policeman," he said unhappily, "not a sodding gardener."

And he walked off, mumbling darkly to himself.

She turned from the window, approached Briggs's closed door and paused. She gathered her thoughts, took a deep breath and stood up straight. Reading wouldn't have been everyone's choice for a transfer, but for Mary, Reading had one thing that no other city possessed: DCI Friedland Chymes. He was a veritable powerhouse of a sleuth whose career was a catalog of inspired police work, and his unparalleled detection skills had filled the newspaper columns for over two decades. Chymes was the reason Mary had joined the police force in the first place. Ever since her father had bought her a subscription to *Amazing Crime Stories* when she was nine, she'd been hooked. She had thrilled at "The Mystery of the Wrong Nose," been galvanized by "The Poisoned Shoe" and inspired by "The Sign of Three and a Half." Twenty-one years further on, Chymes was still a serious international player in the world of competitive detecting, and Mary had never missed an issue. Chymes was currently ranked by *Amazing Crime* second in their annual league rating, just behind Oxford's ever-popular Inspector Moose.

"Hmm," murmured Superintendent Briggs, eyeing Mary's job application carefully as she sat uncomfortably on a plastic chair in an office that was empty apart from a desk, two chairs, them — and a trombone lying on a tattered chaise longue.

"Your application is mostly very good, Mary," he said approvingly. "I see you were with Detective Inspector Hebden Flowwe. How did that go?"

It hadn't gone very well at all, but she didn't think she'd say so.

"We had a fairly good clear-up rate, sir."

"I've no doubt you did. But more important, anything published?"

It was a question that was asked more and more in front of promotion boards and transfer interviews and listed in performance reports. It wasn't enough to be a conscientious and invaluable assistant to one's allotted inspector — you had to be able to write up a readable account for the magazines that the public loved to read. Preferably *Amazing Crime Stories*, but, failing that, *Sleuth Illustrated*.

"Only one story in print, sir. But I was the youngest officer at Basingstoke to make detective sergeant and have two commendations for brav—"

"The thing is," interrupted Briggs, "is

16

that the Oxford and Berkshire Constabulary prides itself on producing some of the most readable detectives in the country." He walked over to the window and looked out at the rain striking the glass. "Modern policing isn't just about catching criminals, Mary. It's about good copy and ensuring that cases can be made into top-notch documentaries on the telly. Public approval is the all-important currency these days, and police budgets ebb and flow on the back of circulation and viewing figures."

"Yes, sir."

"DS Flotsam's work penning Friedland Chymes's adventures is the benchmark to which you should try to aspire, Mary. Selling the movie rights to *Friedland Chymes — the Smell of Fear* was a glory moment for everyone at Reading Central, and rightly so. Just one published work, you say? With Flowwe?"

"Yes, sir. A two-parter in *Amazing Crime*. Jan./Feb. 1999 and adapted for TV."

He nodded his approval.

"Well, that's impressive. Prime-time dramatization?"

"No, sir. Documentary on MoleCable-62."

His face fell. Clearly, at Reading they expected better things. Briggs sat down and looked at her record again.

"Now, it says here one reprimand: You struck Detective Inspector Flowwe with an onyx ashtray. Why was that?"

"The table lamp was too heavy," she replied, truthfully enough, "and if I'd used a chair, it might have killed him."

"Which is illegal, of course," added Briggs, glad for an opportunity to show off his legal knowledge. "What happened? Personal *entanglements?*"

"Equal blame on both sides, sir," she replied, thinking it would be better to be impartial over the whole affair. "I was foolish. He was emotionally . . . *dishonest.*"

Briggs closed the file.

"Well, I don't blame you. Hebden was always a bit of a bounder. He pinged my partner's bra strap at an office party once, you know. She wasn't wearing it at the time," he added after a moment's reflection, "but the intention was clear."

"That sounds like DI Flowwe," replied Mary.

Briggs drummed his fingers on the desk for a moment.

"Do you want to hear me play the trombone?"

"Might it be prejudicial to my career if I were to refuse?"

"It's a distinct possibility."

18

"Then I'd be delighted."

So Briggs walked over to the chaise longue, picked up the trombone, worked the slide a couple of times and blew a few notes, much to the annoyance of whoever had the office next door, who started to thump angrily on the wall.

"Drug squad," explained Briggs unhappily, putting the instrument down, "complete heathens. Never appreciate a good tune."

"I was wondering," said Mary before he had a chance to start playing again. "This detective sergeant's job I'm applying for. Who is it with?"

He looked at his watch.

"An excellent question. In ten minutes we're holding a press conference. I've a detective in urgent need of a new sergeant, and I think you'll fit the bill perfectly. Shall we?"

The pressroom was five floors below, and an expectant journalistic hubbub greeted their ears while they were still walking down the corridor. They stepped inside and stood as unobtrusively as possible at the back of the large and airy room. Mary could see from the "Oxford & Berkshire Constabulary"–bedecked lectern and high turnout that press conferences here were taken with a great deal more seriousness than she had known, which probably reflected this city's preeminence over Basingstoke when it came to serious crime. It wasn't that Reading had any *more* murders than Basingstoke — it just had better ones. Reading and the Thames Valley area was more of a "fairy cakes laced with strychnine" or "strangulation with a silk handkerchief" sort of place, where there were always bags of interesting suspects, convoluted motives and seemingly insignificant clues hidden in an inquiry of incalculable complexity yet solved within a week or two. By contrast, murders in Basingstoke were strictly blunt instruments, drunkenly wielded, solved within the hour — or not at all. Mary had worked on six murder investigations and, to her great disappointment, hadn't once discovered one of those wonderful clues that seem to have little significance but later, in an epiphanic moment, turn the case on its head and throw the guilty light on someone previously eliminated from the inquiries.

She didn't have time to muse upon the imaginative shortcoming of Basingstoke's criminal fraternity any longer, as there was a sudden hushing of the pressmen and a burst of spontaneous applause, as a handsome man in his mid-fifties strode dramatically from a side door.

"Goodness!" said Mary. "That's —"

"Yup," said Briggs, with the pride of a father who has just seen his son win everything at sports day. "Detective Chief Inspector Friedland Chymes."

Friedland Chymes! In *person.* There was a hush as the famous detective stepped up to the lectern. The assembled two dozen newspapermen readied themselves, pens poised, for his statement.

"Thank you for attending," he began, sweeping back his blond hair and gazing around the room with his lively blue eyes, causing flutters when they lingered ever so slightly on the women present in the room, Mary included. She found herself almost automatically attracted to him. He was strong, handsome, intelligent, fearless — the most alpha of alpha males. Working with him would be an honor.

"It was the small traces of pastry around the gunshot wound on Colonel Peabody's corpse that turned the case for me," began the great detective, his sonorous tones filling the air like music, "minute quantities of shortcrust whose butter/flour ratio I found to be identical to that of a medium-size

Bowyer's pork pie. The assailant had fired his weapon through the tasty snack to muffle the sound of the shot. The report heard later was a firecracker set off by a time fuse, thus giving an alibi to the assailant, who I can reveal to you now was . . ."

The whole room leaned forward in expectation. Chymes, his only apparent vanity a certain showmanship, paused for dramatic effect before announcing the killer.

". . . Miss Celia Mangersen, the victim's niece and, unbeknownst to us all, the sole beneficiary of the missing will, which I found hidden — as expected — within a hollowed-out statuette of Sir Walter Scott. Yes, Mr. Hatchett, you have a question?"

Josh Hatchett of *The Toad* newspaper had raised his hand in the front row.

"What was the significance of the traces of custard found on the Colonel's sock suspender?"

Chymes raised a finger in the air.

"An excellent question, Mr. Hatchett, and one that pushed my deducting powers to the limit. Bear with me if you will while we go through the final moments of Colonel Peabody's life. Mortally wounded and with only seconds to live, he had somehow to leave a clue to his assailant's identity. A note? Of course not — the killer would find and destroy it. Guessing correctly that a murder of this magnitude would be placed in my hands, he decided to leave behind a clue that only I could solve. Knowing the Colonel's penchant for anagrams, it was but a swift move to deduct his reasoning. The sock suspender was made in France. 'Custard' in French is *crème anglaise* — and an anagram of this is 'Celia Mangerse' — which not only correctly identified the killer but also told me the Colonel died before he was able to finish the anagram."

There was more applause, and he quietened everyone down before continuing.

"But since anagram-related clues are now inadmissible as evidence, we sent the pork pie off for DNA analysis and managed to pinpoint the pie shop where it was purchased. Guessing that Miss Mangersen might have an affinity for the pies, we staked out the shop in question, and yesterday evening Miss Mangersen was taken into custody, whereupon she confessed to me in a tearful scene that served as a dramatic closure to the case. My loyal, and annoyingly chirpy, cockney assistant and biographer DS Flotsam will of course be writing a full report for *Amazing Crime Stories* in due course, after the formality of a trial. Ladies and gentlemen: The case . . . is *closed!*"

The assembled journalists rose as one and burst into spontaneous applause. Chymes dismissed the adulation with a modest wave of the hand and excused himself, muttering something about needing to open a hospital for orphaned sick children.

"He's amazing!" breathed Mary, somehow convincing herself — as had all the other women present — that Chymes had winked at her across the crowded room.

"I agree," replied Briggs, standing aside as the newsmen filed out, eager to get the stories into the late editions. "Don't you love that 'the case is closed!' stuff? I wish *I* had a catchphrase. He's an asset not only to us here at Reading but also to the nation — there aren't many countries that haven't requested his thoughts on some intractable and ludicrously complex inquiry."

"He's remarkable," agreed Mary.

"Indeed," went on Briggs, seemingly swept up in a paroxysm of hagiographic hero worship. "He's also a hilarious raconteur, has a golf handicap of two, was twice world aerobatic champion and plays the clarinet as well as Artie Shaw. Speaks eight languages, too, and is often consulted by the Jellyman *himself* on important matters of state."

"I'm going to enjoy working with him, I can see," replied Mary happily. "When do I start?"

"Chymes?" echoed Briggs with a faint yet unmistakably patronizing laugh. "Goodness gracious, no! You're not working with *Chymes!*"

"Who then?" asked Mary, attempting to hide her disappointment, and failing.

"Him."

Mary followed Briggs's outstretched finger to an untidy figure who had taken his turn at the lectern. He was in his mid-forties, had graying hair and one eye marginally higher than the other, giving him the lopsided look of someone deep in thought. If he *was* deep in thought, considered Mary, it was clearly about something more important than his personal appearance. His suit could have done with a good pressing, his hair styled any way but the way he had it. He might have shaved a little less hurriedly and made more of an attempt to exude some — *any* — confidence. He fumbled with his papers as he stared resignedly after the rapidly vanishing press corps.

"I see," said Mary, sounding a great deal

colder than she had intended. "And who's he?"

Briggs patted her arm in a fatherly manner. He could sense her disappointment, but it wasn't up to him. Chymes picked his own people.

"That's DI Jack Spratt, of the Nursery Crime Division. The NCD. You'll be on his team. Or at least you and a few others will be the team. It's one of our smallest departments." He thought for a moment and then added, "Actually, it *is* our smallest department — if you don't count the night shift in the canteen."

"And his *Amazing Crime Stories* rating? What about that?"

"He's not rated," replied Briggs, trying to make it sound all matter-of-fact and not the embarrassment that it was. "In fact, I don't think he's even in the Guild."

Mary stared at the shabby figure and felt her heart fall. All of a sudden DI Flowwe didn't seem quite so bad after all.

Jack Spratt looked around the room. Most of the newsmen had by now left, and aside from Briggs and a woman Spratt didn't recognize at the door, there were only two journalists still in the room. The first was a large man named Archibald

Fatquack, who was the editor of the Reading weekly gossip sheet *The Gadfly.* The second was a junior newshound from the *Reading Daily Eyestrain*, who appeared to be asleep, drunk, dead or a mixture of all three.

"Thank you all for attending this press conference," announced Jack in a somber tone to the as-good-as-empty room. "I'll try not to keep you any longer than is necessary. This afternoon the Reading Central Criminal Court found the three pigs not guilty of all charges relating to the first-degree murder of Mr. Wolff."

He sighed. If he was intending it to be a dramatic statement, it wasn't, and it didn't help that no one significant was there to witness it. He could still hear the excited yet increasingly distant chatter of the newsmen as they filed down the corridor, but it was soon drowned out by Chymes's 1932 Delage D8 Super-Sport, which started up with a throaty roar in the car park. Jack waited until he had gone, then continued on gamely, the extreme lack of interest not outwardly affecting his demeanor. After nearly twenty years, he was kind of used to it.

"Since the death by scalding of Mr. Wolff following his ill-fated climb down

Little Pig C's chimney, we at the Nursery Crime Division have been following inquiries that this was *not* an act of self-defense but a violent and premeditated murder by three individuals who, far from being the innocent victims of wolf-porcine crime, actually sought confrontation and then acted quite beyond what might be described as reasonable self-defense."

Jack paused for breath. If he had hoped his misgivings over the outcome of the trial would be splashed all over the paper, he was mistaken. Page sixteen of *The Gadfly* was about the sum total of this particular story, sandwiched ignominiously between a three-for-two Hemorrelief advert and the Very Reverend Conrad Poo's weekly dental-hygiene column.

"Mr. Spratt," began Archibald, slowly bringing himself up to speed like a chilled gecko. "Is it true that Mr. Wolff once belonged to the Lupine Brotherhood, a secret society dedicated to traditional wolfish pursuits such as the outlawed *Midnight Howling*?"

"Yes, I understand that to be the case," replied Jack, "but that was over fifteen years ago. We do not deny that he has been investigated over various charges of criminal damage arising from the destruction of two dwellings built by the younger pigs, nor that Mr. Wolff threatened to 'eat them all up.' But we saw this as an empty threat — we produced witnesses who swore that Mr. Wolff was a vegetarian of many years' standing."

"So what was your basis for a murder prosecution again?" asked Archie, scratching his head.

"We believed," replied Jack in exasperation, as he had made the same point in the same room to the same two uninterested journalists many times before, "that boiling Mr. Wolff alive was quite outside the realm of 'reasonable force' and the fact that the large pan of water would have taken at least six hours to reach boiling point strongly indicated premeditation."

Archibald said nothing, and Jack, eager to go home, wrapped up his report.

"Despite the not-guilty verdicts, we at the NCD feel we have put up a robust case and were fully justified in our actions. To this end we will not be looking to re-examine the case or interview anyone else in connection with Mr. Wolff's death."

Jack sighed and gazed down. He looked and felt drained.

"Personally," said Briggs in an aside, "I didn't think the jury would go for it. The problem is that small pigs elicit a strong sympathetic reaction and large wolves don't. There was a good case for self-defense, too — Mr. Wolff was trespassing when he climbed down the chimney. It really all hinged on whether you believed that the pigs were boiling up a huge tureen of water to do their washing. And the jury did. In only eight minutes. Do you want me to introduce you?"

"I'd prefer tomorrow, once I am officially on duty," said Mary quickly, thinking she might have to go outside and scream or something.

Briggs picked up on her reticence.

"Don't underestimate the Nursery Crime Division, Mary. Spratt does some good work. Not high-profile, you understand, but important. His work on the Bluebeard serial wife killings case was . . . *mostly* good solid police work."

"That was Spratt?" asked Mary, something vaguely stirring in her memory. It hadn't been in *Amazing Crime*, of course, just one of those "also-ran" stories you usually find dwelling in the skim-read part of the dailies, along with city prices, dog horoscopes and "true-life" photo stories. It had been under the subheading "Colorfully hirsute gentleman kills nine wives;

hidden room contained gruesome secret."

"That's him. Jack was onto Bluebeard and was well ahead of events."

"If nine wives died, he couldn't have been *that* good."

"I said it was *mostly* good police work. More notably, he arrested Rumplestiltskin over that spinning-straw-into-gold scam and was part of the team that captured the violently dangerous psychopath the Gingerbreadman. You might have heard about Jack in connection with some giant killing, too."

Something stirred in Mary's memory again, and she raised an eyebrow. Police officers weren't meant to kill people if they could help it — and giants were no exception.

"Don't worry," said Briggs, "it was self-defense. Mostly."

"Mostly?"

"The last one he ran over in a car."

"The last one?" repeated Mary incredulously. "How many have there been?"

"Four. But don't mention it; he's a bit sensitive over the issue."

Mary's heart, which had already fallen fairly far, fell farther.

"Well, that's all I have to say," said Jack to the sparsely populated room. "Are there any more questions?"

Archibald Fatquack stirred, scribbled in his pad, but said nothing. The reporter from the *Reading Daily Eyestrain* had moved slowly forward during Jack's report, until his head was resting on the seat back in front. He began to snore.

"Good. Well, thank you very much for your time. Don't all rush to get out. You might wake Jim over there."

"I wasn't asleep," said Jim, eyes tightly closed. "I heard every word."

"Even the bit about the bears escaping into the Oracle Center and eating a balloon seller?"

"Of course," he murmured, beginning to snore again.

Jack picked up his notes and disappeared through a side door.

"Are there usually this few people for his press conferences?" asked Mary, horrified at the prospect of the career black hole into which she was about to descend like a suicidal rabbit.

"Good Lord, no," replied Briggs in a shocked tone. "Often he has no press at all."

He looked at his watch. "Goodness, is that the time? Check in with me first thing tomorrow, and I'll introduce you to Jack. You'll like him. Not *exactly* charismatic, but diligent and generally correct in most . . . *some* of his assumptions."

"Sir, I was wondering —"

Briggs stopped her midsentence, divining *precisely* what she was about to say. The reason was simple: All the detective sergeants he had ever allocated to Jack said the same thing.

"Look upon it as a baptism of fire. The NCD is good training."

"For what?"

Briggs had to think for a moment. "Unconventional policing. Your time won't be wasted. Oh, and one other thing."

"Yes, sir?"

"Welcome to Reading."

2. Jack Spratt

The Most Worshipful Guild of Detectives was founded by Holmes in 1896 to look after the best interests of Britain's most influential and newsworthy detectives. Membership is strictly controlled but pays big dividends: the pick of the best inquiries in England and Wales, an opportunity to "brainstorm" tricky cases with one's peers, and an exclusive deal with the notoriously choosy editors of *Amazing Crime Stories*. The Guild's legal department frequently brokers TV, movie and merchandising deals, and membership usually sways juries in tricky cases. It seems to work well. The only people who don't like the system are the officers who are non-Guild.

— Excerpt from *Inside the Guild of Detectives*

Jack drove home that evening with a feeling of frustration that would have been considerably worse had it been unexpected. He and the prosecution had tried to present the pig case as well as they could, but for some reason the jury didn't buy it. Briggs hadn't said anything to him yet, but mounting prosecutions such as *The Crown v. Three Pigs* was undeniably expensive, and after the failed conviction of the con men who perpetrated the celebrated emperor's-new-clothes scam the year before, Jack knew that the Nursery Crime Division would be under closer scrutiny by the bean counters. Not that the NCD was consistently racked with failure — far from it — but the fact was that few of his cases attracted much publicity. And in the all-important climate of increased public confidence, budget accountability and *Amazing Crime* circulation figures, Friedland's crowd-pleasing antics were strides ahead of Jack's misadventures — and hugely profitable for the Reading police force, too. But all of this was scant comfort to Mr. Wolff, who went to his casket unavenged and parboiled.

He drove along Peppard and took the left fork into Kidmore End.

"Shit," muttered Jack under his breath as the whole wasted six-month investigation sank in. He didn't *want* murder cases, of course — he would be happier not to have any, ever — but there was a slight frisson that went with them that he welcomed.

The NCD, after an early rush of celebrated cases, had settled down into something of a workaday existence. There is a limit to how many lost sheep you could track down, how many illegal straw-into-gold dens you could uncover, how many pied pipers arrived in town trying to extort money from the authorities over pest control and how often Mr. Punch would beat his wife and throw the baby downstairs. He knew there was not much prestige, but there was an upside: He was left pretty much to his own devices.

He stopped the car outside his house and stared silently into his own kitchen, where he could see his wife, Madeleine, attempting to feed the youngest of their five children. They had brought two children each from previous marriages — the two eldest, Pandora and Ben, were Jack's, and Megan and Jerome were Madeleine's. As if to cement the union further, they had had one that was entirely down to the pair of them — Stevie, who was a year old.

"This is why I do this," he muttered under his breath, opening the car door. Pausing only to place a block of wood under the rear wheel to stop his Allegro from rolling down the slope, he picked up his case, bade good evening to his neighbor

Mrs. Sittkomm, who was glaring suspiciously at him from over the fence, and took the side entrance to the house.

"Honey," he yelled without enthusiasm as he dumped his case on the hall table, "I'm home!"

She coo-eed from the kitchen, and the sound of her voice made all the stresses of the day that much more bearable. They had been married almost five years, and neither of them had any regrets over their choice. She bounded in from the kitchen, gave him a kiss and hugged him tenderly.

"Otto called me about the Wolff thing," she whispered in his ear. "Bum deal. The pigs deserved to fry. I'm sorry."

And she hugged him again.

"I'd say 'you win some,' but I don't seem —"

She placed a finger on his lips and took him by the hand to walk him through to the kitchen, where Stevie was attempting to reduce his dinner to a thin film that might, through careful skill, be made to cover the entire room.

"Hi, kids!" Jack shouted, summoning a small amount of enthusiasm.

"Hullo!" said Jerome, who was just eight, was enthusiastic about everything and smelt strongly of fish fingers. "I can wiggle my ears!"

He then attempted to demonstrate his newfound skill, and after about a minute of grunting and going bright red and with his ears not wiggling even the tiniest bit, said, "How was *that?!*"

"Awesome," replied Jack, rolling his eyes dramatically. "Wiggle them any more and you'll be able to fly."

"Jack!" began Megan, her mouth full. "My teacher Miss Klaar eats . . . puppies!"

"And how do you know that?"

"Johnny said so," she replied intensely, all curls and big questioning blue eyes the color of a Pacific lagoon.

"I see. And does Johnny have any corroborative evidence?"

"Of course," said the ten-year-old, knowing a few technical police terms herself. "Johnny said that Roger told him that a friend of his who lives next door to someone who knows Miss Klaar said it's a fact in her street. Do we have a case?"

"Oh, yes," agreed Jack. "I often go to court with far less."

"Da-woo!" screamed Stevie, waving a spoon as he scattered food around the room, much to the pleasure of the cat, with whom, it was generally agreed, Stevie had an "understanding." Ripvan — as in "Winkle," naturally — was the laziest cat that had ever lived, *ever.* She would sleep in corridors, roads, paths, puddles, gutters — anywhere she suddenly felt tired. She would rather sit in the cold and have to be revived from near hypothermia with a hair dryer than trouble herself to use the cat flap. If she hadn't had the sense to lie on her back under Stevie's high chair with her mouth open, she would probably have starved.

Madeleine sidled up to where Jack was absently staring at the children gorging themselves and wrapped an arm around his waist.

"How are you feeling?" she asked.

"Deflated," he replied. "And Friedland got another standing ovation at the press conference."

"Don't worry about Friedland," said Madeleine soothingly. "He only gets the good cases because he's in the Guild of Detectives."

"Don't talk to me about the Guild. Heard the saying 'If you're in, you're made. If you're out, you're traffic'?"

"Many times. But you're not traffic."

"Check in again a week from now."

"Did you apply like we discussed, darling?"

"Yes."

"Really?"

"No. Listen, I'm not really Guild material. How many people want to read about three disreputable pigs and a dopey wolf with a disposition towards house demolition?"

"If you were in the Guild, maybe lots."

"Well, I'm not so sure. The Guild won't want someone like me. The NCD conviction record is . . . well, *shit*."

"That's because the force doesn't appreciate what you're doing. If you were Guild, Briggs and the Crown Prosecution Service would soon change their tune. *Aside* from that, Ben and Pandora will *both* be at university in two years, so we could do with the extra cash."

"That's true. The cost of mac and cheese, subsidized beer and cannabis these days is simply scandalous — think I can get a cheap deal from the drug squad?"

"I'm serious, Jack."

"Okay, okay. I'll apply tomorrow, I promise."

"You won't need to. I took the liberty of doing it for you. Here."

She handed him a sheet of paper.

Jack accepted it with misgivings, unsure of whether to be angry at Madeleine's intervention or glad that she had taken the burden of responsibility from him.

"It's a conditional acceptance," he said, reading the short letter twice to make sure he understood what was going on. "They need a day's observation in order to calculate my sleuthing quotient — if it's higher than a six point three, they'll put my name up to the board."

He turned the sheet over. "It doesn't say when this observation day will be."

"I think it's done on a random basis in case detectives try to 'spice things up a bit' with a head in a bag or something," observed Madeleine. She was quite correct. Desperate Guild-wannabe detectives had been known to borrow cadavers from medical schools and then dump them in a chest freezer for later "discovery" to impress Guild observers.

"Well," said Jack, "I'm just amazed that I got even as far as a conditional acceptance."

"That's easily explained," she replied. "I told them you were a chain-smoking vintage-Rolls-Royce-driving divorced alcoholic with an inability to form lasting relationships. And with a love of Puccini, Henry Moore and Magritte. And a big pipe."

"What about a deerstalker hat?"

"No — do you think I should have?"

"Absolutely not. Why did you tell them all that?"

"I had to write *something* interesting about you. If your investigations are going to be written up in *Amazing Crime Stories*, you're going to have to have a few interesting foibles. I don't think 'happily married father of five' quite cuts the mustard these days."

He sighed. She was right.

"Well," he said, giving her an affectionate hug, "if I'm going to be a womanizing, pipe-smoking opera fanatic with a vintage car and a drinking problem, I better practice getting into character. I could make a start chatting up that new assistant of yours — what was her name again?"

"Diane? Sure, you could try that. She said yesterday she thought you were really nice."

"She did?"

"Reminded her of her dad, she said."

"Hmm. What sort of pipe did you have in mind for me?"

They laughed. The Guild. What the hell. He'd cross that bridge when he came to it.

"Bums!" said Madeleine, glancing at the wall clock. "I'm late."

"Late for what?"

"The Spongg Footcare Charity Benefit. It's on the calendar."

Jack walked over to look. It was there in black ballpoint. He didn't look closely enough at these things and was always being caught out.

"Schmoozing or snapping?"

She slapped him playfully on the shoulder. "Snapping, you dope. Someone has to take pictures of all the dazzling Reading socialites shaking hands with whatever D-class celebrity Lord Spongg has managed to dredge up."

"Is that an improvement on the Thames Valley Fruit-Growers Ball, where you were merely photographing 'low-grade celebrity wannabes'?"

"Of course, dear — it's called upward mobility. By the summer I could be doing portraits of chinless twerps at the Henley Regatta."

"Well, you'd better dress up a bit, then."

"All in good time, husband dearest. Can you take Megan to Scouts?

"Sure. When is it again?"

"Seven," said Megan, and excused herself from the table.

"What did you do at school, Jerome?" asked Jack when Madeleine had gone upstairs to change into something a little smarter. It didn't do well to turn up at a charity bash dressed scruffy, even if you were only the photographer.

"Nothing much."

"Then it's a bit pointless sending you, isn't it? Why don't we just cancel school, and you can stay at home and — I don't know — just eat chocolate and watch TV all day?"

Jerome perked up at this gold-edged scenario. "Really?"

"No, not really."

His shoulders slumped. "But school's *sooooooo* boring."

"Agreed. But it's almost perfect training for a career at Smileyburgers."

"But I'm not going to work at Smileyburgers."

"You will if you do nothing much at school."

"Da-woo!!" yelled Stevie, jumping up and down. In the absence of anything more productive to do, he grasped large handfuls of scrambled egg and squeezed until it oozed between his fingers like yellow toothpaste.

"Yag," said Jerome, "and you tell *me* off for picking my nose!"

"It's not the picking," explained Jack, who secretly liked a good dig himself and didn't want to be a hypocrite, "it's the *eating.*"

Talk abruptly halted as Ben walked into the kitchen looking very self-conscious in his college orchestra uniform. He was sixteen, gangly and awash in a toxic sea of hormones. He had joined the orchestra less through the love of music than the love of Penelope Liddell, who played the harp.

"It's those slender fingers plucking on the strings," he had explained while confessing the object of his adoration to Jack a few days before, "and that *concentration!* Hell's teeth! If she looked at me like that, I think I'd explode."

"Well, mind you don't," Jack had replied. "It could be very messy."

Ben was actually a very competent tuba, but since the tuba player is about as far away as you can get from the harp and the tuba doesn't exactly *ooze* macho sexuality — except, perhaps, to another tuba — he had joined the percussion section to bring him closer to the object of his affections. He dragged two heavy cases out from the cupboard under the stairs and put on a parka.

"Do you need a hand with those?" asked Jack.

"Thanks, Dad. My ride will be here soon."

A car horn sounded outside.

Jack tried to pick up one of the cases, but it was so heavy it felt as though it had taken root.

"What the hell have you got in here?"

"We're doing *Il Trovatore*," Ben explained. "Mr. Moore said we should experiment — so I'm using *real* anvils and *real* hammers."

Between the two of them, they managed to drag the cases across the floor and heave them over the doorstep and down the path to the trunk of the waiting car, which sank alarmingly.

Half an hour later, Madeleine came back down dressed in a strapless red ball gown kept up by nothing but faith. All eyes were on her as she did a twirl for them in the kitchen.

"How do I look?"

"Whoa!" said Pandora who had just walked in. "Maddy's in girl clothes!"

"Beautiful," said Megan wistfully, clasping her hands together and holding them at her chin, dreaming of a time when *she* could dress up in ball gowns, go to parties and be kissed by a handsome prince — although she would accept a knight, if there were problems regarding availability.

"It's very bright," was Jerome's only comment.

"Da-woo," said Stevie.

"I thought you were the one doing the photographing," said Jack. "I mean, how do you actually get in your own photographs? Press the shutter and then run around *really* fast?"

"It *is* the Spongg Footcare Charity Benefit, darling. While I've still the tattered remnants of youth and good looks, I might as well use them to drum up some work. Debs' parents pay good money for portraits."

"Well," said Jack, "just don't allow yourself to be chatted up by Lord Spongg — you know what a reputation he has."

"I have *every* intention of being chatted up by Lord Spongg," she responded with a smile. "I need all the work he can give me." She curled a hand around Jack's chin and neck, brought her lips to his ear and whispered, "These dresses are notoriously tight, and the zips are *always* faulty. You may have to tear it from my body."

She kissed him, smiled and withdrew.

"I'll wait up."

"Oh, no need for that is there?" she returned playfully.

"Yes."

She laughed and was suddenly a burst of energy.

"Megan, get your shoes on — NOW! If you can't find a woggle, use an elastic band. The rest of you behave yourselves with Jack. I'll be back after your bedtime."

She kissed them all, grabbed her camera bag, which spoiled the illusion of sophisticated socializing, and was out of the door in a flash.

"Da-woo," murmured Stevie, clearly impressed.

It was after ten, the younger children were all tucked in, and Jack and Pandora were sitting in the living room. The telly was on, although they weren't paying it much attention, and Pandora was doing some revising, as several textbooks on theoretical particle physics were strewn around the sofa. Pandora was almost twenty and still at the sort of age where she didn't really care what her father thought of her life choices and wanted him to know it — which naturally meant she cared a *great deal* what he thought but wasn't going to let on. And Jack, for his part, couldn't help giving her advice that he thought valuable and pertinent but was actually useless — mostly because it had been a long time since he was her age, and he hadn't been able to figure it out either. But there *were* small triumphs. For a start, Pandora didn't have any piercings or tattoos. This was partly due to Jack's relaxed attitude, something that took the wind out of her semirigged rebellious sails. Sometimes she thought Jack was using reverse psychology on her, which meant that she should double-bluff *his* double bluff, and she might have done so except that the idea of a tattoo or a piercing made her feel queasy.

Jack stared blankly at his crossword. It was the 344th consecutive puzzle he had failed to complete. A new personal best.

"Hey," said Pandora, "tough break on the three-pigs case. I'm a committed holier-than-thou-meat-is-murder-bore-the-pants-off-all-and-sundry vegetarian, and even *I* thought they should have been served up boiled with new potatoes, peas and parsley sauce."

"Well," replied Jack, taking a swig of beer, "we thought we might have got Gerald — that's Little Pig A — to squeal on his elder brothers for a lesser sentence, but he wouldn't play ball. How's school?"

"I'm nearly twenty, Dad. I don't go to school anymore. It's called uni-ver-sity, and it's good. Can you help me with my quantum-particle homework?"

"Sure."

"Okay. Here's the question: 'Solve the Schrödinger equation explicitly in the case of a particle of mass *m* in a constant Newtonian gravitational field: $V=mgz$.' "

Jack thought for a moment.

"*Definitely* B."

"Eh?"

"Box B, *unless* the previous answer was box B, in which case it'll be box C. This *is* multiple choice, yes?"

Pandora laughed. "No, Dad. Particle physics is a little more involved than that."

"Box A?"

She slapped him playfully on the arm. "Dad! You are so no help at all!"

The local news came on. There was a piece about Chymes and the Peabody case, of course, and more about the Jellyman's visit on Saturday to dedicate the Sacred Gonga Visitors' Center. There was also a bit about the Spongg Footcare Charity Benefit, live from the Déjà Vu Ballrooms. They both craned their necks to catch a glimpse of Madeleine in her red dress and saw her lurking in the back of a shot where Lord Randolph Spongg, the CEO of Spongg Footcare PLC, was doing a piece for the live broadcast.

". . . as well as representatives from Winsum and Loosum's and QuangTech, we've seen a galaxy of Reading celebrities tonight," said the handsome peer cheerfully, "in order to help us raise funds to replace the outdated and woefully inadequate St. Cerebellum's mental hospital. We are very grateful indeed to Mr. Grundy, Mr. Attery Squash, the Blue Baboon, Mr. Pobble, Lola Vavoom and of course the Dong, who so generously agreed to entertain us with his luminous nose."

"Ah, yes, Miss Vavoom," said *The Toad* reporter as he crossed to the retired star of screen and stage, "so good to see you out in Reading society again. How do you react to the epithet 'formerly gorgeous'?"

"Like *this*," she said, downing the reporter with a straight right to the jaw. There was a cry, a flash going off, and they cut the live broadcast back to a bemused anchorman who hid a smile, told a heartwarming story about the efforts of the fire service to rescue a kitten stuck in a pipe, then introduced Reading's favorite weathergirl, Bunty McTwinkle.

"Reading will once again experience a cloudy day with little sign of sunshine," said Bunty without much emotion, "a bit

51

like living inside Tupperware."

Pandora keyed the remote, and the TV went silent.

"I was hoping I *might* make the local news this time," said Jack despondently, "even if it was to be trashed."

Ben finally drifted in at eleven and made a little too much noise. A light switched on in Mr. and Mrs. Sittkomm's bedroom, which was always a bad sign. Jack beckoned him in as quickly as he could.

"Have you been drinking?"

"To excess. I had *two* shandies."

"Almost an alcoholic. How did it go with the harpist? Did she like your anvils?"

"Oh, *her,*" he sniffed, taking off his parka and chucking it in the cloakroom. "She's going out with Brian Eves, who plays the tuba. She says it's the sexiest instrument in the brass section."

"Oh, Ben," said Jack, "I'm so sorry!"

"Shit happens," he replied, making his way toward the staircase, his room and the welcome oblivion of low-alcohol-induced lovelorn unconsciousness. "Yes indeed, shit happens."

Jack went to bed at midnight and was awoken in the small hours by Madeleine, who came to bed smelling of champagne, canapés and hard work.

"Guess what!" she whispered, not at all quietly in his ear.

"The house is on fire?"

"No. I snapped Lola Vavoom slugging a journalist. It'll be on the front page of *The Mole* and *The Toad* tomorrow. She packs quite a punch — they had to wire his jaw!"

Despite the feisty and provocative talk earlier about the red dress's having to be torn from her body, they both fell fast asleep doing nothing about it. Besides, it was rented.

3. The Fall Guy

PROMOTION FIRST FOR
NURSERY CRIME DIVISION

History was made yesterday when DCI Friedland Chymes was promoted out of the Nursery Crime Division, the first occasion of this happening in the department's twenty-six-year history. It has traditionally been a depository for loners, losers, burnouts, misfits, oddballs and those out of favor with higher authority, but Chymes's elevation has finally shown that the NCD can hold its own in the production of Guild-quality officers to protect, serve and entertain the nation.
    — From *The Gadfly*, August 10, 1984

"The Japanese film crew is waiting to interview you again," said Madeleine, interspersing stuffing spoonfuls of mashed banana into Stevie with taking surreptitious glances outside. "What do they want anyway?"

"To talk to me about Friedland Chymes and the Gingerbreadman," replied Jack, sorting through his post and finding a notice from the Allegro Owners' Club about checking wheel-bearing torque settings.

"Why don't you speak to them?"

"Darling, they don't want the truth. They want me to back up Chymes's version of events where he 'saved the day' and single-handedly caught the deranged psychopath."

Jack finished his toast and looked at Madeleine's picture on the cover of *The Toad*, which had the headline WASHED-UP HAS-BEEN WITH WEIGHT PROBLEM VICIOUSLY ATTACKS JOURNALIST. *The Mole*, whose journalist *didn't* get a broken jaw that night led with SOCK IT TO HIM, LOLA!

"Whatever happened to him?" asked Madeleine.

"Friedland Chymes? No idea."

"No, silly. The Gingerbreadman."

"Last I heard, he was still in St. Cerebellum's Secure Wing for the Incurably Unhinged. Four-hundred-year sentence. It should have been five hundred, but we never proved his one hundred and fourth victim."

"He couldn't escape, could he?" asked Madeleine. "After all, he did promise to do unspeakable things to you and Friedland."

"If he did, I'd be the first to know." He

sighed. "No, I guess I'd be the second."

Jack's mobile vibrated across the worktop and fell into the compost bin with a *plop.*

He picked it up, wiped off the spaghetti hoops and frowned at the text message.

" 'Gngbdmn out 2 get U,' " he murmured. "Now, that's a coincidence."

Madeleine dropped a spoon, and Jack chuckled.

"Just kidding. It actually says, 'Big egg down — Wyatt.' What does that mean?"

"I don't know," replied Madeleine, "but if the husband with the dopey line in practical jokes wants to still be breathing in ten minutes, he better be out of the house."

Wyatt was Briggs's deputy and not the most polite of men.

"Are you coming in today?" he asked as soon as Jack called.

Jack glanced at his watch. It was barely nine.

"Of course. What's the problem?"

"Wall fall over at Grimm's Road. Looks like one of yours. Briggs is on his way and wants to see you there pronto."

Jack replied that he'd be over as soon as possible, scribbled down the address and hung up.

"What was it?"

"One for the NCD, apparently."

"Another Bluebeard copycat?"

"I hope not. Are you interviewing any more potential lodgers today?"

"Two."

"Good. No one weird, remember. I'll call you."

He kissed her, then looked over Stevie to find the area of least sticky. He eventually found a small patch on the top of his head and kissed that and was out of the door.

Jack's car was an Austin Allegro estate Mark 3 painted in a gruesome shade of lime green that had been designated as "Applejack" by an unnamed marketing executive with an odd sense of humor. Detectives driving vintage or classic cars was a Guild-inspired affectation that Jack thought ludicrous. Friedland Chymes's 1932 Delage D8 was a not-untypical choice. As a small, pointless and totally unnoticed act of rebellion, Jack drove the dullest car he could find. His father had bought it new in 1982 and looked after it assiduously. When it passed to Jack, he continued to care for it. It was just coming up to its twenty-second birthday and had covered almost 350,000 miles, wearing out two engines and four clutches on the way.

He didn't drive straight to Grimm's

Road. He had an errand to run first — for his mother.

She opened the door within two seconds of his pressing the doorbell, letting out a stream of cats that ran around with such rapidity and randomness of motion that they assumed a liquid state of furry purringness. The *exact* quantity could have been as low as three or as high as one hundred eight; no one could ever tell, as they were all so dangerously hyperactive. The years had been charitable to Mrs. Spratt, and despite her age she was as bright as a button and had certainly not lost any of her youthful zest. Jack put it down to quantity of children. It had either made her tough in old age or worn her out — if the latter, then without Jack and his nine elder siblings, she might have lived to one hundred ninety-six. She painted people's pets in oils because "someone has to," collected small pottery animals, Blue Baboon LPs and Jellyman commemorative plates. She had been widowed seventeen years.

"Hello, baby!" she enthused merrily. "How are you?"

"I'm fine, Mother — and I'm not a baby anymore. I'm forty-four."

"You'll *always* be my baby. Did the pigs dangle?"

Jack shook his head. "We did our best. The jury just wasn't convinced we had a case."

"It's hardly surprising," she snorted, "considering the jury was *completely* biased."

"The defendants might be pigs, Mother, but they do have the right to be tried by their peers. In this instance twelve *other* pigs. It's a Magna Carta 1215 thing — nothing to do with me or the Prosecution Service."

She shrugged and then looked furtively around. "Best come inside. I think the aliens are trying to control my thoughts using the mobile network."

Jack sighed. "Mother, if you met an alien, you'd quickly change your mind; they're really just like you and me — only blue."

She ushered him in and shut the door. The house smelled of lavender water, acrylic paint and fresh baking, and it echoed with the stately *tock* of the grandfather clock in the hall. A quantum of cats shot out of the living room and tore upstairs.

"It's the diet I have them on, I think," she murmured, passing Jack a canvas wrapped in brown paper. She didn't really want to sell her Stubbs painting of a cow, but since she had discovered all the must-have goodies on eBay, there was really no choice.

"Remember," she said firmly, "take it to Mr. Foozle and get him to value it. I'll make a decision after he's done that."

"Right."

She thought for a moment.

"By the way, when are you going to remove those three bags of wool from the potting shed so I can have it demolished?"

"Soon, Mother, I promise."

The rain had eased up after the previous night's deluge, and puddles the size of small inland seas gathered on the roads where the beleaguered storm drains had failed to carry it all away. Grimm's Road was in an area that had yet to fully benefit from the town's prosperity. There were terraced houses on either side of the potholed road, and two large gas holders dominated the far end of the street, casting a shadow over the houses every month of the year except July. The houses had been built in the latter part of the nineteenth century and were typical of the period: two up, two down with kitchen behind, an outdoor loo, a yard at the rear and a coal house beyond this. A door at the back of the yard led out into an alley, a cobbled track scattered with rubbish and abandoned cars, a favorite playing ground for kids.

The traffic had slowed Jack down badly in the latter part of the journey, and it was about twenty minutes later when he drove slowly down Grimm's Road trying to read the door numbers. He had received two other calls asking where he was, and it was fairly obvious that Briggs would not be in a sympathetic mood. Jack parked the car and pulled on an overcoat, keeping a wary eye on the darkening sky.

"Nice car, mister," said a cheeky lad with a grubby face, trying to bounce a football that had a puncture. His friend, whose face his mother had cruelly forgotten to smear with grime that morning, joined in.

"Zowie!" he exclaimed excitedly. "An Austin Allegro estate Mark 3 deluxe 1.3-liter 1982 model. Applejack with factory-fitted optional head restraints, dog cage and Motorola single-band radio." He paused for breath. "You don't see many of those around these days. It's not surprising," he added, "they're total shit."

"Listen," said the first one in a very businesslike tone, "give us fifty quid and we'll set it on fire so you can cop the insurance."

"Better make it a tenner," said the second

lad with a grin. "Fifty is all he'd get."

"Police," said Jack. "Now, piss off."

The boys were unrepentant. "Plod pay double. If you want us to torch your motor, it's going to cost you twenty."

They both sniggered and ran off to break something.

Jack walked up to the house in question and looked at the shabby exterior. The guttering was adrift, the brickwork sprouted moss, and the rotten window frames held several sheets of cardboard that had been stuck there to replace broken panes. In the window the landlady had already put up a sign saying "Room to Let. Strictly no pets, accordion players, statisticians, smokers, sarcastics, spongers or aliens."

Waiting for Jack was a young constable who looked barely out of puberty, let alone probation, which was pretty near the truth on both counts. He had made full constable and was sent to the NCD for three months to ease him into policing. But someone had mislaid the paperwork, and he was still there six months later, which suited him just fine.

"Good morning, Tibbit."

"Good morning, sir," replied the eager young man, his blue serge pressed into a fine crease — by his mother, Jack guessed.

"Where's the Super?"

Tibbit nodded in the direction of the house. "Backyard, sir. Watch the landlady. She's a dragon. Jabbed me with an umbrella for not wiping my feet."

Jack thanked him, wiped his feet with great care on the faded and clearly ironic "Welcome" doormat and stepped inside. The house smelled musty and had large areas of damp on the walls. He walked past the peeling wallpaper and exposed lath and plaster to the grimy kitchen, then opened the door and stepped out into the backyard.

The yard was shaped as an oblong, fifteen feet wide and about thirty feet long, surrounded by a high brick wall with crumbling mortar. Most of the yard was filled with junk — broken bicycles, old furniture, a mattress or two. But at one end, where the dustbins were spilling their rubbish onto the ground, large pieces of eggshell told of a recent and violent death. Jack knew who the victim was immediately and had suspected for a number of years that something like this might happen. Humpty Dumpty. The fall guy. If this wasn't under the jurisdiction of the Nursery Crime Division, Jack didn't know what was. Mrs. Singh, the pathologist, was kneeling next to the shattered remains dictating notes into a tape recorder. She waved a greeting at him as he walked in but did not stop what she was doing. She indicated to a photographer areas of particular interest to her, the flash going off occasionally and looking inordinately bright in the dull closeness of the yard.

Briggs had been sitting on a low wall talking to a plainclothes policewoman, but as Jack entered, he rose and waved a hand in the direction of the corpse.

"It looks like he died from injuries sustained falling from a wall," Briggs said. "Could be accident, suicide, who knows? He was discovered dead at 0722 this morning."

Jack looked up at the wall. It was a good eight feet high. A sturdy ladder stood propped up against it.

"Our ladder?"

"His."

"Anything else I need to know?"

"A couple of points. Firstly, you're not exactly 'Mr. Popular' with the seventh floor at present. There are people up there who think that spending a quarter of a million pounds on a failed murder conviction for three pigs is not value for money

— especially when there is zero chance of getting it into *Amazing Crime Stories*."

"I didn't think justice was meant to have a price tag, sir."

"Clearly. But it's a public-perception thing, Spratt. Piglets are cute; wolves aren't. You might as well try and charge the farmer's wife with cruelty when she cut off the mice's tails with a carving knife."

"I did."

"And?"

"Insufficient evidence."

"A good thing I never heard of it. So what you're going to do here is clean up Humpty's tumble with the minimum of fuss and bother. I want it neat, quick and cheap — and without hassling any more anthropomorphized animals."

"Including pigs?"

"*Especially* pigs. You so much as look at a bacon roll and I'll have you suspended."

"Is there a third point?"

"The annual budgetary review is next week, and because of that pig fiasco, the NCD's future is on the agenda. Stir up any more trouble and you could find yourself managing traffic volume on the M4."

"I preferred it when there were only two points."

"Listen, Jack," went on Briggs, "you're a

good officer, if a little overenthusiastic at times, and the Nursery Crime Division *is* necessary, despite everyone's apparent indifference. The bottom line is that I want this ex-egg mopped up neat and clean and a report on my desk Wednesday morning. The Sacred Gonga's new visitors' center is being dedicated by the Jellyman on Saturday, and I need all the hands I can get for security — and that includes your little mob hiding down there at the NCD."

"You want me to head up Jellyman security, sir?" asked Jack with a gleam in his eye. He liked the idea of being near the great man; guaranteeing his safety was even better.

"No, we need someone of unimpeachable character, skill and initiative for that; Chymes is already drawing up security plans. I want you to ensure the safety of the Sacred Gonga itself. Anti-Splotvian protesters might try to disrupt the dedication ceremony. Protect it with your life and the lives of your department. Solomon Grundy paid forty million to keep it in the country, and we wouldn't want to upset him. You should go and look over the visitors' center; there'll be a Jellyman security briefing on Thursday at 1500 hours."

"Sir, I —"

"I would consider taking the assignment with all enthusiasm, Jack," observed Briggs. "After that three-pigs debacle, you'll need as many friends as you can get."

"Is this where I say thank you?"

"You do." Briggs beckoned the policewoman over. "Jack, I want you to meet Detective Sergeant Mary."

"Hello," said Jack.

"*Mary* Mary," said Mary Mary.

"Hello, *hello?*"

"Don't play the fool, Spratt," cut in Briggs.

"It's Mary Mary," explained Mary. "That's my name."

"Mary Mary? Where are you from? Baden-Baden?"

"First time I heard that one, sir — today."

Jack sighed. He smiled mechanically, she smiled mechanically, and they shook hands.

"Pleased to meet you, sir," she said.

"And you," replied Jack. "Who are you working with?"

She looked across at Briggs rather pointedly.

"Mary is your new detective sergeant," said Briggs. "Transferred with an A-one record from Basingstoke. She'll be with you on this case and any others that spring up."

Jack sighed. "No offense to DS Mary, sir, but I was hoping you could promote Ashley, Baker, or —"

"Not possible, Jack," said Briggs in the tone of voice that made arguing useless. He looked up at the ominous sky. "Well, I'm off. I'll leave you here with Mary so you can get acquainted. Remember: I need that report as soon as possible. Got it?"

Jack did indeed get it, and Briggs departed.

Jack shivered in the cold and looked at her again. "Mary Mary, eh?"

"Yes, sir."

"Kind of an odd name."

Mary bit her lip. It was a contentious point with her, and the years had not diminished the hot indignation of playground taunts regarding contrariness. It *was* an odd name, but she tried not to let her feelings show.

"It's just my name, sir. I come from a long line of Mary Marys — sort of like a family tradition. Why," she added, more defensively, "is there a problem?"

"Not at all," replied Jack, "as long as it's not an affectation for the Guild's benefit — Briggs was threatening to change *his* to Föngotskilérnie."

"Why would he want to do that?"

68

"Friedland Chymes's investigations usually end up in print, as you know," explained Jack, "and Briggs is habitually *not* referred to. He thought a strange name and a few odd habits might make him more . . . *mentionworthy.*"

"Hence the trombone?"

"Right."

There was a short silence, during which Jack thought about who he would have preferred to have as his DS and Mary thought about her career.

"So the NCD disbanded?" she said, using her best woeful voice to make it sound like terribly bad news. "That would mean all the staff would have to be reassigned to other duties, right?"

"Along with the chairs and table lamps, yes, I suppose so."

"When is this budgetary meeting?"

"The Thursday following next."

Mary made a mental note. The sooner she could get away from this loser department, the better.

Jack turned his attention to the shattered remains of Humpty's corpse.

Mary took her cue and flicked open her notepad. "Corpse's name is —"

"Humpty Dumpty."

"You knew him?"

"Once," Jack sighed, shaking his head sadly. "A very long time ago."

Humpty's ovoid body had fragmented almost completely and was scattered among the dustbins and rubbish at the far end of the yard. The previous night's heavy rain had washed away his liquid center, but even so there was still enough to give off an unmistakably eggy smell. Jack noted a thin and hairless leg — still with a shoe and sock — attached to a small area of eggshell draped with tattered sheets of translucent membrane. The biggest piece of shell contained Humpty's large features and was jammed between two dustbins. His face was a pale white except for the nose, which was covered in unsightly red gin blossoms. One of the eyes was open, revealing a milky-white unseeing eye, and a crack ran across his face. He had been wearing a tuxedo with a cravat or cummerbund — it was impossible to say which. The trauma was quite severe, and to an untrained eye his body might have been dismissed as a heap of broken eggshell and a bundle of damp clothing.

Jack knelt down to get a closer look. "Do we know why he's all dressed up?"

Mary consulted her notebook. "He was

at something called the Spongg Footcare Charity Benefit —"

"What?" interrupted Jack. "The Spongg bash? Are you sure?"

"The invite was in his shirt pocket."

"Hmm," mused Jack. He would have to talk to Madeleine — she might even have a few pictures of him. "It was an expensive do. We'd better speak to someone who was there. We should also talk to his doctor and find out what we can about his health. Depression, phobias, illness, dizzy spells, vertigo — anything that might throw some light on his death."

Jack peered more closely at Humpty's features. He looked *old,* the ravages of time and excessive drinking having taken their toll. The face of the cadaver was a pale reflection of the last time they had met. Humpty had been a jolly chap then, full of life and jokes. Jack paused for a moment and stared silently at the corpse.

Mary, to whom every passing second was a second not spent furthering her career, had made a choice: She would keep her head down and then try to get a good posting when the division was disbanded. If she did really well with Jack, perhaps Chymes would take notice. Perhaps.

She said, "How did you know him?"

"He used to lecture on children's litera-ture and business studies at Reading Uni-versity. Good company and very funny, but a bit of a crook. He was being investigated by the university in 1981 when Chymes and I questioned him —"

"Whoa!" said Mary suddenly. "You worked for Friedland Chymes?"

"No," replied Jack with a sigh, "Fried-land and I worked *together*. You didn't know he started at the NCD, did you?"

"No."

"He doesn't spread it around. I've had some good officers through here, but they don't stay for long."

"Really?" said Mary, as innocently as she could.

"Yes. It's a springboard to better things — if you consider that *anything* is better than this. Unless you run it, in which case —"

He didn't finish the sentence, but Mary knew what he meant.

"So . . . how long have you been here?"

"Since 1978," mused Jack, still staring at Humpty's unseeing eye.

"Twenty-six years," said Mary, perhaps with a little too much incredulity in her voice than she would have liked. Jack looked at her sharply, so she changed the subject.

"I heard Friedland Chymes was a joy to work with."

"He's an ambitious career officer who will lie, cheat and steal as he clambers over the rubble of used and discarded officers on his way to the top."

"Boy, did I read *that* wrong," she replied, not believing a word — she knew how the brightest stars always invoked jealousy from those left behind.

"Yes, you did. You've heard, I suppose, about the murder of Cock Robin?"

"No."

Jack sighed. No one ever did these days. Chymes made certain of it. It had been two decades ago anyway.

"Well, it doesn't matter — it's ancient history. To get back to Humpty, Friedland and I questioned him about a racket in which he imported eight containerloads of spinning wheels the week before the government ban. The compensation deal netted him almost half a million, but he'd done nothing illegal. He was like that. Always up to something. Ducking and diving, bobbing and weaving. He was fired from the university when they suspected him of having his hands in the till."

"They couldn't fire him over suspicion, surely?"

"No, but he'd made the m⌐
having an affair with the dean's w.
didn't go down too well. Last I h⌐
him, he had hit the sauce pretty badly
was into commodity speculation."

Jack looked at Humpty's features again.
"How old was he?"

Mary consulted his driving license. "He
was . . . er, sixty-five."

Jack looked up at the wall again.
Humpty had always sat on walls, it was his
way. He'd even had one built in the lecture
room where he taught, a plaster and
wooden mockup that could be wheeled in
when required.

"Have uniform been round to break the
news to Mrs. Dumpty?"

"Yes, sir."

"We should have a word with her. Find
out what state she's in. Good morning,
Gladys, what does this look like to you?"

Mrs. Singh stood up and stretched her
back. She had just celebrated her fiftieth
birthday and was the pathologist allocated
by default to Jack and all his cases. In real
life she was an *assistant* pathologist, but
the chief pathologist wouldn't do NCD
work in case he got laughed at, so he sent
along Mrs. Singh and rubber-stamped her
reports without reading them. Like Jack,

she was doing the best she could on limited resources. Unlike Jack, she loved cats and people who loved cats and had six grandchildren.

"They hung us out to dry over the pig thing, Jack," she said. "I'm sorry."

"Were you surprised?"

"To be honest, no. When *was* the last time we got a conviction?"

"Five years ago," replied Jack without even having to think about it. "That guy who was running the illegal straw-into-gold dens. What was his name again?"

"Rumplestiltskin," returned Mrs. Singh with a faint smile at the memory. "Twenty years, no remission. Those were the days. Who's the new blood?"

"DS Mary Mary," said Jack. "Mary, this is Mrs. Singh."

"Welcome to the house of fun," said Mrs. Singh. "Tell me, did you actually *request* to work here?"

"Not . . . as such."

Mrs. Singh flashed an impish smile at Jack. "No," she said, "they never do."

She waved a rubber-gloved hand at Humpty's remains. "That's a lot of shell. I never saw him alive — how big was he?"

Jack thought for a moment. "About four-foot-six high — three foot wide."

She nodded. "That makes sense. He would have been quite heavy, and it's a fall of over twelve feet. I'll know a bit more when I get him back to the lab, but I can't see anything that would preclude a verdict of either accidental death or suicide."

"Any idea on the time of death?"

"Difficult to say. The rainstorm last night pretty much washed everything away. There are scraps of inner and outer membrane — and this." She held up a gelatinous object.

"A jellyfish? This far inland?"

"I'm no expert when it comes to eggs," confessed Mrs. Singh, "but I'll try to identify it."

"What about time of death?"

She dropped the section of Humpty's innards into a plastic Ziploc bag with a *plop* and thought for a moment. "Well, the remaining viscera are still moist and pliable, so sometime within the last twenty-four hours. Mind you, the birds would have had most of it if he'd fallen off the wall yesterday, so if you want me to make a guess, sometime between 1800 hours yesterday evening and 0300 this morning. Any later than that and the rain wouldn't have had time to wash away all that albumen."

Mary jotted it down in her notebook.

Jack was sure there must be relatives, and they would almost certainly ask him one important question.

"Was it quick?"

Mrs. Singh surveyed the wreckage. "I think so. When he hit the ground his lights, quite simply, went out."

Jack thanked her as she spoke a few words in Hindi to her assistant, who very gently — as befits the deceased — began to lift the larger pieces of shell into a PVC body bag.

Jack carefully climbed up the ladder and looked at the top of the wall. It was barely a foot wide, and he could see an oval dip that had been worn by Humpty's pro- longed use. He climbed back down again, and both he and Mary went into the yard next door to look at the wall from the other side.

"What are you looking for?" asked Mary.

"Anything that might have been used to push him off."

"Pushed? You suspect foul play?"

"I just like to keep an open mind, Mary, despite what Briggs said."

But if Jack expected to find anything in- criminating, he was to be disappointed. The yard was deserted, and a precarious heap of rubbish and full garbage bags was stacked against the wall underneath where Humpty had sat. An assailant would have had to clamber over the heap but the rubbish was undisturbed. Jack was just looking in the outhouse for a rake or something when he noticed a small boy staring at him from the kitchen window. Jack waved cheerfully, but the little boy just stuck his middle finger up. He was grasped by the ear and pulled away, only to be replaced by a very small man in a nightgown and nightcap. He looked a bit bleary-eyed and fumbled with the latch before opening the kitchen window. Jack showed him his ID card.

"Detective Inspector Jack Spratt, Nursery Crime. You are . . . ?"

The small man rubbed his eyes and squinted at the card. "Winkie," he replied, blinking with tiredness. "William Winkie."

"Mr. Winkie, there was an accident last night. Mr. Dumpty fell off the wall."

"I heard."

"Him falling off?"

"No, the news I mean. He was a nice fella. He used to play ball and that with the kids in the alleyway. My kids are well choked by his death."

One of the "well-choked" kids continued to pull faces at Jack through the window.

Mr. Winkie gave him a clip round the ear, and he ran off bawling.

"Did you hear anything out of the ordinary last night?"

Willie Winkie yawned. "Pardon me. I got in from my shift at Winsum's at about two and went straight to sleep. I have a sleeping disorder, so I'm on medication."

"Anyone else in the house?"

Willie turned and shouted. "Pet! Did you hear anything strange last night? It's about Mr. Dumpty."

A large, florid woman came to the window. She wore a purple nylon dress and had her hair done up in rollers. A small unlit rolled cigarette was stuck to her lower lip and bobbled as she spoke.

"There was a truck reversing sometime in the small hours — but that's not unusual around here. I sleep in a separate room to Willie so he doesn't wake me. Sorry, love, I'd like to be able to help, but I can't."

Jack nodded and started on another tack. "When did you last see him?"

"Last night at about seven-thirty. He asked me to iron his cravat."

"Cravat?"

"Or cummerbund. It's difficult to say with him."

"How did he appear to you?"

"Fine. We chatted about this and that, and he borrowed some sugar. Insisted on paying for it. He was like that. I often ironed his shirts — on a wok to get the right shape, of course, and he always paid over the odds. He helped us out with a bit of cash sometimes and sent the kids on a school trip to Llandudno last summer. Very generous. He was a true gent."

"Did you ever see him with anyone?"

"He kept himself to himself. Liked to dress well, quite a dandy, y'know. One for the ladies, I heard. Come to think of it, there was a woman recently. Tall girl, quite young — brunette."

Jack thanked them and gave Willie his card in case he thought of anything else, then returned to the yard, where Mrs. Singh was still searching for clues as to what had happened.

"Where was his room?" asked Jack.

Mary pointed to the window overlooking the backyard.

They entered the house and climbed the creaking staircase. There was damp and mildew everywhere, and the skirting had come away from the wall. The door to Humpty's room was ajar, and Jack carefully pushed it open. The room was sparsely furnished and in about as bad a state of repair as the rest of the house. Hung on the wall was a framed print of a Fabergé egg next to a copy of Tenniel's illustration of Humpty from *Through the Looking Glass*. There was a shabby carpet that looked as though it hadn't been hoovered since the turn of the last century and a wardrobe against one wall next to a sink unit and a cooker. A large mahogany desk sat in the center of the room with a small pile of neatly stacked bricks behind it which Humpty had used as a seat. On the desk was a typewriter, some papers, a fax and two telephones. The previous week's edition of *What Share?* was open at the rare-metals page, and an undrunk cup of coffee had formed a skin next to Humpty's spectacles. There was a photo in a gilt frame of Humpty with his hand on the leg of a pretty brunette in the back of a horse-drawn carriage in Vienna. Jack knew because he'd been there once himself and recognized the Prater wheel in the background. They were both well dressed and looked as though they had just come from the opera.

"Any name?"

Mary checked the back of the picture. There was none.

Even from a cursory glance, it was obvious that not only had Humpty been working the stock market — he had been working it hard. Most of the paperwork was for a bewildering array of transactions, with nothing logged in any particular order. The previous Thursday's *Toad* had been left open at the business news, and Jack noticed that two companies listed on the stock exchange had been underlined in red pencil. The first was Winsum & Loosum Pharmaceuticals, and the second was Spongg Footcare. Both public limited companies, both dealing in foot-care products. Winsum & Loosum, however, was blue chip; Spongg's was almost bust. Mary had chanced across a file of press clippings that charted the downfall of Spongg's over the past ten years, from the public flotation to the fall of the share price the previous month to under twenty pence. Jack opened another file. It was full of sales invoices confirming the purchase of shares in Spongg's for differing amounts and at varying prices.

"Buying shares in Spongg's?" murmured Jack. "Where did he get the money?"

Mary passed him a wad of bank statements. Personally, Humpty was nearly broke, but Dumpty Holdings Ltd. was good to the tune of ninety-eight thousand pounds.

"Comfortable," commented Mary.

"Comfortable and working from a dump."

Jack found Humpty's will and opened it. It was dated 1963 and had this simple instruction: *All to wife.*"

"What do you make of these?"

Mary handed Jack an envelope full of photos. They were of the Sacred Gonga Visitors' Center in various states of construction, taken over the space of a year or more. But the last snap was the most interesting. It was of a young man smiling rather stupidly, sitting in the passenger seat of a car. The picture had been taken by the driver — presumably Humpty — and had a date etched in the bottom right-hand corner. It had been taken a little over a year ago.

"The Sacred Gonga," said Mary, thinking about the dedication ceremony on Saturday. "Why is Humpty interested in that?"

"You won't find anyone in Reading who isn't," replied Jack. "There was quite an uproar when it was nearly sold to a collector in Las Vegas."

They turned their attention to the wardrobe that held several Armani suits, all of them individually tailored to fit Humpty's unique stature and held up on hangers shaped like hula hoops. Jack checked the pockets, but they were all empty. Under some dirty shirts they found a well-thumbed copy of *World Egg Review* and *Parabolic and Ovoid Geometric Constructions*.

"Typical bottom-drawer stuff," said Jack, rummaging past a signed first edition of *Horton Hatches the Egg* to find a green canvas tool bag. He opened it to reveal the blue barrel of a sawed-off shotgun. Jack and Mary exchanged glances. This raised questions over and above a standard inquiry already.

"It might be nothing," observed Mary, not keen for anything to extend the investigation a minute longer than necessary. "He might be looking after it for a friend."

"A friend? How many sawed-off shotguns do you look after for friends?"

She shrugged.

"Exactly. Never mind about Briggs. Better get a Scene of Crime Officer out here to dust the gun and give the room the once-over. Ask for Shenstone; he's a friendly. What else do you notice?"

"No bed?"

"Right. He didn't live here. I'll have a quick word with Mrs. Hubbard."

Jack went downstairs, stopping on the way to straighten his tie in the peeling hall mirror.

4. Mrs. Hubbard, Dogs and Bones

The Austin Allegro was designed in the mid-seventies to be the successor to the hugely popular Austin 1100. Built around the proven "A" series engine, it turned out to be an ugly duckling at birth with the high transverse engine requiring a slab front that did nothing to enhance its looks. With a bizarre square steering wheel and numerous idiosyncratic features, including a better drag co-efficient in reverse, porous alloy wheels on the "sport" model and a rear window that popped out if you jacked up the car too enthusiastically, the Allegro would — some say undeservedly — figurehead the British car-manufacturing industry's darkest chapter.

— *The Rise and Fall of British Leyland,*
A. Morris

Jack knocked politely on the door. It opened a crack, and a pinched face glared suspiciously at him. He held up his ID card.

"Have you come about the room?" Mrs. Hubbard asked in a croaky voice that reminded Jack of anyone you care to mention doing a bad impersonation of a witch. "If you play the accordion, you can forget about it right now."

"No, I'm Detective Inspector Spratt of the Nursery Crime Division. I wonder if I could have a word?"

She squinted at the ID, pretended she could read without her glasses and then grimaced. "What's it about?" she asked.

"What's it about?" repeated Jack. "Mr. Dumpty, of course!"

"Oh, well," she replied offhandedly, "I suppose you'd better come in."

She opened the door wider, and Jack was immediately assailed by a powerful odor that reminded him of a strong Limburger cheese he had once bought by accident and then had to bury in the garden when the dustbinmen refused to remove it. Mrs. Hubbard's front room was small and dirty, and all the furniture was falling to pieces. A sink piled high with long-unwashed plates was situated beneath yellowed net curtains, and the draining board was home to a large collection of empty dog-food cans. A tomcat with one eye and half an ear glared at him from under an old wardrobe, and four bull terriers with identical markings stared up at him in surprise from a dog basket that was clearly designed to hold only two.

Mrs. Hubbard herself was a wizened old lady of anything between seventy-five and a hundred five. She had wispy white hair in an untidy bun and walked with a stick that was six inches too short. Her face was grimy and had more wrinkles in it than the most wrinkled prune. She stared at him with dark, mean eyes.

"If you want some tea, you'll have to make it yourself, and if you're going to, you can make one for me while you're about it."

"Thank you, no," replied Jack as politely as he could. Mrs. Hubbard grunted.

"Is he dead?" she added, looking at him suspiciously.

"I'm sorry to say that he is. Did you know him well?"

She shuffled across the room, her short walking stick making her limp far more than was necessary.

"Not really," she replied, settling herself in an old leather armchair that had horse-hair stuffing falling out of its seams. "He was only a lodger." She said it in the sort of way that one might refer to vermin. Jack wondered just how fantastically unlucky you would have to be to have this old crone as a landlady.

"How long had he a room here?"

"About a year. He paid in advance. It's nonreturnable, so I'm keeping it. It's very hard getting lodgers these days. If I took in aliens, spongers or those damnable statisticians, I could fill the place twice over, but I have standards to maintain."

"Of course you do," muttered Jack under his breath, attempting to breathe through his mouth to avoid the smell.

At that moment one of the dogs got out of its basket, pushed forth its front legs and stretched. The hamstrings in its hind legs quivered with the effort, and at the climax of the stretch the dog lowered its head, raised its tail and farted so loudly that the other dogs glanced up with a look of astonishment and admiration. The dog then walked over to Mrs. Hubbard, laid its nose on her lap and whined piteously.

"Duty calls," said Mrs. Hubbard, placing a wrinkled hand on the dog's head. She heaved herself to her feet and shuffled over to a small cupboard next to the fridge. Even Jack could see from where he was standing that it contained nothing except an old tin of custard powder and a canned steak-and-kidney pie. She searched the cupboard until satisfied that it was devoid of bones, then turned back to the dog, which had sat patiently behind her, thumping its tail on an area of floor that had been worn through the carpet and underlay to the shiny wood beneath.

"Sorry, pooch. No bones for you today."

The dog strode off and sat among its brethren, apparently comprehending every word. Mrs. Hubbard resumed her seat.

"Now, young man, where were we?"

"What sort of person was he?"

"Nice enough, I suppose," she said grudgingly, the same way a Luddite on dialysis might react to a kidney machine. "Never any trouble, although I had little to do with him."

"And did he often sit on the wall in the yard?"

"When he wasn't working. He used to sit up there to — I don't know — to *think* or something."

"Did you ever see him with anyone?"

"No. I don't permit callers. But there *was* a woman last night. Howling and screaming fit to bring the house down, she was. Really upset and unhappy — I had to threaten to set the dogs on her before she would leave."

He showed her the photo of the woman in Vienna. "This woman?"

Mrs. Hubbard squinted at it for a few moments. "Possibly."

"Do you know her name?"

"No."

Another dog had risen from the basket and was now whimpering in front of her like the first. She got up and went to the same cupboard and opened it as before, the dog sitting at the same place as the first, its tail thumping the area of shiny wood. Jack sighed.

"Sorry, dog," she said, "nothing for you either."

The bull terrier returned to its place in front of the fire, and Mrs. Hubbard sat back in her chair, shooing off the tomcat, which had tried to gain ascendancy in her absence. She looked up at Jack with a puzzled air.

"Had we finished?"

"No. What happened last night after the woman left?"

"Mr. Dumpty went to a party."

She got up again as *another* dog had started to whimper, and she looked in the cupboard once more. Considering the hole in the carpet and the area of shiny wood that the dogs' tails had worn smooth, Jack supposed this little charade happened a lot.

"When did he get back?" asked Jack when she had returned.

"Who?"

"Mr. Dumpty."

"At about eleven-thirty, when he arrived in the biggest, blackest car I've ever seen. I always stay up to make sure none of my lodgers bring home any guests. I won't have any sin under *this* roof, Inspector."

"How did he look?"

"Horribly drunk," she said with disgust, "but he bade me good evening — he was always polite, despite his dissolute lifestyle — and went upstairs to his room."

"Did he always spend the night here?"

"Sometimes. When he did, he slept on the wall outside. The next time I saw him, he was at peace — or in *pieces,* to be more precise — in the backyard when I went to dump the rubbish."

She had expected Jack to laugh at her little joke, but he didn't. Instead he sucked the end of his pencil thoughtfully.

"Do you have any other lodgers?"

"Only Prometheus upstairs in the front room."

"Prometheus?" asked Jack with some surprise. "The Titan Prometheus? The one who stole fire from the gods and gave it to mankind?"

"I've no concern with what he does in his private life. He pays the rent on time, so he's okay with me."

Jack made several notes, thanked Mrs. Hubbard and beat a grateful retreat as she went to the same cupboard for the fourth time.

5. Prometheus

TITAN ESCAPES ROCK, ZEUS, CAUCASUS, EAGLE

A controversial punishment came to an end yesterday when Prometheus, immortal Titan, creator of mankind and fire-giver, escaped the shackles that bound him to his rock in the Caucasus. Details of the escape are uncertain, but Zeus' press secretary, Ralph Mercury, was quick to issue a statement declaring that Prometheus' confinement was purely an "internal god-Titan matter" and that having eagles pick out Prometheus' liver every day, only to have it grow back at night, was "a reasonable response given the crime." Joyous supporters of the "Free Prometheus" campaign crowded the dockside at Dover upon the Titan's arrival, whereupon he was taken into custody pending applications for extradition.
— From *The London Illustrated Mole*,
June 3, 1814

Jack walked up the creaky steps to the upstairs landing. He had just raised his hand to knock on the door opposite Humpty's when a deep male voice, preempting his knock, boomed, "One moment!"

Jack, puzzled, lowered his hand. There was a sound of movement from within, and presently the door opened six inches. A youthful-looking, darkly tanned man with tightly curled blond hair answered the door. He had deep black eyes and a strong Grecian nose that was so straight you could have laid a set-square on it. He looked as though he had just got out of the shower, as he had a grubby towel wrapped around his waist. On his muscular abdomen were so many crisscrossed scars on top of one another that his midriff was a solid mass of scar tissue. He was so cleanly shaven that Jack wondered whether he had any facial hair at all, and his eyes bored into Jack with the look of a man used to physical hardship.

"Yes?" he asked in a voice that seemed to rumble on after he had spoken.

"Mr. Prometheus?"

"Just Prometheus."

"I'm Detective Inspector Spratt, Nursery Crime Division. We're investigating Mr. Dumpty's death. I wondered if I might talk to you?"

Prometheus looked relieved and invited

him in, his voice losing its rumble as he no longer took Jack to be a threat.

The room was similar to Humpty's in levels of shabbiness, but Prometheus had tried to make it look a little more like home by pinning up holiday posters of the Greek islands. Stuffed in the frame of the mirror was an assortment of postcards from other Titans and minor demigods, wishing him well with his ongoing asylum application. A mattress covered with rumpled sheets lay on the floor, and on the bedside table, next to a copy of Plato's *Republic*, was an empty bottle of retsina and a small bowl of olive stones. A copy of Shelley's account of Prometheus' escape from the rock in the Caucasus lay open on the only table, and Jack picked it up.

"A bit fanciful," remarked the Titan. "He took a few liberties with the truth. I had only ever met Asia and Panthea once at a party and I certainly was *never* in love with Asia. As I recall, she was myopic and couldn't pronounce her *r*'s. The bit about us having a child was pure invention. I would have sued him for libel, but he died — which was *most* inconvenient."

"Yes," agreed Jack, knowing that to an immortal such as Prometheus, death really *was* something that only happened to other people, "it generally is."

"I was sorry to hear about Humpty," said the Titan, thumping the vibrating pipes with a wooden mallet to get the water flowing out of the rusty tap and onto his toothbrush.

"You knew him well?"

Prometheus squeezed the remains of a toothpaste tube onto the brush. "Not really, but well enough to know he was a good man, Inspector. Good and evil are subjects I know quite a lot about. He had righteousness in spades, despite his criminal past."

Prometheus rinsed his mouth, popped the toothbrush back in its glass, immodestly dispensed with the towel and wrapped himself in a dressing gown that had once belonged to the Majestic Hotel.

"We chatted quite a lot when we bumped into each other," continued the Titan. "He was always busy but made the effort."

"When did you last see him?"

"Last night at about six. He called me over to help him tie his cummerbund."

"Cummerbund?"

"Or cravat. It's difficult to tell with him. He'd had an argument with his girlfriend. Did Mrs. Hubbard tell you?"

"She mentioned it. Do you know her name?"

"Bessie, I think," replied the Titan.

"No surname?"

"I'm sure she has one, but I don't know it. I don't think she was a serious girlfriend, but she was the most regular."

"There was more than one?"

"Humpty was probably the least monogamous person I've ever met. I couldn't agree with his lifestyle, but despite it I think he had a good heart. I can't imagine Grimm's Road was a great place to bring women, but, knowing him, he enjoyed the sport of sneaking them past Mrs. Hubbard."

"What else did you and Humpty talk about last night?"

"Not a lot, but he seemed upset, or annoyed, or unwell. Put it this way: He looked pretty pasty. When it was time for him to go, he thanked me for my companionship and shook my hand. He didn't usually do that, and, looking back on it, I suppose he might have been saying . . . good-bye."

"Did he seem depressed or anything recently?"

The Titan thought for a moment. "Less talkative. Preoccupied, perhaps."

"When did you see him again?"

"I didn't. I heard him go into his room

about ten-thirty, and the next thing I knew, Mrs. Hubbard was banging on my door and asking if I wanted Humpty's room for an extra fifty quid a week."

There didn't seem to be anything more Jack could learn, at present.

"Thanks for your help. I can usually find you here?"

Prometheus sighed. "Humpty was paying half of my rent. I can't afford this dive any longer. You could always leave me a message at Zorba's — I wait tables there three times a week."

Jack had an idea.

"We need a lodger. Come around to this address and meet my wife tonight at about seven."

Prometheus took the proffered scrap of paper.

"Thank you," he said. "I think I might just do that."

Mary had been speaking to the neighbors. They were suspicious at first but soon became keen to help when they found out it was Humpty who had died. He had, it seemed, been very generous in the neighborhood.

"What have you got?"

"Couple of people thought they heard

dustbins, though no one can put a time on it. I got a statement from Mr. Winkie. I think he's narcoleptic or something; he fell asleep as I was talking to him. SOCO didn't come up with much. No prints on the shotgun, but some unusual traces on the carpet — and a single human hair."

"Brunette? Like the woman in the Vienna photograph?"

"No, red — and twenty-eight feet long."

She passed him an evidence bag with a long piece of auburn hair wrapped carefully around itself like a fishing line.

"Now, that *is* unusual. Rings a bell, too. What about Mrs. Dumpty?"

"Not really the grieving widow. In fact, technically speaking, not a widow at all — they divorced over a year ago. She said to drop in at any time."

"Then we'll do just that. We *really* need to find the woman in the Viennese picture. She and Humpty had a row last night."

"What about?"

"We'll ask her when we find her. Her name's Bessie."

"I'll get the office onto it," said Mary. "Was that Prometheus upstairs?"

"Yes. Creator of mankind to Mrs. Hubbard's lodger. Makes Humpty's fall look like a stumble, doesn't it?"

Jack unlocked the car and pushed some papers off the passenger seat so that Mary could get in. She looked at the baby seat in the back.

"You have children, sir?"

"Lots of people do. I have five."

"Five?"

"Yup. Strictly speaking, only two are mine. Two more belong to my second wife, and we share the other. You married?"

"Me? No. I collect ex-boyfriends — and more than five, at the last count."

Jack laughed, started the engine and selected first gear. There was an ominous growling from deep within the gearbox, and they pulled out into the road to head off to the Caversham Heights district and Mrs. Dumpty.

"So what do you reckon?" asked Mary, still not having come to terms with her new job. She thought she wouldn't tell her friends back at Basingstoke about this quite yet — if at all.

Jack thought for a moment. "How about this: 'Big egg gets a shellful, throws himself off wall in fit of drunken depression.' Or this: 'Humpty goes to party, gets completely smashed, comes home and . . . gets completely smashed.' "

Mary's mobile rang. She looked at the

101

Caller ID before answering. Arnold *again.*

"I can't speak right now," she said before Arnold had a chance to say anything. "I'm at work. I'll call you back tonight. Promise. Bye."

She pressed the "end-call" button angrily, and Jack raised an eyebrow.

"I have a mother like that," he observed.

"It *wasn't* my mother," replied Mary sullenly. "It was an ex-friend who doesn't know the meaning of the phrase 'I never want to see you again.'"

There was a pause as they negotiated a roundabout, and Jack decided it was time to embark on his usual induction speech.

"I know that the Nursery Crime Division isn't everyone's cup of tea, but you should know the basics. The NCD's jurisdiction covers all nursery characters, stories, situations and directly related consequences of same. If a civilian is involved, then the regular CID *can* take over, but they generally don't. I answer to Briggs, but otherwise I'm independent. Because we cover well-established situations, patterns do begin to emerge. You can never *quite* tell how something is going to turn out, but you can sometimes second-guess the investigation."

"Such as?"

"Aside from people like Mrs. Hubbard? Well, there's usually a rule of three somewhere. Either *quantitative,* as in bears, billy goats, blind mice, little pigs, fiddlers, bags of wool or what-have-you, or *qualitative,* such as small, medium, large, stupid, stupider, stupidest. If you come across any stepmothers, they're usually evil, woodcutters always come into fame and fortune, orphans are ten a penny, and pigs, cats, bears and wolves frequently anthropomorphize."

"I wondered why Reading had talking animals," mused Mary, having never really thought about it before.

"The Billy Goats Gruff are a blast," said Jack. "I'll introduce you one day."

"No troll?"

"In the clink. Eight-to-ten-year stretch for threatening behavior."

"Do they know?"

"Do they know what?"

"Do they know they're nursery characters?"

"I think sometimes they *suspect,* but for the most part they have no idea at all. To the Billy Goats, Jack and Jill and the Gingerbreadman, it's all business as normal. Don't worry — you'll get into the swing of it."

Mary went silent thinking about how

nursery characters could possibly *not* know what they were when Jack, suddenly remembering something, picked out his mobile and pressed autoredial 1.

"Hiya, Mads. It's me. Tell me, did you get any pictures of Humpty Dumpty at the Spongg Footcare Charity Benefit? . . . No, Humpty *Dumpty*. . . . Sort of, well, like a large egg but about four foot six. . . . Yeah, but with arms and legs. I'd appreciate it. See ya."

He pressed the "end-call" button.

"As chance would have it, my wife was photographing the Spongg Charity Benefit last night. She may have some snaps."

They drove on for a moment without talking. Mary thought she should grasp the bull by the horns and explain that she really wasn't suited for the NCD; perhaps Jack could have a quiet word with Briggs and she could get out without being seen as something of a quitter. She bit her lip and tried to think of how to frame it, but luckily Jack broke the silence and saved her from the opportunity of making a fool of herself.

"Where did you say you were from?"

"Basingstoke."

"That's nothing to be ashamed of."

"I'm not ashamed of it."

"How many years in the force?"

"Eight, four as detective sergeant. I worked with DI Flowwe for four years."

"As Guild-Approved Official Sidekick?" asked Jack, surprised that Briggs had offloaded a pro on him. "I mean, Hebden was Guild, right?"

"Right. Only one of my stories got printed in *Amazing Crime*, though."

"You know I'm not Guild, Mary?" said Jack, just to make sure there wasn't some sort of embarrassing mistake going on. He didn't think he'd tell her quite yet that Madeleine had applied on his behalf.

"Yes, sir, I knew that."

"What was the case you had printed?"

"Fight rigging at the Basingstoke Shakespeare Company."

"Tell me about it."

Mary took a deep breath. She didn't know how much he knew and wondered whether it wasn't a test of her own humility; she had been commended for her part in the inquiry and was naturally proud of her work. She looked across at Jack, but he was concentrating on his driving.

"We didn't know there was a fraud going on at all for about a year," she began. "It all started on the last night of a Home Counties tour of *Romeo and Juliet*. All went well until the fight between Romeo and Tybalt at the beginning of act three."

"What happened?"

"Tybalt won."

Jack frowned. He was no culture vulture, but he could see the difficulties. "So the play ended?"

"There was almost a riot. A fencing referee who happened to be in the audience was called onto the stage, and he declared it a fair fight. The play finished with the company improvising an ending where Paris married Juliet, then was led to his own suicide by his failure to compete successfully with the love that Juliet held for her dead first husband."

"Quick thinking."

"You said it."

"So where's the crime?"

"At the bookies'. Tybalt, never a strong favorite, had been pegged at sixty to one, and someone pulled in an estimated three hundred grand. We were informed, but it seemed as though the bookies were just complaining that they had to pay out. It wasn't until a matinee performance of *Macbeth* three weeks later that the gang struck again. At the final big fight, Macduff was the clear favorite at even money. The bookies, now more vigilant, had placed Macbeth at three to one. It seemed a foregone conclusion; Macduff had fifty-eight pounds and eight years on Macbeth, not to mention some crafty footwork and a literary precedent that stretched back four hundred years."

"So Macbeth won?" asked Jack.

Mary shook her head. "No. It was smarter than that: *Banquo* did."

"Banquo?" echoed Jack in surprise. "Doesn't he get killed off earlier in the play?"

"Usually," replied Mary, "but this time he returned to the stage and made a brief speech explaining why he faked his own death, then slew Macbeth."

"I bet the bookies weren't pleased," observed Jack.

"You could say that. They hadn't suffered such a devastating loss since David beat Goliath. A rash of late bets had dropped Banquo's odds from five hundred to one down to a hundred to one, but it wasn't enough."

"How much did the gang make?"

"Ten million."

Jack whistled softly, and Mary continued: "This time there could be no mistake; someone was rigging the fights. Flowwe was put in command, and I went undercover as Lady Anne in their up-coming production of *Richard III*. It didn't take long before we caught them in the final act. After a matinee performance, I saw the theater director giving out script revisions. I alerted Flowwe, and that evening we had eight undercover officers hidden in the audience, disguised variously as popcorn salesmen, tourists from the Midlands and critics from the *Basingstoke Bugle*. I had sneaked a look at the 'revisions' and knew what they were up to. At a suitable moment, we pounced, halted the Battle of Bosworth Field and arrested not only Richard III, but Lords Richmond and Stanley as well. Plots had been laid to call the battle a draw and then form a governmental coalition, a surprise result that would have netted the perpetrators over three million quid. It led directly to Flowwe gaining an extra twelve places on his *Amazing Crime* ranking to a creditable twenty-fifth. No Basingstoke officer had ever been higher."

"And a commendation for you?"

She blushed and tossed her head modestly. "That, too."

Jack remembered now where he had seen her name before. She had been commended not only for her sterling police

work but also for her memorable performance as Lady Anne.

"Impressive. Is there anything you want
to know about me apart from the fact that
I'm not Guild?"

"Yes," replied Mary. "What happened to
your last DS?"

"His name was Alan Butcher. A good
man. He died in a car accident."

"I'm sorry."

"Not as sorry as I was; I was the one that
ran over him in my wife's Volvo. But it
wasn't my fault — he stepped out in front
of me."

"Was he . . . tall?" asked Mary a bit reck-
lessly.

Jack shook his head sadly. "You've heard
about the giant killing *already?* Sometimes
I think the station talks of almost nothing
else. Well, hear it from the horse's mouth:
Aside from Butcher, they were all self-
defense. When someone that big comes at
you with a knife, you don't stop to worry
about using lethal force. It was him or me.
Same as the other two. Mind you, only one
of them was *technically* a giant — the rest
were just tall. But you know what really
annoys me?"

"No, what really annoys you?"

"Well, did you hear about the time I

saved Hansel and Gretel from being eaten alive by a witch?"

"No, I'm afraid I didn't."

"Or the time I rescued a hundred children from the Pied Piper of Hamelin?"

"Don't . . . *think* so."

"What about dealing with serial wife killer Bluebeard?"

"Only when Briggs mentioned it yesterday."

"How about the time I closed down the illegal straw-into-gold den?"

"Not really."

"Convicted Jill of aggravated assault against Jack?"

"Nope."

"Stopped Mr. Punch throwing the baby downstairs?"

"Must have missed *that* one."

"This is my point. I've worked hard at the NCD for twenty-six years, trying to bring justice to everyone within my jurisdiction. I deal with most things within the NCD, and I like to think I make a difference. Is *any* of that remembered? Not a bit of it. I kill a few tall guys and all of a sudden I'm nothing but a giant killer."

They reached Mrs. Dumpty's house a few minutes later. It was named, ironically, the Cheery Egg.

6. Mrs. Laura Dumpty

OYSTERS ONE STEP CLOSER TO VOTE

Animal rights took a giant leap away from the dark ages yesterday with the passing of the Animal (anthropomorphic) Equality Bill. The act will guarantee the rights of animals considered human enough to function within Homo sapien society. Applicants are required to take a "speech and cognitive ability" test and, if passed by the five-strong board, are issued with an identity card that allows them to live unmolested within the designated safe haven of Berkshire. "It's a major triumph," said Mr. Billy Gruff, one of the main lobbyists. "For too long now we have been marginalized by society." The rights of standard nonanthropomorphized animals are unaffected by the act, and they may still be hunted, killed, farmed and eaten with impunity.

    — Article in *The Owl*, January 13, 1962

"He had it coming. Who was it, a jealous husband?"

"We never said he was murdered, Mrs. Dumpty."

The ex-Dumpty residence was a large mock Tudor dwelling. It was cheaply elegant, the furniture and pictures all reproductions, and they trod on marble-effect linoleum in the entrance hall. Mrs. Dumpty spoke to them sitting at a faux-wood Formica table in the large kitchen, wearing a mock-leopardskin jacket and smoking a Sobranie through a silver gilt cigarette holder with affected grace. Her hair was dyed jet black, and her last face lift had pulled her features into a grimace. She spoke in elocuted upper-class tones and looked as though her tan had been applied with a roller. Everything in the house was false, and that included Mrs. Dumpty. She fixed Jack with a stern eye.

"What difference does it make? He's dead isn't he?"

"So you weren't close, then?"

She laughed again. "Once upon a time, Inspector. 'Fidelity' was not a word in Humpty's word stock as much as —" She paused, trying to think up a suitable word.

"Vocabulary?" suggested Mary.

"Right. Fidelity was not a word in Humpty's word stock as much as 'vocabulary' isn't in mine. I knew he was sleeping around. He had great charm, and any moppet that came his way he used to regard as fair game."

She paused for a moment, thinking. Neither Jack nor Mary said anything, so she continued:

"He married me for my money. My family name is Garibaldi. I suppose that means something to you?"

"Indeed it does," said Jack. He knew as well as anyone that the Garibaldi family was big in biscuits. Yummy-Time Cakes and Snacks (Reading) was valued at over £130 million, and its Reading manufacturing facility churned out five thousand packets of chocolate digestives a day — and that was just the milk chocolate variety.

"When my father died, he left the biscuit concern entirely to me. It was my money that attracted Hump."

"For high living?" asked Jack, wondering why Humpty had been working from a dive in Grimm's Road.

"Speculation," replied Mrs. Dumpty, taking the spent cigarette from the holder and stubbing it out in a mock-tortoiseshell ashtray.

"What did he speculate in?"

"Mostly bankrupt stock, that sort of

thing. He bought shares when they went low before a possible merger and then sold when the shares rose — if they did. It was a very high-risk venture. He spent over eight million pounds of my money on his harebrained schemes. South American zinc, North American zinc, Canadian zinc. . . . In fact" — she paused for a moment — "I don't think there was much zinc he *didn't* speculate in. Some he made a killing on; most of them failed. We lived together for eighteen years, and in that time he made and lost five fortunes. His philandering always got worse when he was worth a lot of money. I thought it would blow over, small indiscretions that only served to prove he could still charm the ladies. It carried on, Mr. Spratt, grew more and more blatant, until I told him it had to stop. He refused, so I told him he couldn't have any more of my money."

"What did he do?" asked Jack.

Mrs. Dumpty paused for a moment. "He did what any other man would do in the same situation. He walked out. He went that same morning."

She lit another cigarette. "I changed the locks. I got a divorce. An ironclad prenuptial against adultery denied him any of my Yummy-Time fortune. I know nothing about his tawdry affairs because I chose not to be interested. I'm afraid to say I cannot tell you anything more." She paused and stared at the end of her cigarette.

Mary consulted her notebook.

"Do you know where he stayed after he left you?"

"I have no idea. With one of his conquests, I imagine."

"Do you have any idea what he was up to?"

"None. He was out of my life."

"Did he ever get depressed?" asked Jack.

She visibly started at the question and said with some surprise, "Depressed? Are you considering this might be *suicide?*"

"I'm sorry to have to ask you these questions, ma'am."

She pulled herself together and assumed an air of haughty indifference. "Why should I care, Inspector? He is no longer part of my life. Yes, he often got depressed. He was an outpatient at St. Cerebellum's for longer than I had known him. Easter was always bad for him, as you can imagine, and whenever he saw a cooking program featuring omelettes or eggs Benedict, he would fly off the handle. Whenever the salmonella recurred, I know he found life very painful. Sometimes he would wake up at night in a sweat, screaming, 'Help, help, take me off, I'm boiling.' I'm sorry, Officer, do you find something funny?"

She directed this last comment at Mary, who had let out a misplaced guffaw and then tried to disguise it as a sneeze.

"No, ma'am, hay fever."

"Mrs. Dumpty," continued Jack, unwilling to lose the momentum of the interview, "do you recognize this woman?" He placed the Viennese photo in front of her.

"No."

"It would help if you looked at the picture before answering."

Her eyes flicked over to it, and she inhaled deeply on the Sobranie, blowing the smoke up in the air. "One of his tramps, I daresay."

She looked at Jack, her eyes narrowing. "I haven't seen him for two years, Mr. Spratt. We were divorced."

She got up and walked to the window and paused for a moment with her back to them before asking in a quiet voice, "Do you think he was in any pain?"

"We don't believe so, Mrs. Dumpty."

She seemed relieved.

"Thank you, Inspector. It is good to know that, despite everything."

She gazed out the window. In the middle of the lawn was a large brick wall. It was six feet high, three feet wide and two feet thick; the bricks were covered in moss, and the mortar was beginning to crumble.

"He loved his walls," she said absently, looking away from the structure in the garden and staring at the floor. "He had an extraordinary sense of balance. I had seen him blind drunk and asleep, yet still balanced perfectly. I had that one built for him on his fiftieth birthday. He used to tell me that when he had to go, he would die atop one of his favorite walls, that he would remain there, stone-cold dead, until they came to take him away."

She cast another look at the brick monolith in the back garden.

"It's his tombstone now," she said, in a voice so low it was almost a whisper.

Jack peered beyond Humpty's wall at a large wooden construction with a glass roof. Mrs. Dumpty guessed what he was looking at.

"That was his swimming pool. He had it built when we came here. Keen swimmer. It was about the only physical activity he excelled in. Good buoyancy and natural streamlining, you see — especially backward, with his pointy end first, if you get what I mean. If you have no other questions . . . ?"

"Not for now, Mrs. Dumpty. Thank you."

"Mrs. Dumpty?" said a voice from the door. "It's time you did your thirty lengths."

They turned to see an athletic-looking blond man aged about thirty dressed in a bathrobe. He had curly hair and large brown eyes like a Jersey cow.

"This is Mr. Spatchcock," explained Mrs. Dumpty quickly, "my personal fitness instructor."

Spatchcock nodded a greeting. They left her to his attentions and walked back to the car.

"Think she's over Dumpty?" asked Mary.

"Not really. She didn't believe he was likely to fall by accident. What did she say: 'blind drunk and still perfectly balanced'? I think she had more to say, too. *Secrets.* Perhaps not to do with his death, but secrets nonetheless."

"Most people do," observed Mary. "Where are we going now?"

"To the Paint Box to see Mr. Foozle."

"How is he to do with Humpty?"

"He isn't."

Mr. Foozle was a large man with a ruddy complexion whom Jack knew quite well, as their sons played football together. The shop was also a gallery; on the walls at present was a collection of abstract paintings.

"Mr. Spratt!" said Foozle genially. "I didn't expect to see you in here."

"Me neither, Mr. Foozle. Do you sell any of these things?" he asked, waving a hand at the canvases splashed with paint.

"Indeed. Two hundred eighty pounds a throw."

"Two hundred eighty pounds? It looks like a chimp did them."

Foozle gasped audibly and looked to either side in a very surreptitious manner. "Extraordinary! You detective johnnies have an uncanny sixth sense! You see, a chimp *did* do them — but that's our secret, right?"

Jack laid the painting on the counter. "It's my mother's," he explained. "It's of a cow. She says it's a Stubbs."

Foozle unwrapped the canvas. "How is Mrs. Spratt? More cats?"

"Don't ask."

"And your delightful wife? Her cover this morning was a real corker — Oh!"

It was said with a surprised tone that

made Jack wonder whether it was an "Oh!" good or an "Oh!" bad. Foozle took a magnifying glass from his coat and examined the painting minutely, hunching over it like a surgeon. He grunted several times and finally stood up straight again, taking off his spectacles and tapping them against his teeth.

"Well, you're right about one thing."

"It's a Stubbs?"

"No, it's a cow."

"Don't tell me it's a fake?"

Mr. Foozle nodded. "I'm afraid so. It's painted in his style and dates probably from the early years of the nineteenth century. It's interesting for the fact that it's a prize cow. Stubbs usually painted horses, so it's unusual that a forger would copy work in his style yet not his favorite subject."

Jack ventured a theory. "Is it possible that it was painted in his style quite innocently, and then someone else added the signature, intending to pass it off as a Stubbs?"

Foozle smiled. "You should be a detective in our business, Mr. Spratt. I think you're probably right. In any event I don't suppose it's worth much more than a hundred pounds, perhaps more if an auction house would take it."

Jack sighed. His mother would be mortified when she heard. He pulled the picture back across the counter and looked at it. It was a good painting and the only one of his mother's that he would have had on his own wall.

"Do the best you can, Mr. Foozle."

Foozle smiled and placed the picture behind the counter, then had an idea and pulled out a small cardboard box. "I wonder whether your mother would be interested in . . . *these?*"

He opened the box. Inside were six brightly colored broad beans about the size of walnuts. They flashed and glowed as the light caught them. They were exceptionally beautiful, even to Jack's jaundiced eye.

"What are they?"

A smile crossed Mr. Foozle's face. "I got them from a dealer the other day. He said they were magical and very valuable. If you planted them, something wonderful would be sure to happen."

Jack looked at him dubiously. "He said that, did he?"

Mr. Foozle shrugged. "Take them to your mother and if she likes them, we'll call it a straight swap. If she doesn't, I'll give you a hundred pounds for the painting. Fair?"

"Fair." They shook hands, and Mr. Foozle replaced the lid of the box, then wrapped a rubber band around it for safe-keeping.

It was the sort of thing Jack's mother liked. Her house was almost full to capacity with knickknacks of every size and description; something this unusual might take the disappointment out of the Stubbs-that-wasn't.

Jack walked out of the shop and paused on the pavement as a curious feeling welled up inside him. "Magic *beans* for a Stubbs *cow*," he murmured to himself. There was something undeniably familiar about what he had just done, but for the life of him he couldn't think *what*. He shrugged and joined Mary in the car.

7. The Nursery Crime Division

The Nursery Crime Division was formed in 1958 by DCI Horner, who was concerned that the regular force was too ill-equipped to deal with the often unique problems thrown up by a standard NCD inquiry. After a particularly bizarre investigation that involved a tinderbox, a soldier and a series of talking cats with varying degrees of ocular deformity, he managed to prove to his confused superiors that he should oversee all inquiries involving "any nursery characters or plots from poems and/or stories." He was given a budget, a small office and two officers that no one else wanted and ran the NCD until he retired in 1980. His legacy of fairness, probity and impartiality remain unaltered to this day, as do the budget, the size of the offices, the wallpaper and the carpets.
— Excerpt from *A Short History of the NCD*

"Make yourself at home, Mary."

She looked around at the close confines

of the NCD offices. They were cramped and untidy. No. They were *worse* than that. They had gone through cramped and untidy, paused briefly at small and shabby before ending up at pokey and damp. Dented and chipped steel filing cabinets ringed the walls, making the room even smaller than it was. There was barely enough space for a desk, let alone three chairs.

"How long has the NCD been in these offices, sir?"

"Since they started the division. Why?"

"No reason. It just seems a bit . . . well, *close*."

"I like it," replied Jack mildly, taking a telephone from one of the filing cabinet drawers. "We have a room next door as well, but Gretel and the filing take up most of that. It's generally okay, as long as we don't all want to walk around at the same time."

"Gretel?"

"She's a specialist in forensic accountancy, but she helps us out when we're short-staffed, so we consider her one of ours. You'll like her. She's good with numbers and speaks binary."

"Is that important?"

"Actually, it is. Constable Ashley gener-ally understands everything we say, but complex issues are best explained to him in his mother tongue."

"Ashley's a Rambosian?"

"Yes, first ever in uniform."

There was a pause.

"Do you have any problems with aliens, Mary?"

"Never met one," she replied simply. "I take people as I find them. What's that smell?"

"Boiled cabbage. The canteen kitchens are next door. Don't worry; by the third year, you'll barely smell it."

"Hmm," murmured Mary, looking disdainfully around the small room and the piles of untidy case notes. "I might have an issue with the window."

"What window?"

"That's the issue."

At that moment a cloud of cold germs loosely held together in the shape of a human being walked in through the door. This, guessed Mary, was another part of the NCD. She was right.

"Good morning, sir," said the sickly-looking individual. He took a sniff from a Vick's nasal spray and dabbed his red nose with a handkerchief.

"Good morning, Baker," replied Jack. "Cold no better?"

Baker's cold *never* got better. A semi-dripping nose seemed to be a permanent fixture since a bout of flu eight years earlier. He wore a scarf even when it was quite warm, and his skin seemed pale and waxy. Despite looking as if he had barely three weeks before a terminal illness mercifully carried him away, he was actually extremely fit — he passed his annual medical with flying colors and completed the Reading Marathon every June in a creditable time.

"This is Charlie Baker, the station hypochondriac. I call him the office terrier. I give him a problem to solve and he won't let go until it's done. He's also convinced he has only a month to live, so he doesn't mind going through the door first on a raid."

"How do you do?" said Mary, shaking his hand.

"Not terribly well," replied Baker. "The dizzy spells have got worse recently, I have a rash on my scrotum, and a twinge in the knee might be the onset of gout." He showed her his forearm. "Does this look swollen to you?"

"Have you seen Ashley or Gretel?" asked Jack, trying to change the subject before he *really* got started.

"Ashley's burning some spinning wheels that were handed in as part of that amnesty thing," said Baker as he squeezed a few drops of Visine into his eyes and blinked rapidly, "and Gretel is having the morning off — I think she's being checked for Orzechowski's syndrome, a curious disease that plays havoc with the central nervous system and causes rapid movements of hands, feet and eyes — incurable, you know."

Jack and Mary stared at him, and he shrugged.

"Or maybe she's just waiting in for a plumber."

"Right. Mary, call St. Cerebellum's and get the name of Humpty's doctor, and, Baker, dig up some background info on Humpty — we should know what he's been up to and if he has a record. I'll be back in half an hour, and I take my coffee white with one sugar."

Jack picked up the evidence bag that contained the shotgun and walked out the door.

The Nursery Crime Division, it seemed, didn't generate many headlines — the framed news clippings that hung on the wall were just short, faded sections of newsprint culled from the few papers that carried the stories. There were clippings about Bluebeard's arrest, Giorgio Porgia, the notorious crime boss, and several others, going back over four decades. Uniquely, there was one regarding the Gingerbreadman from the front page of *The Toad*, but since it described Jack as "Chymes's assistant," Mary could understand why it was the least prominent.

"I figured you were a coffee person," said a voice. Mary turned to find the young constable she had seen earlier at Grimm's Road doing house-to-house. They had spoken, but only about work. She didn't even know his name.

"Thank you," replied Mary, taking the coffee gratefully and waving a hand at the press cuttings. "What do you know about all this?"

"Before I was even born," replied Tibbit, "but according to Gretel, the Giorgio Porgia collar was more DI Spratt's than Chymes's. The Super got funny about it when things got dirty. No one gives a damn about the nurseries as long as they kill one another. Porgia made the mistake of taking out *real* people. The Guv'nor had all the evidence, but Chymes closed the case — and got the credit."

"No wonder Jack doesn't like him."

"It goes back further than that. He doesn't talk about it much."

Mary's mobile started ringing. She dug it out of her pocket and looked at the Caller ID. Arnold *again.*

"This is a guy named Arnold," said Mary, handing the still-ringing phone to Tibbit. "Can you tell him I'm dead?"

Tibbit frowned doubtfully but took the phone and pressed the answer button anyway.

"Hello, Arnold?" he said. "PC Tibbit here. I'm afraid to tell you that DS Mary has been killed in an accident." He winced as he said it, and there was a pause as he listened to what Arnold had to say. "Yes, it *was* very tragic and completely unexpected." He listened again for a moment. "That's no problem, I'll tell her. Good day."

He pressed the end-call button and handed the mobile back.

"He said he was very sorry to hear about your accident and he'll call you later. I don't think he believed me."

"No, it's going to take more than my death to put him off, but thanks anyway. What's your name?"

"Constable Tibbit."

"Sergeant Mary Mary," said Mary,

shaking Tibbit's hand, "pleased to meet you."

The young officer thought hard for a moment, then said, "Arrange a . . . *symmetry.*"

Mary arched an eyebrow. "Pardon?"

He didn't answer for a moment but again thought hard and finally said in triumph, "Many . . . *martyrs* agree."

"Are you okay?"

"Of course!" replied the young constable brightly. "It's an anagram. If you take 'Sergeant Mary Mary' and rearrange the letters you get 'Arrange a symmetry' or 'Many martyrs agree.' The trick is to have them make sense. I could have given you 'My matey arrangers' or 'My artery managers,' but they sort of *sound* like anagrams, don't you think?"

"If you say so."

She had thought that perhaps Tibbit might have been a life raft of normality that she could somehow cling to for sanity, but that hope was fast retreating. It was little wonder he had been allocated to the division.

"It's a palindrome," continued the young constable.

"Sorry?"

"Tibbit. Easy to remember. Reads the

same backwards as forwards. *Tibbit.*"

Mary raised an eyebrow. "You mean, like 'Rats live on no evil star'?"

He nodded his head excitedly. "I prefer the more subtle ones, myself, ma'am, such as 'A man, a plan, a canal, Panama.' "

Mary sighed. "Sure you're in the right job?"

Tibbit appeared crestfallen at this, so Mary changed the subject.

"How long have you been here?"

"Six months. I was posted down here for three months, but I think they've forgotten about me. I don't mind," he added quickly. "I like it."

"First name?"

"Otto," he replied, then added by way of explanation, "Palindrome as well. My sister's name is Hannah. Father liked word games. He was fourteen times world Scrabble champion. When he died, we buried him at Queenzieburn to make use of the triple word score. He spent the greater part of his life campaigning to have respelt those words that *look* as though they are spelt wrongly but aren't."

"Such as . . . ?"

"Oh, skiing, vacuum, freest, eczema, gnu, diarrhea, that sort of thing. He also thought that 'abbreviation' was too long for its meaning, that 'monosyllabic' should have one syllable, 'dyslexic' should be re-named 'O' and 'unspeakable' should be respelt 'unsfzpxkable.' "

"How did he do?"

"Apart from the latter, which has met with limited success, not very well."

Mary's eyes narrowed. She feared she was having her leg pulled, but the young man seemed to be sincere.

"Okay. Here's the deal. You stay out of my way and I'll stay out of yours. Get me St. Cerebellum's number and make Jack a cup of coffee."

8. The Armory

The Forensic Department in Reading was an independent lab and covered all aspects of forensic technology as well as being an R&D lab for Friedland Chymes's sometimes eccentric forensic techniques. The department serviced not only the Oxford & Berkshire Constabulary but also the Wiltshire and Hampshire forces, too. Chymes had insisted long ago that they should be close enough for personal visits, which always made for more dramatic stories than sending material off and receiving technical reports in return. It pissed off Inspector Moose in Oxford no end, but that might have been the reason Chymes did it.
— Excerpt from *Chymes — Friend or Foe?*

The armory and ballistics division was run by George Skinner. He was a large man with a bad stoop, graying hair and a permanent hangdog expression. He wore pebble specs and a shabby herringbone suit that seemed as though he had inherited it from his father. Looks can be deceptive and were definitely so in Skinner's case. Not only was he an inspired ballistics and weapons expert, able to comment expertly and concisely on everything from a derringer to a bazooka, he was also highly watchable in the documentaries that often followed one of Chymes's investigations. But despite his somewhat sober appearance, he was also a lively fixture of Reading's nightlife. He could outdrink almost anyone, and if there was a report of someone dancing naked on the tables down at the Blue Parrot, you could bet safe money it was Skinner.

Jack knocked on the open door. "Hello, George."

"Come in, Jack," said Skinner without turning around.

Jack walked over and watched him for a moment. Like Mrs. Singh, Skinner was one of the few officers who didn't treat the NCD with the derision that seemed to hallmark Jack's association with the rest of the station. Friedland swore by Skinner, and Friedland expected the best — it galled him something rotten that Skinner was so chummy with Jack. Jack waited patiently while Skinner finished what he was doing, and then he produced the sawed-off shotgun.

"What do you make of this?" he asked.

"Ah!" said Skinner thoughtfully, signing the evidence label before removing the gun and carefully checking to make sure it was empty. "I make this a Marchetti twelve-gauge pump-action shotgun. Illegal, as all pumps are, and shortened like this, it's a nasty piece of work."

Skinner replaced his glasses, making his eyes appear twice as big as they were. He peered at Jack for a moment and then pulled a file off a shelf. He looked up the make against reported stolen or missing guns.

"Oh," he said in a tone that made Jack nervous.

"What?"

He looked at the frame number again.

"Bingo. Jack, meet the weapon that was stolen from Mr. Christian. It could be the murder weapon in the Andersen's Wood murders. That was one of Friedland's, wasn't it?"

"One of the many," replied Jack with a sigh.

The wood murders had all the characteristics of the sort of drama that Chymes liked to unravel. Mr. Christian had been murdered along with his wife eighteen months earlier in Andersen's Wood, a large forest to the west of Reading. The only possible motive was connected to the substantial amount of cash that had been found at their humble dwelling on the edge of the forest. Mr. Christian was a poor woodcutter, yet close to seven thousand pounds was found in their house, and no clue as to how they came by it. Friedland, in a typical display of bravado, had uncovered a sinuous trail of money laundering that led from East Malvonia and involved several hitherto unheard-of and only marginally plausible secret societies and ended up implicating the Vatican. During a daring raid on an address in Cleethorpes, the two prime suspects were killed and a large quantity of arms and cash recovered. The investigation was so complex that it had to be published as an annotated two-parter in *Amazing Crime Stories*. The only survivor of the raid confessed a few weeks later and was currently doing time in Reading Gaol.

"This gun was used to kill the Christians?"

"No, this gun *belonged* to the woodcutter. I can tell you if it was the one used to kill them by comparing the two spent cartridges they found at the scene. Who had it?"

"Humpty Dumpty."

"As in 'sat on a wall'?"

"No, as in 'had a great fall.' He was found dead this morning."

"Ah," replied Skinner knowingly. "I thought murdered woodcutters were NCD jurisdiction?"

"Friedland insisted they were *real* woodcutters, and Briggs agreed with him. As it turned out, he was right. Thanks, Skinner, you've been a lot of help."

Jack walked back into the station, stepped into the lift and pressed the button to go down to the basement. The lift, however, was already programmed to go up, so he went on an excursion to the seventh floor. The shotgun puzzled him. Humpty was undeniably shady, but he'd never been *violent.*

The lift stopped at the sixth floor, where Jack's least favorite person at Reading Central walked in: Friedland Chymes. They had once been partners together at the NCD until Friedland thought it was beneath him and jumped into the fast lane of the Guild of Detectives on the back of two cases that were more to do with Spratt. It had been Jack and Wilmot Snaarb who caught the Gingerbreadman that night, not Friedland, as he liked to claim. So it was no surprise that they didn't even look at each other. Friedland pressed the first-floor button and then stared at the indicator lights above the door. After a twenty-year enmity, the best either of them could manage was a single-word greeting.

"Jack."

"Friedland."

But, Friedland being Friedland, he couldn't resist a small dig.

"I knew the pigs would walk, old sport," he said loftily. "I didn't think the premeditation argument solid enough."

"It *was* solid," retorted Jack. "The defense had the jury loaded with other pigs. I wanted a wolf in the box, but you know how busy they are."

"You can't play the speciesist card every time you lose a case, Jack."

They were silent for a moment as the lift passed the fourth floor.

"I understand you've applied to join the Guild," remarked Chymes with a small and patronizing chuckle.

"Any officer can *apply*, Friedland."

"No need to get defensive, old boy."

"I'm not getting defensive."

"What will be your figurehead case? Finding sheep for Bo-peep? A failed conviction of three pigs?"

"I'll think of something."

"Of course you will. I hear Humpty took a nosedive. Suicide?"

"It's early days," replied Jack quickly, not wanting to relinquish any details, no matter how trivial.

"Humpty . . . wall . . . suicide . . . *murder,*" muttered Chymes thoughtfully. "Sounds like it could be a corker. Want me to take over?"

"No."

"I'll swap it for a strangling over in Arborfield."

"I said no, Friedland."

"Okay, the strangling in Arborfield *plus* a botulism poisoning by a vicar — with potential sexual intrigue thrown in. Proper stuff, Jack. None of your dozy nurseries."

"The answer's still no. You couldn't wait to get out of the NCD. Where were the offers of help when Mr. Punch was beating his wife? What about Bluebeard? I could have done with some assistance *then.*"

"Listen," said Chymes as the friendly horse-trading banter vanished abruptly, "let's cut the crap. I want this investigation — and I *will* have it."

"Which part of 'no' don't you understand?"

"Is that your final word?"

"You don't want to hear my final word."

"Well," said Chymes with a condescending smile, "I hope you won't regret your decision."

The lift stopped at the first floor. Friedland walked out, turned to Jack and said, "Just a spot of advice from an old soldier — don't build the case up. Word in the station says they should have left some room in Mr. Wolff's coffin for the NCD."

He started to walk away, but Jack wasn't done.

"I found the woodcutter's shotgun," he said in a low voice. "I want to check to see if it was the murder weapon in the woodcutter case."

Friedland halted abruptly, pressed the "door-hold" button and stared at Jack.

"I don't think that's very likely. Haven't you read the write-up in *Amazing Crime*? It was the Kiev mafia trying to muscle in on the Reading drug trade via Cleethorpes with the help of several all-powerful and unfeasibly ancient secret societies. It's a done deal, Jack — Max Zotkin is doing time as we speak."

Jack was unfazed. "Even so, I'd like to check. Do you have the cartridges from the murder scene? Skinner can check them against the gun we found."

Chymes stared at him for a moment, then appeared to soften. "I'll have them sent down. Good-bye, Jack."

The doors slid shut. Jack closed his eyes and took a deep breath. Suddenly, he remembered why he had never really wanted to be in the Guild.

9. Back at the Office

van Dumpty, Humperdinck (Humpty) Jehoshaphat Aloysius Stuyvesant. Businessman, philanthropist, large egg. Born/laid 6th June 1939, Oxford, England. Edu: Llanabba Castle. Uni: Christ Church. Career: Lecturer at Balliol, 1959–1964. Chief Financial Controller, Porgia Holdings, Inc., 1965–1969. Head of Reading Prison's laundry department, 1969–1974. Ogapôga Development Council, 1974–1978. Professor of Children's Literature, Reading University, 1980–1981. CEO Dumpty Holdings Ltd., 1983–present. CEO World Zinc, PLC, 1985–1991. CEO Splotvian Mineral and Mining Corporation, 1989–1990. Married 1: Lucinda Muffet-Dumpty 1962–1970 (Died). Married 2: Laura Garibaldi, 1984–2002 (Divorced). No children. Hobbies: reading, oology.

— Mr. Dumpty's entry in the 2002 edition of *Who's What?*

Mary looked up as Jack entered the room, but Tibbit actually *stood*, which seemed to her pointlessly correct protocol.

"Any luck with the shotgun?"

"You could say that. Remember the Andersen's Wood murder?"

"Of course," replied Mary. "It was titled 'From Russia with Gloves' and appeared in *Amazing Crime*, issue 12, volume 101, reprinted in *Friedland Chymes Casebook XVII*. It was an extraordinarily complex case. He —"

She stopped as she saw Jack glaring at her.

"I suppose you know the page number, too?" he asked.

"Sorry, wasn't thinking. Seriously, I thought Chymes had found the weapon that killed the woodcutters. After all, it was the discovery of the engraved Holland and Holland that led him on an unnecessarily complex jaunt around Europe before he solved it."

"It was never *proved* it was the weapon. He's sending the cartridges down so we can check."

"But if Humpty's shotgun *was* the murder weapon used to kill the woodcutters . . ."

"Yes," replied Jack, "Chymes would be *wrong*. Unthinkable, isn't it?"

Mary thought about agreeing with him

wholeheartedly but said instead, "A few things for you."

"Shoot."

"Mrs. Singh rang with some figures. They can't be certain, as so much of Humpty's albumen was washed away by the rain, but indications show he was twenty-six times the legal limit for driving. Even so, she reckons he would still have been conscious — it's something to do with his coefficient of volume."

"That's one seriously pickled egg," murmured Jack. "What else?"

"I've been collating the highlights from police databanks along with some background details Baker gleaned from a contact at the *Reading Mercury*."

"Go on."

She looked at her foolscap notepad, cleared her throat and began: "Humperdinck Jehoshaphat Aloysius Stuyvesant van Dumpty was born on the sixth June, 1939," she read. "His father was Gaylord Llewelyn Stuyvesant van Dumpty, a minor baronet and lecturer in classical Greek at Oxford. There seems to be some doubt over his mother. Schooled at Llanabba Castle, then Christ Church College reading mathematics and children's literature. He played rugby for Oxford and just missed being chosen to play for England owing to a knee injury."

"He'd make a pretty unstoppable player," said Jack, thinking it would be like trying to tackle a cannonball.

"As long as he didn't have to run, on those short legs," added Mary. "Anyway, he married Lucinda Muffet in 1962, and we don't hear anything about him until he is asked to leave a lecture post at Balliol in 1964 after being charged with a crooked property deal. Released through lack of evidence, he was not so lucky in 1969, when he was jailed for five years on a charge of money laundering for the Porgia family crime syndicate. He was questioned closely by the Serious Crime Squad about his connections but didn't talk and, when he was released three years later, was given an apartment, reputedly a gift from Giorgio Porgia himself. His first wife died in a car accident while he was in prison, in 1970. He spent the next few years living and working in Ogapôga and was heard of next in 1978, when he requested asylum at the British consulate in Pôga City. The Ogapôgian government had charged him with smuggling gems, and, following some swift diplomatic dealing, he was deported. He returned to England in 1979 and in

1980 moved to Reading to lecture at the university. Questioned by NCD officers over spinning-wheel profiteering in 1981, then fired from the university in the same year over allegations of embezzlements. In 1984 he married Laura Garibaldi. In 1989 he shifted his interests to world development and raised forty million pounds on a limited-share issue to buy a monopoly on mineral rights in the Splotvian Republic. Six months later a coup there lost him everything when the incoming administration nationalized the land. Investigations followed complaints by the shareholders, but again he was never charged. Made a fortune in zinc between 1985 and 1991, then lost it all in 1993 when he tried to corner the market in talcum powder on the Hong Kong commodities exchange. Questioned about insider trading on the Tokyo stock exchange in 1999 but again, never charged."

There was a pause.

"That's all we have."

"So . . . a few investigations and one conviction? For the Porgia money laundering?"

"I only gave you the *highlights*. He's been pulled in for questioning on one hundred twenty-eight occasions, charged twenty-six times, but, as you say, only convicted once."

"Well, we knew he was a bit of a crook."

"There is a flip side. He has undertaken numerous charitable assignments over the years and has spent a great deal of time raising money for a myriad of good causes, St. Cerebellum's being a notable favorite."

"I'm sure the people defrauded by the Splotvian mineral-rights scam would be overjoyed to hear that. How long had he been an outpatient there?"

"He'd been a patient there for over four decades," replied Mary, looking at a note she had made. "His doctor at present is someone named . . . Quatt."

Both Jack and Tibbit stopped what they were doing and stared at her. There was a sudden silence in the room. You could almost hear the skin forming on the custard in the canteen next door.

"You're joking? Not Dr. *Quatt* of all people?"

"I'm missing something here," she said slowly. "Who is he?"

"*She* used to be head of her own genetic research establishment until a scandal involving ethically dubious medical experiments."

"What sort of experiments?"

"Keeping monkey brains alive in jars, re-animating dead tissue — usual stuff. We probably won't get much sense out of her — she's as mad as a barrel of skunks."

A clerk came in and handed Jack a manila envelope. It contained five black-and-white glossy eight-by-tens and a note from Madeleine to say that he should call her if he was going to be late for dinner.

"Hah!" said Jack, going through the photographs. "There's our man!"

Two of the pictures were of other celebrities with Humpty in the background. In one he was sitting at a table pouring himself a drink, in another walking past, out of focus. The third was of him at the lectern giving some sort of speech.

"He does look drunk, doesn't he?" commented Mary.

The fourth photo was of him shaking hands with a distinguished-looking man in his sixties whom Jack recognized instantly.

"That's Solomon Grundy, the CEO of Winsum and Loosum Pharmaceuticals and ninth-wealthiest man in the country. He'll be pressing flesh and doing the buddy-buddy thing with the Jellyman on Saturday. Who else have we got?"

The fifth picture was of Humpty gazing a bit unsteadily at the camera while shaking hands with a somber-looking man in his early fifties.

Jack turned the picture over and read Madeleine's caption. " 'Local celebrity Mr. Charles Pewter meets local celebrity H. Dumpty at the 2004 Spongg Charity Benefit.' Charles Pewter. Anyone heard of him?"

Tibbit disappeared into the next room to find out.

Jack pinned Dumpty's photo on the board and stared at it for a moment.

"Jack?" said Briggs, who had appeared at the door. "Can I have a quick word?"

"Of course."

Briggs beckoned him out of the door and down the corridor a few yards. He looked left and right before speaking and lowered his voice.

"I've just had a call from DCI Chymes —"

Jack sighed audibly. "No way. No way on God's own earth, sir. NCD is *my* jurisdiction. Humpty is *my* jurisdiction. This is what I do." He felt his voice rising.

"I know that," said Briggs, trying to be conciliatory and authoritarian at the same time, "I just wanted you to *reconsider*. Chymes is Guild and high-profile. If you let him take over the Humpty investigation, it might bode well for the division."

"No, sir. I've been shafted once too often by Friedland. You'd have to suspend me before I'd let go."

Briggs took a deep breath and stared at him for a moment.

"Jack, please! Don't piss Chymes off. If the Guild of Detectives gets involved, it could all get really messy."

"Then," said Jack, "it's going to get messy. Are we done, sir?"

Briggs glared at him, then nodded, and Jack departed. He loosened his collar and felt his heart thump inside his chest. Humpty. Something told him it was going to be a tricky one.

As he walked back in, Tibbit and Mary were waiting for him with a hefty volume of *Reading Who's What?* Mary looked at him quizzically, but Jack didn't say anything.

"Pewter," said Tibbit, "Charles Walter. He's a commodities broker. Has been partnered to Mr. Perkupp at Perkupp and Partners since 1986. Active on the charity scene, married, with one son. Special interests: Victoriana, walking. Lives and works from Brickfield Terrace."

Jack picked up the phone and dialed Pewter's number.

After only two rings, a woman with a

cultured voice answered the phone. "Perkupp and Partners. May I help you?"

"Yes," he replied, "this is Detective Inspector Spratt, Nursery Crime Division. I wonder if I might speak to Mr. Pewter?"

"Certainly, sir. Please wait a moment."

She put him on hold, and a rather poor recording of Vivaldi came down the line. A moment later she was back.

"I'm sorry, sir, Mr. Pewter is in a meeting. Can he call you back?"

Jack knew when he was being fobbed off.

"Tell him I'm investigating Humpty Dumpty's death."

There was a short pause, and then a man's voice came on the line.

"DI Spratt? My name is Charles Pewter. Perhaps you'd better come around."

10. Charles Pewter

DANGEROUS PSYCHOPATH CAPTURED

The incredibly dangerous homicidal maniac known as "the Gingerbreadman" was captured almost single-handedly by Friedland Chymes last night. The cakey lunatic, whose reign of terror has kept Reading in a state of constant fear for the past six months, was brought to book by DI Chymes and some other unnamed officers in a textbook case of inspired investigation. "It really wasn't that hard," declared Chymes modestly. "Myself and some colleagues just did what was expected of any member of the police force." The flour, butter, ginger and sugar psychopath, whose penchant for literally pulling his victims apart, is currently in a secure wing of St. Cerebellum's, where he will doubtless remain for the rest of his life.

— From *The Toad*, March 23, 1984

Brickfield Terrace was a tree-lined avenue of houses built in the late 1890s and was situated only a few miles from the town center. Mr. Pewter's house, Jack discovered, was the last one in the street and also seemed to be the only house not dissected into undistinguished flats. As he tugged on the bellpull, he noted an ugly hole where the boot scraper should have been. After a moment, the door opened, and a tall man with Victorian clothes, a large beard and a face like a bloodhound stood on the threshold.

"If you're from *The Owl*," began Mr. Pewter without waiting to see who either Jack or Mary was, "you spelt my name wrong on the guest list for the Spongg Footcare Charity Benefit. It's not Pooter but *Pewter,* as in tankard."

His deep voice showed little emotion and was about as salubrious as his features.

Jack held up his ID card. "Detective Inspector Jack Spratt, Nursery Crime Division. This is Detective Sergeant Mary Mary."

"Ah!" he exclaimed. "Mr. Dumpty. You'd better come in."

Jack thanked him, and they stepped inside. It was like walking into a museum, for the whole house was decorated and furnished in a middle-class Victorian fashion. There was no expensive furniture; all the pieces were of low-quality boxwood and poor veneer. A pair of plaster of paris antlers painted brown were waiting to be put up on the wall, and fans and other Victorian knickery-knackery filled every vacant space. Mr. Pewter contemplated Jack's curious gaze with pride.

"It's all original, Mr. Spratt. Every single piece, from the screens to the bedstead to the fans on the sideboard. As very little of poor-quality Victorian furniture survives, for obvious reasons, it's of almost incalculable value. I bought these plaster of paris antlers at Christie's last week for seven thousand pounds. I had to beat off stiff competition from Japan; they love this stuff almost as much as I do. Shall we repair to my study?"

"Please."

Mr. Pewter led them through to a library, filled with thousands of antiquarian books.

"Impressive, eh?"

"Very," said Jack. "How did you amass all these?"

"Well," said Pewter, "you know the person who always borrows books and never gives them back?"

"Yes . . . ?"

"I'm that person."

He smiled curiously and offered them

both a seat before sitting himself.

"So how may I help?" he asked.

"You were at the Spongg Footcare Charity Benefit last night at the Déjà Vu Ballrooms?"

"I was."

"And you spoke with Mr. Dumpty?"

"Indeed I did, Inspector. Although, to be honest, I didn't really get much sense out of him."

"Was Mr. Dumpty drunk when he arrived?"

"Mr. Dumpty was a bit drunk all the time. He had a brilliant mind, but he wasted himself. I sat next to him, as I thought I could get him to join one of my self-help groups. You may not know, Mr. Spratt, but I run the Reading Temperance Society. We do what we can for people like Mr. Dumpty, using a combination of group reliance, prayer and electroshock aversion therapy. I spoke to him sternly about his habit when he joined the table."

"What did he say?"

Mr. Pewter coughed politely. "He said, 'Pass the Bolly, old trout, I've got a tongue like the Gobi Desert.' I refused, and he got Marjorie to pass it over instead. I tried to make him see reason, but he just told me not to be an old, er . . ."

"Fart?" inquired Mary helpfully.

"Exactly so, young lady. I tried again to make him see sense but he became sarcastic. I warned him about that, too, as I also run Reading's branch of Sarcastics Anonymous —"

"And *after* he became sarcastic? Then what happened?"

"He drank more and more until he was picking arguments with just about anybody on any subject. The whole sordid business came to a head when Lord Spongg approached the lectern and announced he was starting a fifty-million-pound fund for the rebuilding of St. Cerebellum's, the woefully inadequate mental hospital. Mr. Dumpty got up before any of us could stop him and pledged the full fifty million plus any 'brown envelopes' that might be necessary. There was an embarrassed hush, and his lordship made a joke of it. Mr. Dumpty told him he would be coming into a lot of money in the next couple of months, called Randolph a clot and then fell flat on his face."

"Unconscious?"

"Not quite. Lord Spongg escorted him outside with a waiter. Upon his return he apologized for his absence and explained that he had sent Mr. Dumpty home in Spongg's own car."

"What time was this?"

"About eleven."

"Did you know Mr. Dumpty well?"

"Socially, hardly at all. But in the course of my professional life, I had reason to see quite a lot of him."

Jack and Mary leaned closer. "Go on," said Jack.

Pewter pressed a lever on the office intercom and said, "The Dumpty file, please, Miss Hipkiss."

He then turned back to Jack and Mary and continued. "Humpty approached Perkupp and Partners about eighteen months ago with respect to some share dealings he was interested in. Since he had a considerable sum of money to invest, it was thought best that a partner in the firm should advise him. I was allocated as his personal broker." He shook his head sadly. "Mr. Dumpty dead! What a dreadful business. Who inherits his estate?"

Jack and Mary glanced at each other. Neither of them had considered probate. His will had dictated "all to wife," but he was divorced, so it seemed a bit gray.

"We don't know yet. Why do you ask?"

"Only because I have to move fast to try

to sell these shares. Barring miracles, Spongg's will be bankrupt within the next two months, and Mr. Dumpty's shares will be worth nothing. If we could get probate sorted out straightaway and I could start selling, then I might make something out of this whole dismal mess."

Jack was still in the dark. "Just how many shares did he have?"

At that moment Miss Hipkiss entered with a heavy buff folder. Mr. Pewter thanked the secretary with a badly concealed wink and then consulted the file.

"At a rough estimate I'd say about . . . twelve million."

Jack had to get him to repeat it. He wrote it in his pad and underlined it. "Twelve million shares? In how many companies?"

"Oh!" said Mr. Pewter. "I thought you knew. *Every single one of them is in Spongg Footcare PLC!*"

There was a pause as Jack and Mary took this in.

"So the egg had all his eggs in one basket," observed Mary. "Is that normal?"

"It's against *all* logical thinking, Miss Mary. If you have a large portfolio of shares, it is always considered prudent to spread the risk."

"So how much is all that worth?" asked Jack.

Pewter picked up a calculator and consulted a list of stock-market prices in a copy of *The Owl*. He pressed a few buttons.

"At current rates a little over a million pounds."

Jack whistled. "That's a very good portfolio."

Pewter didn't agree. He leaned back in his swivel chair, which creaked ominously.

"No, Inspector. It's a very *bad* portfolio. He spent about two and a half million pounds on its acquisition."

"You're losing me I'm afraid, Mr. Pewter."

The stockbroker thought for a moment. "Against my advice he continued to buy even when the share price dropped hourly. He holds — *held* — thirty-eight percent of Spongg's."

Jack was not too familiar with the machinations of share dealings, but one question seemed too obvious not to be asked.

"Why?"

There was a pause.

"I have no idea, Mr. Spratt. I can only think that he wanted Spongg shares to recover and to then sell them at a profit."

"How much *could* they be worth?"

Pewter smiled. "At the all-time high in the sixties, Humpty's share would have been worth almost three hundred million. But the possibility of that, given the downward trend of Spongg's fortunes, is infinitesimally small. He might as well have smeared the cash with gravy and pushed the bills into the lions' enclosure at the zoo."

Jack thought for a moment. "Did Mr. Dumpty seem naive in money matters?"

Pewter looked quite shocked. "Oh, no. He was quite astute. He had been playing the stock market for a lot longer than I've known him, although I understood he had a bit of trouble in Splotvia. He floated a company to exploit mineral rights, but a left-wing government took power and nationalized the land. *Badly* burned."

Pewter paused for a moment and played absently with a pencil from his desk.

"So what was he up to?" asked Jack.

"I have no idea," replied the stockbroker. "He became obsessed with Spongg's about eighteen months ago. I never found out why. Spongg's *will* go under; it's only a question of time. Unless," he added, "there was *another* plan."

"Such as?" returned Jack, craning forward and lowering his voice.

Mr. Pewter fixed him with a steely gaze. "Winsum and Loosum Pharmaceuticals would have paid a lot of money to get hold of the shares. They've been trying to take over Spongg's for years. They might pay him a good return on his investment."

"How much?"

"Today? Ten million. Fifteen if he got Grundy in a generous mood. But I must say if that was his plan, I'm surprised he left it so long. Spongg's demise is pretty much inevitable, and Winsum and Loosum can just wait until it goes and then pick up the pieces."

"Solomon Grundy was at the Spongg benefit, wasn't he?"

"He never misses them, Inspector. Along with Randolph Spongg and the Quangle-Wangle, he's Reading's most generous philanthropist. Did you know that he *personally* paid forty million pounds to keep the Sacred Gonga in Reading when the museum threatened to sell it?"

"Of course," said Jack, "everyone knows. Thank you for your time, Mr. Pewter. You've been most helpful."

"Delighted to be of service, Inspector. I am always here if you need to talk again."

Mr. Pewter saw them to the door, and they walked back to the Allegro.

"You can drive," said Jack, tossing the car keys to Mary.

She got in and looked around the spartan controls dubiously.

"Seventies design classic," said Jack. "The Allegro was a lot better than people give it credit for. The clutch is on the way out, so it bites high, and don't be too aggressive with the turn signal — I broke it the other day, and I'm still awaiting a replacement."

She turned the key, and the little engine burst into life. Jack was right, the clutch did bite high, but aside from that it drove very well — and with a surprisingly comfortable ride, too.

"Hydrogas suspension," commented Jack when Mary asked. "Best thing about it."

"So," said Mary as they made their way back towards the city center, "Humpty was buying shares in a company that is heading rapidly downhill — why do you suppose that is?"

"I don't know. Perhaps he wanted a staff discount on corn plasters. Perhaps he liked Randolph. Perhaps he'd gone mad. Speaking of which, let's see if we can get any sense out of Dr. Quatt. But not quite yet. Take a right here and pull up outside Argos. I said I'd drop in and check out the Sacred Gonga Visitors' Center — we're on duty there Saturday."

11. The Sacred Gonga

SACRED GONGA UPGRADED

Hearts rose at the Sacred Gonga Visitors' Center yesterday when the World Council for Venerated Objects upgraded the much-revered Splotvian artifact to "most sacred" status, effective immediately. "It's a tremendous honor," said Professor Hardiman, whose grandfather smuggled the Sacred Gonga out of war-torn Splotvia in 1876, "and just in time for the Jellyman's dedication on Saturday." A spokesman from the WCVO pointed out that the "most" prefix was purely ceremonial, and the twelfth-century relic could still be referred to as "the Sacred Gonga" without disrespect.

— From the *Reading Mercury*,
April 6, 2004

They pulled up at the curb, and Mary switched off the engine. It rattled on for a bit before it finally died.

"*Must* get that seen to."

They climbed out of the car and looked

at the glass-and-steel structure built on Forbury Gardens. If it had been anything other than the dreary day it was, the sun's rays would doubtless have cascaded from the many-faceted glazed roof and given an effect as magical and wondrous as the treasure the building was built to house. As it was, the only thing cascading from anywhere was the rainwater running into the drains from the downpipes.

"Ugly as sin if you ask me," said Jack.

"Beautiful piece of architecture," said Mary, precisely at the same time. "We agree to differ," she added. "A fine building should always court controversy. Isn't that traffic warden staring at you?"

"Oh, shit," said Jack. "Keep moving and pretend you haven't seen her."

But it was too late. The traffic warden, a woman about Jack's age but whom the years had not blessed as kindly as, say, Lola Vavoom, trotted up to him. And she didn't look very happy.

"Jack!" she said with an overblown sense of outrage. "You *never* call me!"

"Hello, Agatha," said Jack with as much politeness as he could muster. "You're looking well."

"Don't try and sweet-talk me, worm. Think you can just toss me aside like a . . .

like a . . . like a used thing that needs tossing aside?"

"Steady on, Agatha."

Mary stared curiously at the uniformed bundle of hot indignation — the overdone mascara and lipstick looked more like warpaint.

"Don't you 'steady on' me, Jack. You don't call, you don't write —"

"Agatha, it's *over.* It's been over for a long, long time."

"Maybe for you," she said angrily. "What about if I came and told your wife, Sarah, about it? What would she say, huh?"

Jack sighed. "Sarah is . . . no longer in the picture. I remarried —"

"Remarried?" she asked in a shocked tone. "When?"

"Five years ago. And listen, you and I were finished *long* before I even met Sarah."

"Do you have any idea how this makes me feel?"

"No," said Jack, who had resisted the temptation of humiliating her with a restraining order, since she happened to be Briggs's partner, "I have no idea at all. How's Geoffrey?"

"Not half the man you are. The trombone's driving me nuts — and he wants to change his name to Föngotskilérnie."

"You have my sympathies. I'm busy, Agatha."

She cheered up, blew her nose on a light mauve handkerchief, leaned closer, gave him a coy smile and walked her fingers up his tie.

"I'll be waiting for your call, Jack. Anytime. I'll be waiting. For your call. Whenever."

"Good day, Agatha." And he turned quickly and moved away.

"Yikes," he said in an aside to Mary. "That was Agatha Diesel. Makes Dr. Quatt seem a picture of rationality."

"There's nothing mad about being miffed at rejection," said Mary, who thought that even people like Agatha needed a champion in their corner.

"A week's passion in 1979," he replied wearily, "twenty-five years ago. And she called it off for a fling with Friedland. She doesn't pester him because he has a hundred-yard restraining order out on her."

"Ah," said Mary, suitably contrite. "You're right: mad as a March hare."

They approached the main doors of the Sacred Gonga Visitors' Center, which had been cast in a bronze relief that depicted in

167

detail the turbulent history of Splotvia, from the earliest days of Splotvane I "The Unwashed" all the way through the medieval civil wars to the modern socialist republic, still coming to terms with itself after the overthrow of Splotvane XIV "The Deposed" in 1990.

The heavy doors were locked and bolted, so they walked around the side to the service entrance. This was also shut tight, but at least there was an entry phone and TV camera. Jack picked up the phone and announced themselves. Without a word the door slid open, and they were admitted to an inner cubicle to which there was no exit other than the way they had come or through a second door shut tight in front of them. To their right a uniformed guard sat behind a thick sheet of bulletproof glass. The door shut noiselessly behind them.

"Welcome to the Sacred Gonga Visitors' Center," said the guard in a marked Splotvian accent. "Can you place your IDs in the drawer, please?"

A steel drawer opened beneath the glass, and they did as he requested. He slid the drawer to his side, and after he'd studied the IDs for a moment and compared their likenesses with those on his database, the door to the building opened in front of them.

"Thank you," said the guard as he handed their IDs back. "If you take a seat, Professor Hardiman will be with you shortly."

Mary looked cautiously around. The interior of the building was modernist but subtly mixed with the geometric motifs that one usually associated with Splotvian architecture. It was pleasing, and she liked it.

"DI Spratt?" came a voice from the other side of the room. They turned and rose to meet the Professor, a small and dapper man who had the rosy red cheeks of outdoorsy good health. "My name is Bruce Hardiman. It was my grandfather's expedition that discovered the Sacred Gonga. And you must be DS Mary. How do you do?"

He shook hands with both of them and thanked them profusely for giving up their lives, if necessary, to protect the historic artifact.

"To protect and serve," replied Jack dryly.

"How very *Gonga* of you," observed Hardiman respectfully. "To die in the service of the Sacred Gonga is to die a worthy death indeed."

"Professor," said Jack, "we're not actually *planning* on dying at all; we're just here to protect it. I'm sure nothing will go wrong."

"You must excuse me. I get carried away sometimes. As you can see the Sacred Gonga is housed in a state-of-the-art museum-cum-strongroom that is gasproof, bombproof, thiefproof, shockproof and antimagnetic. It is completely self-contained in every way. Inertial batteries housed beneath our feet can give power for up to three weeks in the event of a power failure, and all air-conditioning, humidity control, halon antifire systems and CCTV security monitoring are masterminded from within the confines of its walls. Let me show you around."

He walked across to a panel on the wall and pressed his thumb onto a small illuminated square, then entered a code on a touch pad. The door slid open, and they found themselves in a large chamber with the bronze front doors behind them and a full history of the Sacred Gonga on the walls with other examples of early Splotvian art.

"This is the part open to the public," explained the Professor. "The doors to the street open behind us, and the queues form in this outer chamber here. As the eager visitors get closer to the Sacred Gonga Containment Chamber, they are searched by guards at these tables and scanned by metal detectors hidden in the walls. They then move through these secure double doors, which gives us an opportunity to close down the facility quickly and easily in the event of an emergency."

He pressed another thumbprint panel, entered a second code, and the three-foot-thick vault door slowly opened.

"One way in, one way out. Floor, walls, ceiling — all of steel two feet thick encased by a concrete outer shell. Bare feet, please."

They sat on the bench and removed their shoes and socks. Sacred Gonga protocol demanded it. Hardiman was wearing loafers without socks and, after slipping them off, he walked barefoot into the chamber before the vault door was fully open. Once they had joined him, they could see that the room was octagonal and paneled in red marble picked out in obsidian trim. In the middle and encased within a large glass dome was the Sacred Gonga itself. It was illuminated from below, and the rest of the room was quite dark, which added to the mystical effect.

"Behold," said Hardiman grandly,

stretching his arms out wide, "the Most Sacred Gonga."

Neither Mary nor Jack had ever seen the Sacred Gonga up close. They'd seen numerous pictures, of course, but nothing ever quite prepares you for the firsthand experience.

"It's . . . it's . . . *amazing,*" said Mary. "What's that bit there that looks like a map of Wales upside down?"

"Ah!" said Professor Hardiman. "That's the Pwaarl, which connects the Qussex to the Limbrell. As you can see, three of the eight Limbrells are missing. It is said that when the eight Limbrells are rejoined within the influencing sphere of the Sacred Gonga, the true Gonga will be revealed to the world. I see you are admiring the Prizzucks, Inspector?"

"So that's what a Prizzuck looks like," murmured Jack. As the light caught them, they sparkled and danced. "Why are they undulating in that strange manner?"

"The strange undulation of the Prizzucks is only one of the many mysteries of the Sacred Gonga." The professor smiled. "Let me show you something."

He positioned Jack on one side of the room and Mary on the other so the Sacred Gonga was directly between them and told them to close their eyes.

"Now think of a number," whispered the Professor in Jack's ear.

"Eight," said Mary as soon as he thought of it. "Four. Six. Twelve."

"Was she right?"

"Quite right. How does it do it?"

"We have no idea. The Sacred Gonga has many secrets, good and bad. Thousands of lives have been lost over the years in the effort to find out. Despite the demands of the Splotvian minister of antiquities, the Sacred Gonga is going to stay here in Reading."

Jack pointed at the clear dome covering the Sacred Gonga. "What's that made of?"

"Toughened glass. It will withstand a grenade, eighty kilos of Semtex, an .88 artillery round. A thief would have to somehow get through the glass, take the Sacred Gonga and be out again in under thirty seconds — always assuming he was not apprehended by the four armed guards or rendered unconscious by the quick-acting nerve gas we can introduce at will."

"Looks like you're not leaving anything to chance."

"Absolutely not. The dedication ceremony will take place in here at midday. At 1400 hours we open to the public. We expect ten thousand visitors that afternoon and over one million in the first six months. It's not surprising; since the attempted theft three years ago, the Sacred Gonga's not been on public display."

They put their shoes and socks back on and were escorted to the exit.

"The Jellyman Security Service will take command from 0900 hours to midday; the rest of the time, security will be down to you and me and the four armed guards on the museum floor."

"Looks like we won't have much to do," observed Jack.

"*Exactly* what I said to Superintendent Briggs," said Hardiman with unwelcome directness. "I told him I could make do with lobotomized monkeys if he had any." He clapped his hands together, indicating that he had used up enough of his valuable time. "Well, thanks for coming around, and I'll see you on Saturday at 1330, but if you're late, don't worry — I'm sure we can manage."

They exited by way of the secure double doors and were soon back out on the street, which felt cold and damp after the precise humidity-controlled environment of the visitors' center.

"Ever felt redundant?" asked Jack as

they walked back towards the car. "I think it's Briggs's way of easing me into the pain of losing the NCD."

Mary didn't answer. It was probably *exactly* what Briggs had in mind.

"Let's go and see what Dr. Quatt has to say for herself. Blast. Agatha's given me a ticket."

12. St. Cerebellum's

SCANDAL ROCKS QUATT FOUNDATION

The Reading genetic industry suffered a severe blow last night when the Quatt Foundation for Genetic Research was closed following its owner's admission that she conducted morally dubious experiments. "So I kept a monkey brain alive in a jar," said the disgraced Dr. Quatt, "so what? It's only a bit of fun." Once the nation's foremost expert in reptilian genome mapping and skilled at grafting frogs' heads onto whippets, Dr. Quatt has been permanently banned from funded research. The disgraced pariah of the medical establishment has been shunned by every decent hospital in the nation, except for St. Cerebellum's, which asked if she could start Monday.
– Extract from *The Owl*, August 2, 1994

The outdated St. Cerebellum's mental hospital had been constructed in 1831 and was considered modern for its day. With separate wards for unmarried mothers, sufferers of milk allergies, unwanted relatives and the genuinely disturbed, St. Cerebellum's once boasted a proud record of ill-conceived experimental treatment. With the high level of fee-paying curiosity seekers the litmus test of its success, St. Cerebellum's even outstripped Bedlam as those requiring lunatic-based entertainment flocked to Reading in droves. But the days when you could pay sixpence to view someone who thought he was Napoleon were long gone, and despite continued and relentless modernization, it was still an anachronistic stain on Reading's otherwise fine record of psychiatric treatment.

Jack and Mary entered the hospital at the main reception area and, after being issued with passes to avoid any more embarrassing accidental incarcerations, were escorted along the plain whitewashed corridors by a burly nurse with a two-way radio and a bunch of keys on his belt.

"You've heard about the plan to rebuild St. Cerebellum's?" asked the male nurse.

"Sure," replied Jack. "Fifty million should do it, yes?"

"And none too soon. We are both an outpatient center and a secure hospital for the criminally unhinged — even though the two halves never meet, it would be better for everyone to separate the two."

"Doubtless," replied Mary as some weird and maniacal laughter echoed up the corridors.

"Dr. Quatt is a brilliant woman," said the nurse as they took a clanking lift to the third floor. "The popular view is that she's as mad as a barrel of skunks, and many people see her as a perverter of all the decent virtues that bind society together, but they said the same about Galileo."

"I must say I don't remember the bit where Galileo grafted sheep's hooves onto amputees," mused Mary.

"Or subjected toads to Iron Maiden's 'Number of the Beast' so loud they exploded," added Jack.

"All her work was to alleviate suffering," retorted the nurse defensively. "When they banned her, a dark veil fell over the medical-research community. We don't expect outsiders to *truly* understand her brilliance."

St. Cerebellum's seemed like a little world unto itself.

A crackling message came over the nurse's radio. He unclipped it and waved them to a stop. There was an almost unintelligible rasp of dialogue about a "patient in transit," and he acknowledged the call before he turned to a nearby room, selected a key and unlocked the door.

"We are moving one of our secure patients," explained the nurse as he ushered them into what had once been a small cell. "It's safer to lock ourselves in while he's being transported."

The lock clunked shut, and the nurse spoke briefly on the radio. Up and down the corridor, they could hear doors slamming and locks being thrown.

"Who is it?" asked Jack.

The nurse indicated the small glass porthole in the door. "Take a look."

Jack peered out cautiously, which seemed daft, considering the door was iron-banded oak. After a few moments, he caught sight of six burly nurses who surrounded a tall figure wrapped in a straitjacket and bite mask. Each of the six nurses held the patient by means of a long pole that was connected to a collar around his neck. As they drew closer, Jack could see the dark brown cakey texture of the prisoner's skin, and with a shiver he knew *exactly* who it was. He had hoped never to see him again but was thankful at least that Cerebellum's was taking no chances. As they walked past, the patient looked at Jack with his glacé-cherry eyes and his thin licorice lips curled up into a cruel smile of recognition. He winked at Jack, and then they were gone.

Jack stepped away from the window, his palms damp with perspiration. Images of the night he and Wilmot Snaarb had tackled the Gingerbreadman filled his head. He could still see Snaarb's look of pain and terror as the cakey psychopath playfully pulled his arms out of their sockets.

"Are you okay, sir?" asked Mary.

"Yes, yes, quite well."

The male nurse laughed and went to the window to check for the all-clear.

"Believe me, you really don't want to get any closer to Ginger than *that*," he said, placing the key in the door and pausing. "He'd kill you as soon as look at you."

"I know," replied Jack. "I was the arresting officer."

"Nah," said the nurse, "everyone knows that was Friedland Chymes."

They were led into Dr. Quatt's office, a light and airy room with a good view of Prospect Park through large floor-to-ceiling windows. There were testimonials and letters of support hanging on the walls, and bottled specimens that contained misshapen creatures covered every work surface. Jack and Mary looked more closely and winced: The carefully bottled specimens looked like some bizarre form of animal "mix and match."

A few moments later, an elegantly dressed woman of Jack's age walked brusquely in from an anteroom, removed a pair of surgical gloves and tossed them in a bin. Under her white lab coat, she was dressed in a wool suit and blouse with a ring of pearls high on her neck. Her features were delicately chiseled, she wore only the merest hint of makeup and had her hair swept up in the tightest bun Mary had ever seen. She didn't *look* as mad as a barrel of skunks; she looked quite sophisticated.

"Dr. Deborah Quatt?" said Jack. "My name is Detective Inspector Jack Spratt of the Nursery Crime Division, and this is Detective Sergeant Mary Mary."

"Jack Spratt?" she asked, staring at him quizzically. "Have we met before?"

"We were in the same year at Caversham Park Junior School," replied Jack, astounded that she remembered.

"Of course we were. You always insisted on being the pencil monitor — a policeman at heart, clearly."

She said it with a slight derogatory air that he didn't like.

"And you were expelled for sewing the school cat to the janitor."

"The joyous experimentation of children," she declared, laughing fondly at the memory. "What fun that was! Did you come all this way for a reunion?"

"Not at all. We wanted to talk to you about one of your patients — a Mr. Dumpty."

Dr. Quatt shook her head slowly. "I never discuss patients' records, Inspector. It is a flagrant breach of doctor-patient confidentiality. However, I could stretch a point given some form of fiscal reparation. Shall we say fifty pounds?"

"Doctor, you do know that he's dead?"

"I was nowhere near him," declared Dr. Quatt haughtily. "If you want to try me for malpractice, you'll have to mount a good case. I've plenty of experience defending them, believe you me." She stared at Jack for a moment. "Mr. Dumpty? *Dead?* What a pity. A very, very great pity."

"His death was tragic, I agree," admitted Jack.

"Death comes to us all, Inspector. No, it's a pity the patient-confidentiality clause is null and void — I could have done with fifty pounds. The price of lab equipment these days is simply scandalous."

She looked around, lowered her voice and leaned forwards. "Did you know that I have successfully grafted a kitten's head onto a haddock?"

"Should you be telling me this?" asked Jack, also in a quiet voice.

She leaned back and raised an eyebrow. "It's not against the law — I just can't get any funding to do proper research because of that damnable Jellyman and his outdated moral principles. In the world of cutting-edge genetic research, you can't make an omelette without breaking eggs."

"Which brings us back to Mr. Dumpty," said Jack. "How long had you been his doctor?"

"For five years," she said as she sat behind her large desk and indicated for them to be seated, "ever since I arrived in this dump. I was a psychiatrist before I moved into genetic research. What do you want to know?"

"His state of mind."

"Ah!" she said, getting up to rifle through a rusty filing cabinet. "You are considering suicide, Inspector?"

"It is possible."

"Indeed it is," replied Dr. Quatt, looking

at the files carefully. "Physically, he was in a pretty ropy state. He was a lifelong salmonella sufferer, with frequent recurrences; when he had a bad bout, it was most debilitating. He drank more than was good for him, frequently overate and didn't get much exercise — he never could walk far on those short legs."

"And mentally?"

"Not good — but functional. He suffered from a sense of extreme low worth that manifested itself in frequent and self-destructive binges of drinking and womanizing. He also had depressive fits that sometimes lasted for days; all he could do was sit on his wall. Aside from that, he sometimes had problems differentiating reality from fantasy. He was particularly fearful that a giant mongoose was after him, was phobic about soufflé, meringue, and egg whisks, and had a recurring nightmare of being boiled alive for *exactly* three minutes."

"When did you last see him?"

"Six days ago. Easter was a bad time for him, as you can imagine, with all those chocolate eggs being eaten and real ones dyed — he was a virtual prisoner in his own home. We had two sessions last week, and I think we really made some headway."

"Did he talk about his work?"

She shook her head. "Never. It was all purely domestic."

"But could he have been suicidal?"

Dr. Quatt thought for a moment. "I'm sorry to say that I can't rule it out, despite my best attentions."

Jack nodded slowly. It was what he had been expecting to hear.

"One more thing: How long had he been coming to St. Cerebellum's?"

"For forty years, Inspector. It was almost his second home."

Jack got up. "Thank you, Dr. Quatt; you've been most helpful. Tell me — and this is just personal curiosity — were you serious when you said you'd grafted a kitten's head onto a haddock?"

Dr. Quatt's eyes lit up, and she looked at them in turn, her youthful enthusiasm boiling to the surface. "Do you want to see?"

"That was pretty gross, wasn't it?" announced Mary as they drove away from St. Cerebellum's a few minutes later.

"Yes, but fascinating in a prurient, icky, dissecting-frogs, brains-in-jars kind of way. I thought keeping the collar and bell was an inspired touch, and it was kind of cute watching it try to play with that soggy ball of wool inside the tank."

"Sir!"

"Just kidding. Yes, it *was* gross, and Dr. Quatt is definitely as mad as a barrel of skunks. And listen, I *never* insisted on being a pencil monitor at school. Where can I drop you?"

He left her outside the front of Reading Central Police Station. They bade each other good night, and she walked into the car park to retrieve her BMW, thinking that perhaps, given the direction of her new career, she should simply drive straight to Basingstoke and give Flowwe another whack with the onyx ashtray — just to be even-steven.

But when she got to her car, there was something unexpected waiting for her: an envelope carefully tucked under her windshield wiper. She thought it might be from Arnold, but it wasn't. She read the note again, then a third time. She thought for a moment and then trotted into the station's changing rooms to check herself in the mirror. If you are invited to the Reading branch of the Guild of Detectives by DCI Chymes *himself,* you should always look your best.

14. Meeting the Detective

First there was *The Strand*, the original magazine for which Dr. Watson so painstakingly penned all Holmes adventures. Following Sherlock's retirement *The Strand* went through a sticky patch and was relaunched in 1931 under the title *True Detection Monthly* and featured Guild of Detectives stalwart Hercule Porridge and newcomer Miss Maple. The summer of 1936 saw both these characters abscond to the newly formed *Real Detective Magazine*. Lord Peter Flimsey and Father Broom, however, favored *Extraordinary Detecting Feats*, which folded after two issues, to be replaced by *Sleuth Illustrated*. The end of the "golden era" saw a shaking up of the true-crime franchise, and *Real Detective*, *Astounding Police*, *Remarkable Crime* and *Popular Sleuthing* merged into *Amazing Crime Stories*, which is now regarded as the world leader in true-crime adventure.

— From *Watching the Detectives*
by Maisie Gray

Mary walked nervously up the steps of the old Georgian town house on Friar Street and presented herself to the porter. He looked at her disdainfully until he saw the note and Chymes's signature, then went through an extraordinary transformation, welcomed her to the club, relieved her of her coat, pointed out the facilities if she felt like a freshen-up and rang a small bell. He talked politely to her for a few minutes, pointed out the many framed newspaper front pages and *Amazing Crime Stories* cover artwork hanging up in the lobby until a footman arrived and gestured for her to follow him. They walked through some frosted-glass swinging doors and down a paneled corridor hung with more framed headlines and letters from celebrities offering their testimonials and grateful thanks. She was ushered into a bar that was elegantly bedecked in dark oak, rich burgundy carpets and brass light fixtures. There were groups of off-duty officers sitting around chatting and laughing, but these weren't just ordinary rank-and-file officers such as you might find down at the Dog and Truncheon. These officers were different — the elite assistants who worked exclusively for the five *Amazing Crime*–ranked investigators in Reading, the most influential and successful being Chymes, of course. Each of the five detectives had his own coterie of dedicated support officers, each led by an Official Sidekick, four of whom were in that room tonight and three of which she could name.

The footman presented her to a group near the bar, bowed and withdrew.

"It's DS Mary, isn't it?" said a man smoking a large cigar as he sized her up and down in a professional sort of way.

"Yes, sir."

"Chymes will be with you in a minute. He asked us to entertain you. Fancy a drink?"

"Thank you; a half of special would be good."

The man nodded to the barman who had been hovering discreetly nearby.

"Do you know who I am?" asked the man.

"Yes, you're DS Eddie Flotsam. You've been Chymes's OS for sixteen years and penned over seventy of his stories. But you're less . . . *cockney* than I imagined."

"Not cockney at all," he admitted, "nor particularly chirpy. It was a marketing ploy FC and I came up with in the early days. I think it works."

"It does. I've been a big fan since before I was in the force."

"You've been an OS yourself, haven't you?" asked Flotsam.

"I was with DI Flowwe for four years."

"We know," replied Flotsam, handing her the beer that had just arrived. "Your file makes for good reading. Cheers."

"Cheers. Um . . . are personal files meant for general distribution?"

He laughed. "This is the *Guild*, sister. Let me introduce the gang."

The "gang," as Flotsam described them, had all received numerous mentions in the Friedland Chymes stories, but their fictionalized counterparts, like Flotsam's, didn't really match up, so they were hard to figure out.

"That's Barnes, Hamilton, Hoorn and Haynes. Seagrove is over there on the blower. Probably the bookies."

They all nodded their greetings. Despite stories to the contrary, they didn't look an unfriendly bunch.

"I read your account of the Shakespeare fight-rigging caper," said the one named Hoorn. "I thought it impressive. The pace was good, you built the tension early, and you managed to keep it sustained throughout the story." He shook her hand and added, by way of an afterthought, "And the police investigation itself was quite good, too — although if I'd been Flowwe, I would have let one member of the gang escape to add a small amount of tension to a recapture. You could have stretched the headlines over another two days."

"It was our biggest case to date," replied Mary defensively. "I don't think he wanted to blow it for the sake of a few good headlines."

"That's what sorts out the good from the greats," said Hamilton, sipping a martini. "If you want to hit the big time and run investigations that fit well into a TV or movie format, you're going to have to take a few risks."

"Does Friedland?"

No one answered, which Mary took to mean that he did. You don't get to number two in the *Amazing Crime* rankings by playing it safe. It wasn't permitted to "alter, embellish or omit pertinent facts" in one's investigation to make better copy, but all of them did it in one form or another. If it got a result, no one minded. The whole thing suddenly seemed that much more exciting and daring. Friedland's team under Flotsam was a close unit and had been through a lot together — and had reaped the benefits, both professionally and financially. Piarno Keyes had played Flotsam in *Friedland Chymes and the Carnival of Death,* and character rights paid handsomely.

"What does DCI Chymes want with me?"

"Barnes retires next month," Flotsam said, pointing to a member of the small clique who was rolling a cigarette. "Network Mole wants to retain him as police adviser on their TV shows."

She couldn't quite believe her ears. "I'm up for inclusion in the team?"

"Nothing's fixed," said Flotsam with a shrug, "but you're qualified and a looker."

"Is that important?"

"For the telly. The Guv'nor wants us to look a bit less male elitist, so we need another girlie. But he doesn't carry dead wood, and there's no one else suitable in the frame."

"I'm working down at the NCD at present."

There was a murmur of impolite laughter from the small group.

"Nothing to be ashamed of. Barnes and Seagrove have both done a stretch down there. How's Jack, by the by?"

"He's . . . *Jack,*" she answered, finding it too much of an easy shot to gain Brownie points by trashing him, something that would doubtless have gone down well. Jack was unremarkable and in a loser department, but he'd treated her well. Chymes's gang took her meaning to be derogatory and laughed. Flotsam's phone beeped, and he glanced at the text message before putting down his cigar and straightening his tie.

"That was the Guv'nor. He'll see you now."

Mary was taken through another door, which led into the inner sanctum, a personal retreat for the great detectives themselves. It was here surrounded by the dark oak paneling that they met nightly to discuss cases, brainstorm ideas or simply just unwind among their intellectual equals. Mary tried not to gawk at the six or seven famous names that she recognized from her initial glance around the room, but it was tricky not to. There had never been this sort of thing at Basingstoke, but then twenty-fifth was the highest ranking a Basingstoke detective had ever got.

"Guv'nor," said Flotsam in greeting to Chymes, who was seated next to a fastidiously dressed detective of foreign extraction who rose to his feet and bowed politely as

Mary was presented. She felt herself go hot at the exalted company and managed to mumble something respectful as the small man greeted her, thanked Chymes, retrieved his small sherry and departed to the other side of the room.

"Charming man, Hercule," said Chymes with a winning grin, adding as soon as the small foreigner was out of earshot, "but a tad overrated. All that 'little gray cells' stuff he goes on about. A lot of the time, he's simply surfing on a rich seam of luck. Take a seat, DS — has Flotsam been looking after you?"

"Extremely well, sir."

"Good. Thank you, Eddie."

Flotsam bowed obsequiously and departed. Chymes stared at Mary for a moment without speaking. He was a large man and had a deep, commanding voice that inspired confidence. He was handsome, too, and his eyes seemed to sparkle at her. The room suddenly began to grow hot.

"You used to work with DI Flowwe at Basingstoke?"

"Yes, sir."

"That's nothing to be ashamed of."

"Flowwe or Basingstoke, sir?"

Chymes laughed and took a sip from his

ice and whiskey. "So how's my friend Jack?"

"I haven't known him that long, sir," replied Mary, trying to sidestep the question. Chymes picked up on it straightaway.

"Loyalty is something I appreciate, Mary, so I'll tell you: Jack is not well at all. He's up shit creek without a paddle. The pig thing was career suicide, even by the somewhat loose standards of the NCD. He has no idea how to approach a tricky case in order to get a conviction and no sense at all about dramatic timing or case construction so it will fit the format demanded by *Amazing Crime*. And now he wants to be in the Guild. Do you see Jack fitting in here, Mary?"

She looked around. Inspector Moose was leaning on the ornate marble fire surround, talking in subdued tones to Rhombus, down from Edinburgh to interview a suspect, apparently.

"Frankly, no," replied Mary, quickly pushing aside feelings of disloyalty in order to make more important room for thoughts concerning promotion and career.

"I concur," replied Chymes, leaning closer. "How's the Humpty case going?"

"Almost certainly suicide."

Chymes shook his head. "I'll bet you it isn't. I can smell a good investigation the way a perfumer can detect a drop of lavender in a locker room. There is something about a crime scene that is like the opening aria of a fine opera — a few lone notes that portend of great things to come. I've made my career upon it. Humpty is more than meets the eye, I promise you. I need something for the Summer Special issue of *Amazing Crime*, and we thought the Humpty case would do well."

"It's NCD jurisdiction, surely?"

"I have only solutions, never problems," replied Chymes quietly. "I'll have the Humpty investigation, but I won't have it yet. I need to time myself well for the increased dramatic effect. And to do this, I need your help."

"Mine?"

"Of course. I need to know how things are progressing. You can be my eyes and ears."

He could sense her slight reticence.

"You will not find me ungrateful. I read your account of the Shakespeare fight-rigging caper, and I was impressed. Your prose is good, and in the not-too-distant future I might have need of someone with a fresh eye and a fresh pen. Barnes isn't the only one up for retirement."

He raised an imperious eyebrow and

stared at her. Mary weighed the pros and cons of what he was suggesting. It didn't take long.

"What do you need to know?"

"Just keep me informed of what's going on. But don't bring it to me. Speak to Flotsam. When the NCD is disbanded, I think we can find you a good posting with us."

"Thank you, sir."

"Good. Well, I'm glad we've managed to have this little talk. It may prove to be highly beneficial to us both."

"I'm sure it will. Thank you, sir."

She was repeating herself, but she didn't really care anymore. She left the inner sanctum and rejoined the group outside, who were telling stories of past investigations — many of which Mary had read about. It was an intoxicating experience, as though Zeus had suddenly invited her up for a quick tour of Mount Olympus and then casually informed her that Neptune was jacking it in — and would she care for the job?

15. Granny Spratt's Displeasure

SPARROW SOUGHT IN ROBIN SLAYING

NCD officers are eager to interview an un-identified sparrow in connection with the murder of Cock Robin in Redhatch Copse last night. A witness who described himself as a Fly, told us, "I saw him die — with my little eye." The alleged murder weapon, a bow, has not yet been recovered. "It's early days," said DS Spratt of the NCD when asked to comment on the case, "but we have a good description and will be wanting to interview all of Reading's 356,000 sparrows." Cock Robin will be buried on Thursday by Parson Rook; floral tributes to Chief Mourner Dove.
— Article in *The Gadfly*, February 22, 1980

"Beans?" said Jack's mother. "BEANS?" she said again, her voice growing louder with rage. "For a Stubbs cow? Have you taken a wild leap away from your good senses? What do I want with these?"

She held the shiny beans in a trembling outstretched hand. They gently changed color in the warmth of her palm, but not even their singular elegance could dull her disappointment and anger.

Jack sighed. He had explained the whole story to her from beginning to end, but she had obviously failed to grasp the essential facts. He started again.

"It was a fake. I —"

She interrupted him. "It was *not.* I had it authenticated in the sixties. It was worth over a grand then!"

"You did?" asked Jack, suddenly feeling a bit stupid.

"Yes. Mr. Foozle must have gone soft in the head. You can go straight back into town tomorrow and sort him out. As for your beans, this is what I think of them!"

And she threw them out the window with a triumphant gesture. There was a pause as they stood and stared at each other, the only sound the steady *tock* of the grandfather clock in the hall and the gentle hum of the indefinable number of cats running incessantly around the furniture.

"Great," said Jack as he turned to walk through the French windows.

"Wait! Where are you going?"

"I'm going to pick them up," said Jack from the garden, "or Mr. Foozle will charge me a hundred quid for them."

"Oh!" said his mother, and joined in the search.

"I think I threw them down near the potting shed," she said, looking around in the light of the garden floodlamp. "Why do we have three bags of wool in there anyway?"

"It's evidence, Mother, but there's no room in the station — Did you see that?" Jack jumped up and pointed at the ground.

"What?"

"The beans. They were glowing and sort of *burying* themselves!"

"Not possible," she said as she patted him on the shoulder. "I'll look for them tomorrow. Come inside, it's raining."

But Jack wasn't so easily put off, and he searched for another twenty minutes before giving up. He promised to do what he could to get the Stubbs back, kissed her and departed.

"Don't worry," said Madeleine as soon as he had returned home and told her about the Stubbs. "It might have been worse."

"How?"

"It could have been raining."

"It *was* raining. You know, when she threw the beans out the window, I got this really weird feeling. Like it felt kind of *familiar.*"

"Déjà vu?"

"Sort of — but more. A feeling of *inevitability.* Does that sound weird to you?"

"You're probably a bit stressed over the Guild thing. Or the pig thing. Or the egg thing. Or the NCD-disbandment thing. Or the Chymes thing. Or an ongoing unspecified thing. Or an —"

"Okay, okay," he said with a smile, "I get the picture."

"Here," she said as she handed him Stevie's bowl, "*you* try and get him to eat it. Can you do supper?"

"Sure."

She took off her apron and sat at the kitchen table for a rest. She was behind with several deadlines but was enjoying Stevie too much to want to start thinking about child care.

"How's work?" she asked.

"Chymes tried to muscle in on the Humpty case, but it all seems to have blown over."

"Be careful of Chymes, Jack," warned Madeleine.

"I can handle him."

He was doubtful about that last statement, but it made him feel better.

There was a knock at the front door, and Madeleine opened it to reveal Prometheus, who was dressed incongruously — given the poor weather — in a rumpled white linen suit and panama hat.

"Mrs. Spratt?" he said as he raised his hat. "My name is Prometheus."

"Jack!" she yelled. "I think it's for you."

He came out of the kitchen in a flash.

"Ah! Prometheus. Welcome. This is my wife, Madeleine. Darling, this is the lodger I was telling you about. He said he'd lend a hand with babysitting if need be."

"One moment," said Madeleine to Prometheus before beckoning Jack off to where they couldn't be heard at the foot of the stairs.

"This won't be like having that tart Kitty Fisher living here, will it?"

"No, no."

"I'm not having the spare room used as a bordello."

"Keep your voice down. No, Prometheus is quite different — besides, Jerome is doing a project on ancient Greece and needs a bit of help. What do you and I know about history?"

Madeleine shrugged, and they returned

to the front door, where Prometheus was still being rained upon.

"Why don't you come in?" said Madeleine. "We can discuss it."

"Thank you."

They walked through to the kitchen. Stevie was given a biscuit, which he promptly dropped on the floor. The cat opened one eye and then closed it again. Stevie then stared at Prometheus with all the seriousness that one-year-olds can muster, which is quite a lot.

"Da-woo," he said at length.

"A-boo," replied Prometheus.

"Woo . . . ?" asked Stevie doubtfully.

"Wa-boo. Oodle-boo," responded Prometheus with a large smile.

"Da-woo!" said Stevie with a shriek of laughter.

"You speak *baby gibberish?*" asked Jack.

"Fluently. The adult-education center ran a course, and I have a *lot* of time on my hands."

"So what did he say?"

"I don't know."

"I thought you said you spoke gibberish?"

"I do. But your baby *doesn't.* I think he's speaking either pre-toddler nonsense, a form of infant burble or an obscure dialect of gobbledygook. In any event, I can't understand a word he's saying."

"Oh."

"Wow!" said Megan, who had just wandered in. She walked up to Madeleine and clasped her hand tightly.

"That's Prometheus, isn't it? Tell me it is. I know it is. He can be my show-and-tell tomorrow at school. Miss Dibble is a big fan of his. Can he come to school and tell us all about how he had his liver pecked out in the Caucasus? Can he, Mum? *Please?*"

"Darling, I —"

Ben walked in. Being sixteen, he was fashionably unimpressed by anybody and everything. Prometheus, however, proved to be an exception.

"The Fire-Giver!" he exclaimed. "Awesome! Like your style, man."

"You are man," corrected the Titan coolly. "I am Prometheus."

Ben gaped. Street-cred overload. Prometheus smiled modestly. He enjoyed a devoted following among the young. He was, after all, the ultimate rebel — it takes a lot of cojones to stand up to Zeus.

"Ben's the name," he said at last. "You here for long?"

"He might be the new lodger," said Jack.

Ben rolled his eyes. "That is so *unbelievably* cool! What do you know about the sort of girls who like to play the harp?"

"Boo!" said Megan petulantly, crossing her arms and pouting. "He's *my* show-and-tell, Ben. Your dopey girlfriends can wait their turn!"

"Can it, shrimp."

Pandora walked in. She was wrapped in a dressing gown and was still damp after a shower. She hadn't realized there was a visitor.

"Oh," she said, blushed, then rushed back upstairs to get dressed, stopping halfway to sneak a second look at Prometheus through the balusters. Prometheus watched her go and had to be nudged by Jack to stop him staring.

Madeleine softened. She had been concerned for the children, but Prometheus seemed to fit in perfectly.

"Welcome, Mr. Prometheus."

"Thank you." The Titan smiled. "And it's just 'Prometheus.' "

Madeleine put the kettle on and continued, "It's not often I have a political refugee in my house. I've followed your struggle with interest. Perhaps we can talk about ancient Greece a little later?"

Prometheus gave another short bow and smiled politely.

"Well," he began, " 'ancient Greece' is a little bit of a misnomer, really; when I was there, it was simply a collection of city-states — Athens, Sparta, Thebes, Delphi and so forth. Sparta was a tough place to grow up in, but Athens was a blast. Full of people wrapped in sheets having good ideas. We used to have this thing called 'ostracism' where you could vote anyone you didn't like out of the city — I think *I'm an Idiot, Get Me on Telly!* uses the same format. *Your* idea of modern Greece really only began with Diocletian's division in 286. I can tell you a bit about harpies, Ben, and Megan — I'd very much like to be your show-and-tell. Jack, I'm also pretty good with torque settings on Allegro wheel bearings."

"Can you cook?" asked Madeleine.

"I *love* to cook. Do you all like Mediterranean?"

They stared at him, awestruck. He was over four thousand years old, and so he knew almost everything there was to know about everything. Truly, he was the tenant of the *gods*.

"Which way is the karzy?" he asked, puncturing his sagelike image somewhat. "I'm dying for a dump."

16. Mrs. Singh Turns the Story

"LOCKED ROOM" MYSTERY HONORED

The entire crime-writing fraternity yesterday bade a tearful farewell to the last "locked room" mystery at a large banquet held in its honor. The much-loved conceptual chestnut of mystery fiction for over a century had been unwell for many years and was finally discovered dead at 3:15 a.m. last Tuesday. In a glowing tribute, the editor of *Amazing Crime* declared, "From humble beginnings to towering preeminence in the world of mystery, the 'locked room' plot contrivance will always remain in our hearts." DCI Chymes then gave a glowing eulogy before being interrupted by the shocking news that the 'locked room' concept had been *murdered* — and in a locked room. The banquet was canceled, and police are investigating.

— Editorial in *Amazing Crime*, February 23, 2001

Jack got to the station canteen for breakfast. He sat at an empty table and stared absently out the window at the traffic on the Inner Distribution Road. The IDR, as it was known, had been built to alleviate traffic but had exacted a price that the town could ill afford. Several fine streets had been demolished to build it, the heart ripped out of the old town. The whole scheme had rendered itself almost redundant when the M4 took most of the through traffic from the A4, a route that was, despite the huge road-building program, still bottlenecked.

"Good morning, sir."

"Good morning, Baker. How are you?"

It was *definitely* the wrong sort of question to ask a hypochondriac, but it was too late.

"Not so bad, sir," he replied, taking a plastic carton out of his knapsack and depositing a bewildering array of pills of all shapes, colors and sizes in a saucer. Jack could have sworn most of them were either Smarties, Skittles or Tic-Tacs, but he didn't say so. "The thing is," continued Baker after swallowing several blue pills and knocking them back with a purple, "I woke up this morning with a runny nose and was, to tell the truth, rather worried."

"Oh, yes?"

"Yes. I thought for a moment it might be TB, leprosy or tertiary syphilis."

Jack humored him, for this was a common source of conversation with Baker. "I thought they checked you for leprosy last year?"

"They did, so it couldn't be that. TB was out of the question, because I didn't have a cough, and syphilis wasn't likely, because I'm rather too young to have it end-stage without the bit in the middle."

"So it was just a cold, then?"

"It certainly looked like it, but then I thought that maybe it wasn't mucus coming out of my nose at all."

Jack raised an eyebrow. "No?"

"No, it could be cerebrospinal fluid. I played football on Sunday and had a hefty tackle. It's possible that I might have a fractured skull."

"Is that really likely?"

Baker looked down and took a few more pills. "No, not really."

He looked up again. "Sir, I hope you don't mind me saying this, but Gretel, Ashley and myself would be more than happy to put in a bit of overtime if it meant having another crack at the three pigs. I know they got off the murder rap and double jeopardy and all that, but if there is a chance of getting them with 'intentional wounding' or 'boiling a large pot without due care and attention,' then we're up for it."

"You know what Briggs says about NCD overtime."

"We weren't thinking of getting paid, sir."

Jack looked at Baker, who was staring at him earnestly. He had even forgotten to sniffle, and the collection of pills and vitamin supplements he was making his way through was, for the moment, untouched.

"I appreciate that, Baker, but I think we're going to have to just walk away from the porkers. We lost."

A voice made them both turn.

"I suppose you think this is clever?"

It was Briggs, and he didn't look very happy.

"Sir?"

Briggs slapped a copy of *The Owl* on the table in front of him.

"Page eight, Jack," said Briggs testily. "Page eight, column four."

Jack turned to the page Briggs had indicated. " 'Splotvian Minister of Antiquities Demands Return of Sacred Gonga'?"

"Below that."

" 'Nursery Favorite Dies in Wall-Death

Drama. Police Ask: Was He Pushed?' "

"It's a good job it's only on page eight," said Briggs angrily. "If you're trying to whip up some public interest to keep your precious division, I won't be pleased. And I don't think the budgetary committee will take to it very well either."

"I didn't breathe a word, sir."

"Then who is asking if he was pushed?"

"No one. Media speculation. He killed himself. Very depressed around Easter — we spoke to his doctor and ex-wife, who confirmed it."

"When do I see some paperwork?"

"As soon as I get a pathologist's report from Mrs. Singh. There's no story, so I think this article will be the first *and* last."

Briggs seemed to accept this and nodded sagely. "Very well. Good work, Spratt — and not a dead giant in sight."

"That's not funny, sir."

"Isn't it? One other thing: Someone's been spreading a practical joke around the station that you've applied to join the Guild of Detectives. Any idea who's behind it?"

"It's not a practical joke, sir."

Briggs looked nonplussed for a moment, then said, "Does Friedland know?"

"What's it got to do with him?"

"Everything. He's on the Guild of Detectives' selection committee for Southern England and probably won't take very well to someone else at Reading attempting to steal his headlines. Still, he's a fine and upstanding man. I expect he'll view your application with all due impartiality."

"I'm sure he will, sir."

Briggs missed the sarcasm, stared at Baker and his pills, shook his head and then left, dictating a note to himself about using the offices vacated by the NCD as a possible trophy room for Chymes.

"What was that all about?" asked Mary as she walked up.

Jack shrugged and pointed at the newspaper.

" 'Mad Scientists Distill Pure Wag from Dog'?" she read.

"Above that."

"Ah! 'Nursery Favorite Dies in Wall-Death Drama.' "

"Read on."

She cleared her throat and began: " 'Humpty Dumpty, well-known nursery character and large egg, was found shattered to death beneath his favorite wall in the east of town. His generous donations to charity had made him a much-loved figure in Reading, and his death will be greatly mourned. Four-time giant killer Detective Inspector Jack Spratt, former assistant to the great Friedland Chymes until demoted for incompetence and more recently noted for his misguided attempt to convict the three pigs of murder, is in charge —"

"I get the picture," interrupted Jack. "Sounds like Chymes is trying to make life difficult for me already."

Mary was silent. Jack was doubtless correct. Chymes would have every reason to keep the story current *and* trash him if he was planning on wrestling the case from him. She swallowed hard and wondered if Jack was at all suspicious that she was, for all intents and purposes, working for Friedland. She looked across at him, but he was occupying himself by trimming all the fat from his bacon.

"Don't like fat?"

"Hate it. My first wife loved it. It made us the perfect couple. All that was left of the joint was a bone."

"Loved fat?" she asked incredulously.

"Yes. Never ate anything else."

"Isn't that very unhealthy?"

"Very. She died."

Mary covered her mouth in embarrassment and went a deep shade of crimson.

"I'm sorry, I didn't know."

"It's okay. It was ten years, seven months and three days ago. I'm completely over it —" He stopped talking as his mobile rang. It was Mrs. Singh. He listened intently for a moment and glanced at Mary and Baker in turn, then told her they'd be over straightaway.

Mary looked uneasy.

"Got a problem with morgues, Mary?"

"No, sir," she answered truthfully. "I have no problems with morgues. It's the dead people in them that I'm not too keen on."

"Good," said Jack cheerfully. "Finish up your deviled kidneys and we'll go and view some corpses."

The smell of formaldehyde reached them long before they had moved past the security desk of the small Victorian building two streets away, and the odor rose to a pungent crescendo as they pushed open the glass-paneled swinging doors. The pathology lab was set out open plan and was lit by a multitude of strip lights that filled the room with a harsh, unnatural glare. In the center of the lab were four large, white-glazed dissecting tables with a stainless-steel trolley next to each laden with saws, scalpels and other instruments the use of which Mary didn't really want to try to guess. A microphone dangled from the ceiling above each table, along with an angled theater lamp. It had been a quiet week; none of the tables had anyone on them — except Humpty. As they drew closer, they could see that Mrs. Singh and her assistant had both been busy reassembling Humpty's shattered shell with surgical tape, the way one might hold a broken vase together while glue was drying.

Mrs. Singh looked up and smiled.

"So you've managed to do what all the king's men couldn't," observed Jack in admiration.

An ordinary pathologist would have given Humpty the most cursory of glances, but Mrs. Singh was different. Nursery Crime Division work was all hers, and she wasn't going to let any possibility of criminal activity slip through her fingers.

"Quite a puzzle," breathed Mary.

"With one hundred and twenty-six pieces," replied Mrs. Singh proudly. "They say dead men can't talk, but this one has spoken volumes. Take a look."

Humpty was lying on his side with his face away from them. She pointed with a forefinger at the area of his lower back, just next to a little lion tattoo. There was a patchwork of much smaller fragments with the cracks radiating out in different directions.

Jack raised his eyebrows. "This is where he landed?"

She said nothing but beckoned him around to the front and pointed to a more random pattern of breakage just above Humpty's left eye, this time with no defined center. A myriad of small pieces made up what seemed to be a second small impact area.

"So he bounced, right?"

"No. Your turn, Mary."

Mrs. Singh looked at Mary, who was taken aback; she wasn't expecting this to be a quiz.

"A blunt instrument?" ventured Mary.

"Wrong. Look closely at the damage on the lower back again."

They dutifully walked back around and peered closer. There was a definite point of impact, very small and discolored at the edges.

"Holy shit," whispered Jack. "He was . . . *shot.*"

"Top of the class," replied Mrs. Singh. "The discoloration is definitely gunshot residue. Someone came up from the other side of the wall and shot him. I've requested pathological information about the effect of bullets traveling through very large eggs, but the Home Office hasn't really got much on the subject — for obvious reasons. I'm hazarding a guess, but as the bullet moved through his liquid center, it set up a hydrostatic shock wave. By the time the bullet exited, the cracks had already encircled his body and . . . *pow.* He exploded into fragments. He was dead before he hit the dustbins."

"Oh, crap," said Jack.

"What?"

"I just told Briggs that Humpty had committed suicide because of depression brought on by Easter. You're sure, right?"

"Of course. People who are depressed *can* get murdered, you know."

Jack sighed and walked to the front of Humpty's patchworked corpse to look at the exit wound again. "Caliber?"

Mrs. Singh thought for a moment. "Difficult to say. Skinner will confirm this, but it would have to be a powerful handgun. The distance between entrance and exit is about four feet. Albumen has a high viscosity, so you'd need a powerful slug to get all the way through. If I was forced to an opinion, I'd say something like a .357 or a .44. The slug must have come to earth not more than fifty feet away; I think there will be barely a scratch on it. Find a weapon and ballistics will have a nice easy one for a change."

"Anything else?"

"Not a lot. We can say for certain that he died between midnight and two in the morning, and you already have my report about the high alcohol levels. There was one other thing that puzzled me, though." She pointed to his body. "It was this section of shell, here on his waistline — or neckline, if you prefer."

They peered closer at what would appear to be a small hole.

"Any ideas?" asked Jack.

"It is *exactly* one-quarter of an inch in width, so I am thinking it was drilled in him — and deliberately, too."

"Why do you say that?"

"There was a Band-Aid covering it."

"Drug abuse?"

"Quite possibly. I've run the usual tests. I'll let you know as soon as I have something."

She handed Jack her preliminary report. It wasn't thick, just a few typewritten pages and a diagram of Humpty's body with the bullet track marked in red pen.

"You're a marvel, Mrs. Singh."

"No," she replied wearily, "I just do long hours."

They walked down the corridor deep in thought. Jack was wondering where he was going to start on the investigation and Mary was thinking about how amazed she was that Chymes had been correct. Humpty's murder *was* a lot more involved than Jack had thought. If anyone could handle it, Friedland could. They had got used to the smell of the formaldehyde, and the streets of Reading smelled sweeter than they ever had before.

17. The Inquiry Begins

ALIENS BORING, REPORT SHOWS

An official report confirms what most of us have already suspected: that the alien visitors who arrived unexpectedly on the planet four years ago are not particularly bright, nor interesting. The thirteen-page government document describes our interstellar chums as being "dull" and "unable to plan long-term." The report, which has been compiled from citizenship application forms and interview transcripts, paints a picture of a race who are "prone to put high importance on inconsequential minutiae" and are "easily distracted from important issues." On an entirely separate note, the aliens were reported to be merging into human society far better than has been expected — the reason for this is unclear.

— Extract from *The Owl*, June 4, 2001

As they walked back into the office, they found Tibbit standing guiltily by Jack's chair, which was still moving. He looked like a puppy that had been caught sleeping on the sofa. Jack hid a smile.

"Red rum, Tibbit," he said.

"Murder?"

"So it appears. Humpty didn't fall, and he didn't jump. Mary, we should speak to his ex-wife again."

Mary picked up the phone, and Jack looked at the photograph of Humpty talking to Charles Pewter, the stockbroker. Humpty's illogical purchase of Spongg shares seemed as good as anyplace to start an inquiry. He looked at the snap of Humpty with Solomon Grundy. Jack had dismissed him earlier, but now anyone who had a vested interest in the financial health of Spongg Footcare PLC had to be a suspect. He pinned the picture of Humpty and Solomon on the board and stared at it.

Tibbit held up a small evidence bag with two spent twelve-bore cartridges in it.

"These came down from Chymes's office, sir. DS Flotsam *himself* brought them in. And do you know what? He's not really chirpy or cockney at all!"

"It's an act for *Amazing Crime*, Otto. Run them across to Skinner, would you? He knows what they're for."

Mary opened her notebook and selected a blank page for Chymes's benefit, then wrote "Grundy," ".44 caliber," "28-foot auburn hair" and "Mrs. Dumpty." She then snapped it shut guiltily and looked up. But no one was watching her.

At that moment two officers walked into the room. One was short and the other long.

The shorter of the two was pale blue in color and had the body layout of a human except with elbows and knees that bent both ways and three fingers and two opposable thumbs on each hand. His police uniform was tailored to fit, but even so he still looked uncomfortable in it. Although Mary had seen pictures of aliens, she'd never actually witnessed one up close before and found herself staring.

"What are you looking at?" asked Ashley innocently, blinking laterally at her, which is unnerving the first time you see it done.

"Nothing," mumbled Mary, trying hard not to stare, and she looked away, which felt awkward and more rude, so she looked back and then felt she was staring — and the whole cycle went around again.

She felt herself begin to flush, but Jack, whether sensing her discomfort or not, rescued her by saying, "PC 100111 is a Rambosian. His full name is 100111100100010011101110010 0100, but that's a bit of a mouthful, so we just call him Ashley. Ashley, this is DS Mary Mary."

"Hullo!" said Ashley, putting out a hand for Mary to shake. His hand was unusually warm and adhered to her palm with a dry stickiness that was odd but not unpleasant. As soon as she touched him, however, she had a fleeting and extremely vivid glimpse of herself and this strange creature rolling naked in a slimy and passionate embrace in a shallow marsh under twin setting suns. Ashley quickly pulled his hand away, went bright blue and blinked nervously.

"Is that the time?" he said quickly. "I've just remembered there's something I need to do. Good-bye."

And he darted out the door.

"Rambosians sometimes project their inner thoughts with touch," explained Jack. "Did you see anything?"

"Nothing," replied Mary, a little too firmly for anyone to believe her.

"A good lad," continued Jack, peering out the door to see if Ashley was out of earshot and lowering his voice. "He's here as part of the alien equal-opportunities program. No one else would work with him, so he came down to us."

"Can he do that thought thing in reverse?" asked Mary. "It might be useful."

"I never asked," replied Jack. "Why don't you bring it up with him? But be careful. The first thing you learn about aliens is that they don't quite . . . get it."

"Get what?"

"*It.* Us. The whole bit. You'll see. The second thing you learn is that they're really not that interesting, so don't strike up a conversation without a good reason to excuse yourself. Despite that, Ashley excels with records, filing, indexing and general data crunching."

"It's not as though I actually *wanted* to be a policeman," said Ashley, who had returned as quickly as he left, "but the filing here is to die for."

"Here as in earth?" asked Mary, without meaning to be patronizing.

"No," replied Ashley without even the smallest trace of taking offense, "here as in Reading."

The other officer was a woman. She was very tall and willowy and had long straight hair made up into a single plait. She looked as though she had been heated up at birth and then drawn out like a soft candle. She was over six foot two, and when she ran, it looked as if she were in slow motion, like a giraffe. In the park where she jogged every morning, there were at least a half dozen men and two women there for no other reason than to watch her.

"Mary, this is Constable the Baroness Gretel Leibnitz von Kandlestyk-Maeker, all the way from Cologne. She doesn't know what she's doing here, and we don't know what she's doing here, but we're glad she is, because she's a damn fine officer. She used to work with Chymes."

"Really?" asked Mary, interested all of a sudden. "What happened?"

"I was — how can I say it? — less respectful than I should have been. If Chymes asks you to do something, refuse it at your peril. I could have been DS by now — just look at me."

"Thank you, Gretel," said Jack, none too happy at the inference. "Gretel's area of expertise is forensic accounting."

"Forensic accounting?" asked Mary. "What's that?"

"It is paper chasing mostly," replied Gretel. "If you want to find where money came from or where it went, you come to me."

"Best in the land," added Jack, "which is why Chymes will still use you even after your — how shall we put it? — vigorous exchange of discourtesies."

Gretel leaned closer to Mary and whispered, "I called him an arsehole."

"Daring."

"No, just *stupid,*" replied Gretel with a sigh.

"Okay," continued Jack, "grab a seat, everyone. I want to tell you what has happened so far."

"Sir?"

"Yes, Ashley?"

"Do we get any more officers this time?"

Jack looked at all of them in turn. "I'll ask, but you know how Briggs feels about the NCD. Short-staffed is kind of standard operating procedure with the division, so we'll have to make our armwork and legwork count. Let's get straight to it, then."

Ordinarily they would all have sat, but there wasn't room, so they leaned against the door and the filing cabinets, except Ashley, who nimbly stuck himself to the wall.

"Welcome to the hunt, all of you. Mary is my number two on this, and even though she is new to Reading, I want you to give her all the help you can. Ashley will be based here to look after the incident room and keep him near his beloved Internet . . . and, Ashley?"

"Yes, sir?"

"No checking eBay for unusual beer mats."

Jack pointed to Madeleine's photo of Humpty with Charles Pewter.

"Victim's name is Humperdinck Jehoshaphat Aloysius Stuyvesant van Dumpty, more commonly known as Humpty Dumpty. He was sixty-five years old and died at approximately one o'clock yesterday morning, killed by a single gun-shot wound to the back. He died instantly. He had a bitter ex-wife and a girlfriend we haven't found; no witnesses, no suspects, no weapon and no motive."

He wrote "MOTIVE — WEAPON — SUSPECTS" on the board with a felt pen and underlined each word.

"For the past year, Dumpty has been operating a business from Grimm's Road, changing a carefully earned two-and-half-million-pound profit into a one-and-a-half-million-pound loss. Yes, Baker?"

"Was he living at Grimm's Road?"

"Good point. It seems not, so we need to find out where he was. He had this photo on his desk."

Jack showed them the photo of Humpty with the woman in the back of the horse-drawn carriage in Vienna.

"We need to find this woman. Dumpty

and she were together in Vienna — and that's all we know about her."

He held up the auburn hair.

"SOCO found this in Humpty's office. It's a single human hair, auburn colored and twenty-eight feet long. Shouldn't be difficult to trace. Tibbit, what have we got on your initial door-to-door?"

Tibbit was delighted. To him, this was *real* police work. He flipped open his notebook and summarized his notes. Eager to make an impression, he had copied them up neatly the evening before.

"Some people heard dustbins being knocked over sometime after midnight."

"And?"

"A box van was seen on several nights prior to the night he died."

Tibbit flipped over some more pages.

"There was a silver VW Polo, too — with a woman in it."

"Nothing else?"

"Nope. Everyone I met liked him, though."

"Okay, we've established that he was popular, and not just with the ladies. We should cross-check any VW Polos with the names 'Bessie' or 'Elizabeth.' Otto and Baker, I want you to go back to Grimm's Road and try to find the slug that killed him; you should liaise with Mrs. Singh and Skinner to estimate where it fell. I want drains lifted and bins searched, along with any other place where we might conceivably find a gun. Ashley, start the usual trace proceedings on Miss Vienna and ring around to hair salons to see if you can match the auburn hair."

He held up a photograph of the Marchetti shotgun.

"And there's this. It was found in Dumpty's office and links to one of Chymes's cases, a double murder eighteen months ago, about the same time that Dumpty starts to buy shares in the rapidly failing Spongg foot-care empire, apparently against all better judgment. The dates might be a coincidence, but equally, there might be a link between the two."

"The shotgun proves that, doesn't it, sir?" ventured Baker.

"Not at all. It could have changed hands a dozen times. Skinner is matching the shell cases as we speak to see if it *was* the murder weapon. Gretel?"

"Where did he get the money to buy all those shares?"

"Another good question. We don't know. He traded in bonds, commodities, currency, scrap, béarnaise sauce, strawberries —

anything he could lay his hands on. I'd like you to unravel just exactly *where* all his capital came from. He made two and a half million from scratch in eighteen months and spent the lot on shares in a failing chiropody empire. I think we should know the reason why."

"I'll get onto it straightaway," said Gretel, rubbing her hands in happy anticipation of all the forensic accounting to come.

Baker had been studying the photo of Humpty. "I think he owned a car, sir."

"What makes you say that?"

"It's those short legs. I don't suppose he could go far on them without getting a bit pooped."

"I'll have a look," said Ashley, twisting the computer terminal towards him and tapping in to the Police National Computer.

"At the same time," continued Jack, "I want you to run the usual checks on his background. I want every single scrap of information on him you can find."

Ashley turned from his terminal. He had found Humpty's car.

"Registered to Mr. H. A. Dumpty, a red 1963 modified Ford Zephyr, registration number Echo Golf Golf three one four.

One owner since new, tax disc renewed a month ago. Grimm's Road address."

"I want this car found. Mary, speak to uniform and put out a bulletin. Baker, I want you to put your ear to the ground in town. He's been lying low this past year, so see if you can find out why and where."

Mary thought of something and rummaged in a box of filed evidence. She located what she was looking for — the pictures that they had found in Humpty's desk of the Sacred Gonga Visitors' Center. They were all pictures taken from the window of a car. A *red* car.

"You're boys," she said, showing the pictures to Ashley and Baker. "Tell me, does that look like a Ford Zephyr?"

"Definitely," replied Baker. "My uncle used to own one."

Jack took the picture that had the young man in it and handed it to Tibbit.

"Then we need to find this chap, too. He's a known associate of Humpty's, and they were together, as this date in the photo would attest, almost exactly a year ago. Tibbit, get copies made and circulate them around the station — if he's a local lad with a record, someone might recognize him."

Tibbit took the picture and hurried off.

"Mrs. Dumpty is his ex-wife, still bitter and still in love with him. Mary, have you spoken to her?"

"Not yet, sir. She's not at home or work. I've left messages."

Jack looked at his watch. "That's all for now. We'll reconvene after lunch."

He picked up his coat and headed for the door.

"Ashley, keep on trying Mrs. Dumpty and let Randolph Spongg and Solomon Grundy know we're on our way. Mary — with me."

He was feeling good again, for the first time in as long as he could remember.

"Where are we going, sir?"

"To learn a bit more about Reading's foot-care empire."

18. Lord Randolph Spongg IV

Spongg Footcare is an island of benevolent industrial practices, slowly being eroded by the sea of change. All the other companies around it are run by hard-nosed businessmen to whom profit is everything and workers merely numbers on a report. Spongg's is, of course, unlikely to survive long.
— Report in *The Financial Toad*, June 11, 1986

Jack parked the Allegro in the deserted visitors' car park, next to a huge stylized sculpture of a foot with a large void through it. He pulled his collar up against the rain and looked up at the Gothic-style redbrick factory. Apart from a few wisps of smoke creeping from its chimneys and the muffled sound of machinery from within, the whole place seemed deserted. It was shabby, too. Large sections of stucco were missing from the walls, the brickwork was badly stained and the windows were cracked and grimy.

They walked up the steps to the grand entrance and noted how the carved stone doorway depicted, in ten stages, the evolution of the foot from a flipper to the appendage of modern man. There was no one around, so Jack pushed open the heavy doors. The interior was similarly deserted; a musty, damp smell that reminded them both of Grimm's Road rose up to meet them. As their eyes became accustomed to the gloom, they could see that they were standing in a vast entry hall dimly lit by roof-high stained-glass windows depicting great moments in chiropody. The foot theme didn't end with the windows — they were standing on an immense mosaic of a foot with one of Spongg's corn plasters on its big toe, picked out in gold and azure tiles. Below the picture, Spongg's easily recognizable logo was written in brass letters a yard high. The walls were similarly adorned with an exquisite mural of mythical creatures in a setting of a forest in summer. There were satyrs, nymphs, cherubs and centaurs, all suffering from various foot problems and bathed in shafts of light. Next to each was a painted Spongg product being lovingly administered by beautiful and appropriately dressed maidens. The expressions of contentment on the creatures' faces left one with little doubt as to the effectiveness of the remedies.

"Guess the product," murmured Jack, gazing around at the curious decor and the large twin marble staircases that rose before them, curving up to the left and the right.

"Yeah, but what a *dump*," replied Mary, pointing out the galvanized buckets that had been scattered about on the steps to catch the rainwater that leaked in.

"My grandfather used to work at Spongg's," said Jack. "He always said it was the best place to work in Reading. He lived in nearby Sponggville, and my father went to a Spongg-financed school. If Granddad ever fell ill, he went to the Spongg Memorial Hospital, and when he retired, he stayed in one of the Spongg retirement homes dotted around the country."

"Was he buried in a corn plaster?"

"You must be Detective Inspector Spratt," boomed a voice so suddenly that they both jumped. They turned to find a tall man dressed in a black frock coat standing not more than a pace behind. He had crept up on them as noiselessly as a cat.

Lord Randolph Spongg IV was a handsome man in his mid-fifties. He had black hair that was streaked with gray and a lined face that fell easily into a smile. His eyes glistened with inward amusement.

"Correct, sir," replied Jack. "This is Detective Sergeant Mary Mary."

He shook both their hands in turn and bowed graciously, then led them towards the staircase.

"Thank you for seeing us, Lord Spongg —" began Mary, but Spongg interrupted her.

"Just 'Spongg' will do, Sergeant. I don't use my title much, and — don't see me as fussy — but the first g is short and the second g long. Just let it roll around for a bit before you let it go."

"Spongggg?" ventured Mary.

"Close enough," replied Spongg with a mischievous grin. "Just put the brakes on a little earlier and you'll be fine."

He pointed his silver-topped cane at a satyr with pustules on its hoof and laid a friendly hand on Mary's shoulder that she didn't much care for — but might get used to, on reflection, given the opportunity.

"A charming picture, don't you agree, Sergeant?"

Mary narrowed her eyes and looked at the strange creature. "Not really, I'm afraid."

Randolph Spongg paused for a moment,

looked at the picture again and sighed deeply. "You're right of course," he said at last. "My grandfather had this all painted in 1921 by Diego Rivera. He suffered terribly from fallen arches, did Rivera. Did you know that?"

"I have to say that I didn't," confessed Jack.

"No matter. The result was a classical study of mythical beasts. My grandfather thought that it should reflect his products more, and he insisted that the creatures be made to suffer from some kind of foot ailment. Rivera quite rightly refused, so a Reading sign writer named Donald Scragg finished it off with all this product-placement stuff. Sometimes I think I will have Scragg's paint removed, but artistic restoration is but the least of Spongg's problems at the present."

They followed Spongg as he ran nimbly up the marble staircase, expertly avoiding several more buckets that had been laid out on the landing. The corridor upstairs was almost wide enough to accommodate two lanes of traffic, but for stacks of old papers pushed haphazardly against the walls.

"Records," explained Spongg, following Jack's look. "We had a spot of bother with damp in the basement. Wait! Have a look at this."

He had stopped in front of an oil painting of a venerable-looking gentleman, one of several that lined the corridor. Spongg gazed at it with obvious affection.

"Lord Randolph Spongg II," he announced. The painting was of an elderly man with divergent eyes standing barefoot on a chair.

"My grandfather. Died in 1942 while attempting the land speed record. A great man and a fine chemist. He devised a trench-foot preparation in 1917 that paid for the company to lead the world in foot-care products for the next thirty years. He was the world's leading authority on carbuncles and was working on an athlete's foot remedy when he died. My father carried on his work, and we cracked it in the fifties; it kept us financially afloat for a bit longer. This way."

He led them along the cluttered corridor until they arrived at a large mahogany door. Spongg pushed it open and stepped back to allow them to enter.

Spongg's office was a spacious room with oak-paneled walls and a high ceiling, dominated by a portrait of a man they took to be the first Dr. Spongg. At the far end was a desk the size of a snooker table cluttered high with reports, and in the middle of the room was a model of the factory within a glass case. The room was lit by a skylight, and several more buckets and an old tin bath were laid around the floor to catch the water that leaked in.

Spongg read Jack's expression as he saw the room and laughed nervously.

"It's no secret, Inspector. We're in a bit of a pickle financially, and I can't afford to have the roof done. Cigarette?"

"Thank you, I don't," said Jack, noticing that there were actually no cigarettes in the box anyway.

Spongg smiled. "Wise choice. My father was trying to prove a link between nicotine and fallen arches when he died."

"Did he?" asked Mary.

"No. There isn't one. But it's due to my father's hard work that we know even that much. I heard of Humpty's death on the news last night. For almost a year now, we have been thanking providence for supplying the company with such an upright benefactor."

He beckoned them both to the window and pointed out a large building of modernist style, a mirror-covered office block surrounded by a high-tech factory.

"Do you know what that is?"

Jack had lived in Reading all his life, and the rivalry between the two companies was well known.

"Of course. It's Winsum and Loosum's."

"Winsum and Loosum. Right. They've been wanting to absorb us for some time. The Spongg family has only forty percent of the company, so a danger exists; we have been borrowing against the assets for the past twenty years to keep the old place alive — even old Castle Spongg is in hock."

He indicated a table that was groaning under the weight of Spongg's varied foot products.

"These are our bestselling lines. The need to remain competitive keeps the profit margin small, and we also suffer the most ironic of marketing difficulties."

"Which is?"

"Success."

"Success?"

"Product success, Inspector, not financial success. Have you ever had cause to use a Spongg preparation?"

"Yes."

"And it worked?"

"Very well, as I recall."

"So you see our problem. We promote

the cure, thus effecting the slow eradication of our own market."

Spongg pointed his silver-topped cane at several charts on the wall behind him.

"This is the reported incidence of verrucas. You see how it's dropped considerably in the last ten years?"

Jack and Mary studied the chart on the wall. Apart from a few upturns now and again during hot summers, the trace headed progressively downhill. Spongg pointed to another.

"Bunions. Down seventy percent since this time a decade ago."

He pointed to a third.

"Athlete's foot. Steady decline these past twelve years."

He faced them again.

"Good for the planet's feet, Inspector, disastrous for Spongg's!"

"And Humpty Dumpty?" asked Jack.

"Ah!" said Spongg with a smile. "Now, there's an egg with faith!"

"Go on."

"He was our major shareholder. At the last takeover bid six months ago, all the nonfamily shareholders voted to take Winsum and Loosum's offer. Humpty held firm. With his support we could rebuff the takeover. I was impressed by his fortitude, but puzzled also."

"Because . . . ?"

"I have no idea why he did so. Humpty's plans for Spongg's are a complete mystery to us all. He was no fool; I've done my homework. But as to what he had planned for Spongg's — I have not the slightest idea."

He sighed again and gazed up at the painting of the first Dr. Spongg, whose likeness scowled out at the world holding the model of a foot in one hand and a pair of toenail clippers in the other.

There was a pause. Spongg stared at the ceiling for a moment, then asked, "Anyhow, what else can I do for you?"

"You helped Dumpty outside after his outburst at your charity benefit?"

"Yes; if I'd known he was going to get so . . . er, poached, I would never have had him at my table."

"He said he could raise fifty million pounds just like that. What do you think he was referring to?"

"A refinancing package? Who knows? As I said, his plans for Spongg's were a complete mystery to me."

Jack looked at Spongg carefully, trying to find a chink in the man's reserve. Pewter had said Humpty might have wanted to sell out to Grundy, so he watched closely for Spongg's reaction to his next question.

"Do you think he was going to sell out to Winsum and Loosum?"

Spongg was unfazed. He shrugged. "Possibly, although I think he might have left it a little late. Grundy's waiting for me to go under so they can buy what they want from the receivers. It's not a question of *if,* it's a question of *when.*"

Spongg looked at them both and raised an eyebrow. "By your line of questioning, I can see that you are not satisfied with the circumstances of Humpty's death."

"Correct, sir. We regard it as suspicious."

"Does this make me a suspect?"

"I view everyone as a suspect," said Jack politely. "Perhaps you would tell us your movements after the Spongg Charity Benefit ended."

Spongg smiled. "Of course. I was driven home to Castle Spongg by Ffinkworth, my valet, at about half past midnight. Past one o'clock until breakfast at seven, I am afraid I can offer no witnesses."

Mary made a note.

"And did you see much of Humpty otherwise?"

"Up until the night of the benefit, I hadn't seen him for over a year. His death benefits no one here at Spongg's, Inspector — quite the reverse."

"Would you have any idea who might want him dead, Spongg?"

"A parade of cuckolded husbands, jilted lovers, disgruntled restaurateurs and unpaid wine merchants — I should imagine the list will be quite long."

"What about Solomon Grundy?"

Spongg thought for a moment. "Did you hear about Humpty's Splotvian mineral-rights debacle?"

Jack nodded.

"If you examine the list of people defrauded, I think you will find Mr. Grundy quite high up on it. I don't think Solomon would resort to *murder,* but you should know about it."

"Indeed we should," replied Jack, taking a note. "Mary, do you have anything else to add?"

"Are you married, sir?" asked Mary.

"Was. I'm single at present."

"Nothing else."

Jack handed Spongg his card. "Thank you for your help, and I hope the company picks up. We'll see ourselves out."

They left Spongg staring at the model of his beloved factory. Jack had meant what he said: No one wanted to see Spongg's go down; it had been a part of Reading for so long that its presence was alive all over the town. Apart from Sponggville, Spongg Villas and the Spongg Memorial Gardens, there was Spongg Street and Spongg Lane. The town hall was dedicated to the first Dr. Spongg, and outside the town was Castle Spongg, a vast country home built in the surrealist style in the thirties.

"What do you reckon?" asked Mary.

Jack thought for a moment. "He seems genuinely confused over *why* Humpty should be buying shares in the company. Humpty's death doesn't help him — with his shares in probate limboland, they can't be sold, either to Grundy or anyone else. Spongg's is going down the tubes, and it's a shame. Next is Winsum and Loosum's — and you're driving."

He tossed her the keys and they were soon motoring towards the exit past packing cases full of unsold foot ointments.

"Mary, why did you ask Spongg if he was married?"

Mary delicately pulled on the turn signal lever and the Lucas relay clicked at her with a soft metallic chirrup.

"I couldn't help myself. Sorry. He *is* kind of attractive."

She pulled into the main road a little too quickly; a small sports car with the top down and a distinctive paint scheme appeared behind them and drove past at great speed, horn blaring.

19. Solomon Grundy

GRUNDY TO WED ON THURSDAY

Billionaire financier, philanthropist and foot-care magnate Solomon Grundy will marry next Thursday, it was announced after Wednesday's charity polo match. The sixty-five-year-old Monday-born financier who was ill last Friday departs for a walking holiday on Tuesday. He has dismissed calls from his board to stay in Reading until the latest acquisition goes through. "I'll be dead tired on Saturday," he quipped to waiting journalists, "but will bury myself in work again on Sunday. Those guys — they'll be the end of me!"
— Report in *The Toad*, April 21, 2000

The security guard at the main gates of Winsum & Loosum was trapped behind toughened glass like a goldfish, and Mary had to speak to the bored and surly individual via a microphone. They were admitted after repeating their names several times and drove up to the crowded visitors' parking area, which was adjacent to an unimaginatively landscaped grass mound.

As Mary locked the car, she thought it odd that the two world leaders in foot-care products were situated within a mile of each other. Almost like two ships, she mused, close enough to fire corporate broadsides.

The Winsum & Loosum headquarters was slick and elegant in a modernistic style, with a bright and airy lobby that rose six stories within the building. Jack and Mary announced themselves at the desk and were asked by the razor-thin receptionist to take a seat. They sat by the fountain and watched the glass lifts move up and down inside the lobby, disgorging hordes of expensively dressed executives who seemed to scurry purposefully in all directions but have very little to do.

Mary's phone rang. She pulled it from her pocket, looked at it and groaned audibly.

"Same guy?" asked Jack. "What was his name? Arnold?"

"Yes, sir."

"Give the phone to me," said Jack. "I'll pretend to be your father."

"I really don't think —"

"Has he ever met your father?"

"No, sir."

"Then hand it over."

She reluctantly handed Jack the phone. He cleared his throat and pressed the "answer" button.

"Arnold?" he said, using his stern, talking-to-children voice, "This is Brian, Mary's father. I must say that I am a little disappointed that —"

He stopped, listened for a moment, smiled and then said, "Well, that's very kind of you to say so, Arnold, but I must make *this* point abundantly clear —"

There was another pause. Jack made a few "uh-huh" and "yuh" noises before laughing and looking at Mary.

"Did she, now? How about that. What's your line of work, Arnold?"

Mary stared at him, aghast. She made throat-cutting signals, shaking her head and mouthing *no . . . no . . . no.*

"Really?" carried on Jack. "Well, of course we are *immensely* proud of her now that she's joined the NCD. . . . Of course. . . . DI Jack Spratt. . . . No, with *two t*'s. . . . That's the one. . . . No, as I understand it, only one was a giant — the rest were just tall. . . . She didn't?"

The conversation went on like this for quite a few minutes, with Mary sinking lower and lower in her seat.

"Well," continued Jack, "you must come around for tea sometime. Myself and Mrs. Mary would be very pleased to meet you." He paused again, put his hand over the phone and said to Mary, "Where do we live?"

She glared at him, crossed her arms and said, "Basingstoke," through gritted teeth.

"Basingstoke," repeated Jack into the mobile. He laughed again. "No, we're not at all ashamed. Call us anytime. Mary has the number. Same to you. Bye."

He pressed the "end-call" button, shaking his head and smiling. He passed the mobile back and caught Mary's eye as she gazed daggers at him.

"What? He sounds like a great guy. I think you should cut him a little slack."

Mary wasn't amused. "I thought you were going to get rid of him for me."

Jack thought for a moment, trying to figure out a plausible excuse.

"No," he said finally, "what I *said* was that I'd pretend to be your father. How did I do?"

Mary sighed. "Spookily accurate, sir."

"DI Spratt?" said a pencil-thin woman who looked as if she'd escaped from the cover of a fashion magazine.

"Yes?" said Jack as they both stood.

"I am Miss Daley, the secretary to Mr. Grundy's personal secretary's assistant's assistant."

She shook both their hands.

"Welcome to Winsum and Loosum's. Mr. Grundy is a busy man but understands the importance of police work. He has delayed a meeting in order to be able to grant you an audience."

"How fantastically generous of him."

"Mr. Grundy is always eager to assist the police in any way he can," said the humorless assistant, who had somehow lost something on the road towards highly cultivated efficiency. She led them across the atrium and into one of the lifts, which then shot them upwards like an express train. It deposited them in a noiseless corridor that led to an oak-paneled boardroom with a large oval table in it. Two well-groomed executives were just leaving as they entered, one of whom Jack thought he recognized. They were efficiently introduced to Mr. Grundy by the assistant, who then seemed to melt away.

Solomon Grundy was everything Spongg was not. He had a limp handshake, a false smile and pallid features that surrounded a pair of eyes that were of the brightest blue but projected no emotion. His suit was hand-tailored from Savile Row but looked out of place on his large, bullnecked frame — he reminded Jack of a gangster desperate to be respectable. He wore a well-fitting toupée, and his hands were liberally covered with heavy gold jewelry.

Grundy had got to his feet as he welcomed Jack and Mary and offered them a seat on intentionally low chairs. He opened a silver cigar box and said, "Cigar? They're Cuban."

Jack declined his offer, but Grundy put one in Jack's top pocket anyway and winked at him, then gave one to Mary and said, "For the boyfriend." He then sat down in his own huge, corporate comfy chair and spun completely around, lighting his cigar as he did so. He stopped facing straight ahead as he clicked off his lighter, then placed his hands on the table and blew out some cigar smoke. It seemed like a well-rehearsed routine.

"This interview, is, I assume, to do with Mr. Dumpty's death?"

"Just an informal chat, Mr. Grundy."

"Why should it be formal? Unless, of course, Mr. Dumpty's death was suspicious. Is this the case, Inspector?"

You don't get to be the ninth-wealthiest man in Britain without being astute, thought Jack — or perhaps he already knew?

"We believe there are suspicious aspects to his death, yes, sir. Who was that leaving as we came in?"

"Two of my junior board members. I expect you recognized Friedland's brother?"

"How long has he been working here?"

"Does this relate to Humpty's death?"

"No."

"I'm a busy man, Mr. Spratt."

Jack grew hot. It was not a very subtle put-down, but effective. Grundy had been leading the conversation since he'd walked in. Jack decided he'd have to get the upper hand again and invoked his secret plan: talk to other people as Friedland talked to him.

"So am I, Mr. Grundy," replied Jack, staring at him coldly. "A man — well, an egg, actually — has died, and I think irrespective of who or what he was, he deserves that I investigate his death to the best of my ability. So tell me, how do you describe your relationship with Spongg's?"

Grundy smiled. A smile of respect, thought Jack. To people like Grundy, straight talking was the answer. He still wasn't going to make it easy, though, and his dispassionate eyes bored into Jack like augers.

"Rivals. That's no secret. We tried to buy them out six months ago but were thwarted by a new shareholder."

"Humpty Dumpty?"

"Indeed. I wager old Randolph is kicking himself. With Mr. Dumpty dead, his shares are wrapped up in probate. They'll go bust, and we'll take all we want from the receivers."

He smiled an ugly smile, and Jack shifted his weight uneasily. He didn't like Grundy one bit.

"Sounds as though his death has benefited you, Mr. Grundy."

"It has benefited the *company*, Mr. Spratt. The same as if he had fallen off a bike or died in his sleep. Corporate business is a dangerous place; I do not own this company any more than you own the Reading police force. The shareholders will view Mr. Dumpty's demise without grief. We thought perhaps Humpty had a refinancing package for Spongg's, but his death will have put a stop to that. In under a year, we will have added their product lines to ours. I hope I am candid, Mr. Spratt."

"Very," replied Jack. "What did you and Mr. Dumpty talk about at the Spongg Charity Benefit?"

Grundy laughed. "Your information is good, Inspector. He offered me his thirty-eight percent share of Spongg's for ten million. I told him the time for deals had long passed, and he told me I wouldn't be laughing this time next year. We'll take what we want from the receivers. I heard his private life was fairly colorful. Why don't you speak to some of his girlfriends? Jealousy is a powerful emotion, Mr. Spratt."

"So is revenge, Mr. Grundy."

Grundy guessed Jack's inference. "You have Splotvia on your mind, Mr. Spratt?"

Jack nodded. "I understand you lost a great deal of money?"

Grundy contemplated the end of his cigar for a few moments.

"It was that damnable mineral-rights scam of his. I should never have become involved, but then again, it was business."

"So you weren't bitter?"

"Of course not. I was *furious.* You'd better know the facts. He raised that share capital and spent it, not on securing mineral rights but on arming the rebels against the military dictatorship that ran the country. I tried to have him charged with fraud, but he covered his tracks well. They even" — he laughed — "made him a colonel in the Splotvian Imperial Guard."

"Sounds like a good motive to me, Mr. Grundy."

"I disagree," replied Grundy evenly. "My loss to Humpty was only *two-tenths of one percent* of my fortune. Consider this: Even if I generously estimated your personal net worth at four hundred thousand pounds, the comparative loss to you would be only eight hundred pounds. Two million may be more money than you'll see in a lifetime, but I could lose that sum *every week for a decade* before I might consider myself ruined. Do I make myself clear?"

Jack gritted his teeth. He'd enjoy bringing this one down.

"Abundantly, Mr. Grundy. I wonder if you could tell me your movements following the Spongg Charity Benefit on Monday?"

"I returned home," he replied, indignant that he should have to account for his actions to anyone, "with my wife. You can ask her, if you so wish, with my blessing."

Jack stared at Grundy, who looked back at him without sentiment. Jack wanted to make him sweat, so he tried a threat.

"I'd like to interview the board of directors and read the company minutes for the past two years."

Grundy rolled his eyes and tapped some

ash into a crystal ashtray the size of a hand basin. "It'll require a court order."

Jack stared at him. "I thought you would be happy to assist, Mr. Grundy."

The bluff failed.

"Of course. What you ask will require considerable expenditure of time and resources. A court order gives me peace of mind that you really need what you ask for. I won't be given the runaround on a non-Guild NCD officer's whim. And I'll tell you now I don't frighten easily. I have been investigated by the FBI, the CBI, the CID, the MCC and the FO. I have weathered four stock-market crashes and suffered monetary losses that exceed the GNP of East and West Woppistania *combined.* I survived all that, and I'll certainly survive you."

His voice had kept the same modulation, although red blotches had been breaking out on his pale face. Jack feared for any junior board member who had this to contend with. Grundy paused for a minute as his face returned to its normal pallid complexion, then spoke again: "Is there anything else?"

"Not for the moment," said Jack as sternly as he could. He needn't have bothered. It came out sounding weak and ineffectual, and Grundy knew it. He gave a smile and bade them good day.

The elegant assistant appeared from nowhere and escorted them back to the elevator, in which they were plunged at freefall speed back to the lobby, thanked and shown the door in under a minute.

"I've never been so efficiently expelled from a building before," murmured Mary in awe as they walked back to the Allegro.

"I imagine that being fired is probably a similar experience," said Jack, "but without the courtesy of the elevator."

20. Press Conference

POPULAR CRIME MAG OUTLAWS TWINS

The bestselling true-crime magazine *Amazing Crime Stories* announced that it would be banning the "identical twins" plot device as part of tough new measures to stave off what it described as "stagnation" within the world of professional detecting. Other plot devices facing the ax are the much-loved "left-handed perpetrator" and anything to do with anagrams. The Guild of Detectives reacted angrily to the ban, complaining that they had "not been fully consulted" and would "vigorously defend the right of detectives to use whatever plot contrivances come to hand in the course of their investigations." The ban will come into effect in August.

— From *The Mole*, March 30, 2004

As soon as they walked into the station, they realized that something was going on. A certain buzz travels around as everyone discusses a prominent case. Friedland might have felt it all the time, as his exploits were routinely grapevined, but Jack had never experienced it before. Ashley and Gretel were waiting for them in the NCD offices.

"What's going on, Gretel?"

"Humpty's murder, sir. Seems like everyone has an opinion about how the investigation should be run. The Superintendent has been calling every twenty minutes wanting to know where you were."

"Ah," said Jack, "no surprises there. Have you found any irregularities in Humpty's finances yet?"

"It's very complex and very confusing," said Gretel, "like being lost in a large forest. But I'm making headway. I'll let you know as soon as I have anything solid."

She turned back to her desk and dialed another number on the telephone.

"Ashley, any luck with that auburn hair?"

"Not yet, sir. I'm running through the telephone directory; there are a lot of hairdressers in Reading."

"Keep at it. Did Tibbit get a name for the lad in the photograph?"

"No," said Ashley, "but we did get a cross-reference match with a silver VW Polo and the Christian name of 'Bessie.'

Her name's Bessie Brooks, veterinarian's assistant, age 11001. Hasn't been seen at work since the morning Humpty was killed. The address is on your desk."

"Excellent. Call Ops and get some uniform around there to bring her in for questioning. If she doesn't want to come, then arrest her as a possible suspect. Mary?"

"Yes, sir?"

"I don't buy that 'two million means nothing to me' crap from Grundy. This is a request for a search warrant for Winsum's headquarters. I want you to —"

"Murder, Jack?"

Briggs was at the door. He didn't look quite as angry as Jack had supposed he might be.

"Yes, sir."

"I could have sworn you told me yesterday it was suicide."

"I made a mistake. I'd spoken to you before Mrs. Singh's initial report. There's a copy on my desk —"

"I've read it, Jack. So he was shot — by whom?"

Jack outlined what had happened in the investigation so far, which wasn't very much. Briggs didn't seem bowled over with enthusiasm, but then Briggs never was. The three pigs he had never been keen on, and the emperor's-new-clothes fraud inquiry had similarly been looked upon with tepidity. Even so, his answer surprised Jack.

"Well," he said as soon as Jack had finished, "seems like you're doing fine. Keep me informed of any developments, and if there's anything you want, *anything* at all, just call me." He paused and then added, "As long as it's not extra manpower, overtime, funds or . . . anything else I don't agree with. I'll have my secretary prepare a list. I meant what I said earlier about fast results. The budgetary meeting is next week, and an early arrest would do a lot towards continued funding. And listen: This doesn't mean you're excused from the Sacred Gonga security duties. I'm short-staffed as it is, and we've overspent this year already."

He thought for a moment.

"One other thing: I've just spoken to the Chief. He's had a call from Solomon Grundy *himself,* who lambasted him for half an hour about your threats. Do you seriously expect me to believe that Grundy is behind all this?"

"It's possible, sir. Winsum and Loosum are set on owning all Spongg's foot-care remedies. Dumpty blocked a takeover bid and then seemed set on some kind of a plan to save Spongg's."

"What sort of plan?"

"I don't know, but with Dumpty out of the picture, there is no barrier to Winsum and Loosum's eventual takeover of Spongg's. They have the best motive I can see, and what's more, Solomon *himself* lost two million in Humpty's Splotvian mineral-rights scam."

"The one in 1990? Fourteen years ago?"

"Yes," said Jack, "that one."

"And the proof?"

Jack stared at Briggs.

"That's what the search warrant is for, sir."

"*What* search warrant?"

"This one," said Jack, holding the request up a bit weakly.

Briggs glared at him, took the application and tore it in half.

"Sorry, Jack. You're going to have to do better than this. Words burnt into the wall. Voices from burning bushes, three witches around a cauldron. Anything. No hearsay, no suspicions and definitely no hunches. You don't pester Mr. Grundy or Winsum and Loosum until I see that proof and sanction it."

"But —"

"But nothing, Jack. The answer is no. We've got the Jellyman coming to town, and that's a big deal. Grundy's forty million to keep the Sacred Gonga in Reading is going to be a big tourism pull for the city — why would anyone want to visit Reading without the Sacred Gonga?"

"The river? SommeWorld? The Friedland Museum? Castle Spongg? Shopping?"

"It's no joking matter. Think of the big picture. Think of Reading." He lightened and laid a hand on Jack's shoulder. "I'm sorry, but it's politics. Seventh floor. Don't forget, if you get any proof, come to me first."

He looked at his watch. "Are you going to attend the press briefing, Spratt?"

"I didn't think I'd bother, sir."

"I think perhaps you should."

"Because they might be interested this time around?"

"Not at all. It just allows Friedland to shine with greater luster."

"Then how could I refuse?"

"Good. And I want a full report on my desk ASAP and not a Jack Spratt keep-the-NCD-going-at-all-costs special."

He clapped his hands together and rubbed them happily.

"Right. Well, I must speak to Friedland

before he goes on. Solved another one this morning, y'know — *remarkable* fellow!"

Briggs gathered up his papers and strode off.

"Well," said Mary, who had returned to Jack's side, "are we still on the case?"

"It seems so," said Jack with furrowed brow, "but Briggs wasn't his usual shouting, screaming, threatening-to-suspend-me self. I hope he's not unwell or anything — or perhaps he's just happy with the way things are going. What do you think?"

Mary felt herself swallow, and her mouth went dry. It could easily be explained. She knew that Friedland was poised to take over the inquiry, and it would be with her help, too.

"I . . . I have no idea, sir."

"Me neither," muttered Jack, "but I'm not complaining. Any news on Mrs. Dumpty?"

"Not yet, sir."

"We can't search through Grundy's boardroom minutes, so do some background delving, would you?"

"Yes, sir."

"Good. What is it, Gretel?"

"Skinner sent down a report."

He read it carefully.

"The cartridges didn't match," announced

265

Jack, handing the report to Mary. "The Marchetti *did* belong to the woodcutters, but it wasn't the one used to kill them. That's a relief. I wasn't keen on having to wade through one of Friedland's old cases. And I was a fool to think he might be *wrong*."

He walked from the room.

Mary wandered over to Gretel. Although she was subordinate to Mary, she had the edge in terms of years and experience. It gave Gretel the upper hand beyond the boundaries of official rank, and they both knew it. Mary would not ever want to pull rank on Gretel, and Gretel would make quite sure that Mary never had to.

"How's it going?"

"Not too bad. Forensic accounting is an underused science. Look here: Last July, Humpty bought a thousand tons of fine-grade copper in Splotvia with money from an account drawn on the Bank of Malvonia. He swapped the copper for a hundred thousand gallons of béarnaise sauce. The sauce was never delivered, and Humpty received a refund. The refund was paid to a subsidiary company in Woppistania, which then used the cash to finance a hotel-development deal in Wozbekistan, which in turn generated a loss that Humpty was able to offer to large multinationals in order for them to offset against tax. In return for this, Humpty was given an eight percent fee. From a dirty forty thousand pounds to a laundered eighty thousand pounds in a few short moves. It would take a phalanx of lawyers a month to figure out whether a law had been broken, and another month to figure out which one."

It wasn't the reason Mary had walked over. She knew next to no one in Reading apart from an aging aunt and a few ex-boyfriends. Gretel, she thought, would be a good person for nothing more unproductive — and necessary — than a chat.

"Are you really a baroness?" she asked.

"Oh, yes," replied Gretel in the sort of way that you might admit to having two cars, "but it means nothing. My family is from East Germany. They had a large house and grounds near Leipzig. When the Russians took over, my family escaped to West Berlin with only the title and a single crested teaspoon. You're from Basingstoke, yes?"

"Born and bred — and it's nothing to be ashamed of."

"Yes," agreed Gretel, "so I heard."

"You're very tall," observed Mary. "Don't you worry about Jack and his . . . reputation?"

"The giant killing? No. His *shortest* victim was at least six inches taller than me, so I figure I'm well beneath his height criteria. When did you make sergeant?"

"Four years ago," replied Mary. "I took my Official Sidekick exams — for all the good it did me. Tell me, you've worked with Chymes. What's the possibility of him dumping that idiot Flotsam? He's sloppy and irritating, and his prose stinks."

"*True Detective* would welcome such a thing, but I'm not sure Chymes would dump him. Flotsam knows a lot about Friedland that Friedland wouldn't want to get out."

"Such as?"

"Nobody really knows — and Chymes wants to keep it that way. Flotsam's here to stay, sadly — unless he wants out. Why, have you got your eye on the top DS job in Reading?"

"*Very* long-term plan," said Mary hurriedly.

"The Chymes detecting machine is a double-edged sword," confided Gretel. "The benefits are enormous. You play to *his* rules, and you sometimes hate yourself for doing so — but six months later it's standard operating procedure and you're looking to see who you can trample over next."

Mary nodded thoughtfully. She often hated herself. Once more here and there wouldn't make much difference.

"And that," continued Chymes triumphantly, "was how we knew that Major Stratton was guilty. By pointing suspicion at himself via the unfinished Scrabble game and the half-eaten macaroon, he hoped to be charged, then released when his alibi was proved, banking on the fact that the police would eliminate him from their inquiries completely. But by analyzing the dried saliva on the back of the stamp, I could prove that Wentworth had *not* sent the letter purporting to be from the mergers commission. So with Dibble's allergy to leeks ruling *him* out, Wilks in custody at the time . . ."

He paused in front of his audience, who were frozen to the spot, spellbound.

". . . it could only be Major Stratton."

There was a burst of applause and a battery of cameras going off as Friedland nodded his appreciation at their appreciation.

"But what alerted you to Major Stratton in the first place?" asked Josh Hatchett.

"Simplicity itself." Chymes smiled. "The Major was an accomplished Scrabble player. He would never have played 'quest' without bonuses when the possibility existed to play 'caziques' on a triple-word score. He must have had something else on his mind — such as *murder!*"

There was another burst of applause.

"You are most kind," he said modestly. "A complete write-up of the case will be published under the title 'The Case of the Fragrant Plum.' Ladies and gentlemen — the case . . . is *closed!*"

Jack was observing from the side door when Mary joined him. They watched Chymes take questions and explain in minute detail how the case was solved.

"What's this about you applying for the Guild, sir?" asked Mary.

"It was my wife's idea. But with Chymes on the selection committee, I think my chances are on the lean side of zero."

Mary didn't answer.

"You might have said *something* in rebuttal," he muttered sulkily. "Like 'Surely not, sir' — if only to make me feel better."

"Surely not, sir," said Mary with a sigh. "Is that better?"

"No. In fact, it's worse."

"Do you know all these people?" she asked to change the subject, staring at the curious array of journalists. There were three news crews, a Japanese film crew, several independents and a small, rather lost-looking man with a camcorder who was obviously a newshound for a local cable channel.

"The thin guy at the end is Josh Hatchett of *The Mole*. Next to him is Hector Sleaze, who writes for *The Toad*. They hate each other. The bloke with the glasses is Clifford Sensible of *The Owl*, who is about the only serious journalist here. The big fellow who looks a bit drunk in the front row is Archibald Fatquack, who edits *The Gadfly*. The two either side of him are Geddes and Pearson, who work for the local papers, the *Reading Mercury* and the *Reading Daily Eyestrain*. The others I don't know, but presumably they're syndicated journalists from the nationals."

There was more applause as Chymes finished answering questions, turned left and right for the photographers to get a few alternative snaps, then strode from the room with a flourish. Within five minutes the pressroom was empty apart from Archibald and Hector Sleaze, who was trying to decipher some of his own shorthand.

"Good afternoon, everyone," said Jack

slowly as he approached the lectern. "Yesterday morning at approximately one a.m., Humpty Dumpty was shot dead as he sat on his favorite wall. He died instantly. Any questions?"

Jack started to leave, but there was a question — and it wasn't from Archibald either. It was from Hector, who had never stayed long enough to even see Jack walk on, let alone speak.

"Who are you?" asked Hector Sleaze.

"Detective Inspector Jack Spratt of the Nursery Crime Division."

"Are you new? I haven't seen you here before."

"Only since 1978, Mr. Sleaze. You're usually out the door before I even stand up."

"Whatever. Humpty Dumpty?" repeated Sleaze incredulously. "You mean the large egg?"

"That's correct."

"Any suspects?"

"No."

"Any motive?"

"No."

"Any weapon?"

"No."

"That's me all questioned out," said Hector, getting up and leaving.

"Anyone else?" Jack asked, addressing the room, which now had only Fatquack in it.

"Inspector Spratt," began *The Gadfly*'s editor, "can you confirm that in 1978 the British government negotiated for Mr. Dumpty's safe exit from Ogapôga in exchange for information about oil reserves in the Ogapôgian Basin?"

Jack sighed. "I haven't heard of any deals with the Ogapôgians or anyone else, Mr. Fatquack. What's your interest in Humpty Dumpty?"

"I'm writing a biography, but I find more questions than answers when I begin to delve."

"Really?" replied Jack warily. He wasn't going to tell Fatquack that he had found exactly the same.

"Yes," continued Archie, leaning closer, "but he wasn't arrested for gem smuggling. I have spoken to a journalist who told me that he was actually trading guns to arm rebels to fight the government-backed land grabbers. Is this true?"

"You tell me, Mr. Fatquack."

"Is this part of your investigation?"

"Mr. Dumpty has a long and colorful history," replied Jack, "from fraud to land speculation in Splotvia. All of these facets are part of our investigation, but we'll be looking closer to home first."

"Like Oxford?" asked Fatquack. "You knew he went to Christ Church?"

"Yes," replied Jack, "1946. Just missed being chosen for the English rugby team."

"1946?" echoed Fatquack with surprise. "Are you sure?"

"Yes. Why?"

Fatquack drew in a dramatic breath. "You know that the Jellyman was at Christ Church between 1945 and 1947?"

"They might never have spoken."

"I doubt it. The Jellyman was captain of the rugby team."

"His Eminence has met many people in the past," said Jack quickly.

"Of course," replied Fatquack awkwardly, eager for Jack to know that he would never accuse the Jellyman of any wrongdoing. "I'm not suggesting for one moment that he had any dealings with Mr. Dumpty, but it is *interesting* nonetheless. Is it true that you've applied to join the Guild?"

"Word gets around, doesn't it?"

"I know it's not likely you'll get in, but if by the remotest chance it happens, you will remember your friends at *The Gadfly* when *Amazing Crime* rejects the manuscript?"

"You have the nicest way of putting things, Archie."

"So it wasn't stealing gems in Ogapôga," murmured Mary as they walked back to the NCD offices. "It was gunrunning to rebels."

"His crimes never seem to benefit *himself,* do they?" Jack nodded his head thoughtfully.

"Diddling the City financial establishments out of forty million pounds in the name of freedom and democracy has the nub of a fine joke about it," continued Mary.

"I agree. It looks as though the egg had a social conscience — and he didn't mind risking everything if he thought it would do some good."

"Like a Spongg share scam that liberated fifty million pounds for the rebuilding of the woefully inadequate and outdated St. Cerebellum's mental hospital?"

"Could be. He might be a crook — but with a noble purpose."

Gretel was hunched over papers and a calculator when Jack and Mary walked in. She gave a cheery wave without turning around.

"Have they found the bullet at Grimm's Road?" asked Jack.

"Not yet."

"I couldn't remember whether you liked tea or coffee," said Ashley, bringing in a steaming mug for Jack, "so I brought both."

"Thank you."

"In the same cup."

Jack sighed. Ashley was still having trouble getting used to the way things were done.

"Thank you, Ashley. Next time it's coffee, white, one sugar — yes?"

"Yes, sir."

Mary was talking to a uniformed officer at the door. After taking a few notes, she thanked him and walked back into the office.

"Bessie Brooks has done a runner," announced Mary, trying to find somewhere to sit in the cramped offices and eventually perching on the table edge. "They had a look around her flat, but she's not been there for a couple of days. Suitcase missing and clothes scattered everywhere from a hurried pack. Can I issue an arrest warrant? It would make things easier if we're to try and track her down though credit cards."

The phone rang and Mary picked it up. She listened for a moment and winced. "Thanks for calling. We'll be straight there."

She put the receiver down and looked up at Jack.

"I've got a feeling this is bad news," he said slowly.

"It's Mrs. Dumpty."

"At last! When can we talk to her?"

"Never — unless you know a good spiritualist. There's been an accident down at the Yummy-Time Biscuits factory. She's . . . *dead.*"

21. RIP, Mrs. Dumpty, and "the Case . . . Is *Closed!*"

CHYMES TO ATTEMPT
WORLD SLEUTH RECORD

Global number-two-ranked *Amazing Crime* sleuth DCI Chymes will attempt to challenge Inspector Moose's two-hour, thirty-eight-minute world speed-solving record set last July for a case involving a triple murder, a missing will, blackmail and financial impropriety. "I think we can manage to shave a few minutes off Moose's record," said DCI Chymes confidently as he went into training for the attempt. Because murders cannot be undertaken to order — even for speed trials, Chymes will have to wait until a suitable slaying arrives on his doorstep. "I've never been more ready," he declared.

— Editorial from *Amazing Crime Stories*,
June 7, 2002

"She was on an inspection of the chocolate digestive production line," explained a very shaken executive less than half an hour later down at the Yummy-Time factory, a clean and efficient facility full of clanking machinery, stainless-steel vats and the smell of baking and hot sugar.

"During our afternoon tour, she asked me to fetch her shawl from her office. When I returned, I found a group of workers clustered around the industrial food mixers. It was no use, of course; Mr. Aimsworth said he saw her jump into the main dough mixer — not just for the digestives but for the entire range of biscuits, all the way from custard creams to Abernethys."

He broke down and gave out a muffled sob, then blew his nose on a bright yellow hankie.

"She'd been a leading light of Yummy-Time since she took over from her father ten years ago," said the executive. "She knew shortbread fingers like the back of her hand and upside-down cakes back to front."

Jack and Mary peered cautiously into one of the vast mixing vats, which, they had been informed earlier, held almost five tons of dough mixture. Of Mrs. Dumpty they could see only a foot and part of a blue dress. Already firemen had put a ladder into the vat and were wading through the sticky mixture to try to retrieve what was left of her.

"You better get a statement from the fellow who saw her jump, Mary. I'm going to look at her office."

He was escorted off the factory floor by the executive, who bemoaned the loss of Mrs. Dumpty and her biscuit expertise. They stepped into the spotless interior of the administration side of the building, up two flights of steps and on to Mrs. Dumpty's office, which would have afforded a fine view of Reading if low clouds hadn't been scudding across the city.

"This is her office," said the executive. "What a terrible thing to happen! I didn't think she would want to . . . *you know* . . . herself. She seemed in such fine fettle."

Jack walked around her desk and noticed a picture of her and Humpty in a gilt frame. There was a computer, telephone, correspondence. He stopped. There, on the blotter, was a single piece of paper folded once, with his name written clearly on the front. He took out a fountain pen and pocketknife to avoid touching it, delicately opened the note and read it. He read it again, to make quite sure.

DI Spratt,

I know you will be the officer to read this, and I want you to know that what I did was out of love, not hate. We had been moving towards a reconciliation, and all was going well — until I saw him with a bimbo and my blood boiled. I went to his home and prayed for God to forgive me as I pulled the trigger. Your visit yesterday made me realize that there would be no escape from retribution. Perhaps I am just saving everyone a lot of time and bother.

PS: Please tell Mr. Spatchcock that I won't be able to make my 9:30 appointment this evening.

It was signed Laura Garibaldi-Dumpty. Jack opened her desk diary and compared the handwriting. It was quite distinctive and there was no doubt in his mind that she had written it. He looked at last week's entries in the diary, but there was nothing of interest, just dinner dates, tennis, that sort of thing. She hadn't been planning anything out of the ordinary.

Mary appeared at the doorway as Jack was going through the desk drawers.

"Have a look," he said, indicating the note.

She read it and gave a low whistle.

"So she *did* kill him."

"Probably with this," replied Jack, pointing at a small nickel-plated .32 automatic pistol he had discovered hidden under some papers. "Better get SOCO over here to take possession of the evidence. We'll need to double-check the handwriting on the note and check the pistol for prints and residue. It kind of surprises me she has a gun, though."

"I don't think so," replied Mary, pointing to one of the many pictures on the wall. It depicted a smiling Laura celebrating a win at the British Small-Bore Rifle Championships. Humpty was in the group, holding a bottle of champagne — and Randolph Spongg was there, too. Pistols, it seemed, were not as alien to her as one might have supposed.

"What did Mr. Aimsworth say?"

"He saw her climb over the barrier, pause for a moment and then jump. By the time they had hit the emergency stop, it was already too late."

SOCO arrived within half an hour, but there wasn't much to do. The note was taken away with three other examples of her handwriting, and one of the officers named Shenstone gently lifted the pistol from the bottom drawer. There were five cartridges missing from the clip, but nothing else that could be found. The team was gone in under forty minutes. It was different on the main biscuit-manufacturing level. It took eight firemen, Mrs. Singh and her two assistants the best part of six hours to find all of Mrs. Dumpty. Biscuit manufacture wouldn't restart for another week.

"It seems fairly clear-cut," said Mary as they drove back to the office in the Allegro.

"Keep talking."

"She kills him early yesterday morning, realizes after we visit her that she will be first in the frame, has a fit of remorse and then . . . kills herself."

"It seems a bit too perfect."

"How can it be *too* perfect?" said Mary, wondering whether Chymes would still want her on his team without the Humpty investigation to poach. "She wrote the note, didn't she?"

Jack shrugged. Mary was right. The case was as clear as it could be, and that was good, because that was what he was there for. But from a purely selfish viewpoint, he felt somehow *cheated.* Murder inquiries didn't come around every week, and he had hoped this one would make up for the pig fiasco. It had welcomed him in with open arms, only to spit him out half chewed. The mystery — such as it was — had rapidly devolved to just another crime of passion, an act of desperation that destroyed two lives and ruined countless others. The investigation was over and with it, as likely as not, him and the NCD. He imagined that this was how Friedland felt when a plum mystery collapsed into a simple case of robbery in front of him. And feeling like Chymes made him feel even worse. Besides, he needed a case like this more than at any time before. To prove to Briggs and his blasted budgetary meeting, if not to himself.

"*Shit,*" he muttered.

"Sir?"

"Shit," he reiterated slightly louder, "and bollocks."

He sighed, finally coming to terms with the fact that the inquiry was over.

"There are always a few unanswered questions at the end of an investigation, Mary. But this one's over, and I'd be clutching at straws to think otherwise. Now, I'd better get this sewn up all nice and neat, just as Briggs wants it."

★ ★ ★

To say that Ashley, Baker and Kandlestyk-Maeker were disappointed would be a severe understatement. This investigation was a holiday from their usual dull duties, and they grumbled and moaned as Jack told them the news.

"We're waiting for the results of hand-writing analysis before we can officially close the case, so I want all notes spick and span by ten tomorrow."

"Sir —" began Ashley, but Jack silenced him with a gesture.

"Is this a pertinent question regarding the inquiry?"

"No, sir."

"Well, then. Let's just keep ourselves to ourselves for a bit and catch up on paper-work. Where's Otto?"

"Still trying to ID the man in those pho-tographs we found in Humpty's desk, I think."

"Better get him back."

Ashley and Gretel looked at each other and sat down quietly to do his bidding, as Mary slipped out the door.

Jack flicked through the message slips stuck to his telephone. There was a request from Bo-peep, who had once again lost her sheep, and another message from the Allegro Owners' Club asking whether he had checked the torque settings on the wheel bearings. There were several from his mother, the last one of which was marked "urgent."

Blast! he said to himself. He had forgotten to do anything about the bean refund. He picked up the phone and rang the Paint Box and was informed by a very helpful assistant that Mr. Foozle had departed unexpectedly and at very short notice to London, where he was to attend a Stubbs auction; he wouldn't be back until Friday. She knew nothing about the beans and had no idea why Foozle would be going to a Stubbs auction, at short notice or otherwise. Jack put the receiver down and stared at his computer terminal blankly. Something about the whole Humpty affair felt wrong, but he couldn't quite put his finger on it. Sadly, "hunches" and "feelings" didn't really sit well with Briggs — unless you were Guild, in which case you could base a thousand-man-hour investigation on one.

"1000 010011 1010010 10010," said Ashley in hushed tones on Gretel's phone in the next room. "10010 11010 00100111 1011."

"Are you talking to your mother on the office phone?" bellowed Jack.

"Sorry," said a sheepish voice, and all was quiet. Jack stared at his "four-and-twenty blackbirds" screensaver in a desultory manner until he left to go to the Jellyman security briefing.

While Jack was attending the briefing along with all the other officers of inspector rank and above, Mary was sitting in the Platters Coffeehouse, feeling a bit nervous — and annoyed. From the way things looked, her chances of working with Chymes had been seriously scuppered, and she might have risked her reputation for being trustworthy for nothing if Chymes decided to drop her. If it got out that she had acted behind the back of her senior officer, she'd probably have to transfer to the sheep-theft unit in Lerwick or something. Chymes must have been wrong about the Humpty case, but it didn't matter. She had fulfilled her part of the bargain — she hoped he would fulfill his. She took a sip of coffee and flicked through her notes. She had even photocopied Mrs. Dumpty's confession.

"Mary?" said Flotsam, who was approaching with a coffee of his own. "You don't mind me calling you Mary? You can call me Eddie if you want."

She smiled and invited him to join her.

"How's it going?" asked Flotsam.

"Haven't you heard? The ex-wife killed him. Motive, opportunity and, best of all, a note."

Flotsam didn't seem overly concerned. "Knowing the Guv'nor, tricky — but not insurmountable. He's resurrected more dropped investigations than I've had hot dinners. All that 'cold case' stuff is really popular these days. Just the sort of thing for the *Amazing Crime* Summer Special — now, what have you got for us?"

"This is a copy of the confession note, and these are copies of her handwriting. I've made a few notes and will talk you through it, if you want."

"Well done," he enthused. "The Guv'nor will be pleased — you're definitely backing the right horse here."

So for the next half hour she talked about the investigation and all the pertinent points that she felt had been raised. All the while Flotsam nodded and took voluminous notes and mentioned every now and then how the Guv'nor would like *that* or the Guv'nor would do something with *this,* and when she had told him everything she knew, he thanked her, told her they would be in touch and left, leaving his coffee undrunk.

She waited a few minutes to gather her thoughts, then walked back to the NCD offices just as Jack was returning from the Jellyman briefing.

"Ah, Mary. I've told Briggs it's a murder/suicide, and I'll be seeing him tomorrow at ten to wrap up the Humpty case. I'll need everyone together tomorrow morning for a heads-up on this Sacred Gonga protection-duty operation, so better make it sometime after that. Yes?"

"Very well, sir."

"Good. I'm going home."

And he left her alone to her thoughts in the tiny offices. Annoyingly for her, they weren't good thoughts. She was about to start a career with Chymes, something she had always wanted — but it somehow just didn't seem *right.* The price tag had been high — and might become even higher.

22. Titans and Beanstalks

BUTLER DID DO IT SHOCK

In a shocking result that has put the world of professional detecting into a flat spin, the butler of the deceased Lord Pilchard was discovered to have actually committed the murder. "You could have knocked me down with a feather," said the Guild-ranked Inspector Dogleash. "I've been investigating for thirty years, and I've never heard of such a thing." The overfamiliar premise of "the butler did it" has ensured that any butler on the scene could be instantly eliminated from inquiries. No longer. Miss Maple, who deduced the butler's guilt, was unrepentant. "Goodness me, what a fuss I seem to have caused!" she commented, before returning to her knitting.
— From *Amazing Crime* editorial, August 22, 1984

As Jack stepped into the house, he noticed that even though it was nearly the children's bedtime, things were unusually quiet.

"Hello . . . ?"

Amazingly, the telly was off. The children usually watched it in shifts, and since it was the only one, fights were not uncommon.

Madeleine was in the kitchen. He kissed her and slumped in his big chair at the head of the table.

"The Dumpty case just folded."

"Solved?"

"Through no skill on my behalf. His ex-wife killed him. She just topped herself over at the Yummy-Time factory. I'd avoid chocolate digestives for a while if I were you."

Jack unclipped his tie and removed one of Stevie's toys from the small of his back.

"What does that mean for the NCD?"

Jack shrugged. "Disbanded, I should imagine. I'll be entitled to a full pension in four years. I'll only be forty-eight. Perhaps it's time to think about a new career."

"What would you do?"

"Lots of things."

"Name one."

Jack thought about this for a while but couldn't really come up with anything. Police work was his life. There was *nothing* he'd rather do. This was too depressing.

He decided to change the subject.

"How are things with you?"

"Good. Prometheus said he'd never seen a photographer at work, so he came and helped me do a portrait of Lady Elena Bumpkin-Tumpkinson. He was telling us all about his life before his banishment to the Caucasus. The kids love him; why he can't get British citizenship, I have no idea. The Home Office must be bonkers."

"Not bonkers — just scared. It's not a good idea to get on the wrong side of Zeus, what with all those thunderbolt things he likes to chuck around. Where is Prometheus at the moment?"

"Have a look for yourself."

She pointed to the connecting door to the living room. Jack opened it a crack and looked in. Prometheus was standing in front of the TV, supplanting and outranking it for the evening. He was miming all the actions as he told the children a story, and Megan, Jerome and Stevie were sitting in an attentive semicircle in front of him. Ben sat on a chair close by and pretended to read a copy of *Scientific American* but was actually as enthralled as they were. No one moved or uttered a sound.

"— when Zeus, Poseidon and Hades had

deposed Cronus, their father, they drew lots out of Poseidon's helmet, the helmet of darkness, you remember, that had been given to him by Cyclops. Anyway, they drew lots to decide who would gain the lordship of the sky, the sea and the dark underworld."

"What about the earth?" asked Jerome.

"That, young man, they decreed they would leave common to all. Hades won the underworld, Poseidon the sea and Zeus the sky. Poseidon set about building his underwater palace in the sea off Euboea, constructing magnificent stables to keep his chariot horses in, horses that were brilliant white and had brazen hooves and golden manes. When they pulled Poseidon in his golden chariot, storms would cease and sea monsters appear and play about them like young dolphins. . . ."

Jack shut the door silently.

"Did you speak to your mother?" asked Madeleine. "She's called about eight times."

"I'll ring her later," said Jack. "She's probably mislaid one of her cats or —"

Jack was interrupted by a loud groan of disappointment as Prometheus called a halt to his story. There was a pause, and then the kids trotted in to have a glass of warm milk before bed.

"Is Prometheus going to stay for good, Jack?" asked Jerome, the milk giving him a temporary white mustache.

"He can leave when he wants. He's our lodger."

"You mean a prostitute like Kitty Fisher?"

"No, not like that at all," said Jack quickly.

After milk, Jack and Madeleine herded them upstairs. They put them all to bed and kissed them one by one. Megan had to be kissed twice, "just in case" and they switched out the lights.

They crept back downstairs, and Jack wandered through to the kitchen, where he found Ben, who was dressed up for a night on the town.

"Where are you off to?"

"Clubbing," replied Ben as he carefully combed his hair in front of the mirror.

"Those poor seals. The leisure center really does cater for just about any minority sporting interests these days, doesn't it?"

Ben gave Jack a withering look. "The comedy never ends," he said sarcastically. "You can be such a dweeb, y'know, Dad."

"Is it the harpist?" asked Jack. "I thought you'd lost her to the orchestra's tuba."

"Not lost, but temporarily *mislaid*," said Ben after a moment's reflection. A car horn sounded, and he ran out.

At that moment the back door opened and Ripvan blew in with a blast of cold air like some sort of furry tumbleweed. Following him was Pandora, who was well bundled up in a large down jacket. She had been at a talk given by a particle-physics professor from CERN, and the questions had gone on a lot longer than she had anticipated.

"Hi, Madeleine. Hi, Dad. Is he still here?" she asked quietly as she peeled off layer upon layer of outer clothing.

"Who?" replied Jack.

"Who? Come off it, Dad. *Prometheus,* of course."

"He's about somewhere. Why?"

She looked at him demurely. "Oh, nothing. See you later."

She ran off upstairs after throwing her down jacket into the cloakroom. As she rounded the newel post, she and Prometheus met face-to-face.

"Good evening," he said with a disarming smile.

"Hello," she said uneasily, "I'm —"

"Pandora. Yes, I know."

It seemed as though he had to force the name out.

"I once knew someone of that name," he

295

continued sadly, "a long, long time ago."

Pandora stared at him, mumbled something incomprehensible that one might have expected to hear from Stevie and disappeared upstairs.

Jack and Madeleine had been watching. Madeleine giggled, but Jack was more serious.

"Did you see that?" he asked.

"She's not a child any longer. If she lived elsewhere, you wouldn't treat her like an eight-year-old."

"I do *not* treat her like an eight-year-old."

"Sure you don't."

The phone rang, and Jack answered it. It was his mother.

"Jack?"

She had her angry voice on. Apology time. "Mother, I'm really sorry about the Stubbs —"

"I know that," she said, interrupting him. "That was yesterday's crisis."

"And today's?"

"It's the beans I threw out the window."

"What about them?"

"They've started to grow!"

She had sounded distressed about the rapid growth of the beanstalk, and as Jack rang the doorbell twenty minutes later, he was expecting to find her in a state of acute anxiety. Strangely, she was precisely the opposite.

"Hello, darling!" she warbled unsteadily. "Come on in!"

She ushered him in, but by the time he had taken off his overcoat and hat, she had vanished.

"Mother?" he called, walking past the gently ticking grandfather clock to the living room, which was full of his mother's ancient friends, most of whom he knew and all of whom had asked him surreptitiously to get them off speeding fines.

"New hip, Mrs. Dunwoody?" said Jack politely as he followed his mother towards the French windows, where he was waylaid by Mrs. Snodgrass. "Is that so?" replied Jack sympathetically. "You should eat more roughage." He hadn't got much further when Major Piggott-Smythe stopped him with the end of his pipe pressed on Jack's lapel.

"Don't think much of these alien-visitor johnnies," he said, his red nose almost a hazard to shipping. "Who invited them here anyway?"

"We did," replied Jack, "by transmitting all those seventies sitcoms. I think they wanted to find out why we never did a third series of *Fawlty Towers*. Excuse me."

He found his mother standing on the lawn staring at the beanstalk. It was a cold, clear night, and the moon had come up, which somehow made the plant seem all the more remarkable. Just next to the potting shed, five separate dark green stalks had grown from the earth and fused into what appeared to be a large and complex plait that reached almost twelve feet into the air. Already leaves had started to unfurl on smaller stalks that radiated from the main trunk, and small pods had appeared with tiny vestigial beans inside.

"Isn't it just the most beautiful thing ever?" asked his mother, her breath visible in the crisp air.

Jack took an eager step forward and then stopped himself. For a fleeting moment he'd felt a strange impulse to *climb* it. He shook himself free of the urge and said, "Stupendous! All this growth in one day?"

She nodded.

"And the party?"

"You know, I was fearful at first about the beanstalk. I thought of the harm it could do to the foundations, the value it might take off the house, that kind of thing. But then all of a sudden I thought,

What the hell! and woke up to how extraordinary it was. And do you know, I'm really quite fond of it. I'm having a botanist here tomorrow to have a look." She glanced around at her friends. "Someone brought over some hooch. I'm afraid to say we're all a little tipsy."

Jack sighed. "Does this mean you want to keep it?"

"Why not? Is it doing any harm?"

Jack had to admit that it wasn't — yet. They both gazed at it for a moment. It quivered every now and then as growing stresses were released; they could almost see it grow larger in front of their eyes. His mother shivered in the cold air, and Jack draped his jacket over her shoulders.

"Do you think it will flower?" she asked.

"I haven't the slightest idea. Are you *sure* you want to keep it?"

Mrs. Spratt patted her son's hand reassuringly. "Let's leave it a couple of days. We can make a decision then."

They went indoors, where his mum's friends harangued him about the positioning of speed cameras until he was finally able to tear himself away.

When he got home, everything was peaceful. The young children were all asleep, Madeleine was in her darkroom, and Pandora was reading in the living room. Apart from the quiet sound of Prometheus playing a sad lament on his lute in the spare room, all was calm in the Spratt household. Jack went into his study, switched on his desk lamp and stared at his iQuang computer. It took him another hour to finish his report. The next morning at ten, he would present it to Briggs and officially close the case.

Or so he thought.

23. Mary's Doubts

DOG WALKERS FACE BODY-FINDING BAN

Citizens who find a corpse while walking their dog may be fined if proposed legislation is made law, it was disclosed yesterday. The new measures, part of the Criminal Narrative Improvement Bill, have been drafted to avoid investigations looking clichéd once they reach the docudrama stage. Other offenses covered by the act will be motorists declaiming in a huffy tone, "Why don't you catch burglars/real criminals for a change?" when caught speeding, if there is a documentary crew in attendance. Civil libertarians, motorist groups and dog walkers are said to be "outraged."

— From *Amazing Crime Stories* editorial, December 9, 1997

Mary couldn't sleep. She sat in the bedroom of her dilapidated flying boathouse and watched the rippled patterns the light made on the ceiling. Chymes seemed confident that the Humpty case hadn't ended, and that bothered her. It shouldn't have been any of her business, and that bothered her, too. At six-thirty she got up, showered and drove into Reading while it was still dark, the languid movements of late revelers and the bustle of early tradesmen the only activity in the sleeping town.

She had a coffee with the end of the night shift and at 8:00 a.m. went over to the Forensic Department to see if Skinner was by chance an early riser. He wasn't, but she wanted to speak to him, so she sat outside his office until he arrived, coffee and papers in hand. He still had his bicycle clips on.

"I'm DS Mary," she said. "I'm working with DI Spratt."

She had expected a smirk when she said it but didn't get one. Skinner was one of the friendlies.

"A fine man is Jack. Come on inside."

He unlocked the door and let them both in. The strip lights flickered on, making Mary blink after the dinginess of the corridor.

"So," said Skinner, guessing her intention almost immediately, "more questions over the Humpty murder? Or is it about Mrs. Dumpty?"

"Both."

He pulled off his bicycle clips. "Shoot."

"Five shots had been fired from Mrs. Dumpty's .32," she began, "yet we can only account for one. What happened to the other four?"

But Skinner didn't seem particularly puzzled.

"The fact they were missing from the clip means nothing, Mary. She might never even had loaded them."

"So it's not suspicious?"

"I'm afraid not."

"What about not finding the spent cartridge in Winkie's garden?"

"Shells are often picked up by astute criminals, Mary. It's fairly common knowledge that we can match a cartridge to a gun as easily as we can match a slug — often easier. Perps often use revolvers for just that reason."

"What about a .32 caliber being able to destroy Humpty?"

He scratched his head. "I tend to agree with Mrs. Singh — I would have thought a larger caliber. He was very badly damaged. But we're both guessing. Data on bullets going through large eggs is a little bit in short supply, as you might imagine."

"But if we had the spent slug?"

"Oh, yes." Skinner smiled. "If we had *that,* we could know for sure."

Mary thanked him and moved to go, but Skinner laid a hand on her wrist.

"Be careful, Mary."

"How do you mean?"

"Just that things are sometimes not always what they seem."

"I'm sorry?"

"You're new to Reading and new to Jack. Don't underestimate him. He's a better man than most people give him credit for."

"I still don't understand."

Skinner stared at her through his thick pebble spectacles.

"Some people at Reading are too powerful for the good of the service," he said slowly, pointing at a buff envelope on his desk, right next to the evidence bag with the two weathered shotgun cartridges that needed to be returned, "and people talk out of turn at their peril. You can take the cartridges with you, but I wouldn't want you to make a mistake and take that buff envelope as well. Do you understand?"

She frowned but nodded her agreement, wished him good day and dutifully took both the evidence bag and the envelope.

She had a look when she was in her car. The envelope contained crime-scene photographs of the Andersen's Wood murder, and pretty gruesome they were, too. She went through them once, then again. If there was something going on, she was definitely missing it. She replaced the pictures inside the envelope, stuffed it under the seat of her car and headed off towards Spatchcock's Gymnasium.

Mr. Spatchcock was giving a morning keep-fit lesson to a group of women who were all a bit puffed and had begun to go red. She could almost hear the silent pleas for him to stop or at least slow down. She was glad to be able to help. She tapped on the glass and hoped Spatchcock recognized her. It didn't do to start flashing police badges around people's place of work — unless you needed to make a point, of course.

But he did recognize her. He told his class to take a much-welcome break and trotted up to where Mary was waiting for him.

"It's DS Mary, isn't it?"

"It is, Mr. Spatchcock. I'd just like to ask you a few more questions."

"Of course. I was very sorry to hear about Mrs. Dumpty. She had been a client for about two years and, like many of my personal charges, a driven woman with appetites the same as anyone else."

"You were intimate?"

"If that is how you like to phrase it, yes. You may not approve of what I do, but no one is hurt by it, and I fulfill an important role. Laura was a lot better than most; I think we even had an affection of sorts for each other. Anyway, I have a friend in the pathology lab who told me they thought Humpty had been murdered, so naturally I thought Laura would be in the frame. Of course, I knew she hadn't killed him — and that's why I called you straightaway."

"I'm sorry?"

"Which part?"

"The 'hadn't killed him' part."

"Well, Sergeant," he said in a quieter voice, "*I was with her the night of the Spongg Charity Benefit.* I have no proof, of course, but that's why I contacted you."

"Wait," said Mary, "I haven't spoken to you at all since we met at the Cheery Egg on Tuesday morning."

"I know that. You weren't there, so I spoke to the other officer."

"DI Spratt?"

"No, the one who is always on TV with that annoying chirpy cockney sidekick."

"Friedland Chymes?"

"That's the one. I told him all about it. Did he not tell you?"

"No," replied Mary, suddenly feeling confused. She thanked him and walked outside to her car. If Flotsam had known about Spatchcock when she spoke to him at the coffeehouse the previous evening, why didn't he tell her? Wasn't she part of their team? Chymes, she knew, conducted his investigations in a strange way — perhaps this was part of some bigger plan — and Flotsam followed orders, just like her. But what if there was another reason for it? What if Chymes was waiting until Jack had closed the investigation before he reopened it? That would fit into his dramatic way of doing things. She pulled out her mobile and started to dial Jack, then snapped it shut again. She needed more information. She started the car and drove rapidly across to Grimm's Road.

She parked in the alleyway and, after consulting the diagram Skinner had sketched for her, attempted to find out where the spent slug had returned to earth. It seemed simple enough. Lining up Humpty's entrance and exit wounds gave Mary a zone of probability the shape of a wedge with a twenty-degree spread up to a hundred feet from where Humpty was sitting when he was killed. She worked from the sharp edge of the wedge back, scouring the earth, rubbish and junk in the back alleyway that the simple plan had indicated. She searched for forty minutes in an increasing state of agitation until a sudden thought had her standing on an upturned dustbin to check in the guttering — and there it was, looking small, gray and innocuous. It had been only slightly deformed — an almost perfect specimen for Skinner to work with. Better than that, it was a .44 caliber. Even if Spatchcock *had* lied — and there didn't seem any reason for him to do so — then Mrs. Dumpty had killed her ex-husband with another gun. Not out of the question, but out of the ordinary. The two facts together would be enough to keep the investigation open.

"Well, well. DS Mary."

She turned around quickly. Standing in the alleyway was Friedland Chymes.

"Sir," she said, trying to hide her feelings of nervousness, and jumping down, "what are you doing here?"

"The same thing as you, I suspect," he replied. "Trying to get to the bottom of Humpty's death. What have you discovered?"

She stared at him, and he stared back. She had stumbled, but she had not yet fallen. She prayed she wouldn't blow it.

"I spoke to Mr. Spatchcock this morning."

Chymes wasn't fazed for even a second. He smiled again.

"You figured there was something hokey about the whole thing on your own, Mary? I'm very impressed. Jack's about to roll over and wee on himself in Briggs's office, but you're out here hunting down the truth. I can't begin to tell you how valuable I think you would be to my team."

Two hours earlier it would have been the single greatest compliment she'd ever received from anyone who wasn't her mother. But he hadn't answered her question. And Mary always liked to have an answer.

"When did you know that Humpty had been shot, sir?"

"Long before you," he said. "Mrs. Singh is highly diligent — too much so, to my taste. She wanted to be a hundred percent sure of what she had before she called you. Myself, I'll go with a seventy percent probability any day."

"You knew," said Mary softly. "You knew the evening before about the shooting *and* about Spatchcock. You withheld *crucial* evidence from our investigation."

"No I didn't. And it would be very wrong and detrimental to your career if

309

you were to mention it again. Tell me what you know, Mary."

She paused for a moment, bit her lip and looked down — the full gamut of someone unable to come to a decision, and Friedland pounced.

"I think you should tell me," he said a little more forcefully. "You should know that I generally get what I want and that people who help me are rewarded. Conversely and contrariwise, people who withhold information from me rarely last the course. I'll ask you once more, and I expect an answer: What have you found?"

She felt herself grow hot as he stared her down.

"Do you really have space for me on the team?"

"We always need new blood," came Flotsam's voice from behind her. "I think it's in your best interest to tell the Guv'nor what he needs to know. He'll find out anyway, and then you will have thrown away the last chance of what might have been a very worthwhile friendship."

"I found the slug," she stammered at last. "It's a .44. With Spatchcock's evidence it's enough to keep the case open."

Chymes and Flotsam exchanged looks.

"We concur. Bravo, Mary. We have underestimated you. A good DS is worth her weight in gold, whoever she works for. Now, the question you have to ask yourself is what *exactly* are you going to do next? Think carefully. Your career depends upon it."

She swallowed hard and held up her head. "Well, I kind of thought I'd call . . . um, SOCO and . . . I don't know — DI Spratt?"

There was silence for a moment.

"That's a very disappointing choice, Mary. You're new to all this, so I'm going to cut you some slack. These sorts of potentially high-profile crimes are good for the justice system. For the most part, the public can't be bothered to understand what we do, so there is nothing like a couple of easy-to-understand, solved celebrity murders to keep them in the picture and supportive of our efforts — especially during the summer season. Police approval always leaps up after the successful conclusion of one of my cases."

"Are you saying I shouldn't call my DI?"

"Look at it this way," said Chymes as he glanced at his watch. "It's ten to ten. Jack will be speaking to Briggs on the hour. If you had found that slug a half hour later, we wouldn't even need to have this conversation. I think it would be better for all concerned that Jack *doesn't* hear about the slug or Spatchcock's statement until he has officially *closed* the case. There is nothing quite like one detective closing a case only for another to awaken it with a dramatic flourish, don't you agree?"

"Is it really necessary to make Spratt look such an idiot?"

"Spratt *is* an idiot, Mary — haven't you figured that out yet? Listen, the public needs its heroes. And I want you on my team. We've got the best facilities and the best cases — the cream of not just the Oxford & Berkshire force but most of the others, too. We often do international consultancies, and His Eminence the Jellyman frequently asks for advice. Do you to want to meet the Jellyman, Mary?"

He put out his hand.

"Here is my hand. Shake it and stand by my side. I won't offer it again."

Mary Mary working for Friedland Chymes. She had dreamed of this since she was nine. She stared at Chymes with his winning smile and perfect teeth. It was the easiest decision she ever made.

24. *Briggs v. Spratt*

Briggs beckoned Jack into his office and had him wait while he spoke on the phone to the workman redecorating his house. After an inordinately long ten minutes discussing the choice of wallpaper for the front room, he hung up and stared at Jack.

"You've got a confession note?" he asked.

Jack slid it across the table. It was in a clear plastic cover, and Briggs put on his glasses.

"Verified by the handwriting people?"

"Yes, sir. It's definitely Mrs. Dumpty's."

"Well," said Briggs removing his spectacles, "I think that's fairly straightforward, don't you?"

"But for the smaller-than-expected caliber pistol and the four missing cartridges, and —"

"And *what?*"

"I just don't think she killed him. We interviewed her at ten-thirty the morning of her ex-husband's death. Less than ten hours. She loved him, sir, even after the split — most people dump their ex's stuff as soon as the papers come through, but everything that was his was still in her house. I'm not convinced that a crime of passion would leave her so *calm.*"

Briggs held up the suicide note. "And this? What do you make of this? I quote: '. . . I prayed for God to forgive me as I pulled the trigger.' She had the motive, opportunity — but, best of all, she wrote a confession. This one's over, Jack."

"She didn't kill him, sir."

"Listen," said Briggs, "I know the NCD means a lot to you, but we can't justify the expense. We've got to make some hard choices, and I'm sure the budgetary meeting can make a generous settlement for early retirement. You've done good work, Jack, but it's a question of priorities."

"I thought it was just the department getting canned?" said Jack, rising to his feet.

"You *are* the department," replied Briggs, also rising. "Where else were you going to work? CID? Don't make me insult you by offering you traffic or something. The Humpty case is closed."

"The budgetary meeting is on Thursday, yes?"

"Yes," said Briggs sharply, wondering what he was up to, "why?"

"Just let me carry on until then to prove she didn't do it and if I can't, I'll call it a day and the coroner can have a murder/suicide."

"No."

"Twenty-four hours, then."

"Sorry."

"Until tomorrow morning?"

"No!"

"Twenty years," said Jack, "twenty years I've run the NCD, and while I admit I have made a few slip-ups and killed a giant or two —"

"Four. It was four, Jack."

"He was barely six foot eight, sir. Listen, I've never asked you for anything before now. Geoffrey, *please.*"

It was the first time he had ever used Briggs's first name. He hoped to God he had remembered it correctly. The Superintendent paused for a moment and stared at him, then finally shook his head.

"I can't do it, Jack. You've got nothing. No, I take that back. You've got *less* than nothing. If you could show me one positive piece of evidence, I'd be happy to keep it open, but as it stands, I think all you've got is a hunch and a strong suit of delusive hope. And that's not enough to keep an inquiry open."

"It'd be enough for Friedland," said Jack rather feebly.

"You," said Briggs slowly, "are not Friedland. Not even close."

"Sir . . . !" pleaded Jack, numbed by his intransigence.

"Interview's over, Jack. And I'm sorry."

"Briggs!"

"You'd better leave, Jack. I can sense you're going to say or do something that you might regret."

Jack sighed and headed for the door.

The intercom beeped.

"Yes?"

It was Sergeant Mary, explained Briggs's secretary. Jack grimaced. She might at least have had the good grace to wait until he was out of Briggs's office before she requested a transfer.

"Send her in."

Mary stepped in rather self-consciously, looked at Jack and then walked past him to face Briggs at his desk.

"I was just telling your senior officer, Mary, that by this time next week, the NCD will be disbanded. You are here to ask for an immediate transfer, I take it?"

Mary bit her lip. She could still back out. Chymes or Jack? Two days ago — no, wait, two *hours* ago it would have been a no-brainer. Now it was different. The NCD? Well, somehow it felt sort of right. That she *belonged*.

"I don't think so, sir."

Briggs raised an eyebrow, and Jack stopped in midstride.

"I found the slug that killed Humpty. It had fallen to earth in a length of guttering two doors down. SOCO are on their way now. The slug is only mildly deformed, but we can tell the caliber. It's a .44. If Mrs. Dumpty *did* kill him, then she used another gun from the one we found in her desk."

She waited a moment for the information to sink in.

"I spoke to Mr. Spatchcock, who is her personal trainer, this morning. He was with her when Humpty was killed. All night. They were lovers."

Briggs stared up at her coldly. "And this?" he asked, indicating the suicide note. "What are you saying? Someone *forced* her to write that note?"

"I'll confess it's a puzzler," said Jack, who had returned to Briggs's desk, "but we're going to find out."

"This Thomas Spatchcock fellow is wholly unreliable," muttered Briggs, clutching at straws. "I don't think we can believe a word he says."

"I never said his name was Thomas," said Mary in a quiet voice.

There was silence. Briggs had dropped himself in it, and he knew it. He rubbed a hand wearily over his face, pushing his glasses onto his forehead.

"Okay," he said as he took off his tacles and leaned back in his chair, "you got me. This isn't my doing. Chymes wields considerable weight with the Chief Constable, and as you know, he wants the Humpty gig. Look, well . . . I'm hanging out on a limb here, but you've got until the end of play Saturday to make some headway. If it's not sorted by the time the Jellyman has come and gone, I'm putting someone else on the case. And if you aren't out of my office in ten seconds, I'll change my mind — and screw the consequences."

As soon as they were in the corridor, Jack turned to Mary.

"In the nick of time. I thought you hated it here?"

"I thought so, too, sir. But you know when you said the NCD grows on you?"

"Yes?"

"Well, it's grown on me. And listen, sir, I have to apologize for something."

"Don't bother. You've more than made up for it, whatever it was."

"No, I *really* want to tell you."

"And I *really* don't want to hear it. If you were at the Guild bar the night before last or speaking to Flotsam at Platters Coffeehouse, I really don't want to kno⌐

— you probably have your reasons. ...ey do the old 'Barnes is retiring, we ...d a replacement' routine on you?"

"You *knew?* Why didn't you say something?"

Jack shrugged. "I don't know. It was your decision. I kind of felt you'd do the right thing, though."

Mary couldn't think of anything to say. He had trusted *her* to do the right thing, and she had almost stabbed *him* in the back.

"I've . . . I've underestimated you, sir — badly."

"Well, I shouldn't worry about it. I've been underestimated before."

She felt anger rise inside her. Anger at herself for being such a fool, and anger at Chymes for taking advantage of her.

"Sir," she said, "Chymes wants the Humpty investigation for the *Amazing Crime* Summer Special — he knew the night before we did about Humpty's murder and has known about Spatchcock from about the same time. We can lodge a complaint about serious professional misconduct!"

"Mary," said Jack quietly, "calm down. Think you're the first person this has happened to? I told you before: He's a com-

plete shit. Don't waste your t
Gretel's career is almost finished, and
she did was call him an arsehole. Have you
any idea what a formal complaint would
do to you? We concentrate on Humpty.
Nothing else matters. Okay?"

She took a deep breath.

"Yes, sir. But I think I've made a lifelong
enemy of Chymes."

"You and me both. Did I ever tell you
why?"

"No."

"His fiancée left him when he pinched the
credit for the Gingerbreadman capture."

"So?"

"She left him for *me*. She was my first
wife."

"The one who passed away?"

"Right. Ben and Pandora's mother."

"Chymes got the Guild, and you got the
girl."

Jack smiled. "In one. I got the better part
of the bargain, and he knew it."

Mary looked up at Jack, but this time in
a different light.

"Why have you stayed at the NCD so
long, sir?"

He shrugged. "It needs me. And I need
it. Can't explain. Just the way it is. Make
any sense?"

"Kind of. Oh, I almost forgot." She pulled the buff envelope from out of her jacket. "I was asked to give you these by someone who doesn't want to be identified."

"Skinner?"

"Yes."

"Usually him. Let's have a look."

He opened the envelope and flicked through the pictures, rubbed his forehead and put them back.

"Don't show these to anyone, do you understand?"

"Yes, sir. What is it?"

"Something bigger than any of us. Just forget about them."

"Sir!" said Baker as they approached the NCD offices. "Just got a message from Ops. It's Willie Winkie."

"Asleep again?"

"Permanently. Over in Palmer Park. Mrs. Singh is already in attendance. Is the Humpty investigation finished?"

"Far from it!" yelled Jack over his shoulder as they hurriedly retraced their steps down the corridor. "It's back on with a vengeance. As you were. I want some answers by the time I get back. *TIBBIT!*"

25. Good Night, Wee Willie Winkie

PRINCE SOUGHT AFTER SLAYING

Police were called to Elsinore Castle yesterday to investigate the unnatural death of one of the King's closest advisers. Married, a father of two, Mr. Polonius was discovered stabbed and his body hidden under the stairs to the lobby, although fibers recovered from his wound match a wall hanging in the Queen's bedroom. DI Dogberry, fresh from his successful solving of the Desdemona murder, told us, "We are eager to integrate a Prince who was absurd in the area shortly after." Sources close to the King tell us that Prince Hamlet has been acting erratically ever since the unexpected yet entirely natural and unsuspicious death of his father eight weeks before.
— Extract from the *Elsinore Tatler*, June 16, 1408

It was raining hard when Jack, Mary and Tibbit pulled up at the perimeter of Palmer

323

Park, a sports field and public amenity site to the east of town. A uniformed officer in a raincoat pointed them towards a white scene-of-crime tent set up behind the grandstand. The rain had discouraged all onlookers, and the only member of the public visible was a lone runner who plodded around the track, seemingly oblivious to the downpour.

"Tibbit, start on some house-to-house, will you? I want to know if anybody saw anything."

Tibbit took out his notepad and walked over to the row of houses that faced the field.

"How far are we from Grimm's Road?" asked Mary as they trudged across the wet grass.

"A couple of hundred yards. The other side of that road."

The immediate area around the crime scene had been taped off. Shenstone was the Scene of Crime Officer, and he had conveniently rigged a narrow "exit and entrance" walkway delineated by white tape so they could all come and go without destroying any potential footprints. Mary started to talk to the officer first on the scene, who was relieved that it was an NCD case; it meant a lot less paperwork.

"Hello, Shenstone," said Jack. "What have you got?"

Shenstone stood up from where he had been examining the ground.

"Good morning, sir. I thought this one might be under your jurisdiction." He pointed at the ground. "Some healthy footprints, but nothing exciting — a size-ten Barbour wellie by the look of it. But what seems odd is that the person in the wellies has tried to obliterate some of the evidence. You can see where they've made an effort to scour the ground." He pointed again. "Just there . . . and again, over there."

"So *two* people, one of whom might have had distinctive shoes?"

"Something like that."

Jack thanked him and stepped into the white tent. Winkie's body was lying facedown in the mud. His nightgown and nightcap were soaking wet and clung to his pale white flesh. The grass and mud around him were darkly stained with blood, and a candlestick was on the ground next to him. His hands had already been bagged, and Mrs. Singh and her assistants were just about to turn him over.

Jack crouched down next to the pathologist, glad for the protection the tent could offer from the rain.

"Hello, Jack," said Mrs. Singh cheerfully. "You certainly know how to show a girl a good time. Know him?" She leaned back so he could get a good look at the body.

"His name's William Winkie. Lived next door to Humpty over at Grimm's Road. How did he die?"

"We'll know soon enough."

She gave a few instructions to her assistants, and they gently rolled the body over. It was not a pretty sight. His eyes were still wide open, an expression of stark terror etched on his features. The cause of death was obvious. Jack looked away, but Mrs. Singh leaned closer. To her this wasn't just a human body but a riddle in need of a solution.

"One slash, very powerful and very deep, from right collarbone to halfway down the midthorax. They even managed to split his sternum."

"Ax?"

"I think not. A broadsword or samurai weapon would be more likely. A cut this deep needs to have a lot of momentum behind it. He died from shock and blood loss, probably between three and six a.m. The assailant came from the front and was violently aggressive in the attack, but *controlled*. One slash and no more. Was Mr.

Winkie part of the Humpty investigation?"

"Not really, but it was from his backyard that Humpty's fatal shot was fired."

Mrs. Singh raised her eyebrows. "That would make sense of what he's holding. Take a look."

Jack looked closely at the dead man's fist. Held tightly between his finger and thumb were the corners of what looked like pieces of paper.

"Several fifty-pound notes," she said helpfully.

"Idiot," muttered Jack.

"He can't hear you," replied Mrs. Singh, busying herself with her task as the photographer took some pictures.

"What makes pathologists so facetious, Mrs. Singh?"

She smiled. "Pathologists are just happy people, Jack."

"Oh, yes? And why's that?"

"No possibility of malpractice suits for one thing." She looked closer at Winkie's mouth and murmured, "What have we here?"

She pushed his mouth open, had a look with a penlight and closed it.

"I was hoping I wouldn't see that again."

Mary stepped into the tent, glanced at the corpse, muttered "Oh my God," held her hand over her mouth and stepped out.

"See what again?"

"They split his tongue."

"Porgia," muttered Jack.

"A *classic* Porgia MO," agreed Mrs. Singh. "I should call the dogs' home if I were you."

"Mary?"

"Yes?" came Mary's voice from outside the tent.

"Call the Reading Dog Shelter and tell them to set aside any anonymous offerings of scraps they might receive."

Mary didn't quite understand what was going on but flipped open her mobile and called Ops to get the number.

"Porgia?" repeated Jack with incredulity. "Is there anything else?"

"I'll know more when I get him back to the lab," said Mrs. Singh, "but while you're here, I'm having a few problems with the dynamics of Humpty's shell breakup."

"How do you mean?"

"You know me — I'm never happy until I have all the answers. Skinner and I have been running a few tests using ostrich eggs. He set them up on the range and fired a .22 bullet through them and then used the data to try to build a usable model for egg disintegration. It's as much for our own interest as for anything else, but we're having trouble equating Humpty's destruction with what we're seeing on the range. It's possible that one shot and a fall might not have been enough to destroy him. I'm looking for other evidence of postfall damage, but with one hundred twenty-six pieces, it's tricky to tell. Mind you, ostrich eggs are like cannonballs, so it might not be a good test. I'll know more in a day or two."

"What about the analysis of his albumen?"

"Inconclusive — but then the Ox and Berks forensic labs are not really geared up for eggs. I've sent swabs from the inside of his shell to the SunnyDale Poultry Farm for an in-depth oological analysis. Couple of days, I imagine."

Jack thanked her and stepped out of the tent. It had stopped raining, but the sky was dark and portended more to come.

"What news, Mary?"

"His wife has been informed," she explained, still looking a little pale. "One of her relatives is going to go around and look after her."

"Who found Winkie?"

"A man walking his dog. He'd seen the body earlier but thought it was just a bundle of rags. He alerted us at ten-thirteen."

"Find out what time Winkie came off shift and have a word with his workmates. See if he was boasting of a windfall or something."

"Connected to Dumpty's murder?" asked Mary.

"Possibly. Here's a workable scenario: Mr. Winkie *did* see something the night that Humpty was killed and tried to blackmail the killer, who then arranged the payoff and a permanent good-night for Wee Willie Winkie."

"Why the bit about the tongue? Unnecessarily gruesome, isn't it?"

"A lot of Nursery Crime work is gruesome, Mary — it comes with the turf. Tongue splitting was a Porgia crime family method of dealing with anyone they suspected of speaking to the authorities. 'Telling tales,' they called it. They used to cut it up so that all the dogs in the town could have a little bit."

"That sounds familiar."

"It's classic NCD stuff. The thing is, Chymes and I jailed them all twenty years ago. But they were very powerful — perhaps they still are. Call Reading Gaol and get us an interview. I think we'll have a word with Giorgio Porgia himself. What news, Tibbit?"

"Not much, sir. Nobody seemed to see anything. There was talk of a white van, though."

"Box van?"

"They couldn't tell."

Jack and Mary left Tibbit to do more house-to-house and walked back to the Allegro in silence. Jack leaned on the car roof, deep in thought.

"Did you find anything on Solomon Grundy?"

"Clean as a whistle. Never been investigated for anything, no criminal record — not so much as a speeding fine. A trawl through the *Mole* archives shows a healthy ruthlessness in his business dealings, but nothing we didn't know already."

"Blast. Winkie worked at Winsum and Loosum's, and Solomon Grundy had a two-million-pound motive to have Humpty killed."

"It's small beer to him, sir," said Mary. "Ninth-wealthiest man in the country. He said he could lose two mil a week for ten years before it would worry him. It's true — I've checked. He's worth over a billion."

"He could have been lying. He might actually be a very vindictive man indeed. Trouble is, Briggs says I can't speak to him until this Jellyman Sacred Gonga thing has come and gone."

"Then why don't we speak to his wife? She might let something slip."

"Are you kidding? I can't think of a better way to piss off Grundy and Briggs."

"Not really," replied Mary. "Grundy told us we could ask his wife about his whereabouts the night Humpty died — and with his blessing."

Jack smiled. This idea he liked.

"Good thought. I think we'll do precisely that."

As they drove away, Mary noticed that the passenger window had let rainwater leak onto her seat.

"Yes," said Jack when she pointed it out, "it usually does that."

26. Meet the Grundys

"UGLY" SISTERS TO SUE FOR DEFAMATION

The stepsisters of Princess Ella are understood to be demanding undisclosed sums from numerous publications over defamation of character, libel and slander. A spokesman for the sisters explained, "My clients are fed up being constantly portrayed as physically repellant obnoxious harpies, and have decided to take action against the 984 publishers that have repeated the allegations without bothering to check their veracity." A spokesman for the Binkum Press, publishers of *The Children's Treasury of Fairy Tales*, told us, "Obviously we will be vigorously defending the action, but we have taken the precaution of pulping half a million copies of the offending story. Following the landmark payout to Snow White's stepmother, we'd be fools not to take this seriously, although we don't believe there is a case to answer."

— Extract from *The Gadfly*,
April 17, 1992

The Grundy residence was an exquisitely restored Jacobean mansion set above the river Thames, with scrupulously maintained oak parkland that stretched to the water's edge. South facing and away from any built-up areas, it ranked alongside Castle Spongg and Basildon House as one of the finest examples of period architecture in the Reading area. As Jack and Mary motored down the long graveled drive, they could see that Maison Grundy had been erected on the site of something much older. The church behind the house was considerably older than the mansion itself, and the barns, outbuildings and stables older still. When they arrived in the courtyard at the rear, stable lads were busily grooming some fine-looking Thoroughbreds whose dark coats shone, even in the gray overcast.

They parked the car and got out to see a woman on a large bay horse come thundering across the parkland towards them, throwing up divots of sod behind her. She slowed her mount to cross the roadway, and as she drew closer, they could see she was dressed in a long skirt that seemed faintly Victorian with a high-collared blouse buttoned up to her throat; on top of this she wore a blue velvet riding jacket.

"Hullo!" she said, dismounting expertly from the sidesaddle and handing the reins to a stable boy. "Are you here about the deathwatch beetle?"

She was barely in her mid-twenties and was extraordinarily pretty in an English rose sort of way, with large eyes, a perky smile and a porcelain complexion. She was slightly flushed and out of breath from her ride.

"No, Mrs. Grundy," said Jack, holding up his ID card. "We're police. I'm Inspector Jack Spratt, and this is Sergeant Mary Mary. We'd like to talk to you about Humpty Dumpty."

She looked shocked for a moment but quickly recovered. She smiled delightfully at them both and said, "Well, you better come inside, then," adding to a stable boy, "Callum, have Stranger made ready for this afternoon and check Duke, would you? I think he might have thrown a shoe."

As they walked towards the house, she placed her whip under her arm and removed her gloves. "We have a deathwatch beetle problem in the church," she explained. "I was hoping you were here to have a look at it. Terrible things, you know, can eat a building away from the inside like cancer, so Solly tells me."

They walked in through the front door to where four dogs of varying sizes and a footman were waiting to greet them. She patted the golden retriever and handed her whip and gloves to the footman, who gave a curt bow. She told him to bring tea into the drawing room and then led them down a hall bedecked with portraits of the Grundy family through the ages, all of whom — male or female — had the same pugnacious, bullnecked Grundy look. The dogs all followed, wagging their tails happily.

"The family resemblance is uncanny," remarked Mary.

"Not really," replied Mrs. Grundy with surprising directness. "Solomon sat for them all. The Grundy family tree in reality leads nowhere — Solly was found wrapped in a copy of the *Reading Mercury* outside Battle Hospital sixty-nine years ago. It makes his achievements all that more remarkable."

She ushered them into the large and opulent drawing room, flopped onto a sofa and put her feet up on an expensive coffee table. A terrier made itself comfortable on her lap and the other dogs jumped onto the various sofas.

"Please," she said, "take a seat. Don't be afraid to push Max off; he's a brute —

Down, Spike! Anyway, what can I do for you?"

"Just routine stuff, Mrs. Grundy," said Jack. "We need you to confirm the whereabouts of your husband on the night of the Spongg Charity Benefit."

"Is he a suspect?" she asked as she blinked her large eyes.

"We need to eliminate your husband from our inquiries, Mrs. Grundy."

"Please," she said as she removed her riding hat and a hair clasp to allow acres of luxuriant auburn hair to tumble into her lap, and the sofa, and the coffee table, and the floor, "call me Rapunzel."

Jack and Mary exchanged glances as her long red tresses lapped at their feet like the incoming tide. They had the same thought: the twenty-eight-foot human hair found at Grimm's Road.

"Very well, Rapunzel. You were with your husband that night?"

"Of course. I escorted him to the Spongg Charity Benefit as I do all social events. I stayed at his side the whole evening — as Solomon likes me to do."

"Then you were with him when Humpty made the offer to sell his stake in Spongg's?"

"I was. I think Mr. Dumpty was very

drunk; in any event, the ten million he offered was quite correctly refused by Solly. It isn't good form to talk business while drunk at a charity do."

"And you were with Solomon until the morning?"

"Yes, here at the house."

Jack thought for a moment. He wasn't going to beat around the bush, and he knew it wasn't likely he'd be able to talk to her again.

"When did you visit Humpty's offices at Grimm's Road?"

She looked stunned for a moment and then glanced around to see whether any of the servants were within earshot. They weren't, but she lowered her voice anyway.

"Solomon can *never* know!"

"I'm not here to cause trouble," said Jack. "I just want to find who murdered Humpty."

"So do I!" she cried, tears welling up in her eyes. "If I even *suspected* that Solly had him killed, I would be out of that door like a shot. No one knows Solomon as I do. He's not as bad as everyone makes out. He might buy venerable old companies and strip their assets, causing numerous layoffs and the odd corporate suicide or two, but that's business. Inside, he's a big teddy bear."

"If he does know about you and Humpty," said Jack, "it gives him a very strong motive."

"Rapunzel!" bellowed a voice from the hall. "Rapunzel, my dove!"

Jack and Mary froze. There was no mistaking the gruff voice of Solomon Grundy, even tempered by domesticity, and they both felt as if they'd been caught doing something they shouldn't.

"In here, my love," called Rapunzel, staring unhappily at Jack and Mary. "I've just let my hair down in the drawing room."

Solomon was smiling as he walked in, but the smile soon dropped from his face when he saw Jack and Mary.

"What the blazes are they doing here?"

"Eliminating you from their inquiries, honey-bunny."

Jack and Mary stood up as Grundy marched across to them. He discarded his briefcase on the floor and stopped only inches from Jack's face.

"I could have you both killed, buried, and they'd never find the bodies," he growled menacingly, "but I won't, because that's not what I do." He took a step back and rested a hand on Rapunzel's shoulder; she held it tightly.

"How dare you come into my house? You're an interfering meddling pain in the arse, Inspector."

"It's what I do, sir."

"And very well, by the look of it."

Grundy paused and thought for a moment. Then looked at Rapunzel.

"I know of my wife's infidelities, Inspector."

Rapunzel gave a small cry and put a hand to her mouth. He sat down next to her. His anger had left him, and the big man spoke now in gentler tones — almost compassionately.

"I am an old man with a young wife," he said slowly, "and I know that younger women have needs. I knew all about her visits to Grimm's Road, but I chose to do nothing. It's better that way. I am sixty-nine and am not healthy — I have perhaps five years of life left in me. I want to spend it with a beautiful wife whom I would give anything to keep — even if it means turning a blind eye and being a cuckolded husband."

"Oh, Solly!" said Rapunzel, pressing her cheek to his large hand and sobbing bitterly. "I'm so sorry!" Despite everything, she had a genuine affection for the man.

"If you want to know whether I had

Humpty killed, the answer is a categorical *no.* I am a businessman. I cannot afford the luxury of violent revenge. I would have been happy to ruin him financially, but murder? I wouldn't get my capital back, and I would inevitably end up in prison. I'm a logical man; I never invest money or time that I can't afford to lose, and I certainly can't afford to lose any years off my life. I found out long ago that you can make a fortune in this world far more efficiently by using the law to your advantage than by breaking it."

He looked away from them and rested his cheek on his wife's forehead. It was a tender moment between a bullying tyrant and an attractive woman young enough to be his granddaughter. Jack suddenly felt as though he were intruding.

"Are there any more questions, Inspector?" asked Solomon without looking up.

"No," said Jack, rising to his feet. "Thank you for your time, Mr. and Mrs. Grundy. We'll see ourselves out."

They left the couple holding each other on the drawing room sofa, accompanied by four dogs and twenty-eight feet of the most beautiful hair either of them had ever seen.

"That was unexpected," said Mary as they walked back to the Allegro.

"Shows that looks can be deceptive. I'm sure his business competitors would be surprised to know that old Grundy had a soft side to his nature. Extraordinary hair, wasn't it?"

"Yes," replied Mary thoughtfully, then adding as a practical afterthought, "but think of all that brushing!"

27. Perplexity, Complexity

FLAUTIST'S SON JAILED FOR PIG STEALING

Tom Thomm, son of Reading Philharmonic's noted solo flautist, was finally convicted of serial pig theft yesterday. "I don't know what comes over me," said Thomm when asked to account for his actions. "I just see a pig, this pink veil falls over my eyes, and next thing I know, I've grabbed it and I'm off. I don't even like pork — I'm a vegetarian." The judge heard that Thomm had been a serial pig stealer for some years, having grabbed a total of 2,341 porkers since he was twelve. In his summing-up, Mr. Justice Cutlett told him, "Despite numerous court orders to attend compulsive behavior-disorder realignment sessions, you are still unable to control your urges. I have no choice but to detain you for two years." Several pigs who attended court were said to be "overjoyed at the outcome."
— Extract from the *Reading Mercury*, July 18, 1990

They hadn't been wasting time back at the NCD offices. It was Ashley who had come up with the first good lead. He had put a name to the man in the photograph, the one in Humpty's still-untraced Ford Zephyr.

"Who?" asked Jack.

"Thomas Timothy Thomm. DI Drood down at Missing Persons found him. I did you a printout of his record — but on *acetate* so you could still look at your desk while reading it."

"Very . . . thoughtful of you, Ashley."

It seemed that Thomm was the son of the Reading Philharmonic's premier flautist. Unable to stop an unexplained compulsion to steal pigs, he was sent at age sixteen to a young offender's institute to "straighten him out." It achieved the opposite, and after being in and out of jail for a number of offenses, he was eventually sentenced to fifteen years for armed robbery. He had been released on parole two years previously.

"Looks like he's prime NCD jurisdiction," murmured Jack. "They should have sent him through to me. Where is he now?"

"That's the thing," observed Ashley. "He's not been seen *at all* for over a year. Didn't turn up for parole meetings —

there is an outstanding arrest warrant, and his parents have put him on the Missing Persons register. I'm trying to contact his parole officer and see what else I can learn."

"More questions!" said Jack in exasperation. "It's about time we had some bloody answers!"

Baker had been in town making inquiries but had drawn a blank. No one had seen Humpty for over a year, leading some wag in Humpty's old local to remark that he was surprised to find that Humpty was still alive to be murdered. Baker questioned him further, but it seemed that the man was only reflecting Humpty's slightly downmarket business reputation. "Shady" was the word the man used, although neither he nor anyone else could say who had actually fallen foul of him. Indeed, everyone Baker met commented on how much he was liked. Humpty's womanizing was well known, but Baker didn't find out much more.

"Out of sight for over a year?"

"Yes, sir," replied Baker. "Apart from his neighbors around Grimm's Road, no one's seen anything of him at all."

"In hiding?" murmured Jack, half to himself.

"It would explain the drab office at

Grimm's Road. No one would expect to see him at that end of town. But if he's in hiding, why pop up blind drunk at the Spongg Charity Benefit?"

"Prometheus said he thought Humpty was saying good-bye to him the last time they met. Perhaps Humpty knew he wasn't long for this world. He offered all his shares to Grundy for ten million. Sounds pretty last-ditch to me. Anything on Bessie Brooks?"

"Still nothing. She withdrew two hundred pounds in cash last night from the city center, so she's still in the area."

"I'll release her name and picture to the press."

"Sir?"

It was Gretel. Jack walked into the filing room that she was using as her office. The small room was awash with papers, faxes and financial reports.

"What news?"

She put her pen down and leaned back in her chair. "Complex, sir, very complex."

"How do you mean?"

"It's about gold."

"Gold?" queried Jack "What is it?"

"It's a yellow-colored precious metal. I'm surprised you didn't know that."

"Old joke, Gretel. What about it?"

"Well, eighteen months ago Mr. Dumpty comes into a large quantity of bullion. No assay marks, the finest available."

She held up a receipt.

"He sells it to buy shares in Spongg's. He does the same thing a week later, then a week after that. He claims it is scrap and it requires no documentation. As he sells more and more, the markets in London get suspicious — they start to offer him a lower price, as they think it might be stolen. He eventually finds a ready market in Wozbekistan, Malvonia, Woppistania and a few other tattered remnants of the former Soviet Union where no questions are asked. Except there's a problem. They can't give him the hard currency he needs. He swaps it for copper, scrap, béarnaise sauce, strawberries, anything that can be sold in the West and realize its value. If you turn up his passport, I think you'll find he has enough frequent-flier miles to go to Jupiter. He's been all around the world selling gold, solely to purchase Spongg shares. Every time he had some cash, he went to Pewter."

"How much gold has he sold?" asked Jack.

"About two and a half million pounds' worth."

"That's a lot of gold. Where do you think he got it?"

"How about another illegal spinning-straw-into-gold den?" suggested Baker.

"Not since we banged up . . . what was his name again?"

"Rumplestiltskin?"

"Right. But check he's still inside, just to make sure. Any other gold missing?"

Gretel shook her head. "That's the problem. Nothing of this volume has been stolen recently, but muse on this: The first batch of Spongg shares was bought four days after the woodcutters' murder."

"So you're saying the woodcutters found some gold, were murdered, then Dumpty — he might not be the actual killer — starts to sell it himself?"

"It's a possibility," observed Gretel.

"Hmm," murmured Jack. "It wouldn't be the first time that anyone was killed over a piece of yellow metal. Good work, Gretel. I owe you several large drinks for this. See if you can find out where he got the gold from. Missing bullion consignments — anything. Go back fifty years if you have to."

Mary had joined them.

"I spoke to Tom Thomm's father. Get this: Tom was sponsored for early release . . . by Humpty."

"Now we're getting somewhere. What else?"

"He got Tom a job as a lab assistant in Goring two years ago. Six months after that, Tom leaves the job and comes into some cash. Buys his father a new car and his mother a new hip. Then, about a year ago, he vanishes from sight."

Jack cocked his head to one side and rubbed his chin thoughtfully. The date of Thomm's enrichment matched the date of the woodcutters' death, and it seemed likely that if Humpty didn't kill the woodcutter and his wife, then perhaps Tom Thomm did.

He addressed the NCD office.

"Listen up, everyone. We have a definite lead and a time scale that seems to fit. Here it is: Tom Thomm and Dumpty meet two years ago when Humpty is sponsoring him for early release. Dumpty gets Thomm a job, which he keeps until the same time as the woodcutter and his wife are murdered."

He paused for a moment.

"I'd say almost certainly that Tom Thomm killed the woodcutter and brought the gold to Dumpty to sell."

"Sir?"

"Yes, Baker?"

"I thought the Russian mafia killed the woodcutter? Chymes's investigation of the case was well documented in *Amazing Crime*."

"Then let's say Tom *stumbles* across the gold *after* the Russian mafia kills the woodcutters and takes it to Humpty. Yes, Ashley?"

"Could Tom Thomm have killed Dumpty?"

"It's possible, but why? Tom Thomm wouldn't have been able to sell the gold any more efficiently than Dumpty. Either way, we need to find this Thomm fellow. He's a strong link in the whole inquiry. Yes, Baker?"

"Rumplestiltskin is still inside," he said, turning from the Police National Computer terminal. "He didn't supply the gold."

"Good. Where was I?"

"Buying Spongg shares?"

"Right. Humpty uses the gold to buy thirty-eight percent of Spongg stock, but for the last year he has been in hiding at Grimm's Road. On Sunday night he has a voluble argument with a Miss Bessie Brooks, who we can't find, goes to the Spongg Charity Benefit, gets completely plastered and offers his entire Spongg holding to Solomon Grundy. Grundy turns him down flat, and Humpty tells him that his stock will be worth a lot more 'this time next year.' Humpty then blurts out that he will pledge fifty million to rebuild St. Cerebellum's, is taken home in Randolph Spongg's own car and six hours later he's shot dead."

"He thought the share price would go up," observed Mary.

"Exactly. Spongg prices are dropping daily, but he's still buying, so he knows something we don't. He goes to sit on his wall to sleep off the booze, and someone comes up behind him and shoots from a range of three to four feet with a .44 caliber. What did Mrs. Singh say the time of death was?"

"Between one and three a.m."

"Right. Humpty collapses stone dead into the backyard of 28, Grimm's Road, where he is discovered by his landlady at seven-thirty a.m. It was raining, so a lot of evidence has been washed away. The following day his ex-wife confesses to his murder and then kills herself — she didn't do it but must have *thought* she had. The twenty-eight-foot-long hair came from Mrs. Grundy, who was having an affair with Humpty. Grundy knew about it and said he didn't mind, which kind of throws the jealous-husband motive out the window."

He stopped and looked at them all.

"I don't think we're halfway there yet. Any questions?"

"Wee Willie Winkie," said Gretel.

"A good point. Winkie was Humpty's next-door neighbor and is violently murdered early this morning. It's possible he saw something and tried to blackmail them, but we don't know for sure. Same as this white van that was seen outside Humpty's and also where we found Winkie. Bear it in mind, but it could be nothing."

"Don't Winsum and Loosum's use white vans?"

"Yes — and half the companies in Berkshire. Any questions?"

There weren't. They all knew what they had to do.

"One other thing," said Jack. "A certain DCI named Friedland Chymes wants to take over this investigation and will do almost anything to do so. I want all approaches from him or a member of his staff reported to me. Let's keep gossip to a minimum, too. Okay, that's it. Find me Thomm and where Humpty has been living this past year, and we need to speak to Bessie Brooks."

There was an unseemly rush for the only available chairs. Gretel, as usual, won.

"What do you think about Winkie?" asked Jack.

"I'm not sure," replied Mary. "If he'd been shot with a .44 caliber, I might be a bit more positive. He might simply have been mugged; the fifty-pound notes could have been his."

"I agree. Listen: If we can discover Humpty's plan for raising his share value, we'll find the motive for killing him."

"Then why don't we speak to Spongg again?" suggested Mary. "After all, he stood to gain far more than Humpty ever did from a hike in the share prices."

28. Castle Spongg

The popularity of Nail Soup continues to spread across Reading this week with the news that Smileyburger has added Nailburger to its product list and the makers of Cup-A-Soup, Pot Noodle and Walkers Crisps are introducing "nail flavor" to their product lines. The tasty and healthy concoction that consists only of a nail and hot water has baffled nutritionists and scientists for some months. "It's very odd," declared a leading food expert yesterday, "but the nutritional benefits of nail soup are indisputable — yet fly in the face of established scientific thought, which states that a nail and hot water should be no more nutritious than hot water with a nail in it, which isn't nutritious at all. I have to admit it's got us stumped." Despite the confusion of the scientific community, the tasty snack continues to find favor with young and old alike, many of whom have improved upon the original recipe with a few garnishings of their own,

such as salt, pepper, potatoes, cabbages, leeks, carrots, lentils and chopped bacon.
— Extract from the *Reading Mercury*, January 4, 1984

Randolph wasn't at the factory that day, he was at home. And "at home" for the Sponggs meant only Castle Spongg, the extraordinary neosurrealist building constructed in the thirties by the brilliant yet certifiable Dr. Caligari. Many people argued over the artistic merits of Castle Spongg, but there was one descriptive word that everyone agreed upon: "bizarre."

Jack and Mary slowed to a stop outside the ornate wrought-iron gates of the main entrance. The gatehouse looked ordinary enough, but it was designed to give the illusion that it had sunk into the earth. The lodge was tilted at thirty degrees and was submerged to the top of the front door; the upstairs window served as the entrance and exit. They pulled through the open gates onto the drive, which was straight and flat but seemed to be a crudely mended patchwork of concrete and asphalt.

"You'd have thought he'd maintain it a bit better," said Mary as the tires rumbled and squeaked on the different road surfaces.

"It's not in poor repair," said Jack, who had been to visit the Castle Spongg grounds on a few occasions. "If you drive at precisely twenty-nine miles per hour, the rumble strips play 'Jerusalem' on the car tires. Listen."

Mary slowed to the correct speed and listened as they drove along. It *did* sound like "Jerusalem." A low, rumbling tune, heavy and brooding, like distant thunder.

"*. . . in ancient times!*" sang Jack.

They drove on through the immaculately kept gardens with not a blade of grass looking out of place. "They call Castle Spongg the 'jewel of the Thames Valley,'" said Jack. "The landscaped park was designed by the less-well-known 'Incomprehensible' Greene. See that reservoir?"

Mary looked to her left, where a footprint-shaped lake stretched away from them. Groves of silver birches grew where the soft, undulating parkland met the water. "Yes?"

"Greene installed large hydraulic rams in the lake bed that move up and down to give the effect of an Atlantic storm in winter. There is a sailing ship complete with torn sails and broken rigging down there — also on hydraulic rams — that can be made to founder and sink at the flick of a switch."

"For what purpose?" asked Mary.

"To entertain Lord Spongg and his guests. In the twenties and thirties, Spongg's was the wealthiest company in Reading — bigger even than Suttons Seeds or Huntley and Palmers — and consequently had the most lavish parties."

"I think I'd be bored looking at a sailing ship sink all the time."

"So was Lord Spongg. The ship can be retracted and replaced by a seventeen-ton Carrera marble fountain depicting Poseidon doing battle with a sea monster. Just over there was the pitch where they played aerial polo with Gypsy Moths. It was quite a lark, apparently."

They drove on in silence for some minutes, staring at the strange wonders that met them at every turn. As the road smoothed and the last strains of "Jerusalem" faded on the car tires, they rounded a corner and came within sight of the bizarre and incongruous Castle Spongg.

The word "surreal" might have been invented for the Spongg residence. Everything about it flew in the face of aesthetic convention. It was impossible to say how many stories Castle Spongg had, for the windows were of varying sizes and shapes and placed randomly in the walls. The five towers all leaned precariously — some in, some out, three of them spiraling as they reached skywards, two of them even entwining at the top. The roof was decorated in seven different shades of slate, and the zinc guttering channeled water through gargoyles modeled on all the British prime ministers since 1726. Part of the roof was supported by flying buttresses, some Gothic, others smooth and looking like living branches of a tree. One buttress stretched seventy feet down, only to stop less than a yard from the ground.

They slowly motored up to the front door and parked where a silver-haired servant in a frock coat and white gloves was waiting to greet them.

"Good afternoon," said the butler, bowing stiffly from the waist, "my name is Ffinkworth. I am the Spongg retainer. If you would follow me?"

They all walked towards the main door, which was the shape of a collapsed trapezoid. Strangely, there seemed to be a gap between the two circular brass strips that ran round the perimeter of the house. Stranger still, the house appeared to be *rotating.*

"Castle Spongg is built on a turntable," explained Ffinkworth with a hint of pride.

"Powerful electric motors in the basement rotate the house to any point of the compass so his lordship might look out of his study and view the rose garden, or the lake, or whatever he wishes. Given less inclement weather," added Ffinkworth, "we could even track the sun and ensure that the morning room was naturally illuminated all day long."

They stepped onto the turntable, which had been so precisely engineered it was impossible to be sure you were moving at all. The butler stood back so they might enter first, and they walked past a pair of giant bronze anteaters that guarded the lopsided front door.

Inside, the hall's high ceiling was supported by a varied muddle of columns. Some were Ionic, some Corinthian, some Doric and some Egyptian. Others were a mixture of all four. The floor was checkered with white and black marble, but each piece was differently shaped. They swirled around the floor with no discernible pattern, and if you looked at it too long, you could become disorientated.

"I wonder —" said Jack, turning to speak to Ffinkworth, but the butler had vanished.

"It's a bit creepy, isn't it?" said Mary, listening to the house utter gentle creaks and groans to itself as it flexed slightly on the turntable. Jack was just tilting his head to one side to try to view the paintings, which were hung upside down, when a familiar voice made them turn.

"Inspector!" said Randolph with a smile. "How nice to see you again! And Sergeant Mary. I trust the corn on the second toe of your left foot is not hurting you too much?"

"How did you know about that?"

He smiled modestly. "I am a fully trained and highly experienced chiropodist, Sergeant. I can tell by the way you walk. Is this your first time inside Castle Spongg?"

They both nodded.

"It's officially one of the seven wonders of Reading," said Spongg proudly. "Will you take tea?"

"Thank you."

"The first Castle Spongg was built in 1892," he explained as he led the way down a mirrored corridor. "It was a Gothic Revival edifice of humongous proportions. The main hall, corridor and doorways were so large that my grandfather took to driving everywhere in a Model T Ford."

"Didn't it damage the place?" asked Mary.

"The odd scuff here and there, but

nothing serious. No, the real damage was done by the 1924 Spongg indoor car-racing championships. A three-car pileup in the main hall destroyed all the oak paneling between the library and the smoking room."

He laughed at the thought of it.

"There was a high-banked corner built next to the staircase. The main hall became the home straight; they tell me the chicane in the orangerie was tricky but that you could really open it up down the picture gallery. My grandfather set a lap record of 86.42 miles per hour in a blown Delage-Talbot S-27. He destroyed the car and his left leg in the attempt."

He stopped next to a glass case containing a piece of twisted metal.

"This was part of the Delage's supercharger. We found it embedded in a tree half a mile from here two summers ago. Glory, glory days. This way."

He took a left turn, opened a riveted steel hatch and led them down a corridor that looked like the interior of a submarine, complete with water dribbling out of the valves and the distant concussion of depth charges.

"It all ended badly, of course. On the eighth lap of the race, Count Igor Debrovnik spun his seven-liter Fiat off the corner of the upstairs landing and out through the stained-glass windows to crash through the roof of the chapel below. A few minutes later, a marshaling mistake in the library caused the Earl of Sudbury to crash his Railton at seventy miles an hour into the antiquarian-book section, causing irreparable damage to some early works by Bacon. By the end of the race, a dozen other mishaps had reduced the inside of the house to a ruin, so in 1926 my grandfather decided to rebuild it with the help of the brilliant yet insane Wolfgang Caligari."

He pushed open a panel, and they found themselves in a large room full of ancient Khmer stone architecture with large strangler fig trees growing across and through it. It was hot, and tropical plants grew in lush abundance. As they watched, a parrot flew across the room and perched on the mantelpiece.

"We call this the Angkor Wat Room," said Spongg. "The roof is medieval spider-vaulted, and those windows are a faithful reproduction of the west window at Chartres — but with a few more feet."

He bade them sit on a sofa that had been incongruously placed on a Persian rug in the center of the room. The tea things were already waiting for them.

"It's remarkable!" said Mary.

"They didn't say that when it was built," replied Spongg, pouring the tea. "It was roundly lambasted, as all great buildings are. From the simple 'ugly' through the more forthright 'wholly lacking in taste or style' to the plainly overstated 'work of Mephistopheles.' It's all of these and none of these and a lot more besides. Sugar?"

"Thank you."

"So," he said as soon as they had their tea, "you still have some questions, Inspector?"

"A few. Have you any idea at all how Humpty might have been planning to raise the value of Spongg shares?"

"I've thought about it a great deal since I saw you last," said Spongg, "but I still can't figure it out."

Jack started on a new tack.

"I've spoken to Mr. Grundy. He said that Humpty *did* offer to sell him his share portfolio that night at the Spongg benefit."

"Did Grundy take up the offer?"

"No."

"Then why would I want to kill him? If that was Humpty's plan, then he misjudged his timing badly."

"Perhaps he wasn't planning to sell them

to Grundy at all. Perhaps he was going to sell them back to . . . *you.*"

Spongg frowned and stared at them both. "For what purpose?"

"To allow you to reclaim the factory for the family."

Spongg laughed. "If that is so, I must have been planning this for twenty years — that's how long we've been in trouble. Besides, Humpty bought those shares, not me. I don't have that kind of cash."

"Mr. Dumpty could have been your front. If you had been buying your own shares back, I daresay City analysts would be asking why — and the price would have increased dramatically."

Spongg laughed again, but anger was rising beneath his genial exterior.

"*If* I were a criminal, Inspector, I could have plundered my employees' pension fund. I and my aged relatives are the sole trustees, so it wouldn't have been difficult. There is over a hundred million in there, more than enough to put this company back on its feet. But it isn't mine. It belongs to the workers. I've been battling Winsum and Loosum's for years, not out of my responsibility as an employer or to maintain the Spongg name but because we have a moral imperative to maintain the supply of foot-care products."

He said it very grandly and without any humor intended.

"The supply of foot-care products *has* a moral imperative?"

"You may laugh, Inspector, but then you don't understand chiropody as I do. The Spongg empire is built on four major foot treatments. Without them we are nothing. Anyone can make special scissors, insoles and corn plasters — our selling point is our successful foot preparations. Winsum and Loosum aren't interested in my factory or distribution. They want my patents. With their sales network and my cures for verrucas, corns, athlete's foot and bunions, they could wipe the world's feet free of ailments forever — or not."

"Not?" inquired Mary.

"*Precisely.* They may retain our patents but decide to withhold them from the world market. Ointments that soothe but don't cure is where the *real* money lies. In contrast, Spongg's has always been committed to a public service in the foot-care market. If I wanted to play it like Winsum's, I could be a multibillionaire by now."

Spongg's voice had been getting higher and higher as he explained all this. He was obviously quite impassioned by the magnitude of the situation.

"Without competition from us, they could charge what they want. Chiropody would become a gold mine, and that greedy bastard Solomon Grundy wants the lot!"

He had gone a bright shade of red but soon calmed himself, took a sip of tea, apologized to Mary for swearing in her presence and then said, "To think the Jellyman will be shaking hands and honoring Solomon on Saturday is *obscene* to my mind, Inspector. If the Jellyman understood anything about feet at all, he would not be honoring Grundy but enacting legislation against him."

"Do you know where Mr. Dumpty had been living this past year?"

"I'm afraid not. Aside from at the charity benefit, I've not seen him."

Jack put down his tea and took the picture of Tom Thomm from his pocket.

"Have you ever seen this man?"

Spongg put on his glasses and stared at the picture.

"Yes, I think with Humpty a couple of times — but not for a while."

"What about him?" asked Jack, passing him a photo of Winkie.

"No, I'm afraid not."

"What about Laura Garibaldi?"

"That was tragic, Inspector. Truly tragic. I introduced them, for my sins. Laura and I were on the Reading clay-pigeon shooting team. She was a fine shot and a good woman. I don't think Humpty really deserved her."

"You've been very kind," said Jack, "and I'm sorry that my questioning seemed harsh at times."

"Please think nothing of it," said Spongg. "Come, I'll see you out."

They rose and walked between the faux-ancient-stone ruins as the parrot took flight and flashed its exotic blue tail feathers.

"That's quite a bird," murmured Mary.

"Norwegian blue," said Spongg admiringly. "*Beautiful* plumage."

29. Lola Vavoom

Lola Vavoom had been one of the greatest British actresses of the seventies and eighties. Discovered in 1969 at the cosmetics counter of Littlewoods, she was cast as Deirdre Furlong in the pilot episode of *65, Walrus Street*. Leaving after four years, she made her break to the big screen as maverick cop Julie Hathaway in the highly successful *The Streets of Wootton Bassett*. A string of hits followed: *The Adzuki Bean Murders, My Sister Used to Keep Geese* and *Fancy Free in Ludlow*, for which she won a Milton. By the middle of the eighties she was commanding two million dollars a picture. Then disaster. A string of flops culminating in 1989's *The Eyre Affair* and unceasing speculation over the contents of her bathroom cupboard caused her to withdraw completely. Her attendance at the 2004 Spongg Charity Benefit was her first public appearance in fourteen years.
— From *Valleyhills Movie Guide*

"How many?" asked Jack, who had taken five minutes out to eat a sandwich after his

return from a brief trip to St. Cerebellum's.

"Ninety-seven — and rising," said Baker. "We don't have time to take statements; Ashley and Tibbit are taking names and addresses and checking to see if they have any 'pertinent information.' "

"Do they?"

"Not yet. They just want to help."

News of Humpty's death had elicited an unpredictable reaction among his ex-girlfriends, paramours, affairs and liaisons. The arrival of floral tributes outside Grimm's Road had begun as soon as his death was announced, and they had now spilled into the road. There was talk of a candlelight vigil that night; the long trail of ex-lovers who wanted to help with the investigation had begun a few hours ago and now absorbed all available manpower, which was never that great to begin with. The one girlfriend they did want to speak to, however, had yet to turn up.

"Thanks, Baker. Tell Ashley and Tibbit to come straight to me if they hear anything potentially relevant."

Baker nodded and picked up his mobile.

"So what did you discover?" Jack asked Mary, who had also grabbed a quick bite to eat.

"Not much," she replied, looking at her

notes. "Winkie's supervisor at Winsum and Loosum's was a man named Whelan, who said that Winkie was an excellent worker and much liked. The narcolepsy was a problem, but they worked around it — Winsum's has a good record of employing people with health issues. I couldn't fault them. There were several occasions when jokes could have been made at a narcoleptic's expense, but no one made them."

"Did he seem to them like the sort of man about to try to blackmail a killer?"

"He had been preoccupied and a bit jumpy — about what, no one could say. Are you still thinking Solomon Grundy might be involved?"

"I don't think so. He laid all his cards on the table for us, and as you say, he's got enough money to write off a two-million-pound scam without thinking. And as Briggs pointed out, it *was* fourteen years ago."

Jack took a swig of tea. His trip over to St. Cerebellum's had been equally inconclusive. Winkie's doctor, a helpful chap named Dr. Murphy, told him that Winkie had been treated for narcolepsy as an outpatient for nearly eight years, with sessions twice weekly. Winkie had missed the previous day's session, so it was *possible* something was on his mind. Jack had also bumped into Dr. Quatt, who asked him how things were going. She had referred to Humpty as "Hump," so Jack wondered whether perhaps she might not have a floral tribute for him, too.

Jack finished his sandwich, wiped his hands and mouth on a hankie and thought for a moment. *All those women.*

"By the way," said Baker, "Giorgio Porgia said he'd see you tomorrow at nine a.m. *sharp.*"

Jack snapped his fingers as he suddenly thought of something. "Of course. Baker, the apartment that Porgia gave to Humpty in return for the money laundering . . . ?"

"What about it?"

"Do we have an address? I know Humpty lived over at the Cheery Egg with Laura for eighteen years, but he might have kept it on. He would have had to take all those girls *somewhere.*"

Baker rummaged through paperwork and eventually came up with an address in one of Humpty's old arrest reports. "Here it is," he announced: "614, Spongg Villas."

Humpty Dumpty's old residence was in a large block of flats that had been built by the Spongg Building Trust in the early part of the century for Reading's trendiest set.

After a period of fashionable existence in the thirties and forties, its popularity had begun to wane. Expensive to maintain, the unprepossessing block had changed hands regularly for ever-decreasing amounts as successive landlords took the rent and never bothered to bring the place up to date or even carry out anything other than essential repairs. It had started out as a good address but was now a shabby wreck, an upmarket version of Grimm's Road, its paint long since faded and the stucco rounded and softened by the corrosive action of the wind and rain.

Jack, Mary and Baker stepped into the musty hall and were greeted warmly by the ripe odor of decay. Out of two hundred apartments, they understood from the ancient doorman, who wore a stained bellhop's uniform, barely eight were still occupied. The others had been boarded up and the basins, baths and toilets smashed to discourage squatters. The owner was a wealthy financier who was waiting for the last tenants to leave before he flattened the site and built a deluxe car park in its place. The doorman pointed the way up the stairs. The lift, he explained, had been out of order since 1972.

Humpty's apartment was on the sixth

floor, and as Baker led the way up the creaking circular staircase, Jack looked over the banisters and up at the domed skylight, whose myriad leaks he could see had been crudely repaired with waterproof tape. The banisters were rickety, and the dust of dry rot rose when they touched them. Padlocked doors greeted them on every landing.

"Which was his apartment again?" asked Jack.

"Number 614," whispered Baker. "This way."

He led them slowly down the hall, through fire doors that were wedged open and past corroded wall lights glowing with bulbs of minuscule wattage. Dust rose from the aged carpet as they approached Humpty's front door. Jack pulled out his penlight to examine it more closely. They could see that the dirt and fluff had drifted against it; the doorknob had a small spider living on it, and everything was veiled with a thin coat of dust.

"No one's been in here for rather a long time," observed Baker.

A low, husky woman's voice answered from behind them. "About a year, actually, dahlings."

They turned to see a woman of perhaps

fifty-five standing dramatically in the shaft of light that shone out of her apartment door and pierced the stygian gloom of the corridor. She watched them all with a well-practiced air of laconic indifference, a half smile on her lips. Her hair was up in rollers, and she was smoking an expensive-looking cigarette. She had hastily covered her mouth with crimson lipstick and wore a lacy blouse that was unbuttoned enough to display a large volume of cleavage. Her shoulders were draped with a light tan cashmere sweater, and she wore a knee-length skirt that hugged her well-proportioned frame tightly. She paused for a moment, leaned on the doorframe and regarded them in a manner that might have been described as "smoldering sexuality" had she been twenty years younger.

"Sorry?" stammered Jack, quite taken aback by the curious vision that had appeared in front of them.

"About a year," she repeated. "I called them about the shower, but they never came. They're arseholes, you know, dahling."

She inhaled on her cigarette and blew the smoke upwards. Jack walked over to her.

"I know who you are. You're Lola Vavoom. You used to be big in movies."

"I will treat that feed line with the contempt it deserves, dahling. I'd never tread on Norma's toes. Who might you be?"

"Detective Inspector Jack Spratt of the Nursery Crime Division. These are Detective Sergeant Mary and Constable Baker."

She nodded in Mary's direction but didn't look at her. She put a languid hand out towards Baker, just out of his reach so he had to step forward to shake it.

"Detective Baker," she cooed.

"*Constable* Baker," he corrected with a small smile.

Despite her faded grandeur and worn poise, Lola had a certain grace and bearing that still made her extremely attractive.

"That's a beautiful name. I had a lover named Baker once. He was hung like a hamster."

"Is that good?" asked Baker, unsure of her meaning.

"It is if you're another hamster."

Jack managed to turn a laugh into a cough. Baker blushed, but Jack quickly took charge of the situation.

"Miss Vavoom — what are you doing here?"

"Here, dahling?" she replied with a smile. "Why, I live here!"

"We thought you'd be in Hollywood . . .

or Caversham Heights at the very least," added Mary, who remembered seeing Lola performing *Anthrax!* live when she was a little girl.

"Hah!" Lola spat contemptuously. "Being waited on by an army of cosmetic surgeons? No thanks. What you see is what I am. I've not had my boobs done or my arse lifted, no nips, no tucks. No ribs removed, nothing. Those little strumpets we see on the silver screen today are mostly bathroom sealant. They buy their breasts over the counter. 'What would you like, honey, small, medium or large?' They give us stick insects and tell us it's beauty. If someone of their size went for an audition in my day, she'd have been shown a square meal and told to come back when she was a stone heavier. What's wrong with curves? Anyone over a ten these days is regarded not as an average-sized woman but a marketing opportunity. Cream for this, pills for that, superfluous hair, collagen injection, quick-weight-loss diets. Where's it going to end? We're pressured to expend so much money and effort to be the 'perfect' shape, when that shape is physically attainable by only one woman in a million. It's the cold face of capitalism, boys and girls, preying on misguided expectations. Besides, I always found perfection an overrated commodity."

Her voice had risen as she spoke, topping her tirade on a high C. She paused and collected herself, then continued in a normal voice.

"Sometime I'll make a comeback, and when I do . . ."

Jack and Baker just stared. Lola looked from Baker to Mary and then back to Jack again. She tapped her heel against the doorframe and lit another cigarette.

"So. You're the police. I heard about Humpty. I was sorry, I thought he was a nice guy. A bit short for my taste, but there you have it."

"When did you last see him?" asked Jack, trying to gather his senses.

She flicked the ash off her cigarette. "About this time last year. I saw Hump come lumbering out; he never could move very fast with those short little legs of his. He looked a bit agitated, and I asked if he was all right. He was a bit startled when he saw me and said everything was fine, then went downstairs. I went back indoors, but I could still hear the shower running. Humpty never came back, and I called the maintenance engineer the following week. He didn't turn up, and it's still running.

My guess is that they're trying to make the building unsafe so we all have to move out."

She looked around the shabby corridor and pulled at a piece of curling wallpaper disdainfully. It tore off easily in her hand, and she crushed the fragment to little pieces.

She suddenly looked bored. "Can I go? If you want me, you know where to find me. I don't go out a lot."

Lola didn't wait for a reply. She just looked at them all, smiled at Baker, went back inside her room and closed the door noiselessly behind her.

Jack sighed and put an ear to one of the glass panes of Humpty's front door.

"We've just met British cinema history," he commented.

"She was rather a cracker in her time, sir," declared Baker.

"I think she still is."

"Well," announced Mary, "if I look that good in my fifties, I'll be a happy girl."

Jack raised a finger to his lips. "Quiet a second, guys."

They all stood in silence for a moment.

"She's right. The shower *is* still running."

He stepped back and gestured to Baker to force the lock. They pushed the door open against a mound of junk mail that had collected in the hall and then went on to the second door that separated the hall from the rest of the apartment. Jack paused and looked at Mary and Baker, seeing his own feelings of foreboding reflected on their faces.

As Jack grasped the door handle, it came away in his hand, and the door itself fell away into a rotten, soggy heap. A wave of damp air blew over them all. The moisture in the air had exacted a terrible toll on the apartment. Everything they could see was in an advanced state of rot. The carpets and furnishings were thickly mildewed, and the paper had peeled off the walls and lay in heaps next to the moldy skirting. The books in the bookcase had rotted down to a dark mulch, and everything in the flat was covered with a thin layer of moisture. There was a heavy smell of damp, and Jack noticed that several varieties of fungi had started to grow on the walls and floors. He felt the floorboards collapse gently under his weight, the patterned carpet keeping him from falling through entirely. He trod gently into the bedroom and saw that the sheets had rotted off the bed and the contents of the wardrobe had fallen off their hangers into a soggy mass. As he called to

Baker to turn off the shower, his eyes settled on a badly corroded cartridge that lay on the wet carpet. He looked closer and found another, then two more. He bent down and prodded one with a pen, but it had stuck fast to the carpet.

Jack heard the shower stop. There was a short pause, and then Baker spoke, his voice solemn and quavering slightly.

"Sir, I think you'd better come and have a look at this."

The SOCO team was there in under an hour. They looked around curiously at the decayed room and walked carefully on a floor that now undulated where the floorboards had partially collapsed. One officer busied himself cutting out the squares of carpet that had the cartridges corroded to them, but the fingerprint boys were sent away almost immediately.

Shenstone scratched the back of his head when he saw the mess. "How long has the shower been going?"

"A year."

It posed severe problems. The photographer was still busy as Mrs. Singh arrived, breathless after hurrying up the stairs. Jack was sorting through the heap of junk mail and private letters, most of which seemed to be either bank correspondence, invitations to functions or pleas for charitable donations. There were hundreds of love letters, too — obviously brief amours hastily cast aside. The oldest postmark dated back almost a year, which seemed to tie in with what Lola had told them.

"Jack, Jack," said Mrs. Singh, shaking her head sadly, "what's going on?"

Jack took her to the bathroom, finding her a safe passage over the rotten floorboards. "Body in the shower. Probably been dead about a year."

"A year? Well, as I said, dead men do —"

But then she saw the body. A flash went off at that moment to punctuate the discovery.

"Not much for me to work on, is there?"

"Not really."

The corpse wasn't much of a corpse. Since the body had been in a shower for nearly a year, the flesh had been quite literally washed down the drain. All that remained of the victim was a yellowish skeleton, held together by hardier pieces of tendon and gristle. Wisps of hair were attached to a small area of scalp on the side of the head, and the left foot, which was the only part of the body outside the oversize shower basin, had putrefied and was now host to a large crop of fungus.

"The shower was on when you found him?" asked Mrs. Singh.

"Yes. Him?"

"Male skeleton. Mid-thirties at a guess, not far off six foot. But this is what interests me."

She pointed at the small collection of lead bullets that lay scattered beneath the corpse. They had dropped from the body as the surrounding tissue rotted away but were too heavy to be moved by the water. Mrs. Singh pulled out a Magic Marker and noted the position of one, and had the photographer take several pictures before she picked it up with a pair of forceps and looked closely at it.

"Looks like a .32. Make any sense?"

"There are .32 cartridges scattered all over the carpet just behind you."

"Any idea who he is?" she asked without looking up.

"We think his name is Tom Thomm, aged thirty-four and a missing person — found his wallet in a pair of rotted 501s. Do I need to ask how he died?"

Mrs. Singh knelt by the shower basin. Jack squatted next to her.

"Not really," she continued. "One shot grazed his lowest rib just here but was not fatal; another bullet that shattered the ulna indicates that he had raised his arm in an attempt to protect himself. There is another slug lodged in the hip joint which probably caused him to fall over, and the last two were fired to finish him off. One lodged in the side of his skull and the other nicked his rib."

"How do you know two shots were fired to finish him off?"

She smiled and with a flourish drew back the shower curtain. It had three bullet holes at abdomen height and then two much lower down.

Jack looked at the holes and got up, rubbed his chin and stood just outside the bathroom door facing the shower. The ejected shell cases had been found there, so it was a fair bet that this was where the shots had been fired from.

"So they fire from here three times, hear the person slump in the shower and shoot twice more?"

Mrs. Singh stood up. "I'd say that's about the tune of it. Get Skinner to have a look. I'll leave the corpse there until he's done." She stared down at the body. "Seems hard to believe that a shower could be run for a year. Didn't anyone complain?"

"Next-door neighbor. Lola Vavoom —"

"The actress?"

"The same. She complained, but they ignored her. No one lives below. It's a mess down there, too. The damp has got into everything."

Mrs. Singh was deep in thought, but not, as Jack found out, about the corpse.

"Lola Vavoom, eh?" she said excitedly. "I was about the only person who liked *My Sister Used to Keep Geese*, and my husband and I saw *Fancy Free in Ludlow* eight times. I must get her autograph."

She hurried off, leaving them both staring at the shower curtain.

"Are you thinking what I'm thinking?" asked Jack.

"Mrs. Dumpty?"

"Bingo. First three shots at abdomen level. Humpty was about four foot six. If she *thought* he was in the shower, that's where she would have aimed."

"What did Mrs. Dumpty say in her suicide note?" mused Mary. " 'I went to his home and prayed for God to forgive me as I pulled the trigger.' "

"Only when we came around to interview her," continued Mary, "she didn't know we were investigating something that had happened that morning — she must have thought we'd just discovered the body."

"It explains why Dumpty had been lying low," added Jack. "He obviously didn't want her to have a second go at him."

He stared at the skeleton in the shower basin.

"I reckon he'd only just discovered Tom Thomm's body when Lola saw him."

"Why didn't he report it?" asked Mary.

"Because," said Jack simply, "he was up to no good — and up to no good *big time*. But it still doesn't tell us where Humpty *had* been living this past year."

"So . . . are we any closer to who killed Humpty?"

"We know they used a .44-caliber handgun, that it's probable Winkie saw them do it and —" He thought for a moment. "And that's about it."

The rain had stopped by the time they stepped out of the building. The sky had darkened even though it was barely mid-afternoon, and cautious motorists had switched on their headlights, causing the wet road to glisten. The doorman, inspired by all the activity, had put his pillbox hat on at a jaunty angle and saluted as they walked past.

"Briggs called," said Baker as he saw them to the Allegro.

"Let me guess. Press conference?"

"In one."

30. Another Press Conference

CRIME BOSS JAILED

Notorious racketeer and underworld crime boss Giorgio Porgia was found guilty yesterday on 208 counts of "undertaking home improvements with menaces." The court heard that Porgia and his gang would routinely use threats, violence and intimidation to sell unwanted home improvements to frightened residents. Loft conversions were carried out where no loft had been; double glazing was replaced up to seven times on the same property, and houses were unnecessarily rewired using string. Porgia was sentenced to thirty-five years in prison, having already pleaded guilty to token charges of wanton lack of taste, poor color harmony and badly aligned wallpapering. He was also banned for life from owning a conservatory.

— From *The Toad*,
March 2, 1984

". . . but what was *actually* said at that fateful tea party, it was impossible to ascertain," continued Chymes while the pressroom stared at him, hanging on his every word, "until I devised a forensic technique which I call 'cake-crumb scatter-pattern identification.' This works on the principle that if someone eats cake while talking, the crumbs are ejected from the mouth at different rates according to the syllables of the words spoken. By analyzing the pattern of crumbs on the tablecloth, I was able to deduce that the conversation was not about the weather, as Mrs. Pitkins claimed, but the subject of the misdiagnosis of botulism poisoning, a line of questioning that we were able to bring to our suspect, who soon confessed everything in a tearful scene that made a fitting end to the whole painful inquiry."

Friedland was greeted by the usual standing ovation, which he modestly dismissed with a wave of the hand. There were a few technical questions about his new technique, regarding varying weights of the component parts of the cake and how far you might project a chocolate sprinkle when pronouncing "psoriasis," something Chymes deftly answered with complicated diagrams on an overhead projector as DS Flotsam gave out printed copies of all the details.

Jack, Briggs and Mary were watching from the door of the anteroom.

"What am I doing here?" asked Jack. "I've got nothing really substantial to add — I don't really know if Winkie's death was even *connected.*"

"It's from the seventh floor, Jack." Briggs said it without enthusiasm. Someone was leaning on him.

"What's going on, sir?"

Briggs looked down and rubbed his forehead. "The Guild is very powerful, Jack. I'm sorry."

Before Jack could even *begin* to think what he might mean, Chymes strode past them as he walked out of the pressroom. He went back on to take a curtain call but then came off again, glared at Jack with a confident smile and said, "You want the heat, Jack? Try the fire."

And he joined Flotsam and Barnes on the other side of the anteroom, where they attended to him as a manager looks after a boxer who has just come out of the ring.

Usually Jack waited for the journalists to file out, as they generally made a lot of noise, and if Archibald or anyone else was polite enough to stay, he would at least be heard. But today was different. *Today no one filed out.* There was silence. For a moment Jack thought Chymes was about to go back on, but he had already started to discuss the possibility of solving the Slough Thuggee cult murders in time for the early-evening news the following day.

"Sir," said Mary as she leaned around the door to peer at their expectant faces, "I think they're waiting for you."

"That's not possible," replied Jack, his heart missing a beat. He looked at Briggs, who wouldn't catch his eye. He'd clearly been set up.

"Shit."

"What?" asked Mary.

"I'm going to be boned out there."

"You can refuse to go on."

"If it's not now, it will be later. No, let's get it over with."

He walked on to the symphonic clatter of camera motor drives.

"Good afternoon," he began, feeling what he imagined was something akin to bowel-moving stage fright. "My name is Detective Inspector Jack Spratt, and I am head of the Nursery Crime Division here at Reading Central. On Monday morning at approximately one a.m., Humperdinck Jehoshaphat Aloysius Stuyvesant van

Dumpty was murdered by a person or persons unknown as he sat upon a wall at his place of work. He died instantly. At present we are unable to state a motive."

Josh Hatchett asked, "How was he killed?"

"He was shot."

A murmur went through the collected newsmen. So far this wasn't going too badly.

"Do you have any suspects?"

"We have a woman named Elizabeth 'Bessie' Brooks. We will be issuing a photograph after the press conference. In a separate development, Mr. William Winkie, Humpty Dumpty's next-door neighbor, was found murdered in Palmer Park this morning. We are not ruling out the possibility of a connection."

"Is Mrs. Garibaldi-Dumpty's suicide connected to Mr. Dumpty's death?"

"It is a direct consequence of it, yes."

Hector Sleaze had been staring at what looked like a hastily photocopied list of press cuttings.

"Detective, I wonder if you could confirm for me that you recently attempted to convict the three pigs of Mr. Wolff's murder?"

Jack shuffled uneasily. Here it comes, he

thought. "That is true, yes."

A ripple of laughter went through the room, and Jack felt himself grow hot.

"And that this failed conviction cost the taxpayers a quarter of a million pounds?"

"I'm not aware of the precise figure."

"Okay," said Hector after a pause, "can you also confirm that you have the lowest investigation/conviction ratio of any department in Reading?"

"Without looking at the records, it would be difficult to say."

"Then let me help you," Sleaze muttered, looking through his list. "Sheep rustling from Miss Bo-peep. Two arrests, no charges. Failure to properly take care of livestock by 'Boy' Blue. One arrest, no charges. Cruelly putting a cat in a well. Johnny Flynn arrested, no charges brought. Kidnapping of Hansel and Gretel with intent to commit cannibalism. One arrest, no charges. Criminal spreading panic of sky falling. One arrest, no charges. Bluebeard. Died awaiting trial. 'Goosey' Gander, freed on appeal. Mr. Punch, arrested for wife battery, throwing a baby downstairs and illegal possession of a crocodile. All charges dropped."

Hector put down the list. "I could go on. Not a very good record, is it, Inspector?"

Jack stared at him. If the Prosecution Service had proceeded, he could have brought convictions on a lot more occasions. If there had been a *will* to have them convicted.

"The NCD is a department fraught with —"

"In fact," continued Hector, "I can only find sixteen successful convictions in the twenty years you have been heading the Nursery Crime Division. One every fifteen months. Friedland Chymes convicts that many *every five weeks.*"

It was an unfair comparison, and Jack clenched his jaw. Friedland had been busy.

"The NCD, Mr. Sleaze, is a unique area of policing where an understanding of the problems of the characters involved often allows me to stop things before they get out of —"

"Inspector Spratt, are you competent to run Mr. Dumpty's murder investigation or are you really trying to work beyond your capabilities?"

"There is no doubt," said Jack slowly, "that this case falls strictly within the NCD's jurisdiction."

"Do you think Chymes might have been able to secure a conviction of the three pigs?"

He would, of course. Juries considered it an honor to work with Chymes. But Jack had paused in his answer, and it gave him away.

"I take that as a *yes,* Inspector. Do you think it would be prudent to hand over the investigation to Chymes so we might see some headway?"

"I am completely in control of the investigation," replied Jack hurriedly, answering for answering's sake and wanting to be out of that room as soon as possible. But they weren't done. They had been well primed. The newspaper headlines were already written, Chymes had made sure of it — and it would sell papers. Lots of them. Jack glanced over to where Briggs was staring at him from the side door. Beyond him Jack could see Friedland Chymes wearing a look of ill-disguised delight. The last detective who had tried to usurp Chymes's dominance of Reading Central and refused to relinquish a case had been a bright spark named Drood. He had been transferred to the unrelenting tedium of the Missing Persons Bureau.

"DI Spratt," resumed Hector, "I understand you have killed several giants in the past, and I would like to ask what you have against people of large stature?"

Jack resisted the temptation to tell Mr. Sleaze to poke his accusations up his nose, took a deep breath and said instead, "I was exonerated of all blame, Mr. Sleaze. The report is a matter of public record. Besides, only one of them was *technically* a giant. The others were just tall. Are there any more questions?"

"Yes," said Sleaze. "Wouldn't it be more appropriate for you to invite a senior officer to assist with the investigation? Someone with talent and an impeccable clear-up rate? Someone like DCI Chymes, for instance?"

It went on in this vein for another twenty minutes until, hot and sweaty and almost shaking, Jack managed to escape.

Briggs and Friedland were talking to each other in the corner of the anteroom but broke off as soon as he entered.

"If you want to relinquish control of the Humpty investigation right now," said Chymes in a very businesslike manner, "I'm sure a way can be found to stop the undeniably harmful headlines from being published tomorrow morning."

"For the good of Reading Central, I would have thought you might do that anyway," retorted Jack.

"Oh, no," said Chymes airily. "My control over the press is *extremely* limited." He turned to Briggs. "Sir, I think you should take Spratt off the Humpty investigation."

Briggs bit his lip.

"Sir?" said Chymes again. "I think you should order —"

"I heard what you said. If there is no headway by Saturday night, you can have it."

"But I want it *now!*" yelled Chymes like a petulant schoolboy. "It's mine, and I want it!"

Briggs rankled visibly. Jack had often seen Briggs start to get pissed off at *him,* but never at Chymes.

"I gave my word, Friedland."

"Even so —"

"Even so *nothing,*" said Briggs sternly. "I am your supervisory officer, and I give *you* orders, not the other way around. Do you understand?"

"Of course, sir," said Chymes, surprised and taken aback by Briggs's actually daring to stand up to him. "Did I read somewhere that you play the trombone? An Urdu-speaking, trombone-playing superintendent strikes me as *just* the sort of character the readers of *Amazing Crime Stories* might be —"

"Friedland?" interrupted Briggs.

"Sir?"

"Get out of my sight."

"I'm sorry?"

"You heard me."

Chymes went scarlet, turned tail and strode angrily from the room, his minions at his heels.

"Thank you, sir," said Jack as soon as they had left.

"What the hell," said Briggs, deflated. "I *hate* the trombone, and I've put in my thirty years. You've got until Saturday."

And he was gone, leaving Mary and Jack in the empty anteroom. Next door they could hear the journalist from the *Reading Daily Eyestrain* snoring.

"Things are going to get hot, Mary. Sure you don't want that transfer?"

"Not for anything, sir. You, I and the NCD are disbanded together."

He smiled as they walked towards the elevators.

"I appreciate it. You can drop me at home and take the Allegro. Pick me up at eight-thirty tomorrow morning, and we'll go and meet Giorgio Porgia."

"The Allegro? For the *whole* evening?" asked Mary in a tone of mock delight.

"Yes. Look after it — and no drag racing."

31. Home, Sweet Home

POSTMAN MUZZLED IN AMUSING JURY-RIG MIX-UP

There were laughs all around at the Reading Central Criminal Court this morning, where a comical jury-bribing mix-up brought a moment of levity to otherwise somber proceedings. Sources close to the judge tell us that through an administrative error, sharpened-chisel-wielding mobster Giorgio Porgia had been paying off the wrong jury in his celebrated trial for demanding home improvements with menaces. "What a mix-up!" grinned Mr. Justice Trousers after adjournment. "It's hilarious moments like this that make the courts such a fun place to work!" The "bought" jury in a nearby court, who were trying a dangerous dog, found the pooch in question not guilty and decided, in an unprecedented move, that the postman had bitten the dog. The postman was muzzled for a month and ordered to pay £10,000 in damages.

— Extract from *The Gadfly*, April 20, 1984

As Chymes had predicted, Jack's suitability to carry on the Humpty investigation was the top story on the radio as Mary drove him home. Friedland had done his work well. Questions of Jack's "competence" and "reliability" were foremost in the report, and they even had a short interview with Chymes himself, who graciously said that he had "every confidence in DI Spratt" but would be more than happy to "offer my own assistance if requested." There was a reporter on his doorstep wanting Jack to confirm for *The Toad* that he was a "stubborn fool with a poor hold on reality." Jack ignored him and went inside.

Madeleine rushed up to give him a hug and said, "I heard all that crap on the radio, sweets. Chymes, was it?"

"In one," he replied. "The bastard is using every trick in the book to poach the investigation. I didn't think even *he* would stoop as low as this. I just wonder what he's going to try next."

"You mean he can do more?"

"He's Guild, darling. Those guys are capable of almost anything."

"What about Humpty? Figured out who did him in?"

"Not even close. I'm not so sure anymore that Grundy had him killed — and

Spongg had more to lose than gain by Humpty's death."

"So who does that leave?"

Jack sighed. "An ex-girlfriend named Bessie Brooks."

"Well," she said, "if it helps putting it all into some perspective, Stevie's got a new tooth."

"Top or bottom?"

"Top."

"Thanks," he said, and held her tight.

"Are we interrupting anything?" said Pandora, who had just walked in the front door with Prometheus.

"No," said Jack as Madeleine returned to the kitchen. "Where . . . where have you been?"

"To the flicks," replied Pandora. "They've got a Lola Vavoom retrospective at the Coliseum. We saw a Lola triple bill: *My Sister Used to Keep Geese*, *The Streets of Wooton Bassett* and *The Eyre Affair*. Prometheus and I are big fans of Lola's."

Prometheus nodded agreement, and they walked into the living room.

Jack watched them go and then ran into the kitchen.

"Madeleine!" he breathed. "Pandora and Prometheus have just been to the cinema — *together!*"

She didn't look up from the photo magazine she was reading. "So? She's twenty — she can go to the pictures with whoever she wants."

"She's *almost* twenty, yes — but he's older than her!"

"You're eight years older than me. What's the big deal? Maybe she prefers older men."

"Four thousand years older?"

"If you could hear yourself! He barely looks over thirty, and he's really nice — and think how it will improve her Greek."

"That's not the point!" he muttered, glancing out through the open kitchen door to make sure they weren't listening. "He's the *lodger.* I can't have my daughter . . . you know, with him . . . sort of Titan, immortal . . . *thing.*"

Madeleine laughed, and he stared at her.

"What's so funny?"

"You. You're funny. Daughters grow up. They don't stay all hair band, My Little Pony and 'Wheels on the bus go round and round' forever, you know."

"I know," he said as he calmed down a bit. "I'm a father. I worry about my daughter. That's what fathers do."

"Well, don't make a fool of yourself."

"I won't. I'll be very open-minded. But

they're not sitting together at dinner so they can hold hands under the table or anything."

"Put them opposite each other, then."

"So they can play footsy-footsy? I think *not,* thank you very much."

Ben walked in reading a copy of *Conspiracy Theorist.*

"Hi, Dad."

"Hi, Ben," Jack replied, still looking out the kitchen door, where he could see Pandora laughing at something Prometheus had said. "How's it going?"

"Welsh cattle mutilations are at an all-time high," he muttered without looking up, "but ball-lightning incidents have dropped. Alien abductions hold pretty steady — although the aliens deny they have anything to do with them."

"I can't imagine Constable Ashley kidnapping *anyone,*" said Jack thoughtfully.

"You have an alien working for you?" asked Ben incredulously, then added with annoyance, "Why didn't you tell me?"

Jack shrugged. "I didn't think it was important."

"Tsk!" said Ben. "Grown-ups."

"Can I help?" asked Prometheus, who had just walked in.

"Ah. Yes . . . you could lay the table. I

thought I'd put you at *that* end and Pandora at *this* end —"

"Phone," said Prometheus, a moment before it rang.

"How do you do that?"

"Do what?"

"That thing when you say something and it happens almost immediately?"

"Do I?" asked the Titan, his brow furrowing in bewilderment. "I don't think I do. It's your mother, by the way."

Jack picked up the phone. It *was* his mother.

"You've done it again!"

"I did?"

"Oh, never mind. Hi, Mum, how are things?"

Jack listened while his mother prattled on at some length about the beanstalk. It was now forty feet high, and she still had no plans to get rid of it. It seemed the British Horticultural Society was sending an expert to view it on the following day. Quite a few people had made special trips to see it, and she had entertained a score or two of them, offering tea and a scone with a guided tour at five pounds a head. She had made a tidy sum and wondered whether Prometheus could come around and help out the following day.

"Yes, okay," he said before Jack had asked him.

"So how's the extradition fight going?" asked Madeleine as soon as they were seated and they all had some dinner in front of them.

"Okay, I think," said Prometheus, pouring some gravy. "Zeus' lawyers are preparing for the case. They claim my punishment was entirely just under Mount Olympus law."

"Hardly fair, is it?" put in Pandora from the other end of the table. "Zeus *is* Mount Olympus law. He makes it up as he goes along."

"Well," continued the Titan resignedly, "they also claim that Heracles went beyond the boundaries of his jurisdiction in releasing me and that destroying the chain that bound me to the rock was technically criminal damage."

"Three thousand years chained to a rock with your liver being picked out every night," said Jack, shaking his head at the thought of the punishment. "Do you really think it was worth it?"

"Stealing fire and giving it to mankind? I still maintain it was the right thing to do. I also gave mankind the fear of death. Did you know that?"

They didn't. It wasn't generally known. It was a delicate subject that Heracles had thought was better kept quiet lest it turn mankind against his client.

"No, why did you do that?" asked Jack, pouring Prometheus and Madeleine some more wine.

"Yes, please," said Ben.

"One's your lot, sunshine."

"So you could value your own life," replied the Titan. "Before that you were under the gods' thumbs, doing their bidding without caring if you lived or died. When you could see that life was worth living by your fear of the unknown that was death, then you could really make things happen. I gave you lot the wisdom of architecture, astronomy, mathematics, medicine and metallurgy. Look at you now. The pyramids, nuclear fusion, CAT scanners, space travel, the Internet, computers, escalators, the La-Z-Boy recliner and cable television. I get to watch *65, Walrus Street* every night. If I miss an episode, it's repeated the following evening on Channel WXZ-23-Reading. You lot truly amaze me, and yes, I think it was all very worthwhile."

He emptied the glass and pointed at the bottle. "Do you mind?"

"No," said Jack, "help yourself."

"What about the side effects?" asked Pandora. "The wars, the deceit, the bloodshed, hate, murder, intolerance? Was all that worthwhile as well?"

Prometheus looked over at her. "Of course not. But you have to look at the big picture. I've seen the alternative. Eternal slavery under the gods. Believe me, this is a bed of roses in comparison. Think of this: If it weren't for greed, intolerance, hate, passion and murder, you would have no works of art, no great buildings, no medical science, no Mozart, no van Gogh, no Muppets and no Louis Armstrong. The civilization that devises the infrastructure to allow these wonderful things to be created is essentially a product of war — death and suffering — and commerce — deceit and inequality. Even your liberty to discuss the shortcomings of your own species has its foundations in blood and hardship."

"That's a depressing thought," murmured Madeleine.

The Titan shrugged again. "Not really. You should look at your own achievements more. When I created mankind, everyone thought of you as slaves, packhorses to do the dirty work. No one thought you'd amount to much. I and my fellow Titans and a few of the more sporting gods had a sweep going on how far you would develop. Clothes were even money, domesticating animals at three to one, grouping into civilization within a thousand years at seven to one, language with irregular verbs at thirty to one and nuclear fusion within four thousand years a thousand-to-one outsider — I won a tidy little profit, I can tell you."

Jack, always on the lookout for some misdemeanor, said, "But *you* gave mankind all that knowledge. Wouldn't that make the contest unfair?"

Prometheus appeared crestfallen and said, "It was only a bit of fun," then lapsed into silence, leaving them all trying to guess which was "only a bit of fun," the betting or the bequest of knowledge.

"Anyway," said Prometheus so sharply they all jumped, "the point is that you have exceeded all my expectations."

They ate for a moment in silence, with Jack's thoughts drifting to other things, such as the Guild, whether Chymes was done trying to poach the investigation and, more important, whether he should sleep on the landing outside Pandora's bedroom. Pandora, still unconvinced by Prometheus' fatalist stance, spoke again.

"Your viewpoint is depressingly callous. Are you saying that there's nothing we can do to improve ourselves?"

"Of course there is. There's lots you can do."

"Such as . . . ?"

"Try to be pleasant to one another, get plenty of fresh air, read a good book now and then, depose your government when it suspends the free press, try to use the mechanism of the state to adjudicate fairly, and employ diplomatic means wherever possible to avoid armed conflict."

"But there will still be wars!"

"Of course. There will *always* be wars. It has been in your nature ever since —"

Prometheus broke off suddenly, put up a hand to quiet everyone and sniffed the air. "Do you smell burning?"

They all inhaled. Prometheus was right — there was a faint smell of burning hair, or, as it turned out, *fur.*

"The cat!" yelled Madeleine. Ripvan had fallen asleep too close to the fire and had started to singe. Jack ran into the living room and snatched him out of harm's way, tossing the half-cooked mog from hand to hand like a hot potato. He placed her on a chair and fanned her with a magazine. Ripvan thought it was a game and purred loudly, completely unaware of the excitement she had caused. Jack left Ripvan on the chair, collected up the plates and stacked them by the sink. When he turned back, Pandora was sitting in his place — next to Prometheus.

"I think I was sit—"

"What about coffee?" said Madeleine. "We can have it in the living room."

She got up, and they all followed her, except Jack, who filled the kettle, and Ben, who went back to reading *Conspiracy Theorist*.

Prometheus sat next to Pandora on the sofa and stared into the fire with a look of deep distraction and loss.

"You were saying . . . ?" she prompted.

Prometheus sighed deeply. "It wasn't important."

But Pandora liked answers and didn't want to let it go. "You said it has been in our nature ever since . . . ?"

Prometheus looked up into her intelligent face, and his eyes glistened as a sad and distant memory surfaced in his consciousness.

"There was a woman once — *Careful, Jack!*" A second later there was a crash from the kitchen as Jack tripped over a stool. "I had put those parts of the human id that I thought undesirable into a large jar and sealed it tightly. I hoped to keep intolerance, sickness, insanity, vice and greed away from mankind. But" — he paused — "there was *this woman* who opened it against my wishes and let them out to taint the race I had created."

"Pandora?" asked Pandora, who knew a bit about her erstwhile namesake.

Prometheus flinched at the sound of her name. "Yes, *Pandora.* She was a woman of extraordinary beauty, the most rare and radiant maiden who ever walked upon this globe. Her skin was as soft as silk, and her eyes shone like emeralds. Her dark and flowing hair tossed joyfully in the wind as she ran, and her laughter was like cherubs singing in the morning breeze."

"Hmm," responded Pandora. "*I* heard she was a bit of a trollop."

"Oh, she was," replied Prometheus hurriedly. "She was as vain, foolish, mischievous and idle as she was beautiful."

"And yet you fell in love with her?"

Prometheus nodded. "I loved her, and she betrayed me. I had no idea she was sent by Zeus to cause trouble to the human race. Alas, I was wrong. The ills were let out of my jar, and you can see the result."

"But hope remained," said Pandora, attempting to raise the spirits of Prometheus, who seemed to have lapsed into depression.

"*Delusive* hope," corrected Prometheus quietly. "I had placed it there as a sort of insurance policy. Delusive hope, by its lies, dissuades mankind from mass suicide."

"And where is she now?"

"I have no idea. After I was sentenced, my brother — fool that he was — married her to avoid a similar fate."

"And you never saw them again?"

"They kept in contact for a bit, but you know how it is — just cards on my birthday for the first three hundred years and then nothing at all. The last I heard of them was in 1268, when Epimetheus was working as a cobbler and Pandora made a living as a translator. I have tried to find them since my release, but to no avail. I have difficulty traveling without a passport."

"And the jar?" inquired Pandora, still curious.

He shrugged. "It's invulnerable to any form of destructive power, so it must still be somewhere. But where that might be, I have no idea."

"Coffee!" announced Jack, wondering whether sitting between Pandora and

Prometheus wasn't taking it too far. It was, so he sat with Madeleine. They all talked animatedly with Prometheus into the night. Pandora told him about studying for her degree in astrophysics; Prometheus mentioned that he thought Robert Oppenheimer had done the same as he — stolen fire from the gods and given it to mankind. The difference between him and Oppenheimer, he added dryly, was that Oppenheimer was never punished. Pandora told him about Big Bang theory, and he told her that Zeus had created the constellations; it was a lively argument and they had just got around to discussing human self-determination when Madeleine announced that she was going to bed and pulled on her husband's hand to make him join her.

"I'll stay for a little longer," said Jack.

"It's perfectly okay, Jack," said Prometheus. "I'm not going to sleep with your daughter."

His directness caught Jack on the hop, and he laughed at his own stupidity.

"Terrific!" he said at last. "I'm going to bed."

Pandora and Prometheus continued talking as the fire gradually burnt itself down. Prometheus pointed out the flaws in evolutionary theory, such as how a bird could possibly have evolved wings without having useless appendages for thousands of years that would have hindered its survival. Pandora countered by saying that rule number one of the cosmos was that unlikely things do happen. Indeed, given the time scale involved and the size of the universe, unlikely things, paradoxically enough, become quite commonplace.

"What do you think?" asked Jack as he took off his shirt in the bedroom.

"About what?"

"Pandora and Prometheus."

"Science meets mythology. It'll be interesting to see what conclusions they draw before the night is out. I'll be fascinated to hear what Prometheus has to say about the fossil record."

"Hmm," said Jack as he climbed into his pajamas and pushed the inert form of Ripvan off his side of the bed. The cat fell to the floor with a thump — and without waking.

Jack slept well that night, curled up with Madeleine like two spoons in a drawer. Below them in the living room, Prometheus and Pandora talked into the small hours, while barely a mile away, in Granny

Spratt's garden, the beanstalk creaked and groaned to itself as it grew, like a bamboo plantation in the tropics.

32. Giorgio Porgia

CRIME BOSS TO RUN PRISON

History was made last week when Giorgio Porgia, Reading's onetime crime boss and self-proclaimed "menace to society," was unanimously elected governor of Reading Gaol. The surprise result followed an equal-opportunities advertisement for a replacement governor to which Mr. Porgia applied. Septuagenarian former blowtorch-wielding sadist Giorgio Porgia was found to be the most qualified to run the prison as he had himself spent much time within such institutions and has an almost unparalleled understanding of the irredeemable criminal mind — his own. The Home Secretary happily endorsed his appointment, and "Governor" Porgia will begin work in March.
— From *The Owl*, January 29, 1999

If the Sacred Gonga hadn't been due for dedication by the Jellyman the following day, the papers would have had nothing else but the Humpty Dumpty case. As it was, they were half Humpty, half Jellyman. Even so, the Humpty part of it wasn't good, and they all followed pretty much the same line: that Jack was an imbecile who was too proud to ask for help from one of the most eminent and upright pillars of the detecting community. Jack took the papers from the breakfast table and tossed them in the bin, then switched off the radio.

"The crowd is gathering," said Madeleine as she looked out the window at the pressmen and TV news crews waiting to get a reaction. "I'm going to take the children to see the Jellyman," she added. "Do you think you'll be able to join us?"

"I'm nursemaiding the Sacred Gonga," replied Jack sullenly. "Sorry."

Stevie screamed "Da-woo!" enthusiastically and hurled his spoon on the floor because he *could.* Mary arrived at eight-thirty on the dot and ignored the journalists as she pushed past them. She was introduced to the family and said her respectful hellos before they both took a deep breath and stepped outside to meet the press.

They were met by the glare of video camera lights and the rapid-fire questions of the journalists.

"When can we expect you to relinquish the case to DCI Chymes?"

"Are you competent to run this investigation?"

"Doesn't Humpty deserve more?"

"Will you plead on bended knee for Chymes's help?"

"Do you really think that tie suits that jacket?"

"Will you resign from the force?"

"How many more people have to die before you ask for help?"

"What *is* your beef with tall people?"

"Is that really your Allegro?"

Jack and Mary pushed their way through the throng, got into Jack's car and drove off with the newsmen still shouting questions.

"Expect more at the station," said Jack, winding down the window as the windscreen began to mist up, then winding it shut again, as he was being rained on. He pulled out something he was sitting on. It was a man's cap. "Whose is this?"

"That?" said Mary awkwardly, "Oh, that's . . . that's . . . Arnold's hat."

Jack laughed. "You're taking him out for the evening in my fine automobile? I thought you were trying to dump him?"

"I told him the Allegro was mine," confessed Mary. "I thought it might put him off for good."

"And did it?"

"No. He has an Austin Maxi — and he asked me if I'd checked the torque settings on the rear wheels recently."

They entered the one-way system in Reading with caution, for even frequent and experienced users of it had been known to become trapped for hours, sometimes days. It was *not* unique in that it took you where you didn't want to go before it took you to where you did, no; what made Reading's system special was that it always spat you out where you didn't want to go no matter how hard you tried to get to where you did. It was the established technique of heading for where you didn't want to go that allowed you to end up, quite by accident, in the area where you did. And it was in this manner that they arrived at Reading Gaol.

Giorgio Porgia's womanizing days were over. He was now seventy-five and in poor physical health. The days when women would swoon at his charms were long gone, the trail of irate husbands long since dried up. Giorgio Porgia had spent the last twenty years of his life in jail, a jail that would be his final resting place. As befits a man of his seniority within the underworld and the prison service, his apartments were large, well appointed and of the highest security. It wouldn't be right and proper to have the governor of the jail in with the other convicts, nor would it be safe to have someone who once used a tire iron to enforce discipline kept under anything but the strictest security. Thus it was that Mary and Jack were handed over by a prison officer at the outside of Governor Porgia's secure office to a disreputable character named Aardvark within it.

"They call me Aardvark," said the shambling, bony character as he led them down the corridor, " 'cause I'm Mr. Porgia's number one. I'm also doing twelve to sixteen for armed robbery, so just watch it."

Aardvark led them into a good-size room that had bars on the window and was tastefully furnished with antiques. A large, high-backed leather armchair faced the open fire away from them. A wrinkled index finger tapped time on the chair's arm to an aria from *Madame Butterfly*.

Aardvark signaled for them to halt, then whispered to the unseen figure in the chair. Jack nudged Mary and pointed to a framed photograph of Porgia and Friedland. There was another figure on the other side of Giorgio, but he had been cropped out.

"You?" mouthed Mary, and Jack nodded.

"You will have to excuse Mr. Porgia," announced Aardvark, "but he speaks only in the language of his heart."

"And what language is that?" asked Jack, hoping that Mary could understand Italian.

"English," replied Aardvark. "He is the son of the Bracknell Porgias. You understand what *that* means."

"Of course," said Jack, without understanding what it meant — or particularly caring.

They walked around the front of the chair to find a decrepit old man sitting with a traveling rug over his knees. He smiled benignly at them in turn, running his eyes up and down Mary with the memory of his amorous youth passing fleetingly in front of him. All those women, all that *kissing.*

"Please," he asked in an affected Italian accent, "please sit down."

They sat on two antique chairs that Aardvark had put out for them.

"Mr. Spratt," he said fondly, "we meet again. How long has it been?"

"Twenty years."

"It seems like only eighteen. How is Mr. Chymes these days?"

"The same, sir."

"He has gone on to great things. I follow his exploits in *Amazing Crime Stories* avidly. Isn't that so, Aardvark?"

"Avidly, sir, yes," replied Aardvark, rubbing his hands.

"And you?" asked Porgia. "You are still at the NCD?"

Jack rankled visibly. "There is still work to be done, sir. That's why I'm here. I want to talk to you about an MO you once used."

Porgia's eyes flashed dangerously. "You are here to talk about my days as a criminal?" he asked sharply.

"Yes, sir."

"Then I cannot, I *will* not, help you. I don't speak about my past. If you wish to discourse on the functioning of this prison of which I am the governor, I will be happy to . . . talk . . . to you. . . ."

His voice trailed off as he suddenly seemed to become more interested in Mary. She glanced nervously at Jack. Mr. Porgia put on his spectacles with shaking hands, and a smile of recognition broke out on his lined features.

"Vouchsafe, divine perfection of a woman," he began in a soft voice that was almost a whisper, *"of these supposed evils, to give me leave, by circumstance,*

but to acquit myself. . . . I did not kill your husband."

"Why, then he is alive!" replied Mary before Jack could ask what was going on. *"O! He was gentle, mild and virtuous!"*

"The fitter for the King of heaven, that hath him, . . ." continued Giorgio grimly, *"for he was fitter for that place than earth."*

"And thou unfit for any place but hell!" replied Mary with vehemence.

Giorgio Porgia smiled at Mary, his eyes moistening. "It's Mary Mary, isn't it?"

"It is, sir."

"I saw you at Basingstoke in *Richard III.* It was the only time I have been out since my incarceration began. The Governor — myself — gave me a special pass to go and see you. You were wonderful, dazzling, inspired!"

Mary blushed deeply, and Jack sighed inwardly.

"Your retirement from the stage was a great loss, Mary."

"I didn't have time for both, sir."

"If ever you return to the stage, please let me know. You will, I trust, take tea?"

"No thank you, Mr. Porgia, but we would like to ask you some questions."

"Of course! Are you sure you wouldn't

like some tea? Mr. Aardvark makes a very good cup."

"Thank you, no."

"A slice of Battenberg, perhaps?"

"We're fine."

"Ah, well," said Giorgio happily, "how can I help?"

His manner had warmed since he had recognized Mary. They could have asked him the color of his socks and he would have answered without a murmur.

"We're investigating the murder of Humpty Dumpty," said Mary.

The old man dropped his eyes to the floor and shook his head sadly. "A tragedy, Miss Mary. I heard about it on the wireless. What has this got to do with me?"

"I was wondering how far your influence extended, Mr. Porgia," added Jack, trying to regain the upper hand after being so badly upstaged by Mary.

Porgia leaned forwards and raised an eyebrow. "What are you saying, Mr. Spratt?"

Jack leaned forwards as well. "A man was found dead yesterday. We think he was killed because he knew who murdered Humpty."

"And you think I might have had something to do with it?"

Jack stared into Giorgio's eyes, trying to divine a spark of guilt. He might as well have stared out the window at the clouds and sheep, for the old man gave nothing away.

"He had his tongue split and fed in small pieces to the dogs. Sound familiar?"

Porgia sucked his teeth for a moment. "We used to do that to people who told tales, yes. Liars had their trousers set on fire, and impertinence was punished by breaking people's legs with sticks and stones. I freely admit what I was, Mr. Spratt, and I shall die in prison as my punishment. I am here for the many hideous crimes I have committed in my futile life, and I am truly penitent for my sins. But I am happy also that I was able to see my parents buried in a decent plot and my children go to university. For that I am not ashamed. I have learnt the virtue of honor in my short tenure on this earth, Inspector, and others have learnt what it means to betray that honor. I've also learnt a bit about home improvements. I tell you now, upon the word of a criminal who will pay his debt with the remainder of his worthless life, I had nothing whatever to do with this murder."

He fixed Jack with a gaze that reinforced his conviction.

"Would anyone want to frame you?" Jack asked.

Giorgio laughed uneasily and started to cough. Aardvark patted him gently on his back with the kind of care that a mother might administer to her child.

"For what?" he continued once the coughing fit had abated. "How can I usefully be punished?"

Jack had to agree that he had a point.

"I think," continued Giorgio, "that someone is trying to throw you off the scent." He sighed unhappily. "I come from a different world, Mr. Spratt, a world swept away by the unsophisticated modes of death meted out by street gangs, pimps, muggers and drug dealers. No one kills anyone with any style anymore. The kids I see now just shoot each other. Setting one's opponents' feet in a bath of cement and then throwing them in the Thames is considered *very* old hat these days. We used to encase people alive in motorway supports. I'm amazed," he added nostalgically, "that the elevated sections of Junction 10 even stay up. They tell me I'm just a sad old romantic. The kids today have no respect for tradition. No dash, no style, no *elegance*."

His eyes glistened. "Those were the

days. Yes indeed, those were the days."

"Thank you, Mr. Porgia," said Jack, thinking it was time to leave. "You've been most helpful."

"I hope you find Humpty's killer," said Giorgio thoughtfully. "I liked the egg a great deal, despite the fact that I am here because of him."

Jack started in surprise. "What do you mean?"

The old man smiled and dabbed at a trickle of saliva that had inadvertently run from the side of his mouth. "You knew Humpty did three years for laundering money for me?" he asked.

Jack nodded.

"When he was working for me, he was also collecting information to bring me down. He thought that his own loss of liberty was a small price to pay for the removal of my crime syndicate. I was completely taken in. I even bought him an apartment in Spongg Villas for not talking. It was he who sent the dossier to you and Mr. Chymes."

He leaned forwards and smiled, holding a bony finger in the air.

"Now, that, Inspector, was *style*. I didn't find out for ten years. An ex-cop inside told me. I could have had him killed, but I thought on reflection the world was a better place with Humpty still in it. He did much good work, I understand."

"It depends on your viewpoint, Mr. Porgia."

The old man wheezed a sad laugh and took a sip of the Guinness that Aardvark had brought for him.

"It does indeed," he replied wearily, "it does indeed."

"One other point, Mr. Porgia," said Jack. "There was a member of the Russian mafia who Chymes hunted down after the Andersen's Wood murder. His name was Max Zotkin."

The Governor looked at him intently. "I know of this man," he said slowly. "What about him?"

"Is he here?"

Porgia took a deep breath and stared at Jack for a moment. "Mr. Zotkin's residency at Reading Gaol is potentially a matter of grave importance. What will you do with this information, Inspector?"

"Nothing unless pushed, sir. Call it an insurance policy."

"You are the first person to ask, and while understanding of the reason for the subterfuge, I am unable to lie to you: There is no one of that name resident at this prison, nor has there ever been. Use the information wisely. Good-bye, Inspector. You will excuse me if I don't get up."

He looked fondly at Mary.

"Mary, *bid me farewell.*"

" *'Tis more than you deserve,*" replied Mary; *"but since you teach me how to flatter you, imagine that I have said farewell already.*"

Giorgio smiled and mouthed a silent "Adieu!"

Jack drove away from the prison deep in thought. If someone wanted to make it look as though Winkie had been killed with a Porgia MO, then it stood to reason that it was to throw them off the scent. And if that was the case, then they were clearly looking in the right direction.

Mary was thinking of other things. "Are you going to tell me where Max Zotkin might be if he's not in prison?"

"No," replied Jack thoughtfully, "and with a bit of luck, I intend to keep it that way."

Mary's phone rang, and she flipped it open, listened to something Baker had to say and then closed it again.

"News?"

"You could say that. It's Bessie Brooks. She was nabbed trying to run away from a hotel in Swindon without paying. They're going to transfer her to Reading Central at midday."

33. What Bessie Brooks Had to Say for Herself

BEAR TO SHIT IN WOODS — OFFICIAL

Following yesterday's passing of the Ursine Suitable Accommodation Bill, bears will no longer have to live in urban housing allocated to them by the authorities. The new deal was greeted with open paws among Reading's bear population. "Really, we're delighted," declared married father of one Mr. Gus Bruin. "No more city for us — we're off to the forest!" Parcels of land will be made available in Andersen's Wood, where humanlike bear family units will be able to live in small cottages, take long walks and eat porridge.

— Article in *The Gadfly*,
September 8, 1989

Jack pressed the two "record" buttons simultaneously.

"This is a taped interview. Miss Bessie Brooks is being interviewed, and the time

430

is twelve-twenty p.m. Detective Inspector Jack Spratt is conducting the interview. Also present are DS Mary Mary, Constable Kandlestyk-Maeker and Miss Brooks's solicitor, Seymour Weevil."

He looked across at Bessie. She was staring at the table and appeared sullen.

Bessie was in her early twenties and an attractive brunette who stood at least six foot one. She had dark brown eyes that were red with tears, and her expensive outfit was rumpled and dirty. She did not lift her head to look at any of them, and a packet of cigarettes that Jack had placed on the table remained untouched, even though they could see from the faint stain on her fingers that she was a smoker.

Seymour Weevil, a short man with his hair combed carefully back from his forehead, watched the proceedings impassively from within a suit that should have been condemned as an affront to human decency long ago.

"Miss Brooks, you have been brought in for questioning regarding the murder of one Humperdinck Aloysius Dumpty. You do not have to say anything. But it may harm your defense if you do not mention when questioned something which you later rely on in court. Anything you do say may be given in evidence. Do you under-stand?"

Bessie Brooks nodded imperceptibly.

"Miss Brooks —"

But Seymour Weevil interrupted him. "My client is very willing to answer your questions but feels that she has been treated like a criminal. She also objects to having her apartment searched. She wishes it to be known that she loved Mr. Dumpty deeply and has no idea who killed him."

Jack ignored Weevil and continued. "Can you tell me your whereabouts on the night of the nineteenth and the morning of the twentieth of this month?"

Bessie didn't answer. Seymour Weevil gave her his handkerchief — a cheap one for her to keep, Jack noted — and said kindly, "It would help the police if you spoke to them, but you have the right to remain silent. Do you wish to exercise that right?"

She lifted her head and stared at Jack and Mary in turn. Her mascara had run badly, and her eyes brimmed with tears. "Do you think he suffered?" she asked in a quiet voice.

"We don't think so," replied Mary without any emotion.

Jack placed the picture of her with

Humpty on the table. It was in a plastic bag. She paused and then picked it up.

"Where did you get this?"

"It was on Mr. Dumpty's desk."

A smile crossed her face momentarily as she realized that he must have liked her enough to have her photo up in his office. She touched Humpty's features on the print with a fingertip and spoke again, yet this time her voice had found a new confidence.

"Vienna, June last year," she sighed wistfully. "Hump was on a business trip selling a thousand tons of Wozbekistanian industrial-strength instant soup powder. He asked me if I wanted to come along."

She cocked her head to one side as she filled herself with fond memories of the trip.

"On the night this photo was taken, we went to see *Madame Butterfly*. In the first act, the tenor singing Lieutenant Pinkerton's part was taken ill and the understudy was drunk. The management came out and apologized profusely and explained that they were unable to continue the performance. To my surprise Hump stood up and sang, without music, the first six lines of Pinkerton's part. He was ushered onto the stage, and ten minutes later the performance continued with Hump as the Lieutenant. I was placed in the royal box with the compliments of the management, and Hump received eight curtain calls. It was a night that I shall never forget." She smiled and shook her head sadly. "Does my story surprise you?"

"Mr. Dumpty ceased to surprise me long ago, Miss Brooks," replied Jack. "Why did you leave town?"

The smile dried on her lips, and she looked down at the photo again.

"I loved him, Inspector, more than any woman ever loved an egg." She paused for a moment. "I should never have become emotionally attached to him, but it was hard not to. Did you ever meet him, Inspector?"

"Only once, a long time ago."

"He was a remarkable man," she said slowly, "quite remarkable. His crimes never benefited himself."

"Did he tell you of his plans?"

"No. He had several schemes in place, but I never knew what they were. On the night of the charity benefit, he told me he had remarried. He asked me if I wanted to carry on our relationship, and I am afraid to say that I was less than polite. We argued. How dare he marry another when we had been together for almost three months!"

"Is that why you killed him, Miss Brooks?"

She collapsed into a choking fit of sobs. Seymour moved farther away, and Jack and Mary exchanged looks. Mary tried to comfort her.

"It's okay, Miss Brooks, take your time."

They waited for a couple of minutes for her to compose herself, then sent out for a cup of tea, which arrived speedily.

"I couldn't live without him, and I couldn't bear the thought of another woman in his arms, caressing his smooth white shell —" She closed her eyes and began to cry.

"Let's just go over the details together," said Jack. "Where did you get the gun?"

"Gun?" she echoed with a puzzled expression.

"Yes, where did you get it?"

She looked at Seymour, who raised his eyebrows and said almost mechanically, "You don't have to answer any questions, Miss Brooks."

"I didn't use a gun."

"No?" asked Jack, beginning to have a nasty feeling. "Then what *did* you use?"

"Three tablets of Dizuppradol. I'm a veterinarian's assistant."

"His *coffee?*" asked Mary.

Miss Brooks nodded her head sadly.

"Damn!" said Jack as they walked along the corridor back to the NCD office.

"Is that attempted murder?" asked Mary, unsure of whether a crime had been committed. "I mean, he didn't even touch his coffee."

"*Technically* it is, but I can't see the prosecutors bothering, if past NCD experience is anything to go by."

Miss Brooks had perked up when they told her she hadn't killed Humpty after all, although surprisingly she knew as little about him as anyone else. When he stayed over, it was always at her flat, which had already been searched and revealed precisely nothing.

It was an anticlimactic ending to what Jack had hoped would be a good line of inquiry. But there was one point that Bessie had told them that *was* of interest: Humpty had remarried. There hadn't been time for the records to get into the system at the national registry, so Ashley and Gretel were ringing around locally to try to find out whom he had married, and where.

"Reject one mystery woman from the inquiry and another pops up in her place," announced Jack. "Humpty has quite a following. How many of his ex-lovers have come forward to offer us their help?"

"One hundred and ninety-two," replied Baker. "It's going to take us weeks to sift through them all!"

"We don't have weeks."

Shenstone put his head around the door. "Hello, Jack!" he said cheerfully. "Want to hear the results of the vacuumings I took from the carpet at Grimm's Road?"

"Sure."

"In a word, it's shit."

"The case? I don't need you to tell me that."

"No, the vacuumings. It's bird shit."

"Bird shit?"

"Shit of birds, sir."

"I know what bird shit is, Bob, but what's it doing at Grimm's Road?"

"I don't know. It had been trodden into the carpet."

"Recent?"

"Some recent, some old. The recent stuff, very recent — exited the back end of a bird less than a week ago."

"That recent, huh?"

Jack took the report and read it aloud carefully. " 'Noted on the carpet were traces of an animal excrement that closely resembled that from aquatic birds such as coots, ducks, geese, etc. . . .' "

He thanked Shenstone, who crept out silently. Jack wrote "Bird shit?" on the board and underlined it. He then added "Gold" and "Spongg shares" and "Willie Winkie." He sat in his chair and stared at the whiteboard. The case was *still* intractable. What in hell's name had Humpty been up to?

"Detective Inspector Spratt?" came an unfamiliar voice from the door. They all turned to find Briggs with a small and weaselly-looking officer.

"You know I am."

"My name is DCI Bestbeloved — IPCC. We need to talk."

The Independent Police Complaints Commission was the police who policed the police. They were the ones who descended from a great height on any officer even *suspected* of wrongdoing.

"Good afternoon, sir," said Jack, thinking perhaps that he would have to give evidence against another officer or something. "How can I help?"

"By cooperating with the IPCC," put in Briggs with a sigh.

"About what? You said I had until Saturday to finger Humpty's killer!"

"It's nothing to do with Mr. Dumpty," said DCI Bestbeloved in a coldly business-like manner. "It's about the three pigs. They are pursuing a case for harassment, mental cruelty and malicious prosecution."

34. Investigated

PIGGY IN ROAST BEEF SHOCK

A piggy was caught eating roast beef yesterday, in direct contravention of rules governing the use of animal-based products' being included in animal feed. The piggy, one of a litter of five, was in isolation yesterday as officers from DEFRA tried to trace the other members of his family. A spokesman for the agency had this to say: "Fortunately for us, one of the little piggies stayed at home, and another, when offered the roast beef, refused. A fourth went 'wee wee wee' all the way home and is now also in quarantine. We are still trying to trace the first little piggy, who, it seems, went to market. Until he is caught, we have instructed the withdrawal of all pork-related foodstuffs from shops and have decided to cull everything in sight, whether porcine or not, just to be sure."
— Extract from *The Gadfly*, March 9, 2001

"Chymes put you up to this, didn't he?" demanded Jack as he sat on a hard plastic chair in one of the interview rooms.

"No one puts us up to anything," replied Bestbeloved stonily. "We will be conducting a full inquiry in due course. You do not have to say anything. But it may harm your defense —"

"I know the score," interrupted Jack. "Can we get on with it? I have an investigation to get back to."

"I think it would be best if you were just to answer the questions," said Bestbeloved, "and don't think you'll be getting back to work for a while."

"Sir?" said Jack, appealing to Briggs, who was standing at the door.

Briggs shrugged. It was out of his hands.

"If you would like legal representation or someone from the Police Federation present," went on Bestbeloved, "then we are very happy for that to be arranged — but would insist that you remain suspended on full pay until such time as that can be finalized."

"I waive all rights to representation," replied Jack steadily.

"Will you state your name for the benefit of the record?"

"Detective Inspector John Reginald Spratt, Nursery Crime Division, Oxford and Berkshire Constabulary, Officer Number 8216."

"And you were the investigating officer in charge of Case 722/B, Possible unlawful killing of Theophilus Bartholomew Wolff aka 'Big Bad'?"

"I was."

Bestbeloved laid several sheets of paper on the table in front of him. They were custody and arrest records. "Is this your signature?"

"Yes."

"Then perhaps you will tell me why Little Pigs A, B and C were kept in cells that were scrupulously clean and tidy and were offered tea, coffee and biscuits instead of kitchen scraps and puddle water, as was their right?"

"Sorry?"

Bestbeloved laid another sheet of paper on the table. It was a letter from Nigel Grubbit, the pigs' lawyer, and it bullet-pointed the complaints against Jack.

"They never indicated to me they had special needs," replied Jack, looking down the list of grievances with a growing sense of unease. If he had won the case, no one would have cared less, but the pigs were eager for revenge — and cash, of course.

"It's not their responsibility to ask for it," said Bestbeloved. "They also maintain that you interviewed them while eating a *bacon* sandwich. Why would you do something like that?"

Jack shrugged. "Probably because the canteen was out of rolls."

Bestbeloved glared at him. "Do you find this whole interview funny, Spratt?" He tapped the pigs' list of grievances. "Any three out of these six points would be enough to finish you, Spratt — and cost the Reading Police Department dear. Look at this: 'DI Spratt and his assistant, PC Ashley, made comments about crackling and applesauce that were intentionally made to be overheard by Little Pig C.' If this is true, Spratt, it constitutes a real physical threat to the well-being of the prisoners under your responsibility and might in fact constitute torture. Grubbit is quoting the Animal (anthropomorphic) Equality Bill of 1996 to us, and we think they have a good case."

Jack sighed. He might be cleared by a tribunal in six months' time, but that was six months too late. He needed to be free to continue the investigation *this afternoon.* The thing was, Jack knew that the pigs could have been sent packing if the IPCC had so wished, but this wasn't about justice for three murderous porkers. It wasn't just about getting Jack suspended and Chymes onto the Humpty case. No, this was about what happens to people who defy Chymes and the Guild. Jack's demise would serve as a warning to anyone else daft or stubborn enough to make a stand.

He turned and looked at the one-way mirror in the interview room. Chymes would be behind it, watching, gloating.

"What do you want, Bestbeloved?" demanded Jack.

"I want all officers to uphold the letter of the law when interrogating prisoners," he replied. "An officer who has gone astray is a stain upon the force and every honest officer in it."

"Uphold the letter of the law?"

"Yes."

"And the highest levels of probity when conducting investigations?"

"Of course."

"*All* officers?"

Jack asked the question so pointedly that Briggs glanced sideways towards the one-way mirror. Jack was right. Chymes *was* in there.

"Then I've got something to say, and I think it would be better for everyone if this tape recorder were *off.*"

He directed the comment towards the

mirror. There was no reaction, so he simply said, "It's about a murder in Andersen's Wood. It's about Max Zotkin."

It worked. Within a few seconds, the door had opened and Chymes strode in with a look of thunder on his face.

DCI Bestbeloved, seeing that things were suddenly becoming a great deal more complicated, hastily announced the suspension of the interview and switched off the tape recorder. He had been led to believe that Jack would be a "lamb to the slaughter" and bow to the inevitable — the idea of Chymes's intervening was not part of the plan. Still, spared the burden of initiative by the appearance of such an eminent officer, he sat back to see how things would turn out.

"Do you see how easily I can bury you?" yelled Chymes. "If it's not this way, it's another. I'm through pussyfooting around — relinquish your case to me now and you may get to keep your pension."

There was a pause as they stared at each other. Chymes was a powerful man, and a bully. Jack had been cowed by him many times, but he'd had enough.

"You couldn't get this case by trying to turn my own sergeant against me," he began in a low voice, choosing his words carefully. "You couldn't get it by with-holding pertinent evidence. You couldn't get it by turning the press against me. And you won't get it by invoking the IPCC."

"It's too late for deals," sneered Chymes. "You're finished."

"I don't *think* so," replied Jack, trying to keep the dread in the pit of his stomach under control. He had once had to stand up to the school bully, and this felt exactly the same. He opened the buff envelope that Skinner had given Mary and placed the pictures on the table.

Chymes went silent.

"These are the crime scene photographs of the Andersen's Wood murders," explained Jack for the benefit of Bestbeloved and Briggs. "They clearly show that the cartridges used were Eley."

He produced the evidence bag that contained the spent cartridges from his brief-case. "These are the ones Chymes sent down to me."

It was clear to everyone in the room they were Xpress.

"Why would Chymes want to prove that the Marchetti shotgun I found at Humpty's wasn't the same one used on the woodcutter and his wife? Because I might have shown up a big hole in his investigation? That it wasn't the Russian mafia at all? That Chymes concocted *every single aspect of the investigation* because he needed a filler for the 2003 Christmas bumper edition of *Amazing Crime Stories*?"

There was a deathly hush. This was heresy of the highest order. The veins in Chymes's temples throbbed, and Briggs and Bestbeloved looked nervously at each other. If Jack could prove it, this was explosive stuff and heads would roll. A lot of them.

Chymes broke the tension by laughing.

"A ludicrous suggestion, Spratt. This is the sort of stuff that conspiracy theories are made of. There has clearly been an error in the continuity of evidence procedure. It is unfortunate but not irredeemable. I will hunt down the culprit and make sure he is suitably admonished."

"You can do all that if you want," said Jack, growing more confident by the second, "but it would be easier just to interview Max Zotkin, the surviving member of the Russian mafia who so eloquently gave evidence at his own trial supporting your every point. Only once he was sent down for ten years, he vanished from view. Who was he? *An actor?*"

There was silence.

"I don't want to bring you down or tarnish the public's perception of the Guild," said Jack slowly. "I just want to find Humpty's murderer without let or hindrance."

Chymes thought hard for a moment and then said, "That's it. He was part of a repatriation deal whereby UK convicts in Russian jails are swapped —"

"You *can't* keep on making it all up," interrupted Jack, "but if you insist, I'll go head-to-head with you and ask embarrassing questions. How many other investigations did you 'embellish' in order to boost your *Amazing Crime* circulation figures?"

There was a pause while Chymes thought about this. Briggs exchanged nervous glances with Bestbeloved. They'd never seen Chymes bested, and to them — although they would never admit it — it was a not-unpleasant spectacle. The great man made to eat humble pie.

"Very well," said Chymes at length, "I withdraw all interest in the Humpty investigation."

"And I want your vote if I ever make it to a Guild final application."

"I can do that," said Friedland grudgingly. He was only one of five on the board, so it wasn't a huge concession.

"And I want you to resign from the force."

Chymes laughed, and Jack realized he'd taken it a step too far. Friedland, for all his faults, was almost untouchable. The Jellyman *himself* had requested him to look after his personal security for his visit on Saturday. The man was a legend. A flawed one, but a legend. And they don't tumble that easily.

Chymes glared at Jack, then leaned closer. "We aren't finished yet, Spratt."

And he left the room. They heard him thump the door farther on down the corridor and a cry as he took out his rage on a subordinate.

"Are we done?" asked Jack.

Briggs and Bestbeloved exchanged another nervous glance. If Jack was capable of talking like that to Chymes, he was capable of anything.

"I will return when I have conducted further investigations," announced Bestbeloved hurriedly, "and I may be some time."

He ejected both tapes, threw them in his bag and left without another word.

"Well, Jack," said Briggs when they were alone, "you really enjoyed that, didn't you?"

"Friedland's a jerk who's become obsessed with circulation figures."

"No," retorted Briggs, "Friedland's a

jerk with power and influence. I hope you know what you're doing. As far as he's concerned, I'm now in your camp."

"So?"

Briggs shrugged. "I just hoped he'd write me into his stories so I could do the rounds of the Friedland Chymes conventions. Watson did almost nothing else when Sherlock retired — made him a fortune. Still, I don't think there's much chance of that now."

Jack relaxed. He had every reason to dislike Briggs, but he didn't. He wasn't bad, just weak.

"If I ever make it to the Guild, *I'll* include you in my stories."

Briggs seemed to cheer up at this. He'd wanted to be like Friedland Chymes for years — yet now he was thinking he'd prefer to be like Spratt. A bit down at heel and almost invisible locked away at the NCD — but honest.

"If you do," said Briggs, a glint in his eye, "will I get to suspend you at least once in every adventure?"

"Of course."

"And should I change my name to Föngotskilérnie?"

Jack smiled and patted him on the shoulder. "Briggs will be fine."

35. Summing Up

STRAW-INTO-GOLD DEFENDANT NAMED

The jury was shocked into wakefulness on the eighth day of the Straw-into-Gold trial by the dramatic naming of the defendant yesterday. The previously unnamed illegal gold-spinner had been making a mockery of British justice by his insistence that the judge try to guess his name before he would agree to plea. After seven days and 8,632 guesses, the judge finally hit upon the correct name, whereupon *Rumplestiltskin* (this reporter can now faithfully record) flew into an inflamed passion, accused the judge of "listening down chimneys" and stamped his foot so hard it went through the floor. The defendant thus identified, the trial came to a speedy conclusion, and he was jailed for twenty years.

      — From *The Gadfly*, April 30, 1999

"What's your prose like, Mary?"

"Rusty — but not too bad."

"Good. There exists the faintest possibility that I might make it into the Guild. If I do, I want you as my Official Sidekick."

"I'm flattered of course, sir — but Chymes is on the selection committee. How would you get him to change his mind?"

"Need-to-know basis, Mary. What news?"

"Mrs. Singh sent up the initial autopsy report on Winkie."

Jack took it from her and read. There was nothing that had changed dramatically since her initial ideas the night before. One cut, very savage, leading to death from shock and loss of blood. The look on Winkie's face, partial rigor and the fact that he had urinated on himself might relate to his witnessing something terrifying.

"Terrifying?" queried Jack. "I suppose someone coming at you with a broadsword *would* be terrifying."

Jack handed the report back. It seemed unusual, but what in this inquiry wasn't?

"Okay, boys and girls," Jack announced to the NCD officers who had waited patiently and a little nervously for him to return from almost certain suspension at the hands of the IPCC, "it's the end of day four. The body count is rising, and we're no closer to finding out who killed Humpty. Here's the story so far: Mr. and

Mrs. Christian, the woodcutter and his wife, find a missing consignment of gold. Ashley, any luck on this?"

"Nothing recently stolen, sir — just the usual urban myths of missing Nazi bullion."

"Keep on it. Small-time criminal opportunist Tom Thomm murders them both with the Marchetti shotgun we find at Humpty's and steals the gold. He takes it to his old friend and mentor Humpty Dumpty, who starts to sell the gold to buy shares in a company that's rapidly going down the tube. All goes well until Humpty comes home to his flat six months later to find Tom Thomm shot dead in the shower. He correctly assumes it was his ex-wife, Laura, and the shots were meant for him, so he goes to earth. Where, we don't know."

"Why didn't he report it?" asked Otto.

"Probably because he's in over his head laundering money from the original theft. It would make him an accessory."

"Ah."

"He then buys shares in Spongg's with the laundered gold money, but not even Randolph Spongg has any idea how he could raise the share value — the company has been sliding downhill for years.

Humpty has a jealous mistress named Bessie Brooks, who tries unsuccessfully to kill him, and this afternoon we learn from her that he remarried sometime in the past two weeks."

He paused for a moment.

"His will had 'all to wife' written on it, so until Humpty's Spongg shares are worthless, she is a wealthy woman and a thirty-eight percent shareholder of Spongg's. On Sunday, Humpty breaks cover and is seen drunk at the Spongg Charity Benefit, offering to pledge fifty million to rebuild the woefully outdated and inadequate St. Cerebellum's mental hospital, somewhere he has been an out-patient for nearly forty years. He offers to offload his shares to Grundy, who refuses. That night someone kills Humpty. It's likely that William Winkie saw the mur-derer from his kitchen window and tried to blackmail whoever it was. So he's killed, too."

"It was a Porgia MO, wasn't it?" observed Gretel.

"It was," conceded Jack, "but I'm pretty sure he had nothing to do with it."

Mary nodded in agreement.

"The killer might have done that to send us off looking in other directions, a logical inference of which is that we just might be looking in the *right* place," said Jack.

Then he paused for a moment.

"We need to know several things: who his new wife is and where he's been living for the past year. Grimm's Road was just his office. He might have spent a few nights there on his wall, but not more. Grundy says he turned down Humpty's offer of ten million, and Grundy's wife, Rapunzel, was having an affair with Humpty — something Grundy knew about and sanctioned. Humpty's car is still missing, and then there's the bird shit."

A brief titter went round the room.

"It's not funny. If he had enough shit on his shoes to bring it all the way to Grimm's Road, he must have been wading in it. And wherever the bird shit was will be the place he's been living the past year. Ashley, any leads on the car?"

"Not good, sir. We spoke to his garage. He had his car serviced three months ago — so we know it's probably still around."

"Okay, what about Humpty's marriage?"

Ashley and Gretel shook their heads. They had exhausted all the registrars in Berkshire and Oxford and were moving farther afield. As Gretel pointed out, he might have got married in Las Vegas.

Jack surveyed their faces. "Any questions?"

There weren't any.

"Okay. Make yourselves comfortable, because we're going to run over tomorrow's job from midday to 1530 hours: looking after the visitors' center for the Sacred Gonga."

He went over what they'd be doing with the aid of a drawing on a flip chart and a hastily photocopied plan. There wasn't much to say, but he tried to make it as important and serious as he could. Besides, there was an outside chance they might get a look at the Jellyman. They all listened to Jack but soon realized they were supernumerary to the Sacred Gonga security staff.

"We're there to make up the numbers, aren't we?" asked Gretel.

"It's orders, so we do our best," replied Jack. "Mary will take questions. That's it for now. I'll see you all tomorrow."

36. Refilling the Jar

KING ORDERS SPINNING
WHEELS DESTROYED

The spinning industry was shaken to its foundations yesterday by the shocking royal proclamation that all spinning wheels in the nation were to be destroyed. The inexplicable edict was issued shortly after the King's only daughter's christening and is to be implemented immediately. Economic analysts predict that the repercussions on the wool, cloth and weaving trade may be far-reaching and potentially catastrophic. "We are seeking legal advice on the matter," said Jenny Shuttle, leader of the Spinning & Associated Skills Labor Union. "While we love our King dearly, we will fight this through the courts every step of the way." The King-in-opposition has demanded a judicial review.
— Extract from *The Mole*, July 15, 1968

As Jack drove towards home, he could see the beanstalk illuminated by two searchlights that swept lazily to and fro, criss-crossing the night sky with their powerful beams. Curious, he altered course and drove up to his mother's, where the streets had been closed and crowds of curious sightseers milled around the neighborhood, taking in the extraordinary spectacle of a giant beanstalk growing in the back garden of an ordinary suburban house.

He parked as near as he could and elbowed his way through the crowd. The closer he got, the more impressive the beanstalk looked. It had entwined itself into a tightly woven, self-supporting stalk of a dark green color and was now at least seventy feet in height. Big umbrella-size leaves like canopies drooped out of the main stalk as it spiraled skywards, and the bean pods were already the size of dachshunds. Jack could understand the crowd's interest. The whole thing was clearly unprecedented; he wondered what the botanists would make of it. As he stared, he once again had the strange feeling that he should climb it, but it soon passed.

"Jack!" said his mother as soon as he had walked up the garden path and knocked on the door. "What a stroke of luck!" She beckoned him through to the kitchen, where a neatly dressed man was sitting at the table holding a brown briefcase. He had small wire-rimmed glasses, seemed to be sweating even though it wasn't hot and had oily black hair combed backwards from the crown.

"This is Percival Quick of the Reading Planning Department. Mr. Quick, this is my son, Detective Inspector Jack Spratt."

"It's just plain Mr. Spratt," said Jack, knowing full well how bureaucrats hate having rank pulled on them. "What seems to be the problem?"

Mr. Quick laid his briefcase on the table as several of Mrs. Spratt's cats shot past his feet in a blur.

"As I was saying to your mother, there is a maximum size of structure that can be permitted to be built without recourse to a planning application. This . . . er . . . 'thing' . . ."

"It's a beanstalk, Mr. Quick," said Mrs. Spratt helpfully.

"Precisely. This 'beanstalk' exceeds those guidelines quite considerably. I'm sorry to have to say that you are in contravention of planning regulations. We will be issuing a summons and require you to have it demolished at your own expense — there might be a fine, too."

"Is that really necessary?"

"I don't make the rules," said Quick, "I just enforce them."

They all stopped as a large bear of a man in a tweed suit and deerstalker hat entered the room. He was barefoot and sported a long, shaggy beard that appeared to have several rare strains of lichen growing in it. Under his arm he was carrying a giant beanstalk leaf.

"This is Professor Laburnum from the British Horticultural Society," explained Mrs. Spratt. The Professor rolled his eyes but seemed uninterested in anything but the plant. Jack noticed that he had dirt not only under his fingernails but under his toenails, too.

"Just in time for tea, Professor!" exclaimed Mrs. Spratt. "What have you found out?"

"Well, it's difficult to say," he began in a deep baritone that made the teacups rattle in the corner cupboard, "but what you have here is a *Vicia faba,* or common broad bean."

Mrs. Spratt nodded, and the Professor sat down, clutching the large leaf lest anyone try to take it away from him.

"For some reason that I have not yet fathomed, it is at least fifty times bigger than it should be. It has a complex root structure and from first indications would seem to be capable of reaching a height in excess of two to three hundred feet. It is quite unprecedented, unique even — extraordinary!"

"And the planning authority," Jack added provocatively, "wants to demolish it."

Professor Laburnum went a deep shade of purple and glared dangerously at Mr. Quick, who seemed to inflate himself like a puffer fish, ready to ward off an attack.

"Not," growled Professor Laburnum dangerously, "if we have anything to do with it!"

"The rules are very clear on this matter," said Mr. Quick indignantly, "and I have a fourteen-volume set of planning regulations to back me up."

"Oh, yeah?" said Laburnum as he got to his feet.

"Yeah."

"Thanks for helping out," said his mother as she showed him to the door. Behind them in the kitchen they could still hear Quick and Laburnum screaming obscenities at each other. A brief bout of fisticuffs had been succeeded by a series of prolonged and increasingly loud and vulgar name-callings.

"I didn't really do much, Mother. Let me know if you need anything else."

Pandora was talking to Madeleine when Jack walked in through the side door of his own house less than ten minutes later.

"A creationist, of course, but what an intellect!"

"If he's a creationist," said Madeleine, "what did he make of the fossil record?"

"Created to maintain our curious nature. He said it was useful to strive for knowledge even though there is no end to the knowledge that we could gain. It might take two hundred years more to figure out how the universe came about, or five hundred to devise a grand unifying theory. But when we finally crack those questions, they will still remain a sideshow, a mere exercise, he said, to offer us valuable groundwork to solve even greater problems of incalculable complexity."

Madeleine frowned. "Such as?"

"Why the toast always falls butter side down. Why you can look for something for hours and then find it in the first place you looked. These are the *real* puzzles that will face humanity. There is, he claims, a single theory that will explain not only why the queue you choose at a supermarket is always the slowest but why trains always leave on time when you are late and leave late when you are on time."

"There isn't an answer to those," murmured Madeleine doubtfully. "It just happens."

"That's what they used to say about lightning," replied Pandora, "and rainbows."

Jack greeted them both, took a satsuma from the fruit bowl and walked through to the living room. He stared out the window and peeled the fruit. He had bested Friedland and stopped him trying to pinch the Humpty investigation, but he didn't feel as good as he thought he would. By unmasking Chymes as a charlatan, he had the feeling that he might have let the genie out of the bottle when it would have been better for everyone concerned to keep it in. Was Chymes the only one, or did *all* Guild detectives make up their investigations? Since Inspector Moose began at Oxford, there had been a huge upswing in the number of intricately plotted murders around the dreaming spires. And what about Miss Maple and the previously quiet village of St. Michael Mead? It was now almost a bloodbath, with every household harboring some form of gruesome secret. Coincidence? Or just some skillful invention by a talented sidekick?

"Your daughter is an exceptional woman."

It was Prometheus. He was standing at the door with the light behind him. He looked ethereal, unreal almost.

"She takes after her mother."

"And her father."

"I was being overprotective last night, and I apologize," said Jack as Prometheus moved forward into a pool of light thrown by the reading lamp.

"I'd be the same, Jack. I want to marry her."

"What?"

Prometheus repeated it, and Jack sat on the edge of a table.

"But you're immortal, Prometheus. I'm not sure I want my daughter marrying someone who will stay young as she grows old."

"It's more of a partnership than a marriage," he explained. "I can get British citizenship and then we can —"

"So it's a marriage of convenience?"

"Let me explain. Remember I told you about the ills of the world that the first Pandora let out of the jar?"

"Sure."

"Your Pandora wants to put them back in!"

Jack frowned. "It seems quite a task."

"A titanic one." Prometheus grinned. "Mythology has been static for too long, Jack, I've decided we've got to get it moving again — and Pandora is the one to help me."

Jack took a deep breath and stared at the ceiling. "I never thought I'd have a Titan for a son-in-law. Promise me one thing."

"Name it."

"Renounce your immortality."

"I shall, after we locate the ills or, failing that, on Pandora's fiftieth birthday. We've got it all planned."

Prometheus smiled, and Jack put out his hand. As he grasped it, a strong feeling of power seemed to emanate from the Titan. There were so many questions still unanswered about him, but now there was plenty of time.

"Drink?" said Jack.

"Nah," said the Titan, "Friday night is strippers night down at the Blue Parrot — Just kidding. Let's have that drink. Let's have several."

37. The Man from the Guild

ALBINOS DEMAND ACTION ON MOVIE SLUR

The albino community demanded action yesterday to stop their unfair depiction as yet another movie featured an albino as a deranged hitman. "We've had enough," said Mr. Silas yesterday at a small rally of albinos at London's Pinewood Studios. "Just because of an unusual genetic abnormality, Hollywood thinks it can portray us as dysfunctional social pariahs. Ask yourself this: Have you ever been, or know anyone who has ever been, a victim of albino crime?" The protest follows hot on the heels of last week's demonstrations when Colombians and men with ponytails complained of being unrelentingly portrayed as drug dealers.
— Extract from *The Mole*, July 31, 2003

Jack got into the station at nine. It was Saturday, and the whole place was buzzing with activity over the Jellyman's visit later in the day. His Eminence's Special Protection Group in collaboration with DCI Chymes had taken charge, and everyone had to go through a metal detector and be issued a color-coded badge that related to how close you could be to the Jellyman. It ranged from red for "close proximity" all the way through the spectrum to violet, which meant "no proximity." Jack's was violet.

After picking up a Jack Spratt no-fat special bacon sandwich and a cup of coffee, he went and sat in his office. He stared at the pertinent points written up on the board. If it had been an ordinary murder inquiry, they would have had armies of officers and an incident room the size of a gymnasium, but this was the NCD. He knew he was understaffed and had to make do with the cast-offs and social misfits that no one else wanted, but he liked to think he did a reasonable amount with not very much.

As he was sitting there trying to figure out exactly *why* Humpty would think Spongg's shares should go up, someone very tall walked past the open doorway. After a second or two, he came back, stooped to look in the door and said, "I say, is this the Nursery Crime Division?"

"Yelblf," said Jack with his mouth full of bacon sandwich. "Can I helbpf you?"

"I'm looking for Detective Inspector, er . . ." He looked at a sheet of paper he had on a clipboard. "Jack Spratt."

"That's me. What can I do for you?"

"Ah!" said the tall man, looking at the clipboard again and then at the tiny office as though there had been some sort of mistake, "My name's Brown-Horrocks. I'm from the Guild of Detectives. I'll be observing you today and reporting back to the selection committee."

It took a moment for Jack to take this in, but when he had, he carefully wiped his mouth with a napkin and rose to shake the man by the hand.

"How do you do?" he said, trying to sound all professional and businesslike. "Won't you come in and take a seat?"

Brown-Horrocks stooped once more and just about managed to get his large frame into the tiny room and sit in Mary's chair by folding his legs in an uncomfortable manner.

"Thank you," said Brown-Horrocks, looking around in an agitated manner. "Aren't these offices a bit small for you?"

"We're moving shortly," lied Jack. "Ashley, would you get Mr. Brown-Horrocks a cup of tea, please?"

He said this as Ashley appeared at the door, more to get him out of the way than anything else.

"What was that?"

"Constable Ashley. One of the NCD staff."

"Is he all right? He looked . . . well, *blue*."

"All Rambosians are blue, Mr. Brown-Horrocks. He's an alien."

"I'm terribly sorry," said Brown-Horrocks. "There must be something wrong with my hearing. For a moment I thought you said he was an alien."

"Is that a problem?"

Brown-Horrocks stared at Jack, reached into his jacket pocket for a pen and made a note on the clipboard. Jack tried to see what he was writing, but Brown-Horrocks leaned away from him so he couldn't.

"Let me explain what my job is," said the Guild man kindly. "As I understand it, you have applied to join the Most Worshipful Guild of Detectives, and your application has been passed to the second stage: a practical demonstration of your skills as a detective and any other attributes that you can bring to the Guild to further enhance and illuminate the Guild's good standing with the public and the publishers of *Amazing Crime Stories*. Now, I understand you have four failed marriages. Is this true?"

"Yes," said Jack. He didn't know what Madeleine had written on the application, so he was going to have to wing it.

"Your application also says you have a drinking problem and are something of a loner."

"Yes. I drink to excess, and my family has abandoned me completely. I make do with short-term flings with totally unsuitable and very dangerous women."

"Hmm," said Brown-Horrocks, and made another note.

"That's good, right?"

"Not really."

"No, I meant for the application."

"I can't give anything away as regards my report, Inspector, and it would be very improper of you to ask."

"Of course. Here's your tea."

Ashley placed the cup and the saucer on the desk and said, "Sugar?"

"Two, please."

Ashley looked embarrassed and glanced at Jack.

"That's 10, Ashley. He's a Rambosian," explained Jack. "They only understand binary."

"Only . . . understand . . . binary," repeated Brown-Horrocks slowly, making a note.

"Yes," replied Jack, trying to act as if it were entirely normal and not strange at all. "If we need something in, say, eight days' time, we just tell Ashley it's needed in 1,000 days. Aside from a few lapses in common sense brought on by cultural differences, as befits a visitor from eighteen light-years away, he's a model officer."

"By the way," said Ashley, pointing at Brown-Horrocks's tea, "they were out of milk, so I used emulsion paint."

"See?"

"Yes," said Brown-Horrocks slowly, making another note and staring at the alien curiously. "Tell me, Mr. Ashley, what's it like being an alien?"

"Well, goodness," he said, tapping one of his thumbs on his temple, "do you know, I've never really thought about it before."

"Thank you, Ashley," said Jack before any more damage was done. "Would you check my pigeonhole for any correspondence, please?"

Ashley got the message and beat a fast retreat.

"Anyway," continued Brown-Horrocks, "I've got a copy of your interim report, so I have an idea what is going on, although, to be honest, I'm a little disappointed. Repeat interviews with prime suspects to eke out the information have *not* been undertaken, and two false confessions does seem to push it a bit. I think the second one could have been played down. In fact," he added loftily, "I've never seen a more badly structured investigation. Did you not consider publication *at all* when you conducted it?"

"It's a new technique," replied Jack hastily, "experimental."

"Well, I'll try to keep an open mind," Brown-Horrocks said in the manner of a man who won't. "What do you plan to do today? Interview all the prime suspects and finger the murderer in a stunning turn of events that will challenge and surprise any potential readers?"

"Brown-Horrocks," said Jack slowly, "this is a *police* investigation — not a mystery writers' convention."

Brown-Horrocks lowered his pen and stared at Jack. "You will find," he said, attempting to keep his obvious dissatisfaction hidden, "that Guild members have many responsibilities. Not only to the victims of crime and the public in need of reassurance against a hostile and dangerous world but also to the publishers of *Amazing Crime*

Stories and the rest of the entertainment business."

Jack thought of telling him to take his clipboard and stuff it up his arse, but opportunities to join the Guild didn't come around every day. Despite Chymes, he still wanted to join. The cash would help. And the kudos. And he might get a few convictions, too. He needed to defuse the situation — and fast.

"Is that tea all right?"

"It's undrinkable."

"Excellent. Ah, Mary," he said with some relief. "Mary, I'd like you to meet Mr. Brown-Horrocks, who is from *the Guild*."

"Oh!" said Mary, who understood the difficulties of the situation at a glance and panicked into saying the first thing that came into her head: "You're very tall."

"Why do people think I might not have noticed?" asked Brown-Horrocks with a trace of annoyance.

"No, it's just that Jack has a reputation for killing —"

"Thank you, Mary. DS Mary is my potential Official Sidekick and has a few interesting character traits of her own that would doubtless make good copy."

"What are they?" asked Brown-Horrocks.

"Yes," said Jack, looking at Mary expectantly. "What are they?"

"Well," said Mary, thinking hard, "I live in a half-converted flying boat."

"So does my uncle," replied an unimpressed Brown-Horrocks.

Ashley returned, and Brown-Horrocks looked at him curiously. "What about you, Constable Ashley? Any strange character traits?"

"None at all," replied the alien wistfully. "I enjoy car-spotting which is like train-spotting but with cars. I keep them in a book and swap the numbers with friends. I collect jam jars, beer mats, buttons, and I'm building a hyperspace-propulsion unit in my garage."

"You're right," muttered Brown-Horrocks, "nothing odd there."

"Good morning," said Gretel as she walked in the door. "They gave me a violet security — Oh!"

"This is Constable Gretel Kandlestyk-Maeker," announced Jack, "another member of our team."

They shook hands. Brown-Horrocks stared at Gretel, and Gretel stared back. Being of greater-than-average height can sometimes be a lonely business.

"Six foot . . . three and a half?" asked Brown-Horrocks.

"Two and a quarter," replied Gretel shyly. "It's these boots."

"Right," said Jack, who was desperate to be anywhere but here. "I'm going to interview Lola Vavoom again to see if she can shed any light on Humpty's new wife. Brown-Horrocks? I suppose you'll stay here and await results?"

"Not at all," he replied with a sigh. "I am here to observe you and your 'experimental' techniques whether I like it or not. Lead on."

38. Lola Vavoom Returns

VAVOOM BREAKS SELF-EXILE TO CLAIM,
"I WANT TO BE ALONE"

The actress Lola Vavoom broke her self-imposed exile of fourteen years yesterday to demand that the press leave her alone. The reclusive fifty-five-year-old former star of screen and stage who has been absent from newspaper columns since 1990 demanded that the press stop hounding her every move and making her life a misery. "I thought she was dead," admitted "Skip" McHale, *The Toad*'s entertainment correspondent, "but now I know she's around and wants to be left alone, we can dig up some of her ex-husbands to spill the beans on her bedroom antics for a crisp twenty-pound note and eight minutes of fame." Miss Vavoom is to give a televised broadcast to eight networks tomorrow evening to decry her "lack of privacy."

— Extract from *The Mole*, April 22, 2004

"Did you ever see *Anthrax! The Musical*?" asked Brown-Horrocks as they climbed up the creaking stairs at Spongg Villas to Lola's apartment.

"No, I think I missed that one."

"Brilliant piece of work," said Brown-Horrocks reverentially. "You would have thought that a musical about the experimental anthrax bombing of the Scottish island of Gruinard would be tasteless but Miss Vavoom's performance of chirpy biological-warfare scientist 'Boobs' McGonagle was both sensitive and touching."

Spongg Villas had been surrounded by journalists, all eager to speak to the actress since Thomm's body had been discovered the day before, but Jack, Mary and Brown-Horrocks had just pushed their way through.

They reached her apartment, and Jack pressed the doorbell. It didn't work, so he knocked instead.

Lola opened it like a whirlwind but seemed surprised to see them. She was wearing a kimono and looked faintly alluring.

"Ah," she said, "it's you, Inspector." She lazily extended a hand for him to shake, then looked at Mary.

"DS Mary, isn't it?"

Mary nodded.

"Well! Haven't we all got *extraordinary* names? Quite unbelievable, don't you think? Who's the giant?"

"This is Brown-Horrocks of the Guild of Detectives, Ms. Vavoom, and he's not technically a giant. He's a big fan of your work."

"Oh, Brown-Horrocks," she cooed, "you are *indeed* my biggest fan!"

"Kjdshdieupw," said Brown-Horrocks, struck inarticulate in her presence.

"Won't you all come in?"

She walked away without waiting for an answer, and they followed. Her apartment smelled of lavender, and the walls were adorned with black-and-white photographs of Lola as a young woman with the stars of the screen and stage in the seventies and eighties.

"So you kept good company?" asked Jack as he pointed at a photo of her with Giorgio Porgia. She pulled down one of the blinds on the window and laughed a high, shrill laugh.

"In the early days. He was a charming man, Inspector. When one searches for exciting men who treat a girl with respect, one is willing to overlook the shadier aspects. Gentlemen like Giorgio just don't exist anymore, either side of the law."

The room was lit mostly by table lamps. There were several drapes hanging on the walls, and all around them were the collected memorabilia of her short yet illustrious film career. Her Milton was on the mantelpiece, in pride of place among an impressive array of other awards. She lay on a chaise longue and indicated the chairs opposite her. "Please."

They sat down.

"A few questions, Ms. Vavoom. You don't mind?"

"Not at all. I was rather hoping you'd have that handsome constable with you. How can I help?"

"We'd like to know a little bit more about Humpty Dumpty — and women."

She looked up at the ceiling and placed her head on one side. "He was devoted to his first wife."

"Lucinda Muffet-Dumpty?"

"Yes; he never really got over her death. She died in a car accident when he was in prison. I don't think he ever forgave himself. If he had been there, he often said, it might have been different."

She sighed. "Whatever his second wife told you, they were never that close. He thought that by marrying again, he could retain some of the stability he had enjoyed with Lucinda and perhaps recoup some of his lost fortunes — I understand Laura Garibaldi had quite a bit of cash."

"She *used* to."

"Sorry, it was dreadful, wasn't it? Anyway, it didn't work. Not more than six months after his second marriage, I noticed him inviting young ladies to his flat next door. I don't think he wanted to upset Laura — he just loved women. He was a very amusing man, Inspector, witty, charming and erudite."

"What would you say if I told you Mr. Dumpty had got remarried?"

Lola looked shocked. "Humpty? Married *again?* I would have thought he'd have learnt his lesson from the last one."

"You met her?"

"No, it was what I was saying earlier. He had hoped the marriage would be as happy as the first time. I think he was disappointed."

"Isn't that the thing about multiple marriages?" commented Jack. "How you always hope the next one will be the perfect one."

Lola flinched. Jack had obviously touched a raw nerve. She flashed a look at him and then got up and walked over to the piano.

"When they were giving out tact, Inspector Spratt, I assume you were at the end of the queue. I've been married sixteen times. Each time, as you say, we wish for the perfect one. My first husband was a plumber from Wantage. We married when I was still behind the cosmetics counter. He gave me more than the Earl of Sunbury ever did. That mean bastard only ever gave me paste jewelery and a dose of the clap. I could still call myself a lady if I wanted, but I'd have to use the Sunbury name, and who wants to be associated with Sunbury in any way, shape or form? He was my fifth husband. We were married for over seven months, and when we divorced, I swore I would never get married again."

Jack, Mary and Brown-Horrocks said nothing, so she carried on.

"Then I met Luke. What a joy. He was young and carefree, funny and gregarious. He was the perfect man."

"What happened?" asked Mary.

"I married his brother. We were having a double wedding, and there was a mix-up at the church. We divorced as soon as we could."

"Couldn't you just have had it annulled?" asked Mary. "If it wasn't consummated, it —"

Lola silenced her with a baleful stare. "The temptation was too great. It might have turned out better, but on balance I think I preferred Luke. Trouble is, by the following morning, he had fallen for his accidental bride. They went to Llandudno and opened a fish shop. Then there was Thomas Pring. When I was being courted by him, he gave me a huge diamond, the fabulous Pring Diamond. They warned me about the curse that went with the Pring Diamond, but I ignored them all and we married."

She held up a cocktail shaker. "Gargle?"

They declined. She shrugged and poured herself a martini.

"It was then that the Pring curse made itself apparent."

"And the curse?"

"Mr. Pring. He was a pig of a man. He used to cut his toenails in bed and rarely washed. I divorced him citing the 1947 Personal Hygiene Act."

She sat down on the chaise longue again.

"How I prattle so! You must be busy. Is there anything else that I can do for you?"

"Only if you can think of one particular girlfriend of Humpty's that he might have liked enough to marry."

"I'm sorry," she said, "I've no idea."

Jack stood up. "Well, I think that's it for now."

"For now?"

"You don't mind if I come back should any other questions arise?"

"Of course not."

"Good. Just one more thing. Would you sign Brown-Horrocks's clipboard? I know he wants you to."

They thanked her and left. As soon as Lola had closed the door, she put a worried hand to her face, strode quickly to the window and raised the blind. She then picked up the telephone.

"It's Lola," she said. "He *suspects*."

39. The Red Ford Zephyr

Blatant red herrings and overused narrative blind alleys could land a detective in hot water if the Limited Narrative Misdirection bill becomes law later this year. The controversial new law called for by readers' groups has few friends among the Guild of Detectives, which still maintains that there is "no problem" and that self-regulatory guidelines prepared in 1904 are "more than adequate." "We're not asking much," explained a representative of the twenty-million-member readers' lobbying group TecWatch. "We just want to see good investigations — not routine rubbish padded out with inconsequential nonsense." The bill follows the successful passing of the so-called surprise assailant act last year, which outlawed the publication of investigations where the murderer is suddenly revealed two pages from the end without a single mention in the previous one hundred thousand words.

— Extract from *The Owl*,
October 1, 1979

Spongg Villas was only a ten-minute walk from Reading Central, and by the time they got back, there had been a development.

"We've just had an anonymous phone call with info on Humpty's car," said Gretel, talking to Jack but looking at Brown-Horrocks.

"Who from?"

"They didn't say. Male caller from a phone box in Charvil. Gave the information and then rang off."

"Headway at last. Whereabouts?"

They stepped closer to the Reading and District wall map, which had to be hung sideways as it was the only way it would fit on the tiny wall.

"They said it could be found . . ." muttered Gretel, looking at the address on the piece of paper and finally jabbing a finger perilously close to the edge of Andersen's Wood. "Here."

Jack looked at the place Gretel had indicated. There were no houses within a mile in any direction.

"Right. Mary and I are going out to have a look. Check out the owners of the closest houses and see if you can spot any link."

The crossroads where they'd been told they could find the Zephyr was in a rural setting to the west of the city, from where they could easily see Andersen's Wood on the next hill. A single signpost with peeling paint sat forlornly at the roadside, and there was no evidence of habitation in any direction. After the bustle of the town over the past few days, the peace of the country was a welcome diversion. The roar of the M4 had been soothed into a gentle rumble by the distance, and for once it wasn't raining.

They stopped the car and got out. Brown-Horrocks had been in the passenger seat, but the small car had not been designed to fit his lanky frame, and he had sat the whole journey with his knees almost around his ears.

"When do you get your vintage Rolls-Royce back from the garage?" he asked. "I don't think much of their loaner."

"Next week," replied Jack as he pulled on a coat against the wind and looked up and down the empty road. "I don't see a car anywhere."

"Hoax?"

"Could be. But let's be sure. You take that road, I'll take this one. Search as you go."

They went their separate ways, with Brown-Horrocks walking behind Jack and asking occasional questions.

"Are you an alcoholic or a *reformed* alcoholic?"

"Reformed . . . but with occasional lapses," said Jack, hazarding a guess as to what would be most acceptable to the Guild.

"Good," said Brown-Horrocks, making another note.

It was Mary who made the discovery. A rickety-looking Quonset hut in a field that was mostly overgrown by brambles. She called Jack over, opened the gate and walked over to the hut. Its doors had sagged and were fastened with a rusty hasp that was secured by a tent peg. Jack carefully lifted out the peg and let the doors swing open. The hut was dry and the floor made of compacted soil; the brambles that covered the outside had also forced holes in the corrugated iron roof and were now starting to take over the interior as well. Sitting in the middle of the hut and looking as clean and new as when it was built was the Zephyr.

Mary delicately tried the doors. "Locked."

"He had no car keys on him," said Jack. "Try the tailpipe."

Mary walked to the back of the car as Jack cupped his hands around his face and peered in the window.

The driver's seat was converted for Humpty's unusual shape, looking a bit like a padded egg cup with a high back. The pedals were all on extensions for his little legs, and the gearshift had been elongated to compensate for his short arm reach.

"Bingo," said Mary, holding up a set of car keys. She inserted one into the door and unlocked it. She grasped the handle and opened the door.

RUN, FOR GOD'S SAKE, RUN!" yelled Jack, sprinting out of the makeshift garage at full speed and hoping that Mary and Brown-Horrocks were behind him. He got as far as the middle of the road when the car exploded. He didn't hear the sound at first, just a shock wave that scooped him up off his feet like an unseen hand and propelled him through the air to the ditch at the other side of the road, where he landed with a thump that knocked the wind out of him. He covered his head with his arms as a shower of debris rained down and a sheet of twisted corrugated iron fell close beside him. His ears were ringing, and in the momentary semideafness that followed, all sounds seemed dead and lacking in detail. He got up, checked he wasn't damaged and divested himself of his singed overcoat. The remains of the car were fiercely ablaze, and the roadway was covered with wreckage. He appeared, apart from a cut on his face from where he had landed in the ditch, unharmed.

"Are you okay?" he asked Mary, who had landed a half dozen paces from him.

"I think so," she replied as she dusted herself down. It was only when Jack started to think clearly again that he remembered there was someone missing.

"Brown-Horrocks?" he said, quietly at first, scanning the roadway for any sign of life. "BROWN-HORROCKS!" he said again, this time louder as he ran towards the shattered building with a sinking feeling. Of the Guild examiner there was no sign, and the car looked as if someone had tried to inflate it with an air hose. The roof bulged outwards, and all the doors had blown off.

"BROWN-HORROCKS!" he yelled once more, now looking around the wreckage for any clue as to what had happened to him, no matter how gruesome.

"Where is he?" asked Mary, who'd arrived by Jack's side.

"I don't know. Shit. Killing a Guild examiner. And he was a giant. I'll never live this down at the station."

"I'm six foot nine," came an indignant voice behind them. "I'm *not* a giant."

They turned to find him staggering up from the side of the road. He had been thrown in a quite different direction and been deposited in a muddy ditch.

"Thank God," said Jack. "Turn around."

He turned around for them, and they checked him over. Apart from some singed hair and a few cuts and bruises, he was fine.

"I expect you'll want to call it a day after that?"

"On the contrary," said Brown-Horrocks in a resolute tone, "I'm curious to see how this turns out."

Jack shook his mobile phone, and some bits fell out. "Buggered. Where's yours, Mary?"

"Car."

They walked back towards the Allegro to find a dent in the hood and a nail that had pierced the door skin like a crossbow bolt.

"Look what they've done to my car!"

"Did someone just try to kill us?" asked

Mary as her mobile hunted for a signal.

"I think so," replied Jack as he opened the door and took a seat.

She got through to the NCD and told Ashley to have uniform close the road and get the fire service down there — and the bomb squad, too. She snapped the mobile shut and sat on the hood. "I owe you, sir. How did you know?"

Jack ran his fingers through his hair and picked out several bits of debris.

"The interior light had been pried off and a small piece of wire ran down the inside of the door pillar. It might have been nothing, but I wasn't going to risk it."

"I have to say I'm very glad you didn't."

"So am I," said Brown-Horrocks, making a note on his muddy and singed clipboard.

"Probably about two pounds of high explosive," explained Lee Whriski, a young major in the bomb squad, "attached to a short time-delay fuse. We'll be able to tell you which explosive it was given a few days, but not much more, I'm afraid. This kind of thing is not hard to do — obtaining the explosives is harder — but when we find out what it was, we might be able to narrow the search. You were lucky."

They were standing on the road surrounded by several drab green army vehicles. The road had been closed while the bomb squad made a detailed search of the area.

Jack thanked him and walked over to where Mary was being checked by a medic.

"You know you're near the target when you start to cop flak," said Mary.

"Yes," agreed Jack. "But which target?"

"Don't you know?" asked Brown-Horrocks.

"Of course," replied Jack hastily. "It was a rhetorical question. I'm just waiting for them . . . to make a mistake. Then we'll have them."

"I see," said Brown-Horrocks, clearly not believing Jack in the least. "And how many assassination attempts do you think you can survive before they make a mistake?"

"It's all in hand, sir," replied Jack unconvincingly.

"I hope so. By the way, how many giants *have* you killed? I ask only by way of curiosity and self-preservation, you understand."

"Technically speaking, only one," replied Jack with a sigh. "The other three were just tall."

"To kill one giant might be regarded as a

misfortune," said Brown-Horrocks slowly. "To kill four looks very much like carelessness."

"I was cleared on all counts."

"Of course," said the Guild man, making another note on his clipboard.

"Sir?" said Mary, who had been going around collecting debris that might have been in Humpty's car. It was surprising how much had survived — explosions are quixotic beasts. Most of it was worthless. A portion of poultry-feed packaging, a charred couple of pages from last week's *Mole*, the remains of the Zephyr's service manual. But one particular item caught Jack's attention. It was part of some promotional material advertising the Goring Foot Museum. Jack and Mary exchanged looks, and Mary called the office to ask Baker whether he knew anything about the museum. She listened intently for a while, then hung up.

"Well?" asked Jack.

"Know the way to Goring, sir?"

"Sure. You going to tell me why?"

"Thomas Thomm was a research assistant there. *That* was the job that Humpty had got for him."

"*That's* the lead we're looking for," said

Jack in the manner that Chymes used.

Brown-Horrocks raised an eyebrow but was otherwise unmoved.

"I'll go in the back," he said. "I'm meant to be just an observer anyway."

And with a sinuous movement of folding arms and limbs, he compacted his large frame sufficiently to fit in the rear seat.

40. The Goring Foot Museum

The foot is, of course, a wonderful piece of engineering. It allowed mankind freedom from quadripedal movement and thus to develop the use of his hands. Without the foot we would have no hands.

    — Professor Tarsus, *The Foot Lectures*

Jack had been to the Foot Museum only once before, when he was at school. It had been considered the low point of the school year, only marginally less interesting than Swindon's Museum of the Rivet or Bracknell's collection of doorstops. The museum was another Spongg bequest and was an impressive structure built in the Greek style, and despite being sandwiched between a supermarket and a fast-food restaurant, had lost little of its imposing grandeur.

    They were met by a white-haired gentleman of perhaps sixty. He had a bad stoop and walked with uncertain steps. He had to look at them sideways, as his chin was almost resting on his chest.

"Professor Tarsus? I am Detective Inspector Spratt of the Nursery Crime Division, Reading Police. This is Detective Sergeant Mary Mary."

"I'll never remember all that. I'll just call you Ronald and Nancy. Who's he?"

"This is Mr. Brown-Horrocks from the Most Worshipful Guild of Detectives."

"Ah. You can be Ronald as well. Took your time, didn't you?"

He had a heavy, gravelly voice that sounded like thimbles on a washboard.

"Pardon me?" asked Jack, unsure of his meaning.

"You chaps don't seem to be interested at all. I had a couple of you johnnies around about three months ago, just after the theft. Ronald and, er . . . *Ronald,* I think their names were. They promised to make inquiries, and that was that. Bad show, I call it."

"We're not here about the theft, sir."

The Professor appeared not to hear and beckoned them to follow him past the rows of ancient foot-orientated exhibits. The interior was as old and dusty as Jack remembered, the leaded windows caked with grime and the hard flags smoothed from three-quarters of a century of bored, shuffling feet. The Professor led them through a door marked "Private" and into a modern laboratory. Racks of jars lined the walls, most of them containing some sort of chiropodic specimen pickled in formaldehyde.

"What's this?" asked Jack, pointing to an acrylic and polypropylene test foot in a worn jogging boot being sprayed with a foul-smelling liquid inside a glass case. The foot and its stainless-steel leg trod a rolling road in a convincing manner.

"Our test foot. I call him Michael. We can program it for any type of walking gait. We can even," he continued excitedly, "simulate a dropped arch to investigate what type of shoe offers the best support. We have it sweating a salt-nutrient mixture and then analyze the bacteria that grows in the gaps between the toes. Would you care to take a look?"

"No thanks," said Jack quickly.

Professor Tarsus grunted, then shuffled to one side of the room and pulled a sheet off a big glass cabinet. The lock had been forced, and inside the empty cabinet was a large cotton pad the shape of an inner tube. On the side were precise controls that monitored temperature and humidity.

Jack's nose wrinkled at the cheesy odor it exuded. Tarsus pointed at the empty case with a petulant air, as if they could somehow magically restore his property.

"I'm sorry, sir," said Jack, "I don't have any details of your break-in. We're investigating several murders in the Reading area, and we hoped you might be able to help."

Tarsus looked at them all suspiciously. "Murders? How can the Foot Museum be connected?"

"Thomas Thomm, Professor," said Mary, "we understand he used to work here?"

"The name means nothing to me, Nancy."

"He worked as a lab assistant — sponsored by Mr. Dumpty. You might have known him as . . . Ronald."

"Then why didn't you say so? Yes, I remember Ron very well. He was Dr. Carbuncle's assistant. Left about a year ago."

"Dr. Carbuncle?" repeated Jack, making a note. "Is he here?"

"He took early retirement," replied Tarsus. "Ron even lived in his house for a bit, I understand. Nancy can tell you more. NANCY!"

He bellowed it so loudly that Mary and Jack jumped. A small voice said, "Coming!"

and presently "Nancy" appeared. She was about the same age as Tarsus but displayed none of his infirmities. She walked with a youthful step and wore bright red leggings, a T-shirt with a picture of a foot on it and a leather jacket. She looked like some sort of aged foot groupie.

"Nancy, this is Ronald, Nancy and — er — Ronald. They're police."

"Hello!" said Nancy. "It's Fay Goodrich, actually."

They introduced themselves as she perched nimbly on one of the desktops. Tarsus looked on disapprovingly.

"Did you ever meet Mr. Dumpty?"

"Yes," she said, as a smile crossed her lips, "he was a pal of Dr. Carbuncle. He used to come in here quite a lot."

"What did they talk about?"

"This and that, feet ailments mostly. They were good friends. Hump was staying at his house."

"Dumpty? With Dr. Carbuncle?"

She nodded. "Humpty said he'd been forced to leave his apartment. Carbuncle was a widower; he lived alone in Andersen's Farm, just on the edge of the forest. I expect he took in paying guests for the company."

Jack thought for a moment. "So when did Dr. Carbuncle retire?"

"Three months ago. We had quite a party. Humpty was there with a tall brunette, and I think almost every chiropodist in the Home Counties turned up — Carbuncle was much respected. Spongg gave a warm speech and presented Dr. Carbuncle with one of his celebrated Bronze Foot Awards for services to the foot-care industry."

"And the break-in occurred . . . ?"

"Two days later," said Miss Goodrich provocatively. The Professor shot her a fierce glance.

"The two events are unconnected," explained Tarsus. "Carbuncle would *never* have stolen it. I have known him for almost three decades."

Miss Goodrich muttered something and stared at the ceiling. This was obviously an argument that had been grumbling on for some time. Jack's attention went back to the broken cabinet as Mary took Fay off for more information.

"Perhaps you'd better tell me what was stolen?"

"In here," said Tarsus proudly, "was my life's work. Thirty years ago I extracted it, nurtured it, fed it, kept it warm and damp, protected it from parasites, even defended it from financial cutbacks in the seventies.

It was the greatest, most stupendous . . . *verruca* in the world."

He sat on a nearby chair and covered his face with his hands and sobbed loudly.

"A verruca?" repeated Jack. "You mean that nasty little warty thing you get on your foot? That's all?"

Tarsus looked up at him angrily. "It wasn't just any verruca, Ronald. Hercules was a thirty-seven-kilo champion. The biggest — and finest — in the world!"

He shed twenty years as he spoke animatedly about what was obviously his favorite subject.

"He was the son I never had. The only other verruca to come close was a lamentable twenty-three-kilo tiddler owned by L'Institute du Pied in Toulouse. Hernán Laso of Argentina claimed that he had a forty-seven-kilo specimen, but it turned out to be a clever fake made from papier-mâché and builder's plaster."

Jack looked at the broken case again, and Tarsus continued. "It was used primarily for research. Dr. Carbuncle was working with it when he retired; some sort of genetic engineering, I believe. Experimenting with a new viral strain of superverruca."

Suddenly things started to come into sharp and terrible focus.

"Isn't that *unbelievably* dangerous?"

"Not if conducted properly. Anyway, it didn't bear fruit. He'd been on the project for nearly two years and eventually called a halt and retired. I came in the following week to find Hercules gone. Its only value is in research. Without precise heat and humidity control, it will dry out and die. And I think, Ron — may I call you Ron? — that even you can appreciate the uselessness of a dead verruca."

"Of course," said Jack uneasily. "I need Dr. Carbuncle's address."

Tarsus grasped Jack's elbow, drew him close and whispered, "You will find Hercules, won't you?"

"Of course," replied Jack. "He was the son you never had, right?"

As Jack, Mary and an increasingly uncomfortable Brown-Horrocks drove towards Andersen's Wood and Dr. Carbuncle's house, they could see a throng of traffic heading into the city center. It was still only ten, and the Jellyman's dedication wouldn't be until midday. That done, he would be driven on a parade route around the town, open several hospitals and an old-people's home, meet members of the community and then have dinner over at the QuangTech facility with the mayor and a roomful of Reading's luminaries, Spongg, Grundy and Chymes among them.

"Hercules is the answer," said Jack as they drove rapidly down the road. "I think I know what Humpty's plan was — I'm just not sure how he was going to execute it."

"You don't think . . . ?"

"I do," replied Jack grimly.

"You do?" echoed Brown-Horrocks, folded up in the backseat. "How, exactly?"

41. Dr. Horatio Carbuncle

DETECTIVES SLAM GENETIC DATABASE PLANS

Plans for a national genetic database could be shelved if the Guild of Detectives gets its way, it has emerged. "Cerebrally based deduction of perpetrators has fallen over the years," wrote Guild member Lord Peter Flimsey in a leaked document to the Home Office funding committee, "and we all have a duty to protect the traditional detecting industry against further damaging loss." MPs were said to be "sympathetic" to the Guild's cause, but Mr. Pipette of the Forensic Sciences Federation was less receptive. "Quite frankly, they've been moaning ever since DNA advances narrowed their field of methodology." A Guild spokesman angrily dismissed the accusation. "We've been moaning a lot longer than that," said Mr. Celery Clean at a hastily convened press conference last night. "If we continue to allow intrusive and narratively boring work practices to flood

the detecting business, we could see an undesirable shift of emphasis from detecting
to forensics — which none of us want."
— Extract from *The Toad*,
March 14, 1997

Andersen's Farm was a small, two up/two
down, redbrick farmhouse with a thatched
roof, surrounded by a vegetable plot and
several outbuildings in various states of
dilapidation. There was a lean-to extension
on the back, and the fields that made up the
smallholding had twenty or so miserable-
looking sheep scattered upon them. An ancient gray mare stood in a muddy pasture
and tossed her head as the Allegro approached, but since she was badly myopic,
it might have been a lime green elephant for
all she knew. She blew out twin blasts of hot
breath in the cold morning air and thought
about the good old days when she chased
across fields with lots of other horses,
leaping hedges and galloping after something that her rider wanted her to catch but
rarely did. She watched the green elephant
drive slowly past and then leaned sleepily
against the gatepost.

They drove into the yard and pulled up
next to a ramshackle barn that contained
an ancient Austin Ten up on blocks. There

was no other car anywhere to be seen, and it didn't look as though anyone was at home. As they got out, Mary drew Jack's attention to a ladder leaning up against a wall with a lot of discarded beer cans at the base. Humpty had definitely been here.

Jack approached slowly and knocked on the front door. After getting no reply, he thumped again, this time louder.

He cupped his hand to look through the window, but there was no sign of life. He beckoned the others to follow him and then walked around to the back of the house where the lean-to section housed the kitchen. He knocked again, then tried the door handle. It was locked.

"Pass me that walking stick, would you?" said Jack.

Brown-Horrocks raised his eyebrows and scribbled a note as Mary passed the stick over. Jack cleared the windowpane with a few well-placed blows of the stick, the sound of shattering glass cutting harshly through the peace of the surroundings. He climbed into the kitchen, checked the back door for any booby traps, then let the others in.

"This is highly questionable procedure," warned Mary. "Anything we find here and want to use as evidence will be disallowed."

"I'm trying to stop a serious crime from being committed," said Jack. "We'll worry about convictions afterwards."

They moved into the front room and nearly jumped out of their skins when a large and very angry goose honked at them and beat its wings in a highly agitated manner. They took a step back as it settled down again on the sofa and hissed at them angrily. The floor was covered in goose shit.

"A goose?"

"It explains the bird shit in Humpty's office."

"Yes, but why indoors?"

As they watched, the goose made itself more comfortable and a flash of something yellow pierced the gloom from within the nest it had made on the sofa. Mary moved forward and rolled up her sleeve. The goose opened its beak and hissed at the intrusion, but Mary made clicking noises with her tongue and very gently pushed her hand under the bird. Jack looked at his watch. He didn't have a lot of time for farm animals; he was more used to seeing them wrapped in plastic at the supermarket or flanked by roast spuds and carrots.

Mary withdrew her hand, and the egg shone brightly even in the relative gloom of the living room. The egg was gold. *Solid* gold. Jack's jaw dropped open. Mary smiled triumphantly, and the goose hissed again as she passed it over to him. The egg was surprisingly heavy and still warm.

"So that's where he got the gold," said Jack. "I should have guessed. The wood-cutters found the goose but weren't too clever about keeping it quiet. Tom Thomm was living here. He hears about it, follows them into the wood, greed overcomes him and pow — that was it."

There was nothing else down here, so Jack turned his attention to the stairs, stepping softly up the treads until he reached the upstairs corridor, which had a narrow carpet running down the center with bare boards on either side. At the opposite end was a leaded-glass window. To the left and right were doors leading off into the bedrooms. The first room they visited was a jumble of chemistry equipment: retorts, dirty beakers and racks of test tubes. There was a pungent smell of decayed cheese in the air, and in the far corner, upon a grimy sofa and surrounded by two three-bar electric fires, was what appeared to be something child-size curled up beneath a dirty bedsheet. It stirred ever so slightly as they watched, and Jack, using his best authoritarian voice called out: "Police! You, under the sheet — move out slowly!"

There was no response, so Jack advanced and slowly pulled the sheet off. But it wasn't a child. It was something that closely resembled a large and very rotten misshapen potato, but about the size of two watermelons. The smell of sweaty feet rose up to greet them, and they all gagged.

"What the . . . ?" murmured Jack, staring at the strange object that seemed to shudder as he watched. He covered his nose and mouth with a hankie and put out a curious hand to touch the gently heaving object. Just as he was about to make contact, Mary's hand deftly grabbed his wrist. He looked up at her with a quizzical expression, but she merely nodded at a warning sign that read: BIOHAZARD — EXTREME CAUTION!

"Good Lord!" muttered Jack, glad that Mary had stayed his hand. "It's Hercules, Professor Tarsus's champion verruca. Would you look at the size of it!"

Mary nodded sagely and passed him an empty bottle that had been lying on a table nearby. It was unused but had been labeled, and Jack shuddered as he read:

CONCENTRATED LIVE VERRUCA SPORE.
USE RATIO 1:100 IN HUMIDITY CONTROL
RESERVOIR EVERY WEEK FOR
MAXIMUM INFECTION.

There was another bottle that confirmed Jack's fears. It was labeled:

SUPERVERRUCA: ANTIDOTE

Humpty hadn't been exaggerating when he'd drunkenly boasted that his shares would be worth a fortune in a few months' time — with an outbreak of verrucas that only Carbuncle and Humpty knew how to cure, they could ask what they wanted for the antidote. With the cure sold to Spongg, Humpty's shares in the ailing foot-care empire would be worth a hundred times what he paid within a few months.

"Get on the phone," said Jack, "and speak to Briggs. Tell him to contact the Communicable Disease Control Center and declare the Sacred Gonga Visitors' Center a hot zone — he needs to have it checked by a biohazard squad before we can even *think* of the Jellyman dedicating it."

"What!?" said Mary.

"It all makes sense. Don't you see? The

Sacred Gonga Visitors' Center is the ideal place to spread the verruca virus. Air-conditioned and with precise humidity control — and everyone having to walk with reverential *bare feet.* Ordinary verrucas are bad enough, but this monster is capable of *anything.*"

"Professor Hardiman was expecting ten thousand visitors this afternoon and more than a million over the next six months," observed Mary, dialing feverishly.

"And every single one of them taking home ultrainfectious superverrucas to spread around their homes. No wonder Humpty was confident he could pledge fifty million to St. Cerebellum's."

"So who killed Mr. Dumpty?" asked Brown-Horrocks.

"Isn't it obvious?" Jack replied. "Dr. Carbuncle. They were partners. Humpty buys the shares, and Carbuncle supplies the virus. Only Carbuncle gets greedy. He kills Humpty in order to keep all the shares for himself. Winkie tries to blackmail him, so Carbuncle kills him, too. Then we get too close for comfort, so he wires the Zephyr. He was good, but not quite good enough."

Brown-Horrocks ticked a few boxes and scribbled a note. "So who did Humpty marry?"

Jack stopped and rubbed his chin thoughtfully. "Not sure about that yet — but when we find Carbuncle, we'll find her, too."

"Then I suppose congratulations are in order," said Brown-Horrocks. "I'll be honest. When I first met you, I thought you were a complete imbecile. But now I'm very glad to be present at the conclusion of what must have been at times a very tricky investigation."

"Well," said Jack modestly, "it was touch and go for a moment there."

"Sir?" said Mary in a hoarse whisper.

"Not now, Mary. So, Mr. Brown-Horrocks, how does your report read?"

"I'm really not at liberty to discuss it, Inspector, but —"

"Sir!"

"Excuse me for a moment."

Jack went out into the corridor and joined Mary. *"What is it?"*

"It's Dr. Carbuncle."

"Where?"

She jerked a thumb in the direction of the second bedroom. "In here."

Jack glanced at Brown-Horrocks, but thankfully he was engaged in making some notes. Jack stepped into the bedroom and stopped. Lying on the floor with a single

512

bullet hole in his chest was Carbuncle.

"Shit! Are you sure it's him?"

"Quite sure. Look at the picture."

He compared it to the photo Professor Tarsus had given them. There was no mistake.

"Blast! I've just told Brown-Horrocks that it was Carbuncle who killed Humpty!"

"Problems?" asked Brown-Horrocks, who was wondering what they were talking about.

"Not really," said Jack, "I just might have been a little overhasty with the summing up I gave you."

"It's Carbuncle in there, isn't it?"

There didn't seem any point in hiding it, so Jack gave up on the possibility of becoming Guild and had a good look around the house. In the room where they found Carbuncle, there was also Humpty's bed, a large divan with an oval cut out of it. There were magazines scattered about, a lot of copies of *The Financial Toad* and several prospectuses that outlined the St. Cerebellum's rebuilding appeal. He pulled up the mattress and found a few love letters from Bessie Brooks but not much else. He walked despondently outside to await SOCO and the biohazard team. Brown-Horrocks was making some notes, and

Mary was on the phone. Jack still wasn't there yet. He had missed something. But what?

He looked up at the sky, which was covered by a thick layer of stratus clouds that moved slowly across the landscape. He couldn't remember the last time he had seen the sun. Then, to the south, a small hole opened up in the cloud and a beam of light spilt to earth, warm and welcoming after the prolonged winter and dismal spring. The pool of bright sunlight fell to earth two fields away, startling some sheep who had forgotten they possessed shadows. Then the hole closed again, and soft, directionless light once more settled on the earth.

"He *lied* to us," said Jack quietly to himself as something clicked in his head. "He lied to us all along. He had all the motive anyone would ever need. I was a fool not to see it!"

He turned, took Mary's phone and hurriedly dialed the NCD offices. If he was right, then he knew who had killed Humpty — and Carbuncle.

The little Austin Allegro sped along the narrow country track with Jack in the passenger seat, Mary driving and Brown-

Horrocks folded up in the rear. Despite the misdiagnosis, Brown-Horrocks seemed determined to see the whole thing through, if not for anything but a strange sort of curiosity to watch what Jack would do next. They left Carbuncle's smallholding as soon as an officer arrived to keep the area secure; Briggs had called Jack to confirm that the Sacred Gonga Visitors' Center had been cordoned off. Chymes, thought Jack, must be kicking himself — he'd never had anything as dramatically complex as a biohazard incident.

The traffic was appalling. No, it was worse than appalling. The news of the Jellyman's visit had had a magical effect, and almost everyone in the Home Counties was trying to converge on Reading for a brief glimpse.

"I expect this sort of thing happens all the time when you're examining potential Guild members?" asked Jack, who felt he had to say *something.*

"No," said Brown-Horrocks, "I have to say this is all quite a new experience."

"Good or bad?"

"You'll find out in due course," replied Brown-Horrocks enigmatically.

Jack turned on the radio and was gratified to hear the news that the Sacred

Gonga Visitors' Center would be closed until further notice.

Mary's phone rang, and Jack answered it. "DI Spratt." He listened for a moment. "Do I?" He pressed his finger on the "mute" button. "It's Arnold. He says I sound uncannily like your father."

"Tell him I never want to see him again, *ever.*"

"Hello, Arnold? She'll call you back."

He flipped it shut and looked at Brown-Horrocks, who raised an eyebrow. Jack pointed out a side street that he knew was a good shortcut as the phone rang again.

It was Ashley.

"Your suspect is at home," he reported. "I had a call from Baker. When he and Gretel knocked at the front door, several shots rang out from an upstairs window."

"Anyone hurt?"

"No. I've requested armed response, but the Jellyman has used up all available manpower. Briggs said that since we were now excused from Sacred Gonga protection duty, we could do it ourselves."

"With what? Using our fingers and making 'bang' noises? Get back onto him and tell him I've *specifically* requested it."

"Righto, sir. Did Mrs. Singh get hold of you?"

They ground to a halt in some heavy traffic.

"Show some blue, Mary. We might not have too much time."

Mary switched on the siren and placed a magnetic blue light on the roof of the Allegro. Jack held on tightly as she swerved across the verge and rapidly overtook the stationary traffic.

"Mrs. Singh?" asked Jack. "What — MIND THE CURB!!"

Mary swerved to avoid a curbstone and took a left the wrong way down a one-way street. Several cars scattered as she drove up the middle.

"Are you still there, sir?" asked Ashley.

"For now. Who knows, I may just live to see the summer."

Jack wedged his feet into the footwell and stamped on an imaginary brake as Mary took a red light at full speed, cut across some grass and entered Prospect Park through a gap in the fence.

"So what did Mrs. Singh want?" Jack asked Ashley.

"She didn't say. But she said it was important. Something about Humpty."

"Anything else?"

"Yes. Did Arnold get hold of Mary?"

Jack held on to the door handle as Mary

bounced through the park and drove out the other side, made a sharp left and then a right and took off over a humpback bridge, on landing transforming an eighth of an inch of the Allegro's sump into a shower of hot sparks. Brown-Horrocks's head hit the roof with a hollow thud.

"Tell Mrs. Singh I'll ring her when I can. Call Baker and inform him we'll be with her" — he looked across at Mary — "soon. Call me back once Briggs has managed to secure an armed-response unit for our use."

Ashley answered in the affirmative and rang off.

They were now driving out the other side of the town, against the heavy traffic — all full of people hoping to catch a glimpse of the Jellyman. They picked up speed, and the needle on the speedometer touched eighty; Jack looked nervously at the temperature gauge, which was already into the red, and then at Mary, who was concentrating on the road. He turned to give a confident smile to Brown-Horrocks, who had wedged himself in the back and was staring grimly at the road ahead. After another ten minutes, they approached their destination: Castle Spongg.

42. Return to Castle Spongg

OWL AND PUSSYCAT TO WED

Following months of heated speculation, the Owl and the Pussycat have announced their plans to wed at the next full moon. The pairing promises to be the celebrity wedding of the year, and guest lists are for the moment being kept secret. Fans of the fearless duo, whose exploits during their record circumnavigation of the globe in the pea-green boat have entered into legend, were ecstatic at the news. "This is, like, so cool," exclaimed one of the many fans who gathered outside the gates of the Owl's mansion yesterday. The couple's PR agent is giving little away, revealing only that the wedding feast will be mostly mince and slices of quince, served up with a runcible spoon. Although the location of the wedding has not been revealed, fans insist that it is most likely to be in the land where the Bong-tree grows, and the min-

The Allegro's tires complained bitterly as Mary turned hard into Castle Spongg's drive and tore across the rumble strips, the "Jerusalem" on the car tires playing this time at *molto prestissimo.* As they passed the rhododendron grove, the car gave an odd shudder and a lurch, and one of the rear wheels sheared off, wobbled for a moment and then, overtaking its erstwhile master, leaped across the lawn like a stone skipping on the surface of a lake, eventually disappearing into the greenhouse with a crash of glass and a tearing of foliage.

"Whoops," said Jack.

The car dropped to the road and slewed sideways, rudely interrupting "Jerusalem" with a metallic scraping noise and cutting a neat groove through the road and into the grass. It came to a stop facing the opposite direction. Mary carefully turned off the engine.

"Wheel-bearing torque settings," explained Jack uselessly in the silence that followed their abrupt halt, "they're quite critical on these cars."

Brown-Horrocks glared at Jack and clambered out. "You don't actually own a vintage Rolls-Royce at all, do you?"

Jack felt stupid all of a sudden. "No, I don't."

"This is your car, isn't it?"

Jack looked at the remains of the Allegro. It had served him well, but a large ripple up the rear body work and across the roof guaranteed that their partnership was at an end.

"Yes, it is."

"You don't have a drinking problem either, do you?"

"No."

"Anything else you might have 'embellished' in your Guild application?"

"I have a wonderful wife and five terrific kids."

"And you — you're quite ordinary, aren't you?"

He was asking Mary, who jumped as though stuck with a cattle prod.

"I have a lot of ex-boyfriends," she said helpfully.

"My superintendent speaks Urdu," added Jack, trying to recoup lost ground, "and he could, if pushed, change his name to Föngotskilérnie. And he plays the trombone."

"Badly," added Brown-Horrocks. "He insisted on playing for me when I went to get your case notes."

He sighed and tucked the clipboard under his arm. "Do you *really* want to be in the Guild, Inspector?"

"I'd like to be," Jack replied, "but I guess it's just that I've spent over twenty years sorting out problems with the nurseries and never getting anywhere. At least if I were Guild, the Prosecution Service might take notice of me — and get some justice for the victims. Give the NCD some balls, if you like."

Brown-Horrocks nodded soberly but gave nothing away. They left the car looking forlorn on the grass and hurried towards the main entrance.

"Why Spongg and not Grundy?" asked Brown-Horrocks as they passed the foot-shaped lake. "Spongg has a philanthropic reputation that is hard to beat."

"Because he *lied.* He said he'd only seen Humpty once in the past year: at the Spongg Charity Benefit. Yet they were both at Dr. Carbuncle's retirement party. Moreover, we saw crates of foot preparations at the Spongg factory. They weren't unsold — they were *stockpiles.* What better way to save his failing empire than engineer a mass outbreak of verrucas?"

"Not bad," said Brown-Horrocks approvingly. "Then who did Humpty marry?"

"Now, that," puffed Jack as they came within site of Castle Spongg, "is something I'm still not sure about."

They found Gretel waiting for them in front of the house behind a large pink marble toe. It was over fifteen feet across and rested on a black marble plinth. A gift from His Royal Highness Suleiman bin Daoud, it was a token of gratitude to the first Lord Spongg for curing his kingdom of a particularly virulent form of athlete's foot in 1878.

Jack glanced around. "Where's Baker?"

Gretel looked uneasy. "He went in. I tried to stop him, but he said armed response wouldn't be here for weeks, and there might be staff in the house that needed to be evacuated. He said it didn't matter because he has a brain tumor and won't last the week anyway."

"Is that true?" asked Brown-Horrocks.

"No," said Jack, "he's a hypochondriac. He's had a self-proclaimed two months to live ever since he started working at the division six years ago. He —"

A muffled shot interrupted Jack's sentence. They peered around the statue at the front door, which was ajar. Nothing stirred from within.

"Call Ops and get the paramedics down here, but don't let them in until I say so — and bring a vest back with you."

Gretel scurried over to Baker's car and relayed Jack's request into the police radio. Jack was all for waiting, but then he heard it. It was the unmistakable sound of Baker. He was hurt, and he was moaning. Gretel returned with the vest. It was designed to stop a knife, but it could just about stop a bullet — as long as it was large-caliber, low-velocity or long-range — ideally, all three.

"You're not going in alone, sir?" asked Mary.

"With all armed-response teams tied up with the Jellyman, it doesn't look like I have a great deal of choice, does it?"

"It's against regulations, sir."

"True, but Baker's hurt, and I don't leave a man down. I'll call when I can." He took Mary's mobile, switched it off and put it in his top pocket.

"Take care, sir."

Jack looked at Mary's anxious face. "Thanks."

Jack approached the bizarre house warily. He knew that his decision went against every police procedural recommendation that had ever been made, but while an officer lay wounded inside, he felt he had to do *something*. He ducked behind one of the giant bronze anteaters and heard Baker cry out again. He ran forwards and stepped carefully inside the house. The lights were off, the interior dingy, and someone, somewhere, was playing the violin. While he paused to let his eyes get used to the gloom, a polite cough made him jump. He wheeled around and came face-to-face with . . . Ffinkworth.

"Good morning, Inspector," said the butler solemnly. "I trust you are quite well?"

"I think you'd better leave, Mr. Ffinkworth. Lord Spongg is armed and dangerous. I don't want any civilians hurt."

Ffinkworth seemed miffed to be referred to as a "civilian." He stared at Jack with his sharp green eyes for a moment.

"Indeed, sir. I hardly think I am in any danger from his lordship. The Ffinkworths have served the Sponggs faithfully for over a hundred years, and I sincerely doubt that his lordship would find it in his heart to end such a favorable alliance. If I get caught in what is referred to as a 'crossfire,' I am quite confident that my Kevlar vest will protect me, sir."

He tapped his chest, and Jack could see

that the butler was indeed wearing body armor. He hid a smile. Ffinkworth looked impassively ahead.

"Even so," returned Jack, "I think you'd better leave."

"In good time, sir. Can I offer you a small glass of Madeira? The house, it is generally agreed, looks easier after a small tot of firewater."

"No thanks. Did you see another officer come in here?"

"Certainly, sir. Constable Baker has, I understand, been shot in the leg. He is in some considerable pain but not yet in danger of expiration. Will that be all, sir?"

"Where are they?"

"His lordship is in the west library. Mr. Baker is with him. He is held, sir, in what I believe is referred to as a 'hostage situation,' sir."

Jack looked at the several corridors that led out of the entrance hall. "Which way is the library?"

"I am sorry sir," replied Ffinkworth loftily, "but I have been instructed not to offer you any help. If you require anything *else*, please do not hesitate to ring."

He bowed stiffly from the waist and disappeared down through a trapdoor like someone in a conjuring trick.

Jack looked around and then walked slowly up the ornately carved wooden staircase. All the steps were of different heights and depths, and it was difficult not to stumble on the polished wood. As he was watching his feet, his head struck the roof of the entrance hall. The staircase went nowhere, the upstairs hall merely a trompe l'oeil that had been painted on the ceiling. Jack retraced his steps back to the front door. He walked off to the right, leaving the entrance hall, and opened a door at random into what seemed to be a drawing room. It was well furnished and lit by electric light, as the shutters were closed. At the far end of the room was another door, so Jack closed the one behind him and made his way cautiously across. The first sign of anything wrong came when he suddenly felt disoriented and fell over. Mary's mobile dropped out of his pocket, and he was about to pick it up when it started to move, quite on its own, back in the direction he had just come. It gathered speed, shot under the table and hit the door he had entered with a sharp thud. Before he could think what had happened, he felt himself being pulled by some powerful force in the same direction. He tried to get up but fell over again and then followed the Nokia back to the door, hitting his chin on a chair leg on the way down. He was now back where he had started, but instead of lying on the floor, he found himself actually in a heap *on* the door, seemingly pulled by some invisible force. He retrieved the mobile and got shakily to his feet. He found, to his astonishment, that he could now stand upright on the wall. The floor had become the wall, the wall the floor. His heart beat faster as his mind tried to make some kind of order of the situation. There was another lurch, and he fell over again, sliding up the wall to the molded ceiling, past two plaster cherubs that grinned at him. He felt panic rise within him, but then a piece of wax fruit from the fruit bowl on the table dislodged itself and fell up to the ceiling, slowly rolling down to where he was sprawled on the cornice. In a flash Jack realized what was happening. *The room was slowly revolving, with him in it.* Once he had figured what was going on, he managed to stand up straight and within a few minutes had walked across the ceiling moldings, past the chandelier and down the opposite wall. Five minutes later the room had turned full circle, and he opened the far door and stepped out into the house again. He sighed a sigh of relief and leaned against the wall.

Jack noticed that the music had become louder, so he slowly followed its source and, rounding a corner, found Ffinkworth playing the violin.

"Hello, sir," the butler said genially, "have you found his lordship yet?"

"N-no!" stammered Jack, running a shaking hand through his hair, noticing the silver salver with his undrunk Madeira upon a small table close by. "How did you manage that?"

"Sir?"

"The violin. I heard it when I spoke to you in the hall!"

"Ah," said Ffinkworth, standing up and untensioning his bow. "As sir has probably found out, Castle Spongg is rarely what it seems. The usual physical laws of time and motion appear to have forsaken its twisting corridors. Caligari was indeed a genius, you know, sir."

He picked up the salver with the Madeira on it and offered it to Jack. "If sir has changed his mind?"

"No thanks, I —"

"If you will excuse me, sir, I have work to do. If you want to know where his lordship is, I should try the dining room. It is down the corridor on your left."

Jack looked down the corridor. It seemed to go on forever. When he looked back, Ffinkworth was gone, whisked away through some secret passage that the infernal place seemed to be honeycombed with. A sound made him turn, and farther down the corridor, just opposite a billiard table screwed to the wall with a game apparently in the middle of play, were two large double doors. One of them creaked, and Jack stiffened. He walked slowly up and put his head round the door. There was no one inside, so he entered.

It seemed to be a dining room of some sort. The ceiling was elaborately decorated with plaster figures of cherubs at a feast, and the walls were covered with a deep red patterned silk. The room was dominated by a large oak table around which sat twelve matching chairs. On one wall, the wall above the door behind him, there was a painting depicting the Relief of Mafeking. On the other side was a large mirror that perfectly reflected the room, painting, table and everything else. Jack was moving slowly across the room when he noticed something that made his heart turn cold. The mirror reflected the room perfectly — but for one thing. *Jack had no reflection.* As he stood staring into the mirror and trying to make some kind of logical sense of it, he saw the door open behind him in the reflection. He turned to see Ffinkworth walking in with some silver candelabras that had just been polished. Jack turned back to the mirror. Ffinkworth was clearly reflected holding the candelabras, yet Jack was *not.* He felt a cold hand grasp his heart, and his throat went dry.

"Can I be of any assistance, sir?"

"My reflection, Ffinkworth — where is it?" he gasped, fear tightening his chest.

"I believe, sir, that it may be found in the mirror."

Ffinkworth stood next to Jack and lifted his arm. His reflection did the same — but was alone in that huge mirror image of the room.

"Can you not see yourself, sir?" asked Ffinkworth with annoying calm.

"No, damn it," replied Jack, his temper rising. "What's going on?"

"I regret, sir, that I have no idea. To my mind the mirror seems to be functioning perfectly."

Jack took a step closer, his voice dropping to a low snarl. "Listen —"

"I have been instructed to ask for your mobile telephone, sir."

"What?"

"By his lordship. He has asked me to inform you that he will answer all your questions — and also release Constable Baker — if you will relinquish said instrument."

Ffinkworth stared passively ahead, and Jack reluctantly handed him Mary's phone.

"Thank you, Ffinkworth. That will be all."

Randolph Spongg's voice was unmistakable, and Jack could see him in the mirror. Spongg was behind him, leaning on the doorframe below the painting of the Relief of Mafeking. Jack turned to where he thought Spongg would be, but Randolph was not in the room with him. Spongg, like Jack, was only on one side of the reflection — the *other* side. Jack turned back to the mirror as Randolph laughed at his frustration and walked to where Jack's reflection should have been, giving Jack the unnerving experience of gazing into a reflection that wasn't his own.

"Hello, Jack," Spongg said brightly. "Thing's aren't going too well for me, are they?"

"What's going on?"

Spongg laughed. "Things are rarely what

they seem at Castle Spongg." He looked around admiringly. "Caligari *was* a genius, you know."

"Where's Baker?"

"He's fine. Not in any real danger."

"Randolph Spongg, you are under arrest for the murder of Humpty Dumpty, William Winkie and Dr. Carbuncle. You do not have to say anything. But it may —"

Spongg laughed again. "You are tenacious, aren't you, Jack? I had a terrier like you once. A Jack, too, a Jack Russell. It used to grab hold of something and wouldn't let go. I admire that. You and I could have been good friends." He picked an apple out of his pocket and bit into it.

Jack said, "The CCDC have declared both the Sacred Gonga Visitors' Center and Andersen's Farm category-A biohazard hot zones. Even without murder charges, you're still looking at life imprisonment for the intentional spreading of a communicable disease. Why not make it easy for yourself?"

Spongg smiled. "I can hardly give myself up, Inspector. I don't think prison would be terribly pleasant for me. I wouldn't be allowed to take Ffinkworth, and the idea of twenty-five years in the clink without the benefit of pâté or grouse or champagne or any of the hundred and one luxuries that make our dreadful lives bearable seems positively depressing. Prison is for small people, Jack. I have no intention of going."

"Why did you do it, Spongg?"

"Well," began Randolph with a curious smile on his lips, "it all began when Tom Thomm *appropriated* the goose. He brought the goose to Humpty — Thomm worshipped him — and Humpty devised the scam with Dr. Carbuncle and myself. Without the cash to buy the shares, it would never have worked, but the potential profits were so large that Humpty just couldn't resist it. He was never happy about the murders in Andersen's Wood, but he was desperate to rebuild St. Cerebellum's. No surprise: The old place had kept him sane for almost forty years. I don't suppose any of us realize what it's like to be a very large egg. Frightful, I imagine."

He thought about this for a moment, smiled and continued. "Humpty got cold feet when he found out how potent Hercules had become. He was essentially a good man, and his heart wasn't in it. I'd been planning to get rid of him for over a month."

"And Dr. Carbuncle?"

"He supported Spongg's and hated

Winsum and Loosum, but murder wasn't in his game plan. As soon as you started to investigate, he made a few assumptions and wanted to blow the whistle. Very regrettable. He was a brilliant research chiropodist."

"And you, Spongg? Everything good that Spongg's stood for. Why risk all that?"

Spongg's eyes flashed angrily as he thumped his fist on the table.

"Don't you understand? I did this to *protect* all that was great about Spongg's. My factory, my workers, Castle Spongg, the Foot Museum, the two hundred charities I give money to every year. Winsum and Loosum would have taken all that and sold everything piece by piece. They had plans to turn this house into a theme park. *A theme park!* I did all this to stop the encroachment of damaging and selfish twenty-first-century business practices. Tell me honestly, Jack, which company did you prefer?"

"Yours."

"Said without hesitation," said Randolph triumphantly. "So you agree."

"Not if murder is involved."

Randolph threw his hands up in the air. "Murder?" he said in exasperation. "If I have to murder a few people, then that's the price we have to pay. The needs of the many outweigh the needs of the few, Mr. Spratt. You work in criminal law; you know the full meaning of that. To run the criminal-justice system, innocent people must, however regrettably, be occasionally sent to prison. It's unfair, but it's for the good of the many. To be efficient, the system can't be fair; to be fair, it can't be efficient. Business is the same. To make profits and benefit the community, then some people, however regrettably, will have to die. My Spongg charity homes look after thousands of retired people and offer better lives than they might enjoy under the government. How many lives do you think I've saved? Ten? One hundred? One thousand? When Spongg folds and the people I look after are cast out, a lot more people will die. You should look at the big picture."

He swept his arms around, indicating the house, the grounds, everything. "All this, Mr. Spratt. How could I afford to let it go?" Spongg stared at him with a manic expression.

"That doesn't explain how you'd get hold of Dumpty's shares."

As if on cue, the door opened behind Spongg. Lola Vavoom entered dressed in a sixties style catsuit. Jack looked around him, but he was still alone in the room; Randolph and Lola existed only in the reflection.

"Hello, Inspector dahling," she cooed, threading an arm round Spongg's waist. "I never liked the idea of a comeback, but for you I'd be willing to make an exception."

She laughed as Jack looked at her in disbelief.

"You two . . . ?"

"Yes, Inspector," replied Lola. "Humpty and I were married; it wasn't hard to persuade him — he *adored* me. I was to own thirty-eight percent of Spongg's following my husband's untimely death in the Zephyr, everyone catches verrucas with help from the Sacred Gonga, and before you can say *Hallux valgus,* Spongg's is back on top!"

"Just through verrucas?"

"At first," said Spongg. "Dr. Carbuncle was working on a corn serum to contaminate Britain's water supply. Athlete's-foot spore was to be introduced into the initial stages of sock manufacture. In under a year, Mr. Spratt, I could have bought out those sniveling dogs at Winsum and Loosum. Sold their company piecemeal as they were going to do to us and then fired all the executives after promising to take them on at increased salary — and then Lola and I could be married again!"

"Again?"

"Indeed," Lola replied slowly, "it will be for the fifth time. Randolph was my third, seventh, tenth, fifteenth and soon my eighteenth husband. It's an on-off sort of romance."

They kissed aggressively on the lips.

"What about Willie Winkie? He saw you at Grimm's Road?"

"I think we've talked enough," said Randolph. "So it's time for you and me to bid each other good-bye."

"Why don't we just call it au revoir?"

Randolph thought for a moment.

"No, let's call it good-bye. My grand-father built a pneumatic railway that leads off beyond the perimeter of the grounds. There I have a Hornet Moth aircraft that will take Lola and myself to Europe. I have friends in Switzerland, and we will be in Geneva in time to hear of my own — and yours, of course — demise on the ten o'clock news. You, the house, that officer upstairs and unfortunately the Ffinkworths will be consumed by the detonation of this device."

He opened a Tupperware container that had been lying on the table and took out a small triangular sandwich on a cardboard plate. It had a piece of foil on its two furthermost corners. Spongg connected each one by way of a crocodile clip to a battery and then in turn to a detonator stuck into six sticks of dynamite bundled together. He then laid a hair dryer on the table, pointed it towards the sandwich and set it to "hot." The sandwich immediately started to curl, and Jack could understand the fiendish simplicity of the device. In a few minutes, the sandwich would curl up completely, the two corners would touch, set off the dynamite and — He shuddered.

"It's a London and North East Railway garlic and lettuce special. They curl more than any others. We were approached in the sixties by the railways to find an anticurling agent. We developed one from our trench-foot remedies. It affected the taste, but that was not a primary consideration. This sandwich, Mr. Spratt, has *not* been treated. If you think this amount of dynamite won't be enough, I have another ton of the stuff under the table. All that will be left of Castle Spongg will be a smoking hole in the ground."

Spongg opened the door on his side of the reflection.

"Adieu!" he said with a cheery wave. "If

it's any consolation, I seriously underestimated you. I wouldn't have dared try
this with Friedland as head of the NCD. I
thought you were just another plod. Oh,
well, pip-pip!"

He and Lola walked out and closed the
door quietly behind them.

"I've been underestimated before,"
growled Jack under his breath.

He ran to the door and tried the handle,
but it was no use — it had been firmly
locked. He checked the chimney, but that
was too small. Then he walked back to the
mirror and stared as the reflection of sandwich curled some more. At the rate it was
going, he had possibly five minutes —
maybe less. He thought of yelling, but that
might bring Mary and the others into the
house, and that would be disastrous. He
sighed, drew out a chair and sat down. He
pulled off the vest, which had grown uncomfortable and was now redundant, and
let it fall to the floor. He thought about
Madeleine and the kids and regretted that
he hadn't been able to say good-bye. He'd
miss Stevie's birthday. All of them. He was
just thinking of some way to leave a message for them that wouldn't be destroyed
when his eye fell upon a servant's call
button next to the marble fireplace. It was

worth a try. After all, Ffinkworth was a gentleman's gentleman, and he did say to call him if he needed anything. Jack ran to the wall and pressed it. Deep in the bowels of the house, a bell sounded, and less than thirty seconds later, Ffinkworth appeared through a trapdoor in the floor, which would not have seemed out of place on a stage. His reflection, Jack noted, did the same.

Ffinkworth brushed himself down and straightened his jacket. "Can I be of any assistance, sir?"

"I need to get out of this room."

"Quite impossible, sir. The door is firmly locked — I made sure of it myself."

"What about your trapdoor?"

"I'm afraid to say, sir, the mechanism for its operation is down below."

Jack looked over at the sandwich. It was now almost completely curled up, only half an inch separating the two corners. He pointed at the mirror.

"Do you see that, Ffinkworth? On the table. It's a bomb. If you don't help me, we'll all be blown to kingdom come. *NOW, HOW DO I GET OUT OF THIS ROOM?*"

Ffinkworth maintained perfect calm. "Prison is a depressing place, I am told, and certainly not the place for a man such as his lordship. He explained it to us both. We think that this is for the best."

Jack was amazed at the man's coolness. He was just about to die, yet he was being loyal to his master to the end.

"Ffinkworth, I —"

Jack stopped and stared at the gaunt butler, who looked ahead of him dispassionately.

" *'Us both'?* " said Jack, the light beginning to dawn. "Who's 'us both'?"

Ffinkworth looked unnerved for the first time, and his eyes flicked across to his reflection. In that instant Jack knew.

"Tell your brother to duck," said Jack, picking up a large marble ashtray and hurling it for all his might at the mirror. Ffinkworth's brother dived for cover, while the Ffinkworth next to Jack raised a hand to his worried face.

Jack ran up to where the glass had been and jumped through into the identical room behind what he had thought had been a mirror. The illusion had been perfectly realized. Even the painting of the Relief of Mafeking had been copied in reverse to create the perfect waking hallucination. Jack didn't stop, his feet crunching and squeaking on the shards of broken glass as he ran up to the table and placed his Allegro Owners' Club card carefully in between the jaws of the sandwich as they clicked shut. He breathed a sigh of relief and pulled the detonator from the dynamite. The second Ffinkworth picked himself up and gingerly brushed himself down. He had been slightly cut by flying glass but was otherwise unhurt. The first Ffinkworth peered through from the room Jack had just come from.

"Will that be all, sir?" the identical Ffinkworth twins asked in unison.

"Yes," replied Jack as he breathed a deep sigh of relief, "except that you're both under arrest."

The Ffinkworths bowed again and also looked relieved.

"As you wish, sir."

Jack brought Baker out of Castle Spongg, and Gretel and Mary and two paramedics ran up to help him.

"If I don't pull through," said Baker in a whisper, "tell Susie that I love her."

"Baker," said Mary, "it's barely a scratch. Don't be such a fusspot."

"You mean I'm not going to die?" he asked the paramedics.

"Not today," remarked the first medic, looking at Baker's inconsequential wound.

"Did you see or hear a light aircraft recently?" asked Jack.

"Circled the building and then headed south about five minutes ago," said Mary. "Was that Spongg?"

"And Lola, on their way to Geneva."

"Lola?"

"It's complicated. I need to speak to Briggs. Anyone got a phone?"

"Well," said Brown-Horrocks a few minutes later, after Jack had reported Spongg's escape and explained everything to him and Mary, "I suppose that wraps up the investigation. Spongg murders Humpty, Carbuncle and then the witness Winkie, attempts to raise the share price of his failing foot-care company by infecting everyone with verrucas. It's not exactly standard *Amazing Crime* material, but I daresay it might be a welcome change for the readership. We may have to play down the identical-twin aspect, but it's not all bad."

"Yes," said Jack thoughtfully, "I suppose you're right."

He got up and walked towards Gretel's car as the two Ffinkworths gave themselves up. They had even changed out of their frock coats and packed two identical suitcases. Brown-Horrocks looked at them disapprovingly as Jack checked his watch. It was almost midday.

"What happened at the visitors' center?"

"Cordoned off to a two-hundred-yard radius," said Mary. "You wouldn't believe the complexity of a biohazard response — everyone turned up, from DEFRA to the Met Office to the Environment Agency. Briggs gave a press conference on your behalf explaining the reason. There isn't going to be a riot or anything; everyone's just hoping there won't be any lasting damage to the Sacred Gonga."

"But the Jellyman will still dedicate it?"

"They've switched locations to the Civic Center."

Jack suddenly felt tired and wanted to speak to Madeleine and the kids more than anything else. He called home, but they were out — probably to go see the Jellyman.

At that moment a van screeched to a halt in front of them. It belonged to the Reading Biohazard Fast Response Team, and two officials dressed in yellow rubberized suits jumped out.

"Who's Jack Spratt?" asked the one with the clipboard.

Jack identified himself.

"Move away from those people and

stand on your own, please, sir. Mary Mary?"

"Yes?"

"You're to join him. Mr. Brown-Horrocks, too. Has anyone else come into contact with any of these three people?"

Baker, Gretel and the two paramedics all meekly put up their hands.

"What's going on?" demanded Jack.

"You've been declared a category-A contamination risk. You're going to have to be showered, scrubbed, examined and inoculated. All your clothes will have to be burned, and any personal effects autoclaved for thirty minutes at one hundred and twenty-one degrees centigrade."

"Even my clipboard?" asked Brown-Horrocks in dismay.

"Everything," said the biohazard agent, with the buoyant tone of someone who has just been given a lot of power and is keen to try it out. "By rights you should never have left the Andersen's Farm hot zone — you might have spread verrucas all over Berkshire. Haven't you read the seven-hundred-and-twenty-page procedure manual for communicable-disease outbreaks?"

"Have you?" asked Jack sarcastically.

"Most of it," replied the biohazard agent with surprising honesty.

They all grumbled but sat obediently in

a small group on the grass while the de-contamination unit cordoned them off and fetched some supplies from the ambulance for Baker, who seemed to be improving.

The fire brigade, ambulance and medical teams arrived within an hour, and the whole process began in earnest. It was a miserable end to an otherwise good day. As Jack waited his turn to be scrubbed down in the portable showers, he suddenly had a disturbing thought about something Lola had said. By the time he was dry, issued a set of blue overalls and finally allowed to go, the disturbing thought had transformed into *doubt.* A doubt that said everything was *still* not quite as it seemed.

43. Loose Ends

PUMPKIN TRANSMUTATION DEVICE TESTED

Scientists at QuangTech were said to be "overjoyed" at the latest testing of their new pumpkin transmutation device, it was reported in the Berkshire Radio News this month. The Reading-based technology company had been experimenting on pumpkins for some years, but until now with little success. The highly technical article outlines for the first time the extraordinary advances made in the world of pumpkin transmogrification. "It is possible," said a QuangTech spokesman yesterday, "to change pumpkins into almost anything one wishes by bombarding them with twin beams of particle-shifting gamma radiation, then moving the charged particles to within a magnetic-contained matrix of the new shape. The successful transmutation of a pumpkin into a coach was undertaken last week and was entirely successful — for a while. At present we have no way of permanently fixing the new shape, and the coach

reverted to a pumpkin around about midnight."
— Extract from *The Mole*, April 19, 1988

Aside from the absence of the Sacred Gonga and the fact that it wasn't held in the visitors' center, the Jellyman's Sacred Gonga Visitors' Center dedication went extremely well. Everyone present commented on how it was conducted with the utmost tact, solemnity and reverence. After the dedication ceremony, the Jellyman went on a procession route through the town, stopping off at various places of interest on the way.

The police estimate for the turnout was nearly three hundred thousand, despite the poor weather and the faint possibility of contracting verrucas. Of that it was estimated that 10 percent actually got a good look, 30 percent saw a man in a white suit waving, a further 30 percent saw only a distant white blob, 10 percent thought they saw something but actually didn't, and the remainder saw nothing at all.

Madeleine, Stevie, Ben, Pandora, Megan and Jerome had been in the unlucky last category. They had left too late and got stuck in the throng, battling with the crowds and dodging street traders who were selling everything from Jellyman key rings to bedside lamps to DVDs of his speeches to dolls that made suitably sagacious pronouncements when you pulled a string at the back of their neck. Pandora and Ben gripped Jerome and Megan's hands lest they get swept away in the crowd. They got to the Civic Center just as the Jellyman had gone in. When he came out two hours later, a police van pulled up and blocked their view, so all they saw was the back of his white Daimler limousine as he drove off to visit St. Septyck's new ward for terminal sarcastics. Madeleine thought of waiting for his return in three hours' time, but the children were tired and it had begun to drizzle. They made their way back home in a subdued mood. It was a bit like visiting the beach one day in the year to find it shut.

"Congratulations, Jack!"

Briggs shook him warmly by the hand, but Jack didn't smile. The decontamination process has that effect on people.

"They got away, sir. It's not much of a result."

"You're wrong," Briggs said, handing Jack and Mary champagne glasses. "It's a very good result. Without you more than ten thousand people would be infected with Dr. Carbuncle's unbelievably infectious superverruca by now — with potentially millions in the coming months. Swimming pools, beaches and sports halls would have become no-go zones and shoe shops places of dread and suspicion. Spongg's would be charging what they want, and we'd all be none the wiser. No, it's a very good result indeed."

Jack took a sip of the champagne to find that it was, in fact, fizzy apple juice.

"We're still on duty," said Briggs in response to Jack's quizzical look. "Cheers!"

"Cheers, sir."

Briggs sat at his desk. It was early evening, and the day's security precautions were being slowly wound down. The Jellyman was at his last official engagement, a banquet over at the sprawling QuangTech facility to celebrate the technological, industrial and artistic achievements of Reading. Jack and Mary had been called up to Briggs's office quite unexpectedly and were surprised to find Brown-Horrocks there, still dressed in the blue overalls, which were too short and showed at least seven inches of white ankle.

"The Biohazard Response Team went to Dr. Carbuncle's house and are going to encase it in conciete rather than risk even *moving* the verruca," said Briggs. "The Foot Museum is being soaked in disinfectant and won't be reopened for six months. I've had a word with the head of the Center of Communicable Diseases. They'd like to shake your hand *without* latex gloves on — that's quite an honor from those chaps."

"Yes, but what about Lola and Spongg, sir?"

Briggs shook his head. "They won't find anywhere they can hide in Europe. The deliberate spreading of infectious diseases is serious stuff; the police forces of the Continent will definitely be on the lookout."

Jack was less than happy. Spongg and Lola's progress had been charted by a series of sightings in the South of England. It seemed they had commenced their Channel crossing at Lulworth, and the French had sent two reconnaissance aircraft to patrol the coast. They were recalled three hours later when the Hornet Moth didn't show.

"Have you seen the late editions?" asked Briggs. He showed Jack a copy of *The Toad*. It carried glowing reports of the extraordinary drama played out in Reading that day and heaped almost as much praise on Jack today as the bile they had dumped on him yesterday. "It's all going frightfully well. The press want you to issue a statement. Perhaps you could make up a catchphrase for yourself — something like . . . 'This inquiry is shut' — or something."

"I'd be lying, sir."

"I'm sorry?"

Brown-Horrocks looked up from where he was transcribing his notes, which had faded badly in the autoclave.

"Something's not right," said Jack despondently. "Spongg *planned* to kill Humpty but *didn't*. Someone beat him to it."

"Why do you say that?"

"Lola said that she would inherit Humpty's thirty-eight percent after her *'husband's untimely death in the Zephyr.'* If she was in on the whole scam from the beginning, she must have known about the shooting — so why mention the Zephyr? It was how they *intended* to kill him, but events overtook them. Then, when we visit her for the second time, asking annoying questions about Humpty's new wife, they decide to use it on *us*."

"That's it?" said Briggs with a laugh. "That's the sole reason for your doubts?"

"Pretty much. Someone else killed Humpty."

"Who?"

"A hit man working for Solomon Grundy."

"Don't be ridiculous! We've gone down that avenue already. Grundy said he knew that his wife fooled around and didn't care. I need proof, Jack, proof!"

"He only *said* he didn't care, sir. Grundy turned down an offer of ten million for Humpty's thirty-eight percent the night of the charity benefit. Charles Pewter told me the price was a snip and he should have jumped at the chance — but he didn't. He knew there was no point, as Humpty had less than three hours to live. He knew *that* because he had paid a gunman to kill him. All the 'understanding husband' act was a sham — Grundy took his wife's affair very badly indeed."

"And Winkie?"

"He must have recognized the shooter. Someone from Winsum's, where he worked."

Briggs drummed his fingers on the desk and exchanged looks with Brown-Horrocks. He took a deep breath and said, "Refusing ten million quid for dodgy foot-care shares is undoubtedly the most tenuous piece of evidence I've ever heard. You could be wrong; Lola might have made a mistake mentioning the Zephyr."

Jack bit his lip. Briggs was right. It *was* conjecture. Sadly, this wasn't about what was true but what was provable.

"I'll concede it's a bit flimsy, sir."

They stared at each other for a moment.

"It's more than flimsy," said Briggs at length, "it's blessed inconvenient. I've got a roomful of press who want to hear *exactly* how Spongg murdered Humpty."

"Can I make a suggestion?" asked Brown-Horrocks.

"Certainly," said Briggs.

"I've spoken to the editors at *Amazing Crime Stories* and they're very taken with the whole chiropody/bioterrorism/nursery rhyme angle, so they'll go with what you've got — sight unseen. I suggest that you make it seem to readers as if Spongg *did* kill Humpty. I'm sorry to say that publication might be seriously compromised if there were any complications, false endings or unresolved plot threads."

There was silence.

"He's right," said Briggs. "Without Spongg in custody, the case remains open anyway. If we announce the findings that Brown-Horrocks suggests, it'll be good for the force — and good for your Guild application."

Jack didn't say anything, so Briggs, sensing reticence, continued: "I've had the Chief Constable on to me twice today already. He thinks we should keep the NCD and promote you to DCI. The Chief is not happy that Chymes fabricated the entire Andersen's Wood murder case and feels that we should advance someone from within the Reading force *just in case.* He is prepared to offer you all the help and assistance that might be required to make the NCD as much of a success as DCI Chymes was. Times change, Jack, and we *have* to change with them. Public approval is a currency we cannot afford to fritter away. Of course, this would all depend on your ability to play ball. You've moved up a notch, Jack. The stakes are bigger — but then so are the rewards."

Briggs and Brown-Horrocks looked at him expectantly.

Jack thought for a moment and stared at the floor. He'd like the respect, the kudos, the extra cash, the parking place. He'd also like to make DCI. But most of all he wanted the NCD to stay as it was. Yet if he'd learned *anything* over the past few days, it was that *Amazing Crime Stories* and the Guild had no place attempting to make murder, tragedy and violence marketable commodities for the edification of the masses — that and never go near a thirty-seven-kilo verruca.

"This must have been how it all began with Chymes," sighed Jack. "A small omission on one case, an 'embellishment' on the next. The question is not about what's *best* but what's *right*. Chymes had confused the two and compromised not only his own integrity but that of the police — and the due process of law. I'll let you have a full report on Humpty by Monday morning, along with my recommendations regarding Solomon Grundy. Now, if you'll excuse me, I must go and thank the team."

Jack walked down the corridor to the elevator and pressed the "call" button. He turned to Mary.

"You know, Sergeant, principles cost money. And if I've learned anything over the past few days, it's —"

"Sir," interrupted Mary before he could embark on what would doubtless have been a very boring speech about moral relativism, "do you really believe that Grundy had Humpty killed?"

"I'm afraid so. But Briggs is right.

Proving it will be tough. We'll have to get a confession from the hit man himself, implicating Grundy."

"We can start to delve on Monday, sir."

Brown-Horrocks dashed up to them as the lift doors opened.

"I'm not going to change my mind," said Jack.

"No, no," said Brown-Horrocks quickly, "the day is not yet over, and my observational duties include your personal life — although from what you've told me about your regrettably abstemious and monogamous existence, there doesn't seem to be much of interest. Still, orders are orders."

Ashley, Tibbit, Baker and Gretel applauded Jack and Mary as they walked into the NCD offices and gave them some real champagne, but in plastic cups. It was too small in there even with Ashley stuck to the ceiling, so Brown-Horrocks and Gretel stepped outside to the corridor, where there was more headroom for them both. They looked at each other again. Brown-Horrocks was the first person Gretel had ever had to look *up* to, and she was the tallest woman Brown-Horrocks had ever seen — and, to him, the most beautiful.

"You're the most . . . *tall* woman I have

ever laid eyes upon," said Brown-Horrocks after a long pause.

Gretel said nothing, went all shy and didn't know what to do with her hands.

"Thank you," she replied. "I like your overalls."

"Well," said Jack, clapping his hands together to get everyone's attention, "any news about Spongg?"

"Latest report," said Baker, who had a large bandage on his leg but didn't seem to be in any pain at all, "is that the French Coast Guard found the wreckage of a light aircraft floating off the Normandy coast. They'll know more when the search continues tomorrow at first light."

"Well, then," said Jack, holding his cup aloft, "this is to all of us — and teamwork. Each and every one of you was exemplary. Long after we are ashes and the great adventures of this small department are chronicled for all to see, people will —"

"DI Spratt?" came a low voice from the door, interrupting what also might have turned out to be a long and tiresome speech. They turned to see three men dressed in dark suits and gray macs. They had sunglasses on and were unmistakably Secret Service.

"That's me."

They looked him up and down. Dressed in the blue overalls he seemed more like a decorator. "You have something we want, Inspector."

"Something of extreme value," said the second.

"A goose," said the third, who was holding a pet carrier.

"What are you going to do with it?" asked Jack, who didn't like the idea of giving anything to the Secret Service, *especially* something that lived and breathed.

"I don't really think that's any of your concern," said the one who had spoken first.

"It will be studied by top scientists," said the second.

"Top scientists," repeated the one with the pet carrier. "Where is it?"

Jack sighed. "Okay, who's got the goose?"

Tibbit led them into the filing room, where there was a sheet of plastic on the floor and a large cardboard box lined with straw. The goose hissed as the third man grabbed it roughly by the neck and bundled it unceremoniously into the pet carrier. It managed to bite him, much to Jack's and Tibbit's delight, and the other agent took the four golden eggs and placed them in a bag.

"She will be well looked after, won't she?" asked Tibbit, who had grown quite fond of the bird.

"They'll want to know how she does it," said the second.

"Don't worry, kid," said the third, "they're all experts. This is for you."

And he handed Jack a receipt for one goose and four golden eggs.

He gave a cruel laugh, and they were all gone without another word.

"Sir," said Tibbit in a hoarse whisper, "I must tell you something."

"Yes?"

"They're going to take the goose apart to see how it works and find that it's just a goose, aren't they?"

"In NCD work you can never be a hundred percent sure the way events might be interpreted, but yes, it seems likely."

He faltered for a moment, unsure of how to put it. Finally he said, "One goose looks a lot like another, don't you think?"

Jack smiled. "Yes," he replied, "I daresay it does. But I know nothing and don't wish to know anything. If anyone swapped the goose, good luck to them as long as they use that wealth wisely. If they don't, then I just might wish to get involved."

Tibbit smiled. "Thank you, sir."

Jack walked back into the office to continue his speech.

"Where was I? Ah, yes: Long after we are ashes and —"

Luckily for the NCD staff, he was once again interrupted, this time by Mrs. Singh, who swept in like a galleon in full sail.

"There you are!" she said. "I've been trying to reach you all day. Don't you ever return calls?"

"I've been busy bringing down the second-biggest foot-care empire in the world and one of Reading's most respected figures — and my mobile was blown up."

"You could have used Mary's."

"It was taken by an identical-twin butler."

"What about that Guild chap's?"

"Melted in the autoclave."

"Never mind. I got Humpty's results back from the SunnyDale Poultry Labs."

"And?"

"Large quantities of alcohol, traces of marijuana, and about sixty-eight different strains of salmonella, four of which would probably have proved fatal within the next six months, and traces of chorioallantoic membrane."

Everyone in the room leaned closer.

"Traces of *what?*"

"Chorioallantoic membrane. It's a highly vascularized extraembryonic membrane that functions as a site for nutrient transport and waste disposal during embryonic development."

"Embryonic development?" echoed Jack. "You mean . . ."

"Right. He didn't die from the gunshot wound *or* the fall. He *hatched.*"

There was a deathly hush as they took this in.

"Hatched? You mean to tell me Humpty Dumpty was *pregnant?*"

"That's exactly what I mean," replied Mrs. Singh, "although 'pregnant' is perhaps the wrong word. He was an egg, Jack, and eggs, when fertilized, hatch."

"I know what eggs do, Mrs. Singh. And what was going to come out? A three-hundred-pound chicken?"

"Not at all," replied Mrs. Singh. "Even my most conservative estimates place the *chick alone* at that sort of weight — the fully grown hen would probably tip the scales at two to three tons."

"I need to sit down."

"You are sitting down. Skinner and I couldn't simulate the extreme breakup of his shell," continued Mrs. Singh, "no matter what we did. The damage was too severe for anything a bullet might have caused. Something hatching, now, that's a different matter."

"So how did the bullet go straight through?"

"Fluke," replied Mrs. Singh. "It must have passed between the body and the wing or the leg — or something."

"Wait a minute, wait a minute," said Mary, trying to get all the information in context. "Firstly, he's a guy, right? Even if he is, to all intents and purposes, a very large egg?"

"Indeed," replied Mrs. Singh, "he had all the necessary equipment."

"And a series of girlfriends, so he wasn't shy on exercising it," added Jack.

"Okay. He's over sixty-five years of age, so I think we can safely say he was born — laid — whatever — *unfertilized.* Most eggs are, right?"

"Right."

"So when *was* he fertilized?"

Mrs. Singh thought for a moment. "This is more the field of avian pathologists, but by comparing the volume of his egg and likening that to a scaled-up model of ostrich chick development, we can safely say . . . about six months ago."

"How?"

"The hole I found drilled in his shell," said Mrs. Singh. "A modified IVF procedure would do the trick."

"But it's *still* murder," muttered Jack. "Whatever grew inside him would have been slowly consuming him from within. The question is: Why?"

"I should imagine the poultry industry might be very interested in a three-ton chicken, sir."

"Don't be ridiculous, Mary. You'd never find an oven big enough. Besides, what misbegotten evil genius would be so cruelly insane as to want to carry out such a bizarre and perverted experiment on a living, breathing creature?"

They looked at each other, snapped their fingers in unison and said, "Dr. Quatt!"

"Spot on. She had the opportunity, the skill, the knowledge. But, more important, the total absence of any ethical standards whatsoever. Gretel and Ashley, take a couple of officers and go to St. Cerebellum's to arrest Dr. Quatt. Baker, call the Ops room and see if anyone has reported seeing a giant chicken loose in Reading — especially near the Grimm's Road area. I want locations, times, size, everything — so we can plot them on a map."

They all dashed off to do his bidding.

Ashley scampered along the roof to the elevator while Gretel bade Brown-Horrocks a shy "well, see you around, then" sort of farewell.

"Thanks, Mrs. Singh, you're a marvel. Stay for a drink?"

She politely declined, as she had to babysit two of her grandchildren, then stared in a medically curious way at Brown-Horrocks and departed.

"At last!" announced Jack. "Some *closure*. I don't know about you, but I'm knackered. I've been blown up, decontaminated, rolled along the top of a room, my Allegro's been written off, and I was almost vaporized by an insane chiropodist. And tomorrow I've got to hunt a giant chicken running loose in Reading. Well, cheers."

"Cheers, sir."

"Do you think Officer Kandlestyk-Maeker would enjoy the zoo?" asked Brown-Horrocks, who obviously had other things on his mind. "They've got a baby giraffe, you know."

44. The End of the Story

BR AK-IN AT PRINT RS

Th polic w r call d last night to th print rs of R ading's pr mi r gossip sh t, *Th Gadfly*, wh r it was discov r d a gang of typ thi v s had mad off with th ir ntir stock of 's. Polic w r initially baffl d by th th ft until n ws of a similar th ft involving th whol sal purloinm nt of th l tt rs A, B, C, and D was r port d from Byfl t. "I think," said DCI Palatino, "that I can s a patt rn b ginning to m rg ." Archibald Fatquack, ditor of *Th Gadfly*, would not l t th th ft halt publication of his v n rabl organ and d clar d, "It's busin ss as usual!"
— From *Th Gadfly*, S pt mb r 1, 1995

It was a cloud, clearless night and the stars brinkled twightly in the heavens. As Jack and Mary motored closer to his hother's mouse, they could see that the mull foon had risen behind the beanstalk and now presented the leaves and pipening rods in sharp silhouette. Attached to the top of the stalk was a steady red light, a safety precaution fitted by the Civil Aviation Authority that afternoon. The crowds had departed from the streets nearby, and litter and soft-drink cans lay scattered about the road. After the busy day, everyone was at home relaxing.

Everyone, that is, except Dr. Quatt, who had not been at St. Cerebellum's or her home when Ashley and Gretel called. Jack had issued a warrant for her arrest and posted uniformed officers at both places. No one had reported a chicken loose in Reading either — of any size.

"Thanks for dropping me off," said Jack as they drove slowly up the road towards his mother's. "Madeleine said she'd be up at Mum's and I should meet her there. Hello, what's this?"

Ahead of them two police cars blocked the street, and two officers in vests held automatic weapons.

"Yes, sir?" inquired one of the policemen in a businesslike tone when Jack got out and walked towards them.

"Detective Inspector Spratt, NCD."

He held up his ID card, and the officer stood to attention respectfully.

"Thank you, sir. And may I say on a personal note how impressed I was by the way you cracked the Humpty case. Once had a verruca myself. Nasty little blighters. Do you always wear blue overalls, sir?"

"It was a decontamination sort of thing. What's going on?"

The officer leaned forward and lowered his voice. "Jellyman on a personal social call, sir. Private viewing of the beanstalk and an audience with the owner."

This was surprising and also a great honor — owing to his tight schedule, the Jellyman rarely did "drop-ins" these days.

"She's my mother, and my family is up there. Can I go in?"

"One moment," said the officer, and he relayed the request through his walkie-talkie.

"Good evening," said Jack to the second officer. "Tell me, how long has that white van been there?"

The officer looked at where it was parked less than fifty yards away.

"Don't know, sir. Why?"

"No reason."

Mary switched off the BMW's engine, and the city was suddenly still and quiet. Not a dog barked, not a car horn sounded. Everyone was indoors. Jack looked at his watch. Five past ten. People would be settling down to catch the edited highlights of the visit on the news. He looked about. At the various parts of the street, other armed police stood on duty, and outside his mother's garden gate was a white Daimler limousine. Mary joined Jack and handed her own ID to the officer. He looked at Jack for his approval, and he nodded.

They waited for a couple of minutes until the walkie-talkie crackled into life.

"Tell them to come on over."

The officer escorted them towards the garden gate, where Friedland Chymes was waiting to meet them. Since he was heading up Jellyman security, it was understandable. *Unwelcome,* but understandable. He was stony-faced but remained professional.

"Good result, Jack," he managed to growl, the feeling that he should have been the one to figure it out all too obvious. "Sergeant, you'll have to wait here. Family only. Baines will take you to the front door."

Jack was handed over to a man wearing an earpiece and a bulge where a gun would be in a shoulder holster. The man asked to see his card.

"Why has your ID card shrunk?"

"Thirty minutes in an autoclave."

"I see," he replied, as though that sort of thing happened every day. "Thank you, Inspector. Follow me."

Jack accompanied him up the path as the officer named Baines with the gun and the earpiece reeled off instructions parrot fashion.

"Only speak when you are spoken to. Do not attempt to shake hands. Bow your head when you are presented. Do not interrupt when he is talking. Do not touch him. Do not sneeze in his presence. Do not discuss politics, and always refer to him as 'Your Eminence.' "

He rapped on the front door, and it opened a crack to reveal another officer with a large mustache who looked at Jack and then ushered him in. As soon as he stepped into the front hall, Jack noticed that the grandfather clock had stopped. He glanced across and was puzzled to see that the pendulum had halted midswing. Stranger still, his mother's hyperactive cats were all sitting quietly in a row by the door, like skittles. He didn't have time to think about it any further, as he was ushered into the familiar surroundings of his mother's front room.

His whole family was there. Madeleine was standing at the back holding Stevie, and the rest of the children were either sitting or standing next to their grandmother. Incredibly, Pandora was wearing a dress, and *more* incredibly, Ben had combed his hair. Megan was standing in front of them all, facing the large leather armchair that used to be Jack's father's. Sitting in that chair, suffused by a soft glow that seemed to emanate not *from* his white suit but *through* it, was the Jellyman.

The Jellyman's physical presence was something that could only be felt, never described. He exuded strong feelings of hope, and his calming personality seemed to envelop all who met him. They said of the Jellyman that a smile from him could brighten the darkest moment and a word could still the most passionate rage. Jack, like many, had remained skeptical about the great man's powers, but in those few seconds he knew that everything they said was true.

The Jellyman was leaning forward in the chair, his fingertips pressed against his chin, and even though he whispered to Megan and the words were indistinct, they seemed to fill the room like chamber music in a hall of mirrors. Megan was nodding eagerly as he spoke to her, and when he finished, he laid his hand on her head and smiled. Megan nearly melted, and Madeleine wiped a tear from her cheek.

The Jellyman's aide rapped a staff on the floor and said, in a loud, clear, voice, "Your Eminence, may I present Detective Inspector Jack Spratt!"

Jack took a step forwards and tried to remember all he had been told on the short walk up the garden path. He'd forgotten everything except the bit about sneezing, but it didn't matter. The Jellyman swung round in his seat and stared at Jack with his piercing blue eyes.

"Mr. Spratt," he said with an enigmatic smile, "you have a most charming family."

"Th-thank you, Your Eminence."

He stood up and approached Jack. He was a large man, but perhaps this impression was due to his overwhelming personality rather than his stature. He spoke plainly and without ambiguity. You could never remember the precise *words* he spoke, but the meaning of them stayed with you forever.

"I want to thank you on behalf of the nation for saving us from a plague of verrucas."

"My duty, sir."

"Even so, you have our thanks. I knew Humpty well, you know — we were at

Oxford together. I heard he had slipped into the darker side of existence, but he was a good egg at heart. Was it Randolph Spongg who murdered him?"

"No, Your Eminence, we suspect a mad doctor named Quatt."

The Jellyman shook his head sadly. "A perverter of the natural order," he said disdainfully. "I had her banned from research, but I see I should have taken more extreme measures. Why did she murder him?"

"She didn't — but death was inevitable once she had decided to use Humpty as a living incubation device. As soon as Humpty Dumpty hatched, it was murder."

"How fascinating! What came out?"

"A chicken. Quatt must have been —"

Jack stopped as nasty thoughts coalesced in his mind. *Why had he supposed it was a chicken?* Images of Winkie's tattered body hove into view. A slash so violent it had split his sternum. Winkie must have heard the shot, come out and seen — not the hit man who was already gone, but *Dr. Quatt,* who had been waiting for several days with her white St. Cerebellum's van. Winkie returned home, read the newspapers, assumed Quatt had killed Humpty and then — poor fool — tried to blackmail her. She had turned up to pay him off with

whatever came out of Humpty's shell —
something so terrifying that, urine-soaked
with fear, Winkie couldn't even defend
himself. A haddock with a kitten's head
was child's play: Dr. Quatt had created
something unspeakably nasty and then
grown it in Humpty's denucleated yolk.
And for what? *To use against the one man
who had ruined her!*

"Inspector?" asked the Jellyman. "Something perturbs you."

"You're in danger. We're all in danger.
Madeleine, Mum, get the children into the
cellar *right now* and lock the door. You
with the mustache, get the officers outside
to check the white van parked down the
street — and get the Jellyman to safety!"

He used the sort of voice where no one
argued, and as Madeleine swiftly guided
the family downstairs to cries of "yes, but
why?" the guard with the mustache spoke
into his radio. The front door opened a
crack. It was Chymes.

"What the hell's going on, Spratt?"

"Quatt has bred some sort of weird
Humpty-beast to try to kill the Jellyman. It
will be immensely strong and have claws
capable of splitting a man open."

"Don't be ridiculous!"

As if in answer, there was a burst of gunfire and a cry. Chymes rapidly opened the door and came in, while the officer with the mustache drew his pistol and spoke on his walkie-talkie. There was a garbled message in return and another five shots, then silence. After a moment there was a knock at the door, and Baines came inside, sweating.

"Did you see it?" asked Chymes.

The officer with the mustache went to the kitchen door as the Jellyman and his aide-de-camp waited patiently.

Chymes opened the front door a crack and looked out. At the garden gate, he could see an armed officer at the rear door of the limo. He beckoned urgently. Chymes shut the door and turned to Baines and Jack.

"His limo is only twenty meters away. If we bunch ourselves around him, we can probably make it."

"It's your show, Friedland."

Chymes opened the door again just in time to see something large and scaly run past the limo and dispatch the armed officer with a swiftness that was impressive, deadly — and gruesome.

"New plan," said Chymes as he closed the door again. "The Jellyman goes in the cellar."

"I refuse," said the Jellyman with finality. "They want *me*. I won't take danger to the innocents."

He meant Jack's children, of course. Since protocol dictated that the Jellyman could *never* be manhandled, there was little they could do but acquiesce.

There was another shot and a cry from outside.

"Now what?" asked Baines.

"*Newer* plan," said Chymes. "You stay here and defend the Jellyman, and I'll co-ordinate the backup response from . . . somewhere else."

And without another word, he opened the door and was gone. Jack watched him as he ran across the street and jumped in-elegantly through the privet hedge of the house opposite.

"Where's the backup?" asked Jack as he closed and locked the door.

"On its way."

"Then we wait."

There were more shots, this time from the garden, and another cry.

"Whoa!" shouted the officer in the kitchen, "I just saw something dark and scaly go past the windows — and I think it got Simpson."

"Controlled fire at anything that comes

in!" yelled Baines. "Make every shot count!"

Baines and Jack moved through to the living room and wedged the door to the hall shut with a chair under the handle. Baines then positioned himself between the Jellyman and the kitchen door.

"Officer Baines," said the Jellyman, "you are excused. I have nothing to fear from death, and they want only me. You, too, Inspector, and you, Mr. Vaughn."

Jack looked at Baines and Vaughn, the aide-de-camp. Neither of them moved.

"Is he always this pleasant?"

"Always," replied Baines, adding over his shoulder, "I'm sorry, Your Eminence, my orders are quite clear on this matter."

There was a crash as the kitchen door was smashed in and loud reports accompanied by muzzle flashes as the officer in the kitchen slowly emptied his weapon into something out of their line of vision. The gunshots stopped, and they heard a faint metallic *clack* as the empty magazine hit the tiled kitchen floor. The officer with the mustache never got a chance to reload. There was another crash of broken furniture, and the officer's arm, still with the pistol held tightly in his hand, slid past the open door and hit the fridge. The Jellyman closed his eyes and spoke quietly to himself, doubtless preparing himself for his physical end.

There was a low hiss from the kitchen and the scrape of furniture as the creature made its way to the living room door. A scaly claw with an elongated central digit like a kitchen knife grasped the doorframe. This was followed by the head of something that looked like an illustration from Jerome's *Bumper Book of Carnivorous Dinosaurs.* It stood upright on powerful rear legs, using a gently lashing tail as a counterbalance, but it was no taller than Jack — just a lot more powerful. The body was covered by a series of bony plates like a pangolin, and it had small dark eyes that darted around until they alighted on the Jellyman. Then it hissed again and trod purposefully into the room, the sharp claws on its feet gouging deep furrows in the highly polished parquet flooring.

Baines fired, but the shot merely ricocheted off the beast's scaly hide and shattered a vase on the sideboard. Jack did the first thing he thought of — he grabbed the creature's tail and attempted to pull it off balance. With a cry the beast snapped its muscular tail like a whip, and Jack was flicked backwards at high speed through the kitchen door and into the furniture, which broke under him like matchwood.

Baines stood his ground and fired at regular, controlled intervals. It didn't help. The beast approached him and with one violent swipe sent him to either side of the room. There was nothing now between the Humpty-beast and the Jellyman, who stared back at it with an expression of detached serenity. Jack looked around desperately for a weapon that would make a dent on the creature's hide, but without luck: His mum's kitchen wasn't generally the sort of place where you'd try to kill bioengineered hell-beasts sprung from the crazed mind of a revenge-fueled fanatic.

Blast. And he'd done so well up until now. If only he'd figured this out earlier, Humpty's degenerate offspring wouldn't be about to kill the only honest politician the planet possessed. He stopped. *Offspring.* Strictly speaking, the creature wasn't anything of the sort, as Dr. Quatt had used Humpty only to *incubate* it, but then again . . .

Jack stood up and yelled: *"HUMPTY!!"*

The creature paused momentarily, thought for a moment and then took a step closer to the Jellyman, who forgave the beast and closed his eyes. The creature raised a powerful arm in readiness to complete Dr. Quatt's revenge when . . . a size-B egg hit it on the back of the head.

The effect was electric. The creature roared so loudly that some of Jack's mother's pottery animals vibrated off the display cabinet. The Jellyman thus momentarily forgotten, the beast swung around to face its new aggressor, its eyes fixing Jack's in the sort of way a cat might fixate on a mouse. Jack had changed from being an annoyance — to being *prey.*

Jack purposefully dropped an egg on the kitchen floor. It made that distinctive cracking ploppy noise, and the beast bellowed angrily and pawed the ground, its sharp talons cutting through the parquet flooring like margarine.

"Oh, dear!" said Jack. "What a *butterfingers* I am." He pointed to his right and shouted, "Watch out! *A GIANT MONGOOSE!*"

The creature flinched and looked to where he had pointed, which gave Jack a chance to take the remainder of the eggs and run to the other end of the kitchen. The beast growled menacingly and took a step closer. Deep within its tiny one-track, kill-Jellyman mind, something vaguely familiar stirred. Small vestigial feelings that had been passed unseen from the egg who

had died to give it life. Humpty's worries
— and his *fears.*

"Oh, dearie me again," said Jack as he
dropped another egg on the floor and
backed towards the shattered kitchen door.
The creature gave a snort and a growl,
took three quick steps closer and raised its
arm to attack. But Jack was prepared. He
pulled his mother's egg poacher from the
cupboard and brandished it the way you
would a crucifix to a vampire. The creature
backed off for a moment, then snapped
and lunged, caught the poacher and sent it
flying across the room.

"Then what about this?" asked Jack,
grabbing the egg timer from beside the
oven. "Three minutes for the perfect egg?
Egg dippy fingers, anyone? With *hollan-
daise?*"

He backed out through the door and
dropped another egg. The creature, en-
raged and confused, followed him into the
back garden and snapped, growled and
lunged while Jack taunted it with an egg
whisk.

"Scrambled eggs on toast!" Jack yelled.
"Fried, poached, boiled . . . *SOUFFLÉ!*"

He backed across the garden and yelled
eggy insults until he walked into something
hard and unyielding. It was the beanstalk.

Shiny dark green, with a beautifully smooth trunk, it seemed almost impossible to resist.

"Tortilla!" he yelled as he threw the egg whisk at the beast with all his strength. The creature caught it in its teeth and then crushed it angrily.

Jack stuffed the three eggs that remained in his overall pocket and started to climb. It was easier than he had thought, and the leaves offered good handholds. But if he had hoped this would offer some sort of escape, he was wrong. The creature snapped the air once or twice when Jack shouted "Eggs en cocotte!" — and then followed him.

Jack clambered up, past the ripening beans and high enough to see the road — and the Jellyman's Daimler being driven off at high speed. He breathed a sigh of relief, something that didn't last long, as he suddenly realized that although His Eminence was safe, Jack personally still had to deal with five hundred pounds of dangerously pissed-off Humpty-beast.

"Actually," said Jack, "I *hate* eggs."

The beast snapped angrily at him again.

"No, no," he added hurriedly, cursing his own stupidity, "I meant that by hating eggs, I don't *eat* them. Meringues — yuck."

It had no effect whatsoever. The creature leaped nimbly to the branch below Jack and swiped angrily at his foot. Jack grabbed the branch above him and pulled himself away — just too late. He felt a stab of pain course through his foot. He looked down. The creature had taken away not only the branch he'd been standing on but also his shoe, sock and, although he didn't yet know it, his little toe. He winced with the pain and resumed the climb, favoring the arch of his damaged foot rather than the ball. He could hear the wail of sirens as the backup units approached, but they didn't offer him much comfort. Within a few minutes, he had reached the red aviation warning light, and he stole a quick look below. He was about a hundred feet from the ground, and his mother's house looked very small. There was a growl from below as the creature continued its pursuit, and Jack hurriedly climbed beyond the red light only to discover a new and dramatically unforeseen problem to contend with: The creature was no less angry, and Jack had just run out of beanstalk.

He hooked a leg around one of the leaves and took the eggs from his pocket. But his hands were shaking, and he fumbled; the three remaining size-B free-range eggs fell from his grasp and dropped away into the darkness. And with them his last possible bargaining chip.

"Bollocks!" he muttered to himself. "What a day."

The creature slavered, hissed and snapped and made another swipe. Jack tried to avoid the lunge and succeeded, but it was a short-lived escape. The beanstalk was smaller and weaker at this height, and the leaf Jack was holding came away from the main stalk. He made a wild grab for another, but this, too, came away in his hands. He overbalanced, lost his footing, and fell backwards into space.

He saw a glimpse of the Humpty-beast bathed in a red glow as he fell past, then a blur of beanstalk leaves and pods accompanied by a loud rushing noise. He just had time to experience a curious mixture of relief and renewed peril when he landed on the potting shed in an explosion of rotting wood, earwigs and perished roofing felt. He was momentarily stunned, and all he could see when he opened his eyes was a gaping hole in the collapsed shed and the beanstalk stretching away into the night sky. He picked himself up from where the remains of the roof had collapsed onto the three bags of wool, groaned and stumbled outside. He had a bad cut above his eye, and his foot and ankle were starting to throb badly. He had to think for a moment as his dazed mind tried to focus on what had just happened. It didn't take long. He looked up and realized that it wasn't a bad dream: The creature was beginning its descent.

Jack shook his head and staggered backwards, his hand falling onto the shaft of an ax that was resting in a block of wood. He knew what had to be done. He hobbled into the shed, rummaged under the broken wood and found his father's old chain saw. He flicked the switch and pulled on the cord. It didn't even fire. He pulled again and again as he walked around to the side of the beanstalk facing the road. If he felled it onto his mother's house, he'd never hear the end of it. On the fourth pull, the chain saw burst into life, and the harsh staccato roar filled the quiet night. The chain saw bit easily into the hard stalk, and he had soon cut out a wedge and then swapped sides to make the final cut. He was halfway through and had already felt a few promising cracks and groans when there was a loud concussion, some sparks, and the chain saw stopped dead. Jack didn't realize what had happened until a voice made him turn.

"I underestimated you," snarled Dr. Quatt.

She stood facing Jack with a smoking automatic and looked as though she would be only too happy to use it again.

"I get underestimated a lot," replied Jack with a wince, as the pain from the thousand and one cuts and bruises he had sustained began to kick in, "and by better people than you."

"Interfering fool!" she spat. "The bastard Jellyman has escaped. Ten long years of planning for nothing. Do you know how long it took me to engineer my little friend up there?"

"You just said. Ten years —"

"Don't patronize me!" she screeched, her eyes flashing dangerously. "My research was only to save lives!"

"And Humpty? Who saved *his* life?"

"Humpty was an egg," she retorted. "What is an egg for — if not to create life?"

"How about an omelette?" suggested Jack with a grimace as a muscle twinged uncomfortably in his back.

"Come here, my child," called Dr. Quatt to the Humpty-beast, still halfway down the beanstalk, which creaked and groaned under its weight. "One more for you."

"But Humpty was your patient!"

"And the worthy recipient of my greatest research project," said Quatt with pride. "I was initially worried that night when the gunman shot him, but he was fine. I just had to help the little darling to hatch."

Jack shivered. She was nastier and more inhuman than he had thought.

"He survived the fall, didn't he?"

"Oh, yes. He recognized me, you know, and asked for help, so I picked up a chair leg —"

There was a loud, dull metallic *clunk,* and Dr. Quatt abruptly stopped talking and pitched heavily forwards onto her face. Mary had struck her a glancing blow on the back of the head with a shovel.

Jack's legs collapsed from under him, and he sat on the ground against the garden swing. The stalk creaked ominously. Mary kicked away Quatt's pistol before running up to him.

"Sorry, sir, but I thought we'd heard quite enough. Are you all right?"

"No, Mary, I feel like shit. I've just fallen a hundred feet and gone through a potting shed — and you need to get out of here."

"Not without you."

She tried to lift him, but he was surprisingly heavy, and weakened. He couldn't stand.

"Go, Mary, before the —"

It was too late. The creature jumped the remaining fifteen feet and landed on Stevie's tortoise-shaped sandbox with a crunch. It lashed its tail angrily and hissed menacingly at them both before looking down at the unconscious body of Quatt. It nudged her gently with its nose, made a quiet whining noise and then very tenderly picked her up. The beanstalk creaked and trembled as the stresses of the huge weight bore down on the badly weakened structure.

Mary grabbed the ax to use as a weapon, but Jack stopped her.

"Leave it," he said shakily. "I think I know how this will all turn out. It's an NCD thing."

The beast hissed at them once more and then bounded clear over the garden fence with Quatt in its arms, snapping angrily at the officers who had just arrived. They weren't armed, but it wouldn't have mattered if they were.

"Tell them to leave it alone," said Jack in a quiet voice.

"Step away from the beast!" yelled Mary. "It won't get far — it's an NCD thing."

Jack nodded gratefully as the beanstalk

cracked again, shook and gently started to fall, while the beast gathered speed in large strides down the road. It had almost reached the first police car and was about to leap over it to freedom when the beanstalk came crashing down on top of it, crushing the hapless creature and Dr. Quatt and scattering sleeping-bag-size bean pods around the neighborhood. The almighty thump reverberated through the ground, split the asphalt and lifted two drain covers. Four cars were cut virtually in half, and there was a spontaneous cacophony of car alarms.

"What do you know?" said Mary with admiration. "It got them!"

"That's the beauty of Nursery Crime work," said Jack, closing his eyes and smiling. "Things generally turn out the way you expect them to, even if the manner in which they do is a bit unpredictable."

"Like who killed Humpty Dumpty?"

"Of course. Mrs. Dumpty thought she had shot him; Bessie thought she'd poisoned him. Grundy thought his hit man had got him, and Spongg wired his car. But none of them killed him, not even that lunatic Quatt. The giant beast that Humpty had become was killed by a man named Jack . . . when he chopped down a beanstalk."

An ambulance picked its way through the outsized beans lying on the road and pulled up alongside the garden.

"You're going to be okay, sir," said Mary, yelling over her shoulder for a medic and placing her hand against a bad wound in his side.

"Call me Jack," he whispered. "We've been through enough."

"You're going to be okay, Jack."

"I'll be honest, Mary —"

"You should call me by my first name too, Jack."

"Sorry. I'll be honest, Mary —"

"That's better."

"I thought you weren't going to last the course."

"Closer than you think. Y'know, I don't know why, but I just feel that I *belong* here. Does that sound weird to you?"

"Nah," said Jack. "I think Briggs, for all his faults, knew that when he sent you to me."

"How do you think he knew?"

"I don't know," he replied with an almost imperceptible shrug as grateful unconsciousness, heavy and black, swept towards him. "Sometimes the name just fits."

Humpty Dumpty was buried that June. Thirty thousand people turned up to see his ovoid coffin being borne through the town. Hundreds of those whom he had helped in the past paid floral tributes, and noted among the guests were the Jellyman's personal aide-de-camp, Mary Mary and Jack Spratt.

Jack Spratt made a full recovery and returned to work at Reading Central. He was promoted to detective chief inspector and presented with the Jellyman's Award for Outstanding Courage in the Face of Something Nasty. Despite numerous pleas from the Guild of Detectives, he has yet to join.

Mary Mary still works with DCI Spratt. The investigation that became known as "The Big Over Easy" was serialized in *Amazing Crime Stories* and is soon to be made into a TV series. She has still not yet managed to dump Arnold.

Lola Vavoom and **Randolph Spongg** were listed as "missing, presumed drowned." Reports of sightings from Alice Springs to Chicago have been dismissed as "unsubstantiated."

Sophie Muffet-Dumpty was written out of an early draft of this novel and does not appear.

Friedland Chymes's infamous "tactical withdrawal" from the attack on the Jellyman led to his retirement from the Oxford & Berkshire Constabulary. He is now president of the Most Worshipful Guild of Detectives.

The Goose was spirited away to a top-secret government research station. It contained only what you'd usually expect to find inside a goose and died on the operating table.

The Stubbs was real after all. Mr. Foozle is helping the police with their inquiries.

Mr. and **Mrs. Grundy** now live in Eastern Splotvia, which conveniently — and *coincidentally,* claim the couple — has no extradition treaty with Britain. They are doing well, and Mrs. Grundy is expecting their first child.

Otto Tibbit never worked with Jack again. He left the force and became a goose breeder, gold dealer and president of a charitable trust. He is currently writing a palindromic book entitled, predictably enough, *D'neeht.*

The Sacred Gonga Visitors' Center was opened to the public after prolonged decontamination. It attracted half a million visitors in the first six months and remains Reading's number-one tourist attraction.

Prometheus and **Pandora** were married six months later. Prometheus gained British citizenship and permanent political asylum. A bolt of lightning hit the church during the ceremony, setting fire to the congregation and badly burning eight people. The event was described as "an act of God," although no specific gods were mentioned.

Castle Spongg was given to the National Trust. It is open six days a week, ten until four, excluding Tuesdays and Christmas Day. Wheelchairs welcome; visitors to the revolving room please bring soft shoes.

The Nursery Crime Division was not disbanded and is still active to this day.

About the Author

Jasper Fforde is the author of the best-selling Thursday Next series: *The Eyre Affair*, *Lost in a Good Book*, *The Well of Lost Plots*, and *Something Rotten*. *The Big Over Easy* is the first book in the Nursery Crime series. Watch for *The Fourth Bear* in 2006. Fforde lives and works in Wales. For more information about both series, visit www.jasperFforde.com.